THE HOUSE OF JANUS

I skirted a lake and crossed a wooden bridge. The mist swirled and moved around me. Overwhelmed by fatigue and mounting vertigo I steadied myself with one hand against a tree. Was Oliver Sutchley the link? The link between Lingfeld and Roehampton? Ideas swirled away from me, as insubstantial as the lakeshore mist. But beyond everything was a hardening certainty. Whoever I was, whatever I had experienced or done in the past, I wanted to know nothing of it. I desperately wanted to be free of an idea which padded after me with the insidious persistence of a pursuing wolf, the fear that I had been involved in some horrendous event, that I had been guilty of some crime of obscene and violent proportions.

DONALD JAMES

· The House of Janus ·

Mandarin

A Mandarin Paperback
THE HOUSE OF JANUS

First published in Great Britain 1990
by William Heinemann Limited
This edition published 1991
Reprinted 1991
by Mandarin Paperbacks
Michelin House, 81 Fulham Road, London SW3 6RB

Mandarin is an imprint of the Octopus Publishing Group,
a division of Reed International Books Limited

Copyright © Donald James 1990

A CIP catalogue record for this title
is available from the British Library
ISBN 0 7493 0192 9

Printed and bound in Great Britain
by Cox and Wyman Ltd, Reading, Berks

To M-F

PART ONE

· Daniel ·

· One ·

I could see light. A rectangle of soft opaque light before my eyes and shadowy figures moving above me. A woman's voice, American, one of the moving shadows, said: 'We'll finish this one and break for coffee, OK?'

A warm, rounded shape leaned over me. For a moment I felt scented breath on my chin and neck. A covering was drawn back from my body. I could feel cool draughts of air set up by the woman's arms and legs moving around me.

'He's been dreaming again,' one of the nurses said. 'Betty Grable by the size of it.'

Warm water sponged my chest; a hand took my erect penis, holding it aside as the sponge flicked between my thighs.

One of the women laughed. 'Carrie told me,' she said, 'that Staff Henderson comes in here to practise on him when she's on night duty.'

'Poor darling.' Soft lips touched my forehead. 'He deserves something better than to be mouthed off by old Mother Henderson.'

For days or hours or minutes I watched the sunlight pass across the gauze that covered my eyes. I seemed content not to try to move. Sleep came in deep drifts from which I awoke to savour the proximity of the women who attended me. I smelt their freshly soaped skins. I imagined crisp white uniforms as the nurses leaned across me. I listened to their talk as they worked around me. I was a blind voyeur, an uncomprehending eavesdropper.

When the doctor came the women's banter stopped. Temperatures were discussed; the regularity of breathing reported on. One nurse claimed that I had been weighed yesterday. How could that have been? I knew nothing of that. Was there a part of my life hidden from me? The doctor's voice announced the start of one course of drugs or the termination of another. The nurses called him 'Colonel'.

Drifting on the wings of sleep I once heard footsteps, the many steps of many feet clattering towards me on a tiled floor. I listened acutely. The high heels of women mixed with the measured heel-rap of men. I distinguished three, four, five different persons.

'So this man could well be the last American casualty of the war,' a deep voice said through the tumbling mists of sleep.

'Could well be, General,' the colonel-doctor answered. I could hear in his voice that he didn't know, or care.

'Is he going to make it? I mean will he pull through?'

I waited indifferent through the long pause. 'He's come through surgery,' the colonel-doctor said. 'In that sense there's no reason he couldn't stand up and walk out of here.'

'I mean will he come out of the coma?' the general said testily.

There were many people round the bed. Pipesmoke and perfumes mingled nauseously.

'I can't say, General,' my friend the colonel-doctor said. 'This is beyond our precise medical knowledge. He was torn to pieces by an explosion. We gave him all the necessary surgery. Now his body and his mind, working together, or maybe fighting it out, for all I know, will either bring him out of the coma. Or not. Sorry, General, I can't say more than that.'

Suddenly time had passed on; there was the yellow haze of night lights through my window of gauze and nurses whispering by my bedside.

'The general today was trying to get Colonel Buck to say he definitely wouldn't wake from the coma. That's what the general wanted. He wanted him to die.'

'So the old bastard could get him for his monument to the last GI casualty of World War II.'

'There must be plenty of other candidates.'

'The general thinks this one's perfect. If he dies without speaking he'll not only be the last GI casualty of the war. He'll be the unknown soldier thrown in. That's why the general wants this one.'

'Screw the general,' the third girl's voice said softly. 'We're not going to let this baby die.' A hand touched my face and I realised for the first time that I had a beard.

When was it now? The next day – the next week? The excitement was terrific. Three or four nurses and the colonel-doctor were there. Curtains ran on rings along a bed-bar as others joined them. 'He moved twice,' a young voice said breathlessly. 'I noted it all down, sir. Two distinct movements.'

'Describe them please, nurse.'

'First . . .' the pages of a notebook fluttered, 'the very slow turning of his palm down on to the blanket. At 0734 hours.'

'That was the first movement?'

'Yes, sir. After that I sat by the bed watching. Thirty-five minutes later he drew his leg up, normal speed, didn't jerk it up, just brought it up like he was getting more comfortable. And his mouth moved at the same time. Not really a word. A sort of croak.'

I could almost *hear* the colonel-doctor smiling. The girls were all clustered round. 'Does that mean he's going to make it, sir?' 'Does that mean he's going to be all right, Colonel?'

I knew from their voices how much they wanted to put one over on that sonofabitch general.

There was no escape now. The light gauze was removed from my eyes and I stared up at Colonel-Doctor Buck to find he was narrow-shouldered in his white coat with blond receding hair and pale eyes. His hands took my shoulders. 'Do you hear me? Do you hear me, soldier?'

I stared at him transfixed. My mouth moved.

'Moisten his lips, nurse,' the colonel said, his voice now edged with excitement.

The colonel bobbed aside from my vision and it was filled with a small, neatly featured nurse, a white cap balanced on her dark slightly frizzy hair. Her large soft breasts, labelled in olive-green stitching 'Nurse C. O'Dwyer', pressed down on my upper arm as she held a china beaker, dipped her hand into the water and gently drew her wet fingertips across my lips.

'Get inside his mouth,' Buck's voice urged from the sidelines.

The girl's fingers worked themselves gently past my lips and between my teeth. Within the secrecy of my mouth I moved my tongue against her fingertips and she smiled down at me.

After this Colonel Buck came back every two or three hours, taking my shoulders and looking pale-eyed down at me. 'Do you hear me, soldier? Who are you? What's your name?'

Each time I stared up at him in terror. I could hear my own breath sloughing back and forth past my lips.

'Can you hear me, soldier? Just tell me your name. Just tell me your name.'

But how could I tell him my name? How could I tell him when I didn't know myself!

My temperature rose and fell erratically. I sweated drops of fear whenever a doctor or physiotherapist came near me. Only Nurse O'Dwyer gave me comfort as she sat beside me asking no questions. Only with Nurse O'Dwyer did I communicate – secretly tonguing her fingertips as she moistened my mouth.

In the following days Colonel Buck's visits became less frequent. I know he was baffled by my resistance. Worse now was the Army sergeant physiotherapist, a mean-eyed southerner who kept up a rattle of questions as he pulled and pushed and pummelled me.

There were no deep drifts of sleep to conceal my hunted self now. All day I lay there listening for the approach of footsteps. When they next came it was a captain-doctor, a colleague of Colonel Buck, a man who stared and mused a lot and went away again whispering secretly with the colonel.

Between visits the days were sweet. I listened to the warm bustle of nurses around me, the clatter of metal instruments in bowls, the soft squeak of a trolley as it was pushed past the open doorway of my room. It was summer and the air was warm. Outside in the gardens GIs talked of home and of the war that had lost them arms or legs. Places and names were mentioned that I knew – the battle for Nuremberg and Pilsen, George C. Patton's Third Army. But none of the things related to me directly. Between me and events that I could describe to myself in quite reasonable detail lay a veil, a thin wall of mist. In no incident of my memory did I myself play any part whatsoever!

Sweetest of all was the morning Nurse O'Dwyer came in smiling and bidding me good morning as she always did, as if I were responding.

'It's a beautiful morning, Daniel,' she said. She had christened me Daniel for reasons known only to herself. 'Now, let's get you all freshened up.'

She drew back the covering and turned away to busy herself with a sponge and bowl of warm water. 'Now, if we knew when it was your birthday, Daniel, all the girls would want to send you a card,' she said inconsequentially.

She turned back towards me, her small hands bubbled with soapy water. 'My! Betty Grable again, is it?' she said as she reached down and smoothed her palm under my testicles. 'I think, Daniel,' she said, 'you must have very naughty dreams.' Her left hand masturbated me with smooth regular strokes. 'Don't pretend, Daniel. Don't pretend you don't like it.'

It was irresistible. My back arched and lifted from the mattress, my fingers twisted the sheets. As the sensation flooded me I jack-knifed my legs groaning with pleasure but also with the knowledge that she had betrayed me. The captain-doctor stood smiling in the doorway. Behind him Colonel Buck's voice said: 'Thank you, nurse. Excellent. Well done!'

I was in hell. It was as if one half of my mind saw myself lying in a hospital bed while another darker element took part in a Dantean scene from the other side of midnight. In my vision yellow fumes rose from everything, from the ground, from the dead trees, from the three long columns of people, men, women and children, their heads lowered, their feet dragging, as they marched through this sulphurous landscape.

Perhaps I was part of these dread columns or perhaps I stood outside them watching, I'm not sure. But I was searching the faces with an intensity of yearning that I can feel even now, fully awake. I was searching for a face which seemed to settle on one pair of shoulders after another, ever moving away from me until it was lost among the columns of the damned.

I can't claim that it came to me often as a complete dream. But the experience of the vision hung about me, appearing not so much before my eyes as in the form of a presence, almost as a memory from the whitened past.

I talked to Captain Baxter, the hospital psychiatrist, about it but he was not really helpful. He tried for ten minutes to dredge from the dark picture some indication that it was set in Idaho or Texas or Vermont but when I told him there was no sense of a setting, no convenient signposts reading Morgan's Creek, 15 miles, he tended to dismiss the whole story. In any case, he said, most young men fantasised about finding the perfect girl, about finding her and losing her and finding her again. What did I think Popeye cartoons were about?

Not, I thought furiously, about the cold horror of those marching columns.

Captain Baxter had his own view of my condition and I came to realise it had not a lot to do with what I had to tell him. I'm not saying he was wrong. I had no way of knowing. When he asked: 'What are you running from?' maybe he was right. Maybe the textbooks told him something I didn't know myself.

I much preferred the company of Colonel Buck. Sitting out on the porch, looking across at the mountain peaks, I watched as Buck crossed the timber planking of the veranda and threw himself into the easy chair beside me. A man small in stature, he liked to behave like a big man. Looking across at the gleaming snow-cap of the Unterberg, he drew in a deep draught of the mountain air. 'Any complaints, Daniel?' he asked.

'It's as good a name as any,' I said.

'I'm talking about real complaints,' he said.

'Like why did you move Nurse O'Dwyer to another section?'

He grunted, took out a pack of Chesterfields and offered me one. I took it automatically, accepted a light from his Zippo and inhaled smoke.

He was watching me, the blue flame of the Zippo wavering around the wick.

'Lots of GIs smoke,' I said.

He grinned wryly. 'It's hard not to play detective.'

'Listen, Colonel,' I said, easing my chair round to half-face him. 'Chesterfields taste fine to me. Maybe I smoked a pack a day or more. I'm holding back nothing. But you know things about me, like where I was picked up, and I can't think for the life of me why you won't speak up.'

'Captain Baxter has advised against it.'

'The man responsible for the nicest experience in my young memory. Give me back Nurse O'Dwyer, Colonel, she has a great effect on my morale.'

He had capped the Zippo. Uncapping it again he spun the wheel and lit his cigarette. 'You were picked up in the middle of a minefield,' he said. 'The field had been set around a big house, a mansion they say, between here and the Austrian border.'

'What were the army units in the area?'

He shook his head. 'None really. No US Army units within twenty miles. No, looks as if you went there alone.'

'I walked?'

'No. You went by Jeep.'

'So the Jeep had unit markings, what's the problem?'

'The problem is the Jeep was blown from under you, exploding one mine after another as it landed.' He paused. 'I guess it was like a firecracker.' He nodded, pleased with the image he had evoked. 'It was ignored after they'd taken you away to the field burial station. There was nothing left of it that wasn't burnt black.'

'Engine number,' I said hopefully.

The colonel closed his eyes to the mountain scenery. 'Now you're playing detective, Dan. When they picked you up the medics thought you were dead. They followed procedure. They cut your ID tags and threw the body on the blood wagon.'

'My body?'

'The one you're sitting in. The ID tags went into the bin with a few hundred others. In those last days the Third Army lost three hundred men dead.'

'Are you telling me you have *nothing* to go on?'

'Not a lot yet. Small things, like damage to your right ankle.'

'With a Teller mine under me I'm not surprised.'

He shook his head. 'Earlier damage. I would say a piece of shrapnel, or small calibre bullet maybe, passed right through the heel. You're lucky to have any tendons left at all.'

'How long ago would you guess that took place?'

He shrugged. 'At least a year. Perhaps longer. You're probably some kind of hero.'

'Where does all this take us, Colonel?'

'Not far yet maybe,' he conceded. 'But when we get full lists of men supposedly killed in action on that last day, all we have to do is check for a previous injury to the ankle. And that guy will be you.'

'I can't wait. Didn't I say anything under anaesthetic?'

'Nothing remotely comprehensible. Nothing in English that is. You've got a pretty solid linguistic background. One of the nurses swore you were muttering in Polish. You certainly speak good French and German. Try it out.' He nodded towards an old man in a faded peaked Wehrmacht cap tending the flower bed beneath the veranda.

I tried a few sentences, passing the time of day. Still I didn't think I'd slipped through the veil. I understood the old man as I might a film I was watching, a film in which the characters were supposedly speaking in German but were in fact Hollywood actors. I knew it meant I was a fluent German speaker. As the old man touched the long peak of his cap and returned to his flower bed I saw that Buck was smiling at me. 'You got more secrets like that tucked up your sleeve, Colonel?'

'Captain Baxter advises we let the rope out slowly.'

'Tell Captain Baxter I want O'Dwyer back on my section.'

'I could maybe arrange it if you really tried hard for your name.'

I couldn't explain to him that I was not, as he and maybe Baxter imagined, consumed with curiosity, desperate to know who I was. Most times my identity was like a piece of landscape somewhere beyond the range of mountains. I knew for sure it existed. But *I* existed here, on this side of the mountain range, more real than anything I could conjure up for my past.

I had been fully conscious for four days now. So far I had been held in a sort of cosseted solitary confinement on my own special veranda. Each day the colonel tried to bribe me, quite specific rewards were to be offered for quite specific efforts. Today I guessed he was making another effort at the core of his problem. He was out again after my name.

'We think maybe you were an officer,' he said.

'You're ringing bells, Colonel,' I said with faked concentration. 'Something pretty senior maybe? Do I aim too low at Brigadier-General?'

He glanced bleakly at me. 'Did you fill in that questionnaire?'

'I gave it to Captain Baxter this morning. What difference will it make if I've ever eaten pâté de foie gras de Strasbourg or drunk Château Haut-Brion?'

'Baxter says he's building up a cultural and personality profile.'

'At the end of which he'll stick a pin into a list of all the poor dead guys whose dog-tags were thrown into the same bin and announce I am Milton F. Fairfax III.'

'Where did you get that name?'

'I made it up, for Christ's sake, Colonel. I may be short on memory but I've still got imagination. You want me to give you a dozen others?'

'No,' he said. 'You feel like a drink?'

I considered. 'Yuh. Scotch and water . . .'

He rang the bell. 'Ice?'

'No thanks. Just water.'

'No ice.' He grimaced. 'Maybe you really are Milton F. Fairfax III.'

Later that week I stood in front of a mirror, the first one I had been allowed to approach. Colonel Buck and Captain Baxter stood to one side as I examined the figure before me. That he was tall and pretty much underweight was no surprise. I could see my thin legs in the hospital bed and I knew I had a good four inches on Buck and even some of the taller nurses. What I was not prepared for was my face. By now clean shaven, the mirror revealed it as long with deep-set eyes heavily eyebrowed. A neat but not too sharp nose led down to a good wide mouth. I bared my lips. The teeth looked good.

'Don't get carried away, Valentino,' the Colonel said. 'We gave you four bottom crowns and a bridge San Francisco wouldn't be ashamed of.'

'How about the nose?'

'I modelled that on my own.'

I looked. The bastard had too.

I hadn't mentioned the hair. I took a few strands and rolled them between fingers and thumb, strong, wiry stuff. 'It's not a wig?' I said suspiciously.

'All your own,' Buck assured me.

'But for Christ's sake, Colonel, it's *white*.'

'That didn't worry Nurse O'Dwyer,' Baxter said.

I scowled at him, found I was really taken by the effect and scowled again. 'Apart from the white thatch,' I said, 'I'm not a bad-looking guy.'

· Two ·

By midsummer I felt good.

I could swim and play tennis. I had put on ten or more pounds. And I looked as fit as any of the young soldiers I saw visiting their wounded comrades in the wards or gardens of our mountain hospital.

I still had scars, of course. As the sun tanned my face and body they became less visible. But I could still not break through the mists that separated me from the past. I had, at first, all sorts of sensations of *déjà vu*. A soldier would round the corner in the hospital yard and I would almost call out to him so close was I to his name. But he would stare blankly and I would be incapable of formulating the word on my tongue. I drove myself one day to visit Captain Baxter in his Munich office and on the outskirts of the ruined city I saw a tented refugee camp I was certain I knew. But I was told it had only been erected the week before.

It took time but in the end I came to recognise my own mind grasping at straws.

Habit, unconscious habit, Baxter said, was different. It was probably the most reliable clue of all. Catch yourself in a habit, he said, and it would be pure you, untainted by recent experience.

Maybe.

I watched myself pretty carefully. The way I shaved. Brushed my hair. Tied my shoes. Nothing of any conceivable use emerged.

Until I first handled money. In these early days we were still using the old Reichsbank bills. The hospital cashier had issued me with a thin packet of tens, when I first noticed it. The habit. I took the bills in one hand and with the other flicked through them to reveal the serial numbers. I was talking at the time. But my mind registered the sequence of numbers.

I did not really notice this the first time but within a week or ten days I became aware of an unusual relationship to money. I tried to tell Captain Baxter but he couldn't rise above a few weak jokes. I checked bills, I folded them, I ran them through finger and thumb. I couldn't put it over to

Baxter. It was not just that I liked money, had some overwhelming desire to possess more. It was quite simply that I, in my past life, had had some special, even eerie connection with paper money.

Grand amnesia of the type afflicting me is still not much understood. The mechanism of recovery tried by Captain Baxter included questionnaires, movies he believed I would have seen, photographs of film stars, politicians, generals, places, events in the historical or recent past, all designed to jolt my memory.

I handled the picture gallery without difficulty. I found I was pretty familiar with the historical and most of the recent events. Most of the movies I knew. But I could not place myself in the context of these experiences. I could never say *where* I had seen a Katharine Hepburn–Spencer Tracy movie, *how* I knew both New York and Kansas City, *why* I was reasonably well informed on the subject of Napoleon's defeat at Waterloo or the details of Sherman's march on Georgia.

Captain Baxter had many other amnesia patients but I shyed away from conversations with them. They were different, all partial amnesiacs desperately worried about facing the world after their treatments.

For me there seemed no such worries.

I was incapable, at this stage at least, of envisaging myself as other than the man I saw in the mirror.

Daniel Lingfield.

My surname chosen from the anglicised version of the house in whose grounds the mine had exploded. I was young, of course, and perhaps would not always feel the same about what had happened. But at the hospital at Unterberg I felt clean, fresh. Unencumbered with a past.

It was Colonel Buck who handled the only real clue to my identity. Together we examined the list of men whose dog-tags had all gone into the same bin. In other words men who had died by military accident or enemy rearguard action along that section of the front on the Austrian–Czechoslovak–German border on the last day of the war. There were 329 names, 54 of them officers.

So if I had been an officer I was one of the following: Aberanjan – Austin – Barton – Broughton – Candlewick – Coburg – Cohen – Dalton – Danzigger – Dickson – Doyle – Doonan – Edelman – Eech – Effol – Evans – Forster – Frankenheim – Ferrano – Franks – Gentry – Giorgione – Harmon – Harris – Harrison – Ignatiev – Jenkins – Kawolski – Kerr – King – Kraft – Lime – Madokolos – Manio – Newson – Ossich – Ozonov – Percentin – Rigatti – Ronson – Sampson – Schultz – Skollar – Solaman – Solomon – Stenton – Strasser – Thompson – Tilney – Vallassy – Wheeler – Yeatman – Ziev – Zoller.

I was there somewhere. I would run my eyes over the list wondering, with that still vague and distant curiosity I had in those early days, which one I was. I tried on each name for size. But none of them seemed to fit.

Colonel Buck had a more scientific approach. My photograph was taken and sent to each army unit and next of kin of the men on the list. Over the weeks the results came in, sad letters of regret from families who had lost a son, crisp negatives from the army units. But then I knew from the colonel that surgery had changed my face. How much, and how essentially, neither he nor I knew.

Colonel Buck was more cast down than I was. Smoothing back his receding blond hair with an impatient motion of the hand I had got to know well, he resolved to take on the US Army.

Fighting the military bureaucracy to a standstill he had me recognised as first a person, name of Daniel Lingfield, secondly as a captain in the US Army due nearly three months back-pay, and thirdly as a US citizen, city and state of birth unknown.

It was an extraordinary achievement.

One day in midsummer I drove down through the ruined streets of Munich to Baxter's office and found him hardly able to suppress his excitement.

'You think you might have found out who I am?'

I fumbled through my shirt pocket for a cigarette. I could feel the disappointment or maybe fear welling up. Even at that early moment in 1945 I was facing the fact that I didn't really *want* to know who I was. I had been presented by chance and a 2.5 kilogram Teller mine with a unique opportunity to construct my own personality, my own being.

And now it seemed I might be about to lose it.

But I should have known Baxter better than that. 'No *hard* facts,' he said, the head bobbing from side to side. 'But a lot of very, very interesting data has emerged from your last tests. For instance, I could say with reasonable certainty what your wife looks like. If you have a wife,' he added hurriedly.

I relaxed.

'From the preference tests I gave you it emerges that you are sexually attracted to tall, slender women with brown hair, a generous mouth and hazel eyes.'

A generous mouth. Why not?

'You require a considerable body of general information rather than an active intelligence. Your relationship with this woman . . .'

'. . . if she exists.'

· 13 ·

'Granted. If she exists, is distinctly professorial. You are, uh, perhaps a little overpersuaded of the qualities of your own mind.'

'Aren't we all?'

He smiled. 'In civilian life I'll bet a hundred dollars you were a teacher. A teacher of languages, principally French and German. You definitely visited Europe before the war. Maybe several times.'

'How do you know that?'

'The menu tests.'

'Maybe I was a chef.'

He smiled generously. 'I don't think so, Dan. You were a teacher, I'll stake everything on that.'

'So where does that get us?'

He smiled contentedly. 'A mighty long way. You see, when I put this data against your reading list questionnaire it emerges that you had a speciality in eighteenth century literature. Particularly eighteenth century *German* literature.'

I had to admit that pointed to a pretty unusual chef.

'So with the army's help,' he enthused, 'I've buzzed off the information to every college in the United States. We're getting answers every day now. Nothing positive yet, but . . .'

A week passed, then another. As the replies came in from college after college across America it became clear that somewhere there was a flaw in Captain Baxter's psychiatric detective work.

I was not disappointed. I didn't *see* myself as a teacher. I didn't see myself as a lawyer or newspaperman or a line-backer for the Chicago Bears either. I saw myself as I was now, revelling in my anonymity, my weightlessness.

I saw myself as Dan Lingfield.

Sometime there would no longer be any reason for me to stay on in Germany. At first I looked forward to returning home, never guessing that it was back in the US that I would be confronted with the awful truth.

In the US officers' club in Munich one night in early August I drank too much whisky. I had been playing poker (a game I had to learn) with a group of young New York Jews, confident, educated fluent German speakers from the interpreters' department. I was a lure to their agile imaginations and during the game we laughed a lot as they put forward fanciful suggestions about my origins. The one I liked best was that I was not American but British, Viscount Rodney Falcon Courtney, the son of the Duke of Gosport, who had been captured in the Italian campaign, taken to

Germany as a POW and escaped in the confusion of the last days of the war. This, Lieutenant Barry Green hypothesised, was why I had no dog-tags when found. Not because they had been removed by some over-zealous US Army battlefield clearance unit but because I had removed them myself to avoid capture.

Leaving the club I regained my Jeep in the motor park and drove slowly through the ruined streets of Munich.

There were people on the sidewalks, mostly old women pushing small wooden carts or perambulators piled high with household goods, a few young pale-faced hookers. I drove on down Leopoldstrasse and turned into the Marienplatz. A post in the centre of the square had nailed to it over twenty black and white painted signboards. The one that caught my eye was Special Services HQ, Lingfeld.

Lingfeld was of course the name of the house in whose grounds my body had been picked up. Daniel Lingfield, in the English form, was the name I now carried.

Of course I had known, for some two months, where the village of Lingfeld was. I had even, from time to time, under the prompting of Captain Baxter, considered going there. But I had felt no wish to be part of an experiment the successful outcome of which might re-commit me for life, might remove from me the glorious freedom of the amnesiac.

So why did I head the Jeep towards Lingfeld that night? Because I was drunk? Because I feared that I was not, as Barry Green had laughingly suggested, a British prisoner of war, nor even an American infantry officer whose broken body had been left for dead. But a soldier, a German soldier who spoke fluent American, rather than an American who spoke fluent German. The thought, in almost every sense unadmitted, I now realised, had gnawed and nudged at me since I first spoke German to the old gardener at the hospital.

Should I continue down the Lingfeld road? Should I continue past the looming signpost which would have directed me back to the hospital? Or should I face my fears and drive on down this narrow way where the trees almost joined above my head and where the long whipping radio aerial of the Jeep sliced off apples that danced and rolled on the moonlit road behind me.

I was afraid. A different sort of fear. I was afraid not of the future but of the past.

Why had I been in the grounds of Haus Lingfeld on 8 May 1945? In the vast sweep of a world at war when inconceivable crimes were committed by simple, ordinary men, what was I running from?

What had I done?

I stopped the Jeep at the entrance to the drive beside a gatehouse of perhaps four small rooms and a gabled roof the tiles of which had been torn and scattered by mortar fire. A green-painted door slumped inwards on a single remaining hinge. Every pane in every window was broken. Before me the drive curved away in parallel lines of linden trees. The gravel surface was pitted with shallow holes. A crudely painted notice said, in English and German: 'The drive to the house has been cleared of obstacles. You are warned that the woods on either side still contain mines.'

Had it been in these woods that I had been blown up? I moved the Jeep down the broken drive at five miles an hour. Just past the first gently curving bend the moonlight caught the full-length statue of a figure in Roman breastplate, chipped where the name might have been, but the date read clearly in the incised stone: 1694.

Gravel crunched under the Jeep tyres. The moonlight brightened as the linden trees seemed spaced wider apart. A screech owl burst into my lights and rose, banking menacingly above my head. In the distance dogs barked and then fell silent. A sense of private menace hung over the place. As the wheels of the Jeep rolled slowly forward the hair on the back of my neck stiffened and rose. I reached over and hauled my webbing pistol belt from the back seat and one-handedly clipped it round my waist.

The drive now opened steeply before me into a cobbled forecourt, enclosed on the three sides by a stone balustrade topped at intervals by weathered stone urns. The roof of a large house gradually became visible.

Haus Lingfeld was a mansion, a manor house the English would have called it, large but not enormous. It was built of stone in a style which in this part of Germany seemed to run straight through from the late-seventeenth to the nineteenth century. Part of the roof had collapsed and window frames hung outwards, shattered by the force of some explosion inside. Along the lower floor the stone was chipped where the façade had been raked by heavy machine-gun bullets.

The house was deserted. No lights shone from even those few windows which were intact. I stopped the Jeep and got out. The steps before me were of worn stone and the wide terrace in front of the house was flagged and balustraded. I climbed the steps and stood on the terrace. Away to the east, high hills rolled towards the mountains. On the west side of the house a huge ornamental lake gleamed in the moonlight. In the middle a wrecked German army truck stood, the water-level above its wheels.

On the far side of the lake a stone pier ran out into an ornate boathouse. I felt some lurch in my chest which may have been recognition. I wished now I'd asked Colonel Buck if there was any record of exactly where I had been picked up.

A stone boathouse on a lake. An auburn-haired girl. A summer day. Of course I knew it was all nonsense, a re-creation of a hundred films or paintings I had seen. I could go on, I said to myself, listing all the other things that completed the picture. The pair of young English setters racing through the shallows. The girl's light muslin dress through which, in certain angles of sunlight, I could catch just momentarily the outline of her legs.

The crunch of gravel somewhere round the side of the house interrupted my romancing. Fear returned as I strained my eyes into the deep shadow beside the house. I could see a shape there, unmoving. Then the crunch of gravel as the figure came forward. Panic surged through me. In the shaft of moonlight the shape seemed to be without a face!

I pulled myself together. I knew I was looking deep into my own fear. I called. The figure came forward two paces and stopped.

In the moonlight I could now see it was a woman. Tall, seven or eight years older than me, her hair drawn back from a hard but beautiful face. She stood, one hand resting on the rusticated stonework of the corner of the house.

'What do you want here?' she said.

She had spoken in English. Turning towards her, looking past her to see that she was alone, I said: 'On the last day of the war, I was blown up by a mine in the grounds of this house.'

She barely moved but with one almost imperceptible lift of the shoulders she indicated her indifference.

'I want to come in,' I said. 'I want to go into the house.'

'Why?'

'I'm an American officer,' I said. 'I don't have to explain why.'

Again she shrugged, this time more obviously. Then she turned and led the way round the side of the house. 'We live in the kitchens,' she said. 'Or what's left of them. The house was hit by shellfire. As you have probably seen most of the roof has collapsed. The upper floors are uninhabitable.'

She turned through a porched doorway and led the way along a passage. The kitchen at the end of the corridor was a huge room, the ceiling height lost in diminishing candlelight. Dark recesses suggested great oak cupboards or other doors which led into the interior of the house. A fire was burning in a tiled stove and woodsmoke drifted into the candlelight and was lost in the darkness above my head. As I watched the shadowed outline of her body before me I was seized by curious, unmeasurable feelings. Distaste? Yes. Familiarity? Certainly.

She turned, the lines of her cheekbones caught in the candlelight. She was in her mid-thirties, dressed in a skirt and flowered blouse of some quality beneath a rough plain farmworker's apron. Her eyes, wary, intensely proud, caught mine. Then some surge passed through my body or brain, far more than familiarity. Instead, an overwhelming sense that I had once slept with this woman.

'Is this your house, or are you squatting here?' I felt no friendliness towards this woman whom perhaps I had slept with. That first single shrug of the shoulders had told me all I wanted to know about her attitude to Americans.

She hesitated a long time before answering the question. 'It's my house,' she said at length.

'What's your name?'

'Frau Elisabeth Oster.' She pronounced it with deliberate emphasis on each syllable.

'You live here alone?'

'No. My husband lives here with me. Tonight he is in Munich preparing for the *Viktualienmarkt* tomorrow. The home farm produces a little extra food. Not much.'

I nodded. 'Were you here in the last days of the war?' I asked.

'Yes.'

'Do you know me?'

'No.'

'Are you sure, Frau Oster?'

'Why should I know you?'

She was trembling faintly which somehow increased this strange intimacy I felt towards her. I had no doubt that I disliked her but for men at least some feelings are more potent than dislike. Again I felt that surge of warmth, that near certainty that I had slept with her, like meeting a woman the morning after an erotic dream in which she had unwittingly played a part.

'The explosion of a Teller mine in the drive of this house,' I said carefully, 'rendered me temporarily incapable of remembering what I was doing here.' I paused then added as a shot in the dark. 'I think you know.'

I was looking at Elisabeth Oster. She was now shaking violently.

I leant forward until my face was only a foot or two from hers. 'Do you know me, Frau Oster? Have you ever met me?'

She shook her head.

'Why had I left my unit? Why was I making my way towards this house?'

But she was recovering, fast. 'I can't help you, Captain,' she said. 'I do not know you. We have never met.' Again she pronounced the words with that same deliberate pacing she had used when she had first given her name. 'We have never met.'

· Three ·

In the days that followed my visit to Lingfeld some images faded. So many irrelevant and impossible scenes seemed familiar that I could have no certainty about the familiarity of Haus Lingfeld. Nothing really meant anything except the fact that I had been travelling up the drive of the house when the mine exploded. Perhaps I had indeed been going to a place I knew from before the war or perhaps I was simply lost on a legitimate reconnaissance or, the thought made me shudder, I had seen the house across the hills and was drawn by the prospect of loot.

The morning after my visit Captain Baxter had not been pleased to discover I had been to Lingfeld off my own bat. He had planned, it now emerged, to take me there without my knowing where I was going. He planned, he said, 'to surprise my memory with the scene'. Failing that he plied me with questions – was the drive familiar, the house, did anything stir when I saw Elisabeth Oster?

My dream-memory of having slept with her seemed too fantastic to tell the captain. I admitted my visit had considerably disturbed me.

'You saw nothing about the house you thought familiar?'

'It was dark.'

'The woman meant nothing to you.'

'No.'

'Sure. . . ?' he prompted eagerly.

'I had some vague feeling of having seen her before.'

'Tell me about it.'

'Doctor,' I said, 'you know I've had that feeling with a dozen people. I've even stopped GIs in the streets of Munich but each one has been a bush.'

'Why did you go last night?'

'I saw a road sign. That simple.'

'I doubt it. You rode over a mine at Lingfeld. I'm personally convinced you were going there for some specific purpose. Something last night sparked you off.'

I relaxed. It was the same old Baxter, half detective half doctor, and maybe not that good in either capacity. 'Listen,' I said carefully. 'Has it occurred to you that the day I was injured I may have been heading somewhere else? Just passing through the area.'

'You were blown up on the *drive* to the house,' he said obstinately.

'Doctor, infantry units don't use the highway in an advance to contact.'

He nodded reluctant agreement. He had become daily, visibly more keen on my case. To him it was a good one. I think he was beginning to see his future speciality in amnesia and he had no intention of letting me go.

He closed up the session for the day with a petulant pressure on his pencil and snapped it in two. 'OK, Dan, OK,' he said. 'But what really bugs me is your lack of curiosity.'

I stood up. 'See you Friday,' I said, making for the door.

Was he right about my lack of curiosity? Was there something strange about that? Not to me. What Baxter couldn't quite grasp was that, apart from a few disturbing images, the past had no existence for me. I didn't miss it because I didn't know it. I *liked* being me, the *me* I knew. The only *me* that existed. I didn't want to become someone else.

What I couldn't work out was the fear. The prickling in the hair when I felt Baxter was maybe getting somewhere. What had I done that made me so scared of my past? So content with the present? That night I talked to Colonel Buck. He occupied two small rooms in a wing of the hospital and I was free to drop in and see him any time. I found him more congenial company than Baxter, perhaps because as a surgeon he felt he had completed his job on me.

He opened a bottle of German wine. 'Dan,' he said pouring me a glass, 'the time has come for you to go back home, you know that.'

'I guess so. What will happen?'

'You'll be honourably discharged and given a pension.'

'To pick up where I left off before the war,' I smiled.

He poured himself a scotch. 'Baxter doesn't want to sign your discharge.'

'He wants to keep hold of me, right?'

'To him you're a case history.' The colonel swallowed his whisky. 'Baxter's been posted back home. He's taking you with him.'

'The hell he is.'

'I can't stop him, Dan. He's got authority to take you back with a number of partial amnesiacs. My advice is to play along with him.'

'You mean *pretend* my memory's coming back.'

'No, I mean don't pick a fight with Baxter. Back home he'll have a regular hospital superior, a colonel or brigadier-general maybe. I'll recommend you're discharged after a month or two. But I can't stop Baxter taking you back with him in a bottle.' He grinned. 'This is the Army, Mr Jones.'

Two days later I began my journey home with a seventeen hour train ride to the Hook of Holland from where I was to be flown to England to embark for New York.

I arrived in London for the November fogs. To be in a strange city is confusing enough. To be a stranger in fog-bound London was a disturbing echo of my own condition. I stayed at the US Officers Club in Bayswater near Hyde Park and for the first four days I didn't dare to venture out. The news was we were sailing from Southampton on the *Queen Elizabeth* in late November but the fact was that at this time hundreds of thousands of GIs were flowing through England on their way home. All held some priority status and I guess nobody knew exactly where to place an amnesiac. I was passed over and assigned to a military hospital in Roehampton, a pleasant area on the western outskirts of London. The hospital, an elegant eighteenth-century building standing on a hill above Roehampton village, was full of badly injured British soldiers in their blue hospital uniforms. There was a small unit for head cases like me, most badly shocked RAF and USAAF bomber crews, most of them barely twenty-one years old.

In this part of London the fogs were quite different, more like autumnal mists rising from the River Thames below us. I was assigned a light high-ceilinged room overlooking a girls' school basketball (they called it netball) court and there are worse ways for a young man to pass the day than reading and watching nubile girls jump and run and shoot for the net.

Among the patients in the psychiatric centre I formed one of those brief military friendships with a young man named Wayne Thomas. He was the epitome of the good, simple side of American optimism. He used phrases like '*Get lucky yet?*' to greet you and '*Strike oil*' to wish you goodbye.

His posting to the 8th Strategic Air Command in England had saved him, he insisted, from a life of diapers and connubial bickering. At twenty years old he already had two children and he saw leaving Europe and returning home to Florida as the end of his freedom. The particular liberty he prized was not among Franklyn D. Roosevelt's four freedoms. Wayne's was the freedom to get laid.

His medical problem was in fact already resolved when I met him. He had been blown out of the belly of a B17 at 20,000 feet by flak. His parachute ring had caught on a piece of protruding metal and by happy chance dragged out the canopy as the aircraft exploded in a fireball beside him. Wayne had landed scared and deaf. The German doctor in his prison camp could find no physical injury. He had been classified at the end of the war as a psychiatric case. In Roehampton he spent half the day telling doctors his ears had popped and he could now hear perfectly but that wasn't good enough for the medical bureaucracy. In Roehampton he was still undergoing 'tests'.

I had my own problems. My medical man was a civilised English civilian doctor whose ruling passion was the history of the US Constitution. 'Tell me,' he said at our first meeting, leaning forward with the intense anticipation of the true academic, 'had the Supreme Court produced no John Marshall who would now be the arbiter of the US Constitution?'

I looked at him uncertainly. To be truthful it occurred to me that he might be a patient who had snatched up a white coat.

'It's quite a poser,' he said.

I agreed. 'My interest, Doctor,' I said carefully, 'is in what the hell I'm doing here.'

He nodded in a friendly manner. 'Sorry about the outburst of enthusiasm,' he said, 'but I can't resist putting a few questions to my American patients. So, what are you doing here? Let's see.'

He took out my file and began muttering his way through it. 'Well, as far as I can see, Captain, you were due to be shipped back to the United States in early November and you suffered a bit of a relapse.'

'A relapse?'

He nodded. 'So your passage was postponed and you were transferred here *pro tem.*'

'What sort of relapse am I supposed to have had, Doctor?'

He shook his head. 'No idea. The notes just say a relapse. To be investigated further at Roehampton Military Hospital.'

'Doctor,' I said patiently, 'I am a one hundred per cent amnesiac. How does a man slide back down from there?'

Again he shook his head. 'Even if you had,' he said, 'we don't really have the facilities to treat you.'

'So why am I here?'

'A mystery, old chap,' he said. 'We're the best plastic surgery unit in the world, but frankly we're pretty hopeless when it comes to your sort of problem.'

'So why am I here?' I repeated.

The doctor looked up at me. 'I think you've been side-slipped, Captain,' he said seriously.

'Side-slipped?'

'Pushed up here to Roehampton.'

'Why should anyone want to do that?'

'I think someone wanted your berth on the *Queen Elizabeth*, Captain. Someone with enough influence to get it.'

Meanwhile Wayne had clocked up some impressive tallies in his favourite pursuit and he didn't see why the female staff of Roehampton Hospital should be any more resistant to his genuine charm. But these young English nurses had seen a lot of American soldiers pass through their wards in the last three years and Wayne was soon bemoaning his lack of significant progress. One day we were sitting under the huge Lebanon cedars in the hospital gardens in a rare shaft of November sunlight when one of the temporary ward doors opened and a woman crossed towards us. For some reason, still unknown to me, Wayne was convinced he had scored. This one, he said pointing to the woman approaching us across the lawn, had given him the big smile once today already.

'She could be my big strike,' Wayne mused. 'Either her or one of the nurses in E block. I'm not sure how to play it.'

She was fifteen years older than Wayne, a tall imposing woman in her late thirties, big in every sense with a round face and dark-red hair worn long. She wore some sort of green uniform which I didn't recognise, a matching skirt and jacket and a beret which she carried in her hand with a silver badge which glinted in the pale sun.

'Look at those thighs,' Wayne said happily.

'For God's sake, shut up.'

'I tell you she can't keep away from me. This morning she was asking about my taste in reading. They like to believe all American airmen are simple. I obliged. I told her *Gone with the Wind*, Clark Gable is my favourite writer.'

'Is that when she gave you the big smile?'

'Sure.'

I stood up. I saw now the woman was carrying a book. 'Good afternoon, Lieutenant,' she said to Wayne. She pronounced it as if there was a double f concealed there somewhere.

'Well, good afternoon,' Wayne said. 'So we meet again.'

'Yes. Stand up,' she said sharply as he lounged back in his seat, one leg thrown over the other.

'Sure.' He scrambled to his feet.

'You were complaining there was so little to read here.'

'For a reader like me, yes.'

'I found a copy of *Gone with the Wind*.' She handed it to him. 'I hope you enjoy it.'

She began to turn away.

'Hold it one moment,' Wayne said. 'I have to thank you for the book and I don't even know your name and telephone number.'

She looked at him with something less than passionate amusement. 'My name is Dorothy Curtis,' she said. 'I'm a member of the WVS, the Women's Voluntary Service. I run hospital records. And the library, such as it is.'

Wayne moved the book back and forth from hand to hand. 'Dorothy Curtis, I like the name.'

Her eyebrows rose in disbelief.

'The only thing you don't tell me is whether it's Mrs Dorothy Curtis or Miss.'

'Neither. It's *Lady* Dorothy Curtis,' she said. 'I hope you enjoy the book. Good afternoon, gentlemen.'

Her high heels hit the concrete path as she headed for the hospital.

'What was she doing,' I said, 'playing hard to get?'

'The hell with it,' he grimaced. 'Let's go and talk to those nurses in E block.'

After a week at Roehampton Hospital Wayne Thomas and I were given permission by our doctors to leave the hospital on thirty-six-hour passes. With hopes high and a pocketful of back-pay, Wayne was eager to spread some of it among the clubs and girls of Soho, London's sleazy red-light district.

We took a taxi from Roehampton, descending the long hill with London lying in a shallow fog below us. Streetlamps just penetrated the fog level and shone through in a crazy pattern of streets, twisting, straight or turning back on themselves. We drove across Putney Bridge and at four in the afternoon could barely see down to the level of the river. Wayne Thomas shivered in his trenchcoat in the unheated back of the taxi. 'Let's just get into a warm pub and with a couple of large scotches we'll plan our next move.'

The cab driver, muffled in the front of the taxi, grunted over his shoulder. 'Pubs don't open till half past five, sir.'

'You can't get a drink before five-thirty?' Wayne asked incredulously.

'Unless you know a place.'

Wayne nodded. 'And you do.'

'It's my job, sir. You want me to take you there?'

'OK. Where is it?'

'Charing Cross, sir. Not far from Soho.'

A few minutes later we turned off the Strand into narrow old-fashioned streets within the sound of the river boats' fog-horns. 'Duke Street,' the cabbie said. 'Buckingham Street.' We came to a stop. 'And that one there is Of Alley. Duke-of-Buckingham. Get it?'

We paid him off and followed his directions down Of Alley. The club was called Druitt's and it was many years before I got the joke. Montague Druitt, barrister of the nearby Inner Temple, had been the prime police suspect for the role of Jack the Ripper.

We presented ourselves at a basement door, were inspected through a wooden Judas which snapped back and forth with all the efficiency of a Hollywood prop and were let in. It was a huge, half-dark, cavernous place with, I swear, water dripping through the ceiling. Three men in frayed and greening tuxedos served behind a long, brass-railed, mahogany bar. On a flagstoned floor, tables and chairs were grouped among puddles which may have been roof-leaks and may simply have been spilled drink. The din was terrific. Girls in short emerald satiny dresses shrieked with laughter at their companion's wit and discreetly ordered another bottle of champagne. It was a clip-joint that the Kansas City Mafia would have been proud of. Wayne thought it was great.

We sat at the bar and were quickly joined by two girls who introduced themselves as Ethel and Wilma. They were *not* cut out for the business of courtesans. Ethel's pinched lips spat venom about every waiter or bouncer in sight. Wilma said little or nothing beyond the word champagne. She was marginally better-looking than Ethel but her legs and arms were as thin as sticks. Her face was drawn and in a different context might have been called tragic. Or haunting.

One sip of the 'champagne' persuaded me I should drink whisky. Ethel had launched into another philippic against one of the bouncers and I ordered two large scotches in succession. Wayne was enjoying himself stroking Ethel's thigh and Wilma sat grinning as she clumsily organised her elbow to knock over the champagne. After that nightly performance she immediately ordered another. I think it was our third.

A corner of the cavern lit up and a band began to play some swing. Glenn Miller melodies were just recognisable. A few people got up to dance, mostly American soldiers and their girls. I ordered another scotch and drank it as I looked around. Perhaps in the Far East it might have been different. Sex for sale in a discreet, bamboo-walled restaurant. The waft of French cooking from the kitchens. Two slender almond-eyed girls silently pouring brandy; the muffled sounds of the port of Haiphong like background music to your imminent decision.

The contrast between Somerset Maugham and the present was too much to take. More than anything I wanted to get out of this awful place.

I leaned over to Wayne and tugged his arm. 'We've got a lot of fun to have tonight. Let's go.'

'Fun?' Ethel's thin mouth worked the chewing gum Wayne had given her. 'Aren't you having fun?'

'We've got to move on.' I signalled to the barman for the bill.

'Just one more bottle before you go,' Wilma said.

I shook my head. 'No, thanks.'

'Your friend wants to stay,' Ethel said in a steely voice.

Wayne had drunk nearly two bottles of the carbonated white wine. He looked easily about him, too drunk to care.

'We're going,' I said. I picked up the bill, glanced at it and reacted. A week in England was enough to know I was being robbed. 'Thirty-five pounds! You could drink champagne in the Ritz all night for less than that.'

'Not very gallant, Yank,' a soft voice said behind me. I turned to face a thick-shouldered bruiser. 'You're forgetting the company of the girls. Ethel and Wilma are our star turns.'

'You're right,' I said. 'But we still aren't paying thirty-five pounds.'

I put ten pounds on the bar and his hands came out to grab me. One of the girls hit me a great slap round the back of the head with her handbag and the bouncer caught my lapels and butted me with his forehead. In a painless, half-fainting mist I slid off the bar stool. Wayne was struggling effectively with another bouncer as my man stood over me with his right foot drawn back. 'Twenty quid more,' he said. 'Make it twenty-five for my trouble.'

The toe-cap was about eight inches from my ribs. As my chest muscles involuntarily contracted I saw, past the shining toe-cap, a figure erupt from one of the nearby tables. Shorter, but if anything broader than the bouncer standing over me, he moved with astonishing speed for someone so heavily built. A chair materialised in his hands. It hung over the bouncer's back like a bad mistake on Damocles' part and an American voice hissed menaces. Meanwhile two British sailors were helping out Wayne and had pinned his bouncer back against the bar. We clearly had a stalemate. To my surprise, my bouncer grinned. 'OK,' he said, 'call it a tenner.' He stretched out a hand and helped me to my feet. 'Now, sod off, the lot of you,' he said not unamiably.

We found ourselves in Of Alley. The British sailors had gone. Wayne was still talking about Soho and more clubs. I was getting hungry.

The mists rolled up from the river as we walked into Villiers Street. The squat American civilian with the huge shoulders and rubbery features introduced himself as Vik Zorubin. I thanked him for his timely intervention and he just grinned, his thick lips moving towards his enormous ears. He was one of the ugliest men I'd ever seen.

Wayne was insistent on getting to Soho. I made him hand over five hundred dollars of his back-pay for safe-keeping then bundled him into a taxi.

I stood with Zorubin on the corner of the Strand. Red buses rumbled through the fog. 'London's a city of many delights,' Zorubin said. 'But her whores are not among them.'

'You saved me a lot of money,' I said, 'not to mention a few cracked ribs. Let me buy you dinner. You know a place?'

We hailed a taxi and Zorubin directed the driver back to the King's Road to a very different club called the Pheasantry. Slightly shabby in a genteel fashion the Pheasantry was housed in a two-century-old building behind a stone courtyard. Zorubin showed his membership card and we were settled quickly at a comfortable table from where we could watch the new arrivals and the bar customers, some of whom looked as if they had permanent reservations on their bar stools.

'Who comes here, Vik?' I asked him.

'This is Chelsea,' he said, 'so it could be anybody: painters, writers, cricketers, members of Parliament. The guy at the bar is Churchill's nephew, Johnny Spencer Churchill. Not a bad painter, they tell me. The very thin guy's a writer named Eliot. Can't understand his stuff. Once tried.'

We ordered dinner. 'What about you, Vik?' I asked. 'What are you doing in London?'

'I use it as a base,' he said. 'I have a forwarding address.'

'Is this where you came out of the war?'

He smiled. 'I was wounded in Italy,' he said. 'When I was invalided out I thought I had to begin looking around for things to do. In a way I realised I'd been lucky. Before all those young, bright guys came out of uniform I had a year or so's start in the job market.'

'What did you do before the war?'

'Boston Police Department,' he said. 'There's no going back there with a stainless steel knee cap.'

'So how did you use your year's start on the other guys?'

'I drank a lot of vodka,' Zorubin said. 'Old family habit.'

'And . . . ?'

'I applied for a job with Pentagon Records. A civilian job.'

'They turned you down?'

'No. In June 1944 I joined the European section. Three days before the invasion of Normandy. After that if I'd had a heart it would have broken. We were inundated with letters from parents of kids who had made the landings and disappeared.' His vast, rubbery face screwed up. 'Missing in action. Harder for the parents than killed outright. At least for some parents, the parents of those who don't come back in the end.'

I ordered another bottle of wine, a 1928 Château Margaux. It cost less than an hour with Ethel and Wilma. Zorubin took a quarter-litre of vodka. He said there were so many Russian *émigrés* among the membership that the Pheasantry stocked the best vodka in London, a Moscow-bottled Royal Stolichnaya.

I asked him if he was still with the Department of the Army.

'No,' he said. 'I resigned the day the war ended and came over to Europe. As an ex-cop I felt our missing persons investigations were worse than useless. They raised false hopes, they confused names . . .' He paused. 'I became a professional searcher.'

'For MIAs?'

'Ghoulish, you think. Like robbing war graves?'

'No,' I said slowly, 'I don't think that. What sort of success rate do you have?'

'Minuscule,' he said. 'But sometimes I find a guy in an old German prison camp in Poland. Or living in a mountain village in Italy not sure yet whether the war's over. Sometimes.'

'It's kind of an odd-ball occupation,' I said carefully.

'I'm an odd-ball.'

'Just MIAs, missing in action.'

He shook his head. 'No. I trace a lot of girls. Guys that were wounded and shipped back ask me to trace a girl they knew in Manchester or Paris or Sorrento.'

We both drank and watched the late-comers drifting in. Now and again Zorubin would recognise a face and offer me a short biography.

'You know, Dan, most people back home don't have the faintest idea what happened in Europe these last five years. They only know armies fought other armies and half the Jews in Europe were killed in concentration camps. But something else happened too. Millions, tens of millions, over a hundred million people lost their homes, driven out by bombing, battles or racial or political crackpots. The Germans did it on a grand scale. The Russians hardly less. And now we're doing it, the Americans and British. Or at least we're condoning it.'

He saw my blank face.

'Germans are being driven out of their homes in Poland, the Baltic States and Czechoslovakia. We've put millions of them on the road, or we've agreed to put millions on the road. Old men and women, children barely old enough to walk. This winter five million Germans will be driven west. God knows how many will perish. Do you know that the Czechs are even pressing old concentration camps into use? Our allies the Czechs. Did you know that, Captain?'

I rocked back at the sheer power of his anger.

'I trace missing soldiers,' he said quietly. 'I trace long lost girl friends. I trace what's left of the families of New York Jews. I trace French men and women who were transported to Germany and have never been seen again. And I trace Germans for other Germans who lost them in the night and the fog that settled over Europe for the last five years.'

'Don't give me a hard time, Vik, because you take on German clients.'

'I'm anticipating,' he said grimly. 'A lot of British and Americans don't think the Germans deserve help.'

That first night I decided not to tell Vik Zorubin my story. I realised well enough that in my own way I was one of the millions lost in this vast European fog.

We were about to leave when the party came in. I was paying the bill. Zorubin had gone to the john. A noisy group of perhaps ten or a dozen people, the men in dinner jackets and the women in long dresses, flowed through the door. I looked up the way people do in libraries or restaurants and found, to my utter astonishment, that I was looking into the face of someone I knew beyond all possible doubt.

Waves of nausea flooded over me. I was gripped by a strange breathless vertigo. I closed my eyes and images flooded in.

A long colonnade in some southern city. Night and the restless drift of streetgirls among the great stone columns.

Then I was looking at the man's face again. For a moment I distrusted what I saw. The tall figure in the dinner jacket seemed some further trick of my elusive memory. But I swear he had recognised me. He bent quickly and said something to a woman in a blue dress, her back towards me, and turned for the door.

I stood up abruptly and plunged through the crowd. He had grabbed up his black overcoat from a hook in the hallway but it had taken precious seconds. At the front door I was level with him. I stuck my foot forward. As he pulled the heavy door inward it stopped against my shoe. He looked down slowly. 'Excuse me,' he said. 'I wish to open the door.'

'In a moment. First I want to talk to you,' I said clumsily.

He raised his eyebrows.

'I know you,' I said.

'Possibly.' He was one of those Englishmen, one of those men, I particularly dislike. He carried with him an assumption of superiority without basis, a dismissive manner that made me want to punch him out. Except this man was scared. Or if not scared, alert, on his guard.

'You know me,' I said.

'Do I?'

'You high-tailed it for the door as soon as you saw me.'

His thin shoulders moved in a world-weary gesture. 'I came back to pick up a coat and drop off an ex-wife. What's your problem?'

I didn't feel good. I leant back against the wall. I knew I was breathing heavily. 'I'm damn sure,' I said, a mixture of apology and aggression, 'that I've seen you before.'

'We've probably had a yarn together, here at the bar. Both of us too pissed to remember.'

I didn't accept that but I didn't know what else to say, or do. 'You don't remember me,' I said lamely.

He lifted the thin shoulders. 'Sorry, old chap,' he said. 'Would normally. That night *I* must have bought the drinks.'

I withdrew my foot and he opened the door. He passed through letting it swing in my face. Within seconds he was swallowed up by the fog.

· Four ·

I came back into the room. The party of newcomers were at the bar. As I pushed past they eyed me curiously. The woman in the blue dress still had her back to me. As I made it past her towards our table I caught the flash of a smile in the mirror behind the bar. I stopped as the woman turned.

'Good evening, Captain,' she said. 'You've lost no time in discovering the Pheasantry, I see.'

'Good God!' I said fighting a confusion verging on craziness. 'Lady Dorothy Curtis.' I mumbled introductions and Zorubin lumbered to his feet.

As she shook hands, leaning forward, her polite but slightly distant smile directed towards Zorubin, I was struck by the extraordinary quality of her attraction. She was a woman in fullest bloom. Next year she might have passed that indefinable divide between late youth and middle age. Today she was poised on that knife-edge between the mature and the matronly. As I offered and she accepted a drink, there was no hint of invitation in her voice or smile. She was cool, friendly, correct.

As she drank a glass of wine with us her attention was mostly concentrated on Zorubin. With a slight twinge, I had to admit there was something very winning about his rubbery face and deep-set brown eyes. I realised, too, that he could talk. Because he felt as strongly as he did about the displaced millions of Europe, people listened. She listened.

'Don't you think, Mr Zorubin,' she said, 'that the German people should have thought of this when they voted for Hitler in 1933?'

Zorubin's face creased and rolled. 'They didn't have a crystal ball.'

'They knew the Nazi Party was evil. They knew Hitler himself was evil,' she said stubbornly.

'A lot of well-placed people in Britain and the United States supported Hitler, until it became obvious that he was gonna fail.'

'In England they were held in jail under a regulation called 18B. In my opinion they richly deserved it.'

'Who was the man?' I said brusquely in a pause in the talk.

She frowned.

'The one that picked up his coat and hit the exit without a word of good night?'

'Oliver? Is that why you rushed out?'

'Oliver who?'

'He doesn't owe you money?'

I shook my head. Zorubin watched inscrutably.

'Oliver Sutchley. My very much ex-husband. Gambles, boozes, tarts around.' She paused. 'He really doesn't owe you money? Honestly?'

'I thought I knew him,' I said.

'I hope for your sake you were wrong.'

'Could be. What line of business is he in?'

'Printing,' she said. 'Banknote printing. My former husband worked for the Bank of England.'

The Bank of England. The images of panelled rooms and hanging portraits came to me in a flood. The hell of amnesia is that you can't distinguish between imagination and memory.

She smiled her rather distant smile at me. 'If you're planning to go back to Roehampton in the next hour,' she said, 'I can drop you. I live just beyond the hospital.'

When she left our table to join her friends Zorubin was silent for a moment. 'One very tough lady,' he said at length. 'Be careful, Dan.'

'Careful of what?'

'She's taken a fancy to you. Or something.'

'Not that I'd noticed. But why would that be so bad?'

'Maybe you haven't come across women like that before,' he said as much to himself as to anyone else.

'I guess not. This is my first time in England.'

He nodded. 'Where are you from, back home?'

It was the question that made me feel intensely uncomfortable. 'Kansas City,' I said.

'Rich family?'

'So-so.'

'Brothers?'

'No.'

Zorubin caught the moment's hesitation and looked up.

'No brothers,' I said awkwardly.

'Sisters?'

'No.'

'Tell me if I'm asking too many questions.'

'Ask away,' I said lamely.

He poured some more wine. 'You taking up Lady Dorothy's offer?' he said.

'Offer?'

'To drive you home,' he said calmly. And then added apparently out of the blue: 'Where did you go to school in the States, Dan?'

'Princeton.' I flailed wildly at an answer.

'Marcus Beveridge.'

'Uh?'

'The President.'

'Oh sure,' I said.

He sat back, finishing his drink. 'None of my business, Dan. Sorry. Fifteen years a cop, old habits die hard.'

What the hell was I holding back for? Why *not* tell him? 'You're getting there, Vik,' I said. 'In a sense I'm one of your people. One of those lost in the fog.'

'Intermittent amnesia?'

I shook my head, relaxed again now. 'Nothing intermittent about it, Vik. I am one of those rare and beautiful cases of what the doctors call global amnesia. They also say it could last.'

Zorubin thought for a few moments. 'Do I offer my services? Or do you ask for them?'

I finished my glass. 'Neither,' I said. 'This is one amnesiac who's far from sure he wants to remember.'

Zorubin shrugged.

I stood up. 'I think I'll talk to my driver.'

He pushed out his heavy-knuckled hand. 'Nice time I had,' he said. 'We'll meet again.'

She drove a pre-war Jaguar six-cylinder Standard Special. I sat beside her in the green leather bucket seat as we roared off down the King's Road. 'Will you tell me about your husband?' I said.

'Tell you what?' She zoomed round a small Ford. There was no other traffic on the road. Her foot touched the gas pedal.

'All you can. All you're prepared to tell me.'

Braking hard she brought the car into the kerb outside Chelsea Town Hall.

'Is there some mystery?' She turned towards me offering a red box of Du Maurier cigarettes.

'I'm certain I knew him,' I said obstinately.

She put a hand on my thigh. 'Come on,' she said, 'I've read your record. Why should you know Oliver?'

'Christ knows.' I lit our cigarettes.

'I chose you,' she said, 'because you're a nice, clean-cut, *sane* American. Was I wrong?'

I drew on the English cigarette. The unmixed Virginia tobacco tasted harsh and flat. 'Nice, clean-cut? I don't know,' I told her. 'But I'm as sane as they come.'

She was patting the inside of my thigh. Her aim was deliberately bad.

'One more question,' I said.

'Must you?'

'What is your husband's job at the Bank of England?'

'Ex-husband!'

'Ex-husband.'

'I'm not really sure.' She turned toward me, white teeth gleaming in the streetlight. 'Can it possibly be important?'

'Yes.'

She sighed and removed her hand. 'He was invited to join the Bank from his collapsing family firm of papermakers, so I assume his role at the Bank of England is something to do with banknote printing.'

I put out my cigarette in the ashtray in the dash and I snapped shut the walnut veneered cover.

Banknote printing!

That too-familiar cold shiver ran up my spine. I thought of all I had never been able to tell Baxter about touching, feeling the bills in my hand, marks, dollars, pounds . . . I sat in the bucket seat of the Jaguar staring ahead, transfixed. Had *I* been at the Bank of England? What had Oliver Sutchley or banknotes to do with me?

We all know fear. We all know that moment when the heart and the breathing panic. But when the mind panics, careering madly away from any sane reference point, then that's real fear. I felt it now.

'Do you have *any* interest in parties?' she said quite gently.

'Only if they're very, very wild,' I said mechanically.

She side-glanced me and her lips pursed. 'I think I can promise you that,' she said, starting the powerful engine and turning, roaring north into Sydney Street.

I was lost by the time we got to the house where the party was taking place. I was even more lost when we entered a large white house with columns on either side of the door. The butler, if he really was a butler, was totally naked; he carried a rampant erection on which was speared a large fig leaf.

'You said you liked wild, wild parties,' Dorothy said with a demure smile.

This was the wildest. Dorothy was set upon by half a dozen naked men and stripped to her bra and knickers within twenty seconds. I was thrown onto a sofa by many female hands. My uniform jacket and trousers were stripped from me as a large naked black guy looked on, murmuring, 'I sure hope you ain't from Alabama, Captain.'

I was already drunk. In self-defence I became very, very drunk. I lay between anonymous young thighs and scrambled away unashamedly from fifty-year-old predator ladies.

I was spent in the first hour. In bed with a pretty young girl in the English women's naval service (this I deduced only from the tags round her neck), she asked me coldly if I would prefer to discuss philosophy.

'We could argue recent modifications to R. H. Tawney's concept of the Protestant ethic,' she said, 'if it really turns you on. God knows, something must.'

I suppose it is the inevitable pattern of all orgies but the women, more sober than the men, more demanding and with more staying power, became the hunters. A new man at the door brought shrieks of excitement and a rush of naked women into the hall. An unfortunate found sleeping under a bed was dragged out and tested for potency by eager mouths.

I saw Dorothy once lying in a bed with several young men and smoking a long cigarette which she claimed was the best hashish obtainable in London today.

I drank more and more. Gradually as dawn broke the frenetic level of activity quietened and died away. Snores overlaid the soft dance music. Champagne bottles rolled along the landings and sometimes down the thick-carpeted stairs. I suppose I had slept too, somewhere. With someone. I smelt the waft of coffee from downstairs and found Dorothy in the kitchen, dressed, made-up, looking as if she hadn't been humping all night. She said: 'Wild enough for you?' and pushed a cup of coffee towards me. It was only then that I realised that I was naked.

It was just before dawn when we left. She drove slowly now, almost dreamily. 'Bacon and eggs?' she suggested as we approached Roehampton. 'I have a flat five minutes from the hospital.'

'I'd like that,' I said. Wrecked as I was by the night, I still wanted to talk more to her. I had the feeling that once back in the hospital she would put on her remote, distant self again.

We drove through Richmond Park, the 300-year-old oaks incomparably beautiful as dawn broke, to an apartment which she rented in a low block near Robin Hood Gate. Within ten minutes I was eating breakfast while she took a shower and changed.

I listened to the sounds of her moving about the apartment and tried to formulate the questions I wanted to ask her. First and foremost, I suppose, when she became as she was. A nymphomaniac? Certainly something close.

A door opened and closed, I heard her steps along the hall and she was standing in the kitchen doorway. In her trim green WVS uniform.

I must have been staring hard. 'An aspirin for your thoughts,' she said. 'How does a nice girl like me . . .'

I nodded, coffee cup poised halfway to my lips.

'Mostly,' she said briskly, sitting down opposite me, 'by having a husband like Oliver Sutchley.'

'He . . . he approved?'

'He initiated,' she said, pouring herself coffee. 'An utter scoundrel. Thoroughly depraved.'

'You don't sound as if you have too many regrets.'

'No,' she said. 'I don't.'

'Somehow,' I said carefully, 'he doesn't seem to fit my image of the Bank of England.'

'Oh, yes,' she said. 'He's frightfully pukka. But he has a darker side, I suppose. Most of us do, I've discovered. Oliver is intensely mysterious. Eventually he allowed me to discover what he had to be mysterious about. He claimed he'd learnt it all in Lisbon.'

'Lisbon?'

'Yes, he was an assistant military attaché at the embassy there. Invalided out of the service when someone attempted to murder him.'

'What?'

'Yes,' she said calmly. 'Too melodramatic for words. Stabbed in a dark alley. By an irate husband, I've no doubt. Would have done it myself if I hadn't been busy dousing fire-bombs in the Blitz.' She finished her coffee. 'I'll give you a lift to the hospital.'

'No, thanks,' I said. 'I'll take a walk through the park. I've never seen anything quite like it.'

She smiled wryly and got up to let me out. 'When we pass the time of day at the hospital,' she said at the door, 'I will not appreciate any reference to last night. Or come to that any sniggering with your friends.'

'Don't worry, Lady Dorothy,' I said, 'nobody would believe it anyway.'

I walked back across Richmond Park. The yellowing leaves of ancient oak trees topped each rise in the land. Sandy bridle paths led through glades of elm and azalea. An old man on a strong white horse doffed his bowler hat to me as he cantered past. Over Pen Ponds a light mist hung. Oliver Sutchley, Brigade of Guards, pre-war employee of the Bank of England, half murdered in a Lisbon alley in 1944. Daniel X, injured at Lingfeld, unclaimed amnesiac, posted to Roehampton Military Hospital – work-place of Dorothy, former wife of Oliver Sutchley.

I skirted a lake and crossed a wooden bridge. The mist swirled and moved around me. Overwhelmed by fatigue and mounting vertigo I steadied myself with one hand against a tree. Was Oliver Sutchley the link? The link between Lingfeld and Roehampton? Ideas swirled away from me, as insubstantial as the lakeshore mist. But beyond everything was a hardening certainty. Whoever I was, whatever I had experienced or done in the past, I wanted to know nothing of it. I desperately wanted to be free of an idea which padded after me with the insidious persistence of a pursuing wolf, the fear that I had been involved in some horrendous event, that I had been guilty of some crime of obscene and violent proportions.

· Five ·

I rang Baxter that morning like a kid asking to be brought home from summer camp. In 1945 transatlantic calls weren't as straightforward as they are today but by 12.30 my time, 7.30 a.m. New York time, I had my call. The captain-doctor was showered, breakfasted and in his office at the Eastlake Veterans Hospital, Eastlake, New York. He was pleased to hear from me.

'Listen, Dan,' he said. 'What the hell's going on over there?'

'You tell me. I thought I was due on a boat at the beginning of the month.'

'You were.' The line crackled. I thought he said heavenly powers had intervened.

'Heavenly powers?' I shouted.

'Don't yell,' he said. 'Somebody pulled rank and diverted you to Roehampton Hospital. Somebody grabbed you, got it?'

'No,' I said. 'Why should someone grab me?'

There was a long pause. This time I thought the line had gone dead. 'Baxter,' I said. 'Baxter . . . ?'

'Still here.'

'OK, why should someone grab me?'

He sighed. 'Because you're the most interesting case of amnesia anybody's come across in years.'

'It can't just be that. Nobody here asks me questions about being a teenager.'

'So what do you want me to do?'

'Get me back home.'

His voice lightened with hope. 'You want to come to Eastlake? You'd sign an application?'

'Put it in front of me.'

'I'll do that, Dan,' he promised. 'Those Limey bastards won't get their hands on you, you rest assured.'

Within a week Baxter was as good as his word. I had time to see Vik Zorubin once when he came over to Roehampton and we walked to the top of the hill together to drink a pint at the King's Head. 'What's your next assignment, Vik?' I asked him. 'Something in Europe or is it back home for a spell?'

'My next assignment?' He gave me a sidelong glance then concentrated on his footing as we climbed the gravel path to the pub. 'I've been asked to check on a young French woman. Her husband served out the war as a submarine captain in the Mediterranean. He got back to Paris to find she'd disappeared.'

We entered the old black-beamed pub. The king's head on the swinging board outside was Charles II's. Men had been sitting in the inglenook, sipping beer by the fire, before the eighteenth century was born. I ordered two pints of bitter.

'You'll take the job of finding what happened to her?'

'No, I don't think so,' he said, scowling up at me over the beer mug.

'Why not?'

'One thing, I'm pretty sure I could tell the guy what happened to his wife without a long, expensive search.'

'And the other thing?'

'I want to work for you.'

'Oh, no, Vik,' I said. 'I'm a happy man. I've got a great future ahead of me. I don't want to be saddled with a past.'

'What are you afraid of?' he asked calmly.

'Nothing.'

'Something you've remembered,' he persisted. 'Something you've half remembered.'

'For Christ's sake, Vik,' I could hear the tension in my voice, 'leave it alone.'

'It's your life,' he shrugged.

'You're right, God damn it.' I knew I was shaking like a madman.

'I can't see you've got a lot to be afraid of.'

I got up abruptly. 'I've got to get back to the hospital,' I said.

'You haven't finished your beer.'

'Sod the beer,' I said and walked quickly and unsteadily towards the door.

I saw Dorothy Curtis once before I left for home. She had been off duty for a couple of days when her Jaguar stopped beside me in the drive. 'I hear you're leaving us,' she said.

'I take the train down to Southampton this afternoon.'

'Pity.' She smiled. 'There's a super party tonight.'

'Don't you ever do anything in ones or twos?'

She inclined her head. 'Not often anymore. But I just might have with you.'

'I'm flattered.'

'Yes,' she said. 'Goodbye, Dan.'

The engine revved and the long polished hood bucked as she released the handbrake. It seemed a somehow not inappropriate comment on our short acquaintance.

Wayne Thomas saw me into the taxi which was to take me to the station. 'No sign of my own transfer coming through,' he said happily.

I congratulated him.

'Something I wanted to ask you,' he said, 'about that Lady Dorothy broad. You think there's anything going on there?'

I hesitated. 'My guess is there's a lot going on – but she's the one who chooses who gets it.'

We shook hands. 'Strike oil,' he said and I climbed into the taxi. I had no wish to strike oil, I thought as we pulled away down the drive, my only wish from now on was to leave the ground undisturbed.

· Six ·

My train arrived in Eastlake amid the first heavy fall of snow in Upper New York State that year. Baxter, waiting on the boarded platform for me, had, I saw from the oak leaves on his shoulder, been promoted to Major. He welcomed me as he might a fragile old aunt, insisting he take my bag, guiding me by the arm past the ticket collector and out onto the forecourt to the waiting Jeep.

'You can't guess how pleased I am to have you here,' he said.

'I can.'

'Is that so? What is it, Dan?' His single track mind told him he'd missed out on something. 'Have you discovered more in Roehampton? What treatment did they give? Hypnosis, uh? Something I was planning myself.'

'Slow down, Major,' I said. 'Nothing's changed. I know no more now than I did when I arrived in London. And here and now I make it clear that I'm not submitting to hypnosis.'

'Dan,' he said earnestly, manoeuvring the Jeep past cars in which wives waited for their commuter husbands, 'you've got to relax, you've got to go with the treatment, whatever it is. It's the only way we're going to crack this.'

'I told you, Baxter,' I said dropping the military niceties of rank. 'Nothing's changed. I'm happy as I am.'

'Still no essential curiosity.'

'None,' I lied.

'OK, OK,' he muttered to himself, screwing his eyes up to peer through the windshield at the thickening snow, 'we'll fix that. Careful diet, exercise, maybe a woman once a month, say. Yup, I think we can soon establish a pretty normal pattern of essential curiosity.'

I wasn't really listening. I was looking out of the side-window of the Jeep as we left the township of Eastlake and took to the rolling hills beyond. A thin covering of snow, drifting and kicking in the wind, seemed to alter the very shape of the hills as we drove through them. I looked down on the whitened shape of Eastlake, a pattern of a few dozen streets, a courthouse, a church, and saw black smoke rise and drift through the falling snow. I knew it was from the steam train standing in Eastlake Station but for an instant the image enclosed me in fear, tightening my chest, flooding my mind. But there was something else too. That sick, vertiginous visitation of the most appalling guilt that I had felt that morning in Richmond Park.

Within the first few days at Eastlake Veterans Hospital I felt comfortable and at home. The building was a nineteenth-century iron and steel magnate's second home, two storeyed, red-brick with quantities of snow-spattered ivy growing up the walls of the two return wings. As Eastlake Vets it housed upwards of a hundred and fifty men, the most disturbed, and they were the majority, in north-wing and my group numbering no more than thirty in spacious comfort in the south wing.

We suffered from a wide variety of physical and mental problems. Some guys had lost arms or legs. Others, there were a dozen or more, had lost their genitals in some of the most bizarre and horrifying circumstances you could imagine. There were half a dozen simple, straightforward nuts among whom I was numbered. I was definitely one of the lucky ones.

The newly promoted Major Baxter was not a bad guy. As an investigator he had none of Viktor Zorubin's frightening ability to keep his own counsel. If Baxter thought something, he said it. Probably several times.

On exercise one afternoon I discovered I was a most expert skier, a detail which upset the laborious picture Baxter had been building of me. I knew the picture was wildly inaccurate because from the moment of my arrival at Eastlake I had begun to lie to him. I claimed familiarity with places I'd only read about in a travel book a couple of days before. I persuaded him that my mother was probably Danish, named Bridget or Birgitta. I played games with the poor man but they were games of serious intent. I was already beginning to erect the barriers I needed round my present.

Baxter was no threat. I could deal with him. But the thought of Zorubin haunted me. Once I had been into Eastlake to buy cigarettes and booze. It was New Year's Eve and I had begun to think about the time when I would leave the hospital. It was snowing hard and on the sidewalks it had been blown into deep sloping drifts against the shop windows. I came out of the department store carrying brown paper bags heavy with cartons of Lucky Strike and my favourite Glenmorangie malt. A hunched figure in a raincoat, snow scattering his shoulders like dandruff, was looking at the window display. The immense width of the shoulders, the short-cropped grey hair, the ungloved hands casually hanging like a skilled bar-fighter by his sides all reminded me forcibly of Viktor Zorubin.

The snow was falling thickly through the light of the streetlamps. I formed Zorubin's name on my lips, perhaps I even shouted it loud enough for the hunched figure to hear. I fancied as I wiped wet snow from my eyes that that broad, rubbery face had turned towards me. I don't know. One of my paper bags was slipping from my arms. A crowd of kids with skis on their shoulders bundled past me. When I looked up the man in the raincoat had gone.

I had few dreams. Mostly erotic fantasies known to any young man. I awoke with erections and squeezed myself into a quick ejaculation. But contentment eluded me. In early February of 1946 I told Baxter I was applying for a medical discharge.

I know he was deeply disappointed in me and he elicited my reluctant permission for him to insert a photograph and an 'If anybody knows this man . . .' advertisement in the *Kansas City Star*. The *Star* because I often talked of Kansas City or used it in my answers. I seemed to know all about Tom's Town and Ernest Hemingway working on the *Star* and a black musician I claimed was the greatest, Charlie Parker, known as the Bird, a New Jazz saxophonist.

I had begun to construct my own background and I wrote it out at night in my room checking reference books and street maps as laboriously as if I were an illegal resident constructing my *storia vitae*.

After two months I checked it and memorised it until I was word perfect. My name is Daniel Lingfield. I was born in 1920 in the West Bottoms, Kansas City. My father was of second generation German extraction and was killed in an accident in the Kaw River packing plant where he worked when I was seven. My mother was Irish. She died shortly after my father and the family was split up. I vaguely remember brothers and sisters but perhaps I'm just romanticising. I joined the US Army in 1939 and was commissioned shortly after the outbreak of war in December 1941. I served in England, near Roehampton village in a hutted camp in Richmond Park. I was shipped to Europe after D-Day and am the sort of reluctant hero that hates talking about his war experiences. I learnt decent French on our progress through France and perfected my German during the time I spent in Germany. I was badly wounded just before the end, hospitalised in Upper New York State and discharged with the European Theatre medal early in 1946.

Not a bad life story. I could fill in most details I wanted from the Goat faction of Kansas City politics to Harry Truman's failed haberdashery venture at Twelfth Street and Baltimore in the 1920s.

I wasn't really too worried about the photograph in the *Kansas City Star*.

Back in Germany I had talked a lot with Colonel Buck about the surgery I had gone through, a great deal of it facial, and I had, in addition, the significant advantage, from the point of view of confusion at least, of a thick mane of white hair. Finally I had myself chosen the photograph. It was a head and shoulders from a group picture. Reproduced in a newspaper, I was sure a man's creditors wouldn't recognise it.

I was wrong. Sometime in the early spring of 1946, Baxter called me to his office. I imagined it was to do with processing my discharge since all real treatment had now ceased. I knocked and entered. He was the cat with the cream, the fisherman with a big one on the line. He could barely control the grin of triumph which fought for existence on his round cherubic face.

'Sit down, Dan,' he said. 'For this one you'll need to be sitting down.'

I sat on the edge of the upright chair opposite his desk. The documentation I had brought with me slipped from my knees scattering pages across the floor. I bent and collected it up. Every glance at Baxter showed the idiot grin breaking out all over his face. He waited until I had finished. The patience of triumph.

'So what is it?' I said sliding back onto the chair. 'What is it? For God's sake, Baxter, what's got into you?'

'The ad delivered.' A long pause. 'The ad in the *Kansas City Star*. It produced.'

There was no nausea like this one churning in my mind. I don't know for how long I was silent. To give him credit, I think Baxter realised the stress produced in me by his brief announcement. He waited, with a genuinely concerned look on his face as I visibly struggled with the news. Then he got up and poured me a large whisky, put it in my hand and sat down again behind his desk.

In front of him was my file. He opened it and took a letter from the top. 'Your name is Hopkins,' he said. 'Ronald Frederick Hopkins.' He looked at me. The smile had returned. He raised his eyebrows twice in quick succession like Groucho Marx. 'How does it feel?'

I was numb.

'OK. Let's leave that time to cook.'

'Wait a minute,' I croaked at him. 'Ronald Hopkins – who says my name's Ronald Hopkins?'

He lifted the letter from his desk and passed it to me. 'Your father-in-law.'

I took the letter. The paper was heavy and discreetly embossed with a Kansas City address. It was written in an elegant copper-plate script. I held it in one hand for a moment.

'Can I get you some more of that whisky?' Baxter asked me.

I nodded, still not able to read the letter.

He took my glass, refilled it and placed it in my hand again. 'What you're feeling is perfectly normal, Dan.' He touched my shoulder reassuringly.

'How the hell do you know?' I snarled at him.

'Read the letter, Dan,' he said softly.

'I don't want to read the fucking letter.'

I had spilled or almost thrown the whisky across the office floor.

'I'll leave you for a few minutes.' Baxter crossed to the door. 'I'll smoke a cigarette outside.'

He was right, of course. I finished what was left of the whisky in my glass and slowly brought the sheet of expensive paper up into view. It read:

> Dear Major Baxter,
>
> I am writing to you after having seen the picture you published in the *Kansas City Star*. I have no doubt, on examining the photograph, that it is my son-in-law, Ronald Frederick Hopkins. There are differences as you suggested there might be. In particular the colour of the hair and I think the nose.
>
> My son-in-law was posted as killed in action in the Munich area in the last days of the war. In practice, I was able to ascertain that his body was never satisfactorily identified.
>
> I will not dwell on my feelings when I saw the photograph. I will only tell you that I have not yet shown it to my daughter, Catherine, because I do accept the very faint possibility that I am mistaken. The newspaper photograph was grainy and inadequate. I would beg you to forward another, or indeed a whole pack of photographs with the greatest possible speed. Only then I would dare to speak to my daughter.

There was more, mostly about the war record of Ronald Hopkins. It seemed to fit. The letter was signed:

> God be with you. Let us pray that we are not mistaken.
>   Yours truly
>   The Rev. John Hunter

Behind me the door opened and Baxter came back into the room. The grin of triumph had gone. He was a decent enough man to know what was before his eyes. 'I'm sorry, Dan,' he said.

I realised there were tears streaming down my cheeks.

'It's best,' he said.

'What's best?'

'It's best you don't live a life of fantasy.'

'Why the hell not?' I managed to say. 'I thought you told me every human being fantasises. If you don't fantasise, you're sick, is what you said.'

'There are nice people out there in Kansas City, Dan, who can be hurt as bad as you can if you're not the man they think you might be.'

I retreated into some ball of protective anger. 'That's their problem,' I said. 'That's their fucking problem. I am me. My past-life name may be Ronald Hopkins, or Benvenuto Cellini or Abe Bronstein, but to me, I'm just me, Dan Lingfield.'

'You got to face facts, Dan.'

'Who the hell faces facts? Who the hell lives or succeeds or even rubs along fairly happily by facing facts? Do great artists face facts? Do business tycoons face facts? Of course not. Do soldiers when they cross a minefield? When you fuck do you face facts – that you might be creating a new life? Of course not. Does the Reverend John Hunter face facts? You bet your sweet ass none of us do.'

Baxter took some papers from his file. 'Try these facts,' he said, tossing them onto my knees.

I caught the papers and unfolded them. There were three or four pages stapled together. The first was five photographs stuck on a single sheet. A young soldier smiled from one, proud of his obviously new uniform. A pleasant-looking guy, bright-eyed . . . there I ran out. Was it me? No. Then suddenly I looked again, back from the photograph of the young man at the wheel of the new Ford, the young man picking apples in the garden, suddenly I looked again at the top picture. Oh my good God, I felt the mouth to be mine. I felt the eyes to be my eyes. I felt the breezy, optimistic thoughts behind those eyes to be my breezy optimistic thoughts. Then. When I was young in blood.

I recoiled, terrified, from the other pages. Birth certificate, US Army KIA certificates. And then to the last page. A photograph of Catherine, a gently nice-looking girl. A preacher's daughter I had to admit. A quiet, respectable, *ordinary* young woman. Eminently violable, as Dorothy Curtis would have put it.

'They're arriving tomorrow,' Baxter said.

· Seven ·

A 1946 model Oldsmobile rolled down the drive. A man got out, medium height, brown hair balding into deep widow's peaks, a tweed suit and clerical collar. A nice guy.

Baxter came forward across the bag of the gravel drive, hand out-stretched. They shook hands. Then the Reverend Hunter turned and opened the passenger door of the car.

A young woman got out and stood blinking in the spring sunshine. She wore a flowered dress under which no breasts swelled. Her shoes were flat-heeled and she wore little make-up. Her hair had that dowdy brownness which had made Blondine a growth industry. She was, however, fairly tall. She had a well-shaped rather than exciting face. She had slim hips and excellent legs. But she held her purse in front of her and smiled spectrally when she was introduced to Major Baxter.

I was watching from the window of my room. I registered every movement, every gesture of the hand to the face, every surface sheen of the sun on the flowered dress. In a despair of unknowing, I left my vantage point and took the long tiled corridor to the main hall. I am, even at the worst times, subject to moments of wry, inappropriate humour. If this is my destiny, I thought to myself, let's take a look. You can always say no.

It was my last relaxed moment that afternoon.

In Baxter's office we stood opposite each other. I knew I felt something for her but I couldn't kiss her and I couldn't take her hand. She was much prettier than I had believed from her photograph or even seeing her in the drive. She blushed as I came into the room. She seemed to wish the ground would swallow her up. She forced a smile.

After drinks in Baxter's office, Cathy and I walked in the Eastlake Gardens. It was late March and the world of bud and root was almost about to break forth.

'It's impossible for both of us,' I said. 'We're strangers to each other. You're a stranger because I hardly remember the past. I'm a stranger because of what's happened in between. The surgery, the life I've been living as someone else.'

'Have you had women?' she asked me suddenly. 'Since you left hospital?'

We stopped before a greening stone fountain. I could never tell her about Dorothy Curtis. I could never tell her about Nurse O'Dwyer. A German woman who came to my room once a week for a small can of Nescafé I found even more impossible to explain. I said: 'Yes, I've had women.'

Her mouth puckered in distaste.

'I didn't know,' I said.

She was crying in that barely controlled, pent-up way. 'Oh God, why did Daddy do it? Why did he see your picture? Why, for God's sake, did he have to interfere!'

'Tell me about the baby,' I said.

'The *baby*'s nearly five years old.'

I guided her through the paths of the English garden. It was a sunny afternoon and when we sat on a bench before a blazing pink azalea bush the wooden slats felt warm.

'Money,' I said. 'You'll need money.'

She brushed it aside. 'I need a husband, Ron,' she said. 'I need you.'

It was arranged by Baxter that Cathy would fly up with her father from Kansas City the following weekend. Meanwhile I was to be sedated to absorb part of the shock.

By about Tuesday I could get up before 3 p.m. Baxter's idiot grin had returned. 'Of course,' he said, 'you can remember everything.'

'I think I remember her,' I conceded.

'And the Reverend?'

'So-so.'

'What does that mean?'

'It means I don't know, you bastard. You seem to think the memory is one of those forever certain issues. You, Baxter, do you remember the first time you got laid?'

'Of course.'

'Of course. But do you remember the first time you ate a chocolate bar?'

'No.'

'You remember what it tasted like even?'

'No.'

'What brand?'

'I told you, no.'

'OK, that's what memory is about.'

'But Cathy's your wife.'

'OK, but the way I remember her is just something slightly more in focus than that chocolate bar.'

The next week was a bad week. Two or three times I took a horse out from the hospital stable and rode up into the hills above Eastlake. As the mare's hooves bit out black horseshoe shapes in the sand track, I was forcibly reminded of Richmond Park in England and the lurking mists and memories.

Sometimes I tried to present myself with the fact that I had killed someone. That some dark Victorian murder was the source of my frightful anxiety. I tried to envisage the possibility that I had been a member of one of the thriving gangs in Kansas City or that I had murdered German soldiers or raped and killed their wives.

Nothing touched me. I began to form a desperate plan. I would disappear. If I could arrange for a lump sum of money to be paid for Cathy and the boy and for Baxter to push through my discharge, I could be away from Eastlake in a month. I had no wish to form any human contact with my past.

I rode back one day after the first shattering weekend and delivered the mare to the hospital groom. Crossing the drive from the stable block I passed the long windows of the original drawing room which the hospital now used as a reception lobby.

Weak sunlight was low-angled across the window panes and I saw little more than black shapes behind the burnished red reflections of the windows. The gravel crunched underfoot, the old window panes juggled light like fairground mirrors, and suddenly out of the red glow I saw and recognised the unmistakable swagger of Zorubin's shoulders. From inside the reception lobby he raised a hand in perfunctory greeting.

I walked on quickly through the double-doors and tracked back towards the main desk. Zorubin was leaning against it. He wore his familiar shabby brown raincoat and held a black-banded grey hat in his hand.

I had to get within a few feet of him before he stirred. 'Hallo, Vik,' I said awkwardly.

'Hallo, Captain.' He made no attempt to shake hands.

'What are you doing at Eastlake?'

'A few enquiries,' he said.

'Anyone I know?'

'I wouldn't think so,' he said, shifting his elbow on the counter.

'Are you here to see Baxter?'

'No, just checking records. I'm a bureaucrat at heart, Captain. I get a client, he outlines a problem. I make suggestions, he tells me do this, do that. Orders are orders, right, Captain?'

'Baxter found out who I am,' I said.

'Is that right, Captain? So at last you've got the *whole* story.'

'I don't think there's a *whole story* for me to know.'

'Simple soldier meets simple maid, uh? Speaking of simple maids I have a message from your friend Lady Dorothy Curtis.'

'You've seen her?'

'Time and a half.'

'What did she say?'

'She said to tell you that she had decided that one-on-one could be fun.'

'What are you doing here, Vik?'

'I had some business at Eastlake and I thought maybe you'd be interested to hear from Dorothy Curtis.'

'Let me get you a drink.'

He shook his head. 'I looked up her ex-husband's war record,' he said. 'Less than heroic. He was imprisoned for eight months in 1941 under a law known as 18B, the Defence of the Realm Act.'

'He was a Nazi sympathiser?' I said in astonishment.

Zorubin pushed himself off the counter. 'You got it, buddy,' he said as he sauntered broad-shouldered towards the door. 'In one.'

The next day, Friday, I drove into Eastlake in the mid-morning. First, I needed to know exactly how much I had in my bank account and, from the local branch adviser of the American Legion, what I might expect in disability pay on the basis of the rating Colonel Buck had obtained for me.

I drove down Main Street and parked outside the brick-built, ivy-covered Bank of New York and Rochester. I already had arranged an appointment with the manager and the teller took me straight through to his office as soon as I gave my name. The manager was a tall, cadaverous figure with a curiously inappropriate effusive manner. As I came into his office he had his arm round my shoulders conducting me to a chair. He offered me whisky, a near unknown politeness for a bank manager of that period. I decided Mr Surridge was one of those amiable eccentrics that Yankee small town life often throws up. I wouldn't have been surprised if he had suddenly started quoting the *Iliad* to me. Or even *Tropic of Capricorn*.

My plan was simple. I would assign as large a lump sum as possible to Cathy's son. I would add further sums throughout my life. But for now it would be one sum, limited to my account as it now stood with the best part of a year's captain's pay. Less some expenditure and some initial disability payments I calculated I was worth something in the region of fifteen hundred dollars.

'Seventy-five thousand dollars,' the bank manager said, 'is a large sum of money. What do you intend to do with it?'

'There's some mistake,' I said fighting greed, hope and a dozen other lesser emotions. 'The Army's generous but I don't have seventy-five thousand dollars in my account.'

'I assure you that you do, Captain,' Surridge said. 'We received a draft for that sum yesterday morning and informed you as a matter of course. Our letter would have arrived at the hospital . . .' he consulted his wristwatch, 'about now . . .'

'A draft,' I said unsteadily.

'As good as cash,' he said briskly. 'Drawn by a specialist house in New York.'

'But where from? Where did the money come from?'

'That I can't tell you.'

'Can't tell me?'

'I don't know, Captain. If you're as baffled as you appear to be we could make enquiries. But these specialist houses are notably tight with their information. It's what their business is based on – discretion. Do you want me to follow it up for you?'

'Yes,' I said, 'if you're sure the money was really intended for me.'

'Captain Daniel Lingfield, Eastlake Veterans Hospital. Is that your service number, Captain?'

He pushed a page across at me. The service number under my name was the one Colonel Buck had assigned to me.

'That's my number,' I said.

'We'll make some enquiries, Captain, but the answer I guarantee you will receive will be that the money was lodged by some law firm in Lincoln, Nebraska, or Seattle or Santa Fe. It's a legacy, Captain. A hundred to one it's a legacy. Lawyers shuffle this sort of money round the country every day. Never seem to shuffle it in my direction, sadly enough.'

I gave the American Legion pensions adviser a miss and drove slowly back down Main Street. Seventy-five thousand dollars was truly a vast sum of money. If some lawyer *had* shuffled it into my account, why so secretively? And how the hell had they learned my name and serial number? Even more important, if it was a legacy, who was the legacy from? Was it really meant for me?

I was so absorbed by my speculations that I took the wrong turning, found myself blocked by a truck loaded with paving stones, turned right and right again and came out on Main Street just beside the bank. Zorubin was leaving the glass-fronted drug-store just opposite. He lifted his hand in that slow, perfunctory wave.

I drove back to the hospital through the awakening spring hills. I could only think of seventy-five thousand dollars and a bottle of scotch and total oblivion. Tomorrow Cathy and her father were coming up to visit. I was filled with dread.

· Eight ·

From my room I watched their Oldsmobile come slowly up the drive and draw to a halt outside the hospital front steps. As he had last week, the Reverend Hunter got out, circled the car and held open the passenger door for Cathy to dismount. It was as if he were conducting her to the altar.

I let myself out of my room and saw the glass door swing at the end of the corridor. Cathy came through it alone. She seemed different, still shy but less mouselike. She waved her white-gloved hands to me down the corridor.

'Hallo, Cathy.'

'Hi, Ronnie,' she said. 'I thought I'd come and take you for a walk. I've got some pictures of little Ronnie.'

As she came out of the blaze of sunlight I saw, with a sense of shock, her thick lipstick and face powder so heavily applied that fine grains fell from the down on her cheeks as she spoke. I realised too that she walked unsteadily on new ankle-strap high heels. Her dress spoke volumes – plunging daringly down a flat breastbone. It was not difficult to figure out. Her soldier husband had come back. He was used to more exotic delights than Kansas City girls. She would have to play up to him. Tempt him.

I felt deeply sorry that she had been reduced to this pathetic exercise, sorry for her and angry at myself.

She took my arm as we walked in the garden and she told me some of the cute things the little boy said. How much he wanted to come up to Eastlake this weekend and how she'd thought that no, it wouldn't be right. Because after all he would expect to be sleeping in a hotel room with his mother, not with his grandfather.

She gave me another of those tight shy smiles as she said it and I found I was trembling too much to light a cigarette. She looked at me. 'It's going to be all right, Ronnie,' she said. 'You'll get your old job back at the plant. They have to give it to you, that's the law.'

She drew me down onto the bench we had sat on before. From the tiny wooden tower perched on top of the hospital building the mess-hall bell tolled. She was holding both my hands tight. I made an attempt to move. 'You must be hungry,' I said. 'I can arrange lunch here.'

She shook her head, her eyes moist. Through the grassy alleys of the gardens we could hear the voices of other patients drifting back to the dining hall.

'Let's wait,' she said. She gave me a ghastly pathetic smile.

I struggled to start talking. 'Listen, Cathy, all this has been a shattering experience for you. You know, to suddenly discover your husband was alive.'

She frowned. 'You always talk about yourself as if you weren't there. *You're* my husband. *You're* alive.'

'I'm alive, Cathy, but I'm a very different guy.'

'Ronnie,' she said, 'you know why you're feeling like this. Come back to the hotel, come back now.'

'No, Cathy,' I said in acute embarrassment.

She threw an arm round my neck. Lipstick scored across my lips, sweet, salty. She forced her tongue into my mouth.

I pushed her away and stood up in shock and shame. 'I'm sorry, Cathy,' I said. 'You've got to understand.'

Her nose and eyes reddened with tears. 'There's another woman isn't there? You're in love with someone else.'

In my desperate desire to escape more fumblings I admitted it. 'There is someone else. A nurse in England,' I extemporised. 'She's coming back to New York this week.'

She dropped her head on her chest. 'And where does that leave me and little Ronnie?'

'Believe me, Cathy, I didn't think it was possible to feel such a heel. But I do honestly believe it's best for both of us. And for the boy.'

She looked up. 'Your son,' she said with as cold a look as she could muster.

'Yes.'

'Say it,' she screamed.

'My son.'

'I'm sorry, Ronnie.' She stood up. 'Take me back to Dad.'

There was not much that was amiable in John Hunter's expression as I sat opposite him in a room Baxter had assigned us.

'Your proposal, as I understand it, Ronald, is that you live apart from Cathy.'

'We would have no contact with each other.'

'None at all?'

'No.' I felt as if I had climbed Everest. 'Now finances.'

His face was wooden.

'I could offer forty thousand dollars,' I said.

His body visibly stopped for a fraction of a second. 'Forty thousand dollars. Forty thousand dollars? Where would you get that sort of money?'

'I saved a bit in the service. More important I invested in poker.'

'You were never a gambler,' he said suspiciously.

'On troopships and in Normandy invasion transit camps you learn to be. I learnt to be a good one.'

'Forty thousand dollars.' His eyes had become greedy. 'You're proposing to pay this in one sum?'

'Yes. I'll draw a bank draft in Cathy's favour on Monday morning and have it delivered immediately to your hotel.'

He stood up. 'In these very strange circumstances, Ronald,' he said, 'I do believe you are attempting to act like a gentleman.'

As soon as I saw the Reverend Hunter's Oldsmobile leave I walked back towards my room. I had a bottle of Glenmorangie malt whisky there and I intended to be able to see through the bottom of the bottle by morning. Baxter was signing some papers in the reception hall as I passed through. 'Dan,' he called. 'One moment.' He came across to me shrugging in embarrassment. 'I just had a word with Cathy,' he said. 'I guess I just want to say I'm sorry.'

'OK,' I nodded. 'You're sorry. You were in the dark too. We both were. You don't owe me any apologies. When can I leave here?'

'I can push it through for Monday.'

'Do that.'

'Where will you go?'

I was forced to smile. 'Do you think I'd tell you?'

I left him and made my way back to my Glenmorangie. I sat in my leather chair, army issue, and studied the understated orange label. Then I tipped the bottle and poured two inches into a glass. I caught the extraordinary smoky flavour of the spirit as I brought the glass to my lips. I got up and put on a scratchy Charlie Parker piece which I'd found in Eastlake. I got out my chess set and started moving the pieces around. Before I even got to my second drink I was asleep.

I awoke God knows how many hours later. Zorubin was standing in the room. He was wearing his old brown raincoat and he kept it on as, uninvited, he poured himself a glass of Glenmorangie. He sat heavily on the arm of the other leather chair and sipped the whisky, his eyes resting somewhere between the door and the window.

'What is it, Vik?' I asked him.

'I wish I knew,' he said. 'I wish I could just make up my mind about you, buddy boy.'

'You don't drink my drink and give me that tone of voice,' I said. 'Get out.'

He drained his glass and stood up. 'I could break your back,' he said.

'I don't doubt it. I still want you to leave.'

He nodded his vast head. 'Tell you what, Captain,' he said. 'I got a bottle of finest vodka in my hotel room. Come and share it with me.'

'I've got malt here.'

He took my arm. 'Sometimes even whisky drinkers need a change.'

I assented because I didn't care. We left the hospital and climbed into Zorubin's rented car.

'Tell me,' I said. 'What the hell *are* you doing in Eastlake?'

'I don't know.' He took the corner onto the main road at speed and accelerated down towards Eastlake. It was perhaps ten or eleven o'clock and the lights of the town appeared and followed the strange shapes of the hills. 'I don't know *yet*,' he said.

'You've got no client here?'

'Not yet.'

'We've been through this before, Vik. Get it clear, I don't want your services.'

'You've got 'em.'

'For Christ's sake, are you crazy?'

'No, I'm not crazy, Captain.'

'So why in God's name are you following me?'

'I trace missing persons, Captain, you know that. As far as I'm concerned, you're missing.'

After the strains of the day, my head was spinning. 'What's in it for you?' I asked savagely.

'That's to be seen.'

'Then, why me? There are eight million missing persons . . .'

'Are you a genuine missing person, Captain? That's what I ask myself.'

'Turn the fucking car round,' I said. 'Take me back to the hospital.'

He stared straight ahead. 'Your stay in Roehampton, England, was carefully arranged,' he said.

'Arranged? Who by?'

'At the end of the line, I don't know yet. But the technicalities were arranged by the hospital records office.'

'Dorothy Curtis?'

'Lady Dorothy Curtis.'

He nodded toward the twisting road ahead.

'Why would anyone want to keep me in England for an extra month?'

'Perhaps for some reason you wanted to *stay* in England for an extra month?'

'You've got an enflamed imagination, Vik. I knew nothing about this. As far as I'm concerned I arrived in England with an officer's berth on the *Queen Elizabeth* on November 7th. A week later I was transferred to Roehampton Military Hospital.'

'And you don't know how?' We were driving into Eastlake.

'No, I don't know how.'

'Administrative error?'

'I guess.'

'Nothing Baxter could do anything about?'

'For God's sake, Vik, I don't know.'

'What happened,' Zorubin said slowly, 'was that someone was switched into your berth on the *Queen Elizabeth*. You, therefore, were consigned to the Roehampton Hospital. The question is, what was the object of this little exercise?'

We pulled up outside Zorubin's hotel, a quiet stone-fronted building, dating from the 1920s.

'So what was the object?'

He shrugged. 'The guy who got your berth was a Lieutenant Anthony S. Spinks of Grapevine, Texas.'

'Why was he put in?'

'Nobody put him *in*. Somebody took you *out*,' Zorubin grunted.

'Listen, Vik, you know the Army. A million things happen every day that no one can account for. And why can't they? Because there's no real reason to find anyway.'

'You may be right.'

'Somebody gets a name wrong. An ID number is crossed up. Clerks cover their asses. In the process Captain D. Lingfield's berth is assigned to Lieutenant A. Spinks from Grapevine, Texas. What's the big deal?'

We got out of the car and crossed to the hotel. Inside the lobby it was small and comfortable, an American hotel at its best. The desk clerk greeted Zorubin.

'I'm taking Captain Lingfield up to my room for a drink,' Zorubin said.

We mounted the stairs. There was only one flight, wide, carpeted in a Victorian pattern on dark blue.

He looked at his watch. 'It's late,' he said. 'Time all respectable folks were tucked up in bed.'

'You want to forget the drink?'

He shook his head.

'Vik, for Christ's sake, if you know anything I don't, will you just give it to me!'

'I know a thing or two,' he said.

'Something that happened to me in the service? Something that happened before I got blown up by that Teller mine?'

He shrugged. We entered a corridor and stopped before Room 312. He reached in his pocket for his keys.

'Vik,' I said, furious, 'will you stop playing games?'

Zorubin smiled. From a bunch of keys he selected one. 'OK.' He put a key in the hotel door lock. 'Let's clear the decks on one issue first,' he said with something between a scowl and a leer.

The door swung open and Cathy rose off the Reverend Hunter's cock as if it were a red-hot poker.

She was naked, still astride him. He wore only his clerical collar, black dicky and a striped flannel shirt.

Zorubin ignored the girl. He crossed to the bed, took Hunter by the loose shoulder of his shirt and hauled him up. Cathy tipped sideways, across the bed and onto the floor.

The Reverend Hunter was propelled through the door, down the flower-carpeted stairway, across the hall, his white legs wildly dancing, and out through the front door.

Zorubin shouldered his way back into the lobby. 'If I see him back in this hotel,' he said to the startled clerk, 'I'll call the Police Department. Tell him that.'

I turned back from the head of the stairs. Through the doorway I could see Cathy rapidly pulling on her clothes. Vik Zorubin joined me, leaning on the door jamb watching her shaking hands fix her bra.

Not for the first time events had moved too fast for me.

'They specialise in the missing person world,' Zorubin said. 'I've seen their work once or twice but this is the first time I ever caught up with them.'

As Cathy, carrying a case half spilling stockings and underwear, passed between us, Zorubin's huge hand came down on her ass with a resounding thwack which propelled her head first across the landing, to stumble down the stairway into the hall.

As she dived for the front door, Zorubin turned back to me. 'Forget the drink I offered,' he said. 'I already saved you forty thousand bucks tonight.'

How the hell did he know that?

At Eastlake the next morning, I received a call from Zorubin. 'I'm going to put your case on hold,' he said abruptly.

'Listen, Vik, please get it into your head. I am very grateful for your intervention with those con-artists last night. But I am not a case. Not one of yours.'

'Not everybody gets to choose whether they're one of mine,' his heavy voice rumbled down the line.

'OK,' I said. 'What made you change your mind?'

'I haven't entirely. What you were up to in those last days of the war I still haven't got to. Members of the US Army, some of them at least, were adept at exploiting a very fluid and promising situation.'

'You think my amnesia is a cover for whatever I was doing at Lingfeld?'

'Not after last night. A forty thousand dollar cheque is enough to convince me you genuinely were taken in by the Reverend and his girl friend. That's why I've put your case on hold. Goodbye, Captain.' The line clicked and purred. That, I imagined then, was the last I would hear of the curious Viktor Zorubin.

· Nine ·

I was a civilian. I could, of course, say that I was a civilian *again*, but it meant nothing to me. I had no life before the military before waking up in that hospital in Germany.

I hung around in New York for a few weeks until the city lost its appeal. In the New Year I moved west to Los Angeles and signed up to teach in a school in Anaheim, successfully bluffing and faking my way through the paper qualifications I was supposed to present. I gave Colonel Buck as my principal witness and he came up trumps. By the beginning of the 1947 school year I was teaching German at St Joseph's High School, living the easy life of southern California on my salary and fifty thousand dollars invested in Coca-Cola, the Boeing Aircraft Corporation and a real estate company which specialised in land for golf clubs. In the evenings I began desultory work on a novel.

I wasn't fully well. Apart from my persistent loss of my past I was, I came to realise, disturbed. I slept well at nights only if I took sleeping pills or five or six malt whiskies. I dreamed dreams of an intensity which made me wake with my heart racing – and yet seconds later no details remained, only a strange sort of vacuum of fear.

In New York I'd developed a mild paranoia, a sense of being followed, an irrational worry about wrong number calls up to my hotel room. In California at first I felt better, freer in a new climate, more relaxed. But it didn't last. I began to note down the number plates of cars riding behind me. I began to pull across suddenly and swerve rapidly into sideroads. Once or twice I blocked off a following car and jumped out to confront a baffled driver.

I don't know what May Butler meant to me at this time and perhaps to the end of my days it will remain a mystery. May worked at the school, taught English and History, was a nice, sensible woman whom the students respected and her colleagues liked. She was school deputy when I joined the staff and we'd sometimes have lunch together on a friendly basis and talk about the good and bad students as teachers always do.

May was thirty, round-faced, spectacled and definitely overweight. She had that Californian lack of curiosity about background. Everybody she knew had come from other parts of the country. She had no family in California, she had no prying wish to know more about my life in Kansas City. My need for invention was minimal. I talked about Germany and England but at that time most young men talked more about their army experiences than anything else because their army experiences were more real to them than anything else.

May enjoyed seafood and had quite a taste in Californian wine. To most wine drinkers at this time Californian wine was strictly for winos, to be consumed while waiting in the dollar-a-pint blood donor line. But May knew differently. We began to go on Sundays to vineyards in the Napa Valley where wine was made of a quality I never knew America produced. She was impressed by my apparent knowledge of European wine. I was astonished at her knowledge of what was then beginning in the fields of California, the beginnings of a quality wine-making industry which would be able to challenge the world.

We became good friends.

I can't pretend that I enjoyed teaching although some of the students were good and some of the teenage girls were definitely attractive.

Pauline-Ann Partoise gave me a lot of trouble. She was pretty in a pert sort of way and she had a body which seemed to have left her teenage self five or six years behind. She also gave me trouble because in that disturbing sixteen-year-old way, I knew she had settled on me.

There's no use pretending I was unaffected. I doubt if any man or woman is really unaffected by the love or lust of another. As I walked back and forth down the corridor Pauline-Ann's pretty dark-blonde, glistening head would follow me as if she were watching tennis. She made no attempt to disguise it. In class she was an averagely good student. At every opportunity she brought up work and pressed against me. The other girls giggled at her daring. I began to react as she stood next to me or leaned over to turn a page.

None of this was more than passing fancy on my part until the night of the UCLA production of Goethe's *Iphigenie*. It was to be performed in German and I was arranging a visit to Santa Barbara for the senior students. Tickets were one dollar, transport was four dollars including a hamburger stop and Cokes. When I found that I had nearly thirty-five takers, mixed boys and girls, I hired a bus. May agreed to come along and as we rode up the coast road I felt in high spirits. I even had a flask of whisky in my inside pocket which I intended to slip to May as soon as we were out of sight of the kids.

The first act went pretty well, the college students lumbering through the German, sometimes muffing lines but making a pretty creditable effort on the whole. The second act provoked yawns. By the time May and I returned for the third act it was clear that there were empty seats where our contingent were supposed to be sitting. I confess I was no longer completely sober. Swallowing quick gulps of whisky in quiet doorways is not the way to be able to measure how much you've had. May seemed pretty OK. I was aware that I was moving toward being fairly drunk.

As I set out to round up the students and force them back to the last act, I stopped in the empty corridor between the theatre and the car park exit and finished the flask. Even within memory I'd drunk a lot of whisky. I wasn't showing the inner warmth I felt as I came out into the car park. It wasn't too difficult to locate the culprits. It was a warm Californian summer night and the giggles and squeaks from behind the bushes which enclosed the parking lot gave me all the leads I needed. I walked down the line of the thick oleander bushes and young couples rose before me, lipstick smudged, hair tussled, a rapid buttoning by some of the girls.

'That's the lot,' I said to Lena Hawthorne as she stamped in embarrassment and pulled hard on her sweater which was riding high on her bra.

'We were just going back,' she said.

'Better hurry if you're going to cátch the last act.'

As her head turned away I could see from her expression that Goethe could not compete with Tom Gallati. Certainly not that evening.

'Lena.' I stopped her and she turned back toward me. 'That's everybody, uh?'

'All 'cept Pauline-Ann,' she said. 'She don't feel so good. She went back to the bus.'

'OK,' I said. 'I'll go and see.'

I watched the couples go back into the building and turned towards the bus. It was dark and the driver was not in his seat. I climbed up the steps and looked down the length of the bus.

I could see no one. The lighted building cast oddly shaped shadows across the back of the seats. I walked down the aisle. 'Pauline-Ann?' I thought I heard something at the back of the bus where a single long bench ran from side to side. 'Pauline-Ann, are you here?'

I reached the end of the bus. The light from outside fell on Pauline-Ann's long legs stretched out on the bench seat. Her head and shoulders were in shadow.

'Lena said you're not feeling good,' I said, standing one hand on the back of the seat in front.

'So-so,' she said. 'But I told Lena not to say anything. I told her I just wanted to lie here quiet for a while.'

'Sure,' I said. 'You'll feel better in a few minutes. You don't want Miss Butler to look in and see how you are?'

'I'm fine now,' she said.

'OK.' I made to turn away.

'Don't go yet.' There was something adult in her tone.

'I'll catch the last act,' I said.

'But you've seen it before.'

'Of course.'

Her hand reached up from the shadow and touched mine. 'Couldn't you sit here a moment and tell me what happens?'

I wouldn't pretend I didn't know what I was doing. I sat on the edge of the double seat, her legs flowing out of the darkness. I put one hand on her thigh and a white arm came up and slid round my neck. Her lips tasted of bubble gum. Mine, I had time to reflect, tasted of whisky.

Under me there was much panting and wriggling. She took my hand with practised firmness from her thigh, lifted her sweater and laid my palm against the silkiness of her Playtex bra. As I reached underneath her to unhook the fastening she pushed on my shoulder. 'Listen,' she said, 'you know my name's Pauline-Ann. You know it's not Alexina or whatever you were calling me.'

I sat up. One hand was awkwardly trapped under the sweater, under her as yet unfastened bra. 'Alexina?' I said. I heard the words. My head was spinning.

'You drunk or something?' She pushed me away. As she did so I saw, under a wall light, the bus driver coming toward us, zipping his fly.

I stood up quickly and retreated a few feet from the back seat. Pauline-Ann had heard the footsteps approaching and I guess feared it was May.

'Listen,' I said as the bus driver mounted the steps, 'you just stay here then, Pauline-Ann, if you're not feeling well.' I turned to the driver. 'Leave the lights on, will you? And don't hesitate to call Miss Butler or myself if she wants us.'

'Yes, sir.' The driver flicked switches and the interior lights came on. He was climbing into his seat as I regained the parking lot. Only as I dabbed at my face with my handkerchief did I realise that my mouth was smeared with lipstick.

I felt badly shaken. Not just by the surge of adrenaline or the realisation of the risk I had taken, but most of all by that moment which I seemed to see like a re-run movie. The girl's light chestnut hair gleaming in a slant of light. Her dark, shapely mouth and the glisten of her even teeth. Alexina. I shuddered. I had called her Alexina. And there was no doubt at all in my mind that this was some face, rising from the depths.

I regained my seat beside May. She was unaware I was shaking and I sat for half an hour in the darkness answering automatically her whispered questions about *Iphigenie*.

We left the theatre and stopped for our hamburgers on the way. Pauline-Ann was polite and friendly as she explained to May why she had missed the last act. I thought Lena's eyes sparkled or her lips curved but I wasn't really sure. May herself was quite unaware that anything had happened.

I drove home slowly; watching, always watching the following cars. I had had a lucky escape, I suppose, but I don't think I really cared. My mind was desperately uneasy. Images, like my tortured dreams, flickered and died: a young blonde girl calling and the nameless horror I was powerless to protect her against. Or did the nameless horror have a name? Was it my own?

In the late summer May Butler and I agreed to move in together. We both needed it, I because I felt it would settle me, save me from the horror dreams of dead women that I had betrayed or killed. She welcomed the move, as we both knew by then, because she was a lesbian.

We lived together for mutual protection and, marvellously, without mutual pressure. Sometimes I would stay out a night or two; sometimes she would bring a girl home and I would happily be reading in bed half listening to the giggles and snufflings coming from May's room. The deal was simple and completely understood by us both: we were, each of us, free to leave when we chose.

Living with May provided a special form of therapy for me. She was a relaxed, balanced, sexually liberated woman who lived on a quiet, even keel. She told me that she had had men but she had never really enjoyed the physical act and found the relationship her male lovers would then attempt to construct completely stultifying and at worst humiliating. She had always preferred girls from the time of her first teenage romance with a girl in the same class. Of course, she said, matter-of-factly over breakfast, being a lesbian narrows the field. But she was confident that one day the right girl would come along. We got a lot of laughs out of the idea of 'When Miss Right shows up'.

Neither I nor May had seen Pauline-Ann Partoise since she had left school and it was to my real surprise that one night when I had just settled in front of the TV to watch the Packers beat the Bears, the apartment door opened and May ushered Pauline-Ann in. She was nearly twenty now, as pretty as she ever was, a trainee journalist on a local paper.

The first thing I noticed was that they were both a little drunk. Pauline-Ann shook hands with me with a wry smile of remembrance and May bustled about opening a bottle of wine.

'How did you two meet up again?'

May's smile may have been slightly suppressed; Pauline-Ann's was downright secretive. Then she laughed. 'The thing is, Dan – is it all right to call you Dan? – the thing is I was working on a school piece for my paper. Where are they now, sort of thing. And May was the natural link.'

May poured the wine. 'Matter of fact,' she said, 'we've been working on this some time.'

I raised my glass and drank. A 1945 Margaux, far too young but marvellous all the same. What was May doing pouring 1945 Margaux? 'You didn't say anything about it.' My mind was on the superb taste of the Margaux as it rolled across my tongue.

'You were away fishing when it first came up.'

I stopped concentrating on the wine. 'That was six weeks ago.'

'That's right,' May said calmly, going to sit on the couch next to Pauline-Ann. 'We decided that we pretty much like each other.'

The penny dropped. Or rather crashed with the weight of a cannon ball. I think I must have been staring open-mouthed because both of them began to grin.

Her hand still round her wine glass, May pointed with a stubby index finger to Pauline-Ann. 'Miss Right,' she said, 'finally showed up.'

Again the expression on my face must have been less than cool. 'Miss Right?' I said and we all three burst out laughing.

Pauline-Ann moved in with May that spring and I looked for another apartment. At least I moved into an apartment hotel and spent some good evenings alone, drinking Glenmorangie, and asking myself what I really wanted to do.

I was on a short-term engagement at the school. I had approaching seventy thousand dollars in stocks and, for the first time since that day I woke up in hospital in Munich, I felt some faint urgings of curiosity about who I really was.

The nightmares had faded in my time with May. I had told her the truth shortly after we moved in together and she was kind, patient and reassuring. Her argument was simple. I might have lost my memory but I had not changed my personality. At least not to the extent that I might have committed some appallingly violent acts which I would not dream of now. Living with me, she said, was not living with a psychopath.

I had said I was glad to hear it. And I was.

'What it's all about, Dan,' she said sometime toward the end of our period together, 'is how complete you can feel with no memory of your past.'

I was uncertain about that myself. However much I feared the truth, I knew I could never resist it if the chance came.

May was looking at me like a schoolteacher poised over some not too bright pupil.

'I'm happy as I am, May,' I said unconvincingly, getting up from the sofa.

She turned down the corner of her mouth. 'No curiosity about your past?'

'I can live without knowing.'

'You sure?'

I shrugged. It was like being carpeted in sixth grade.

'I think you know that's crazy, Dan,' she said. 'We all get a kick out of hearing something new about ourselves, a family story about how cute we were aged one, some goofy uncle's opinion of us even though it's not worth a damn. You're different?'

'I could be,' I said. 'I've lived here without a goofy uncle's opinion.'

'A respite,' she said dismissively. 'We both needed to duck from the world for a few months. It's been great.'

I poured her a drink. 'I know it's time to move on, May,' I said. 'The question is, where to?'

She raised her glass to me. 'Go looking,' she said.

When I thought seriously about it the idea excited me. I wasn't that different from anyone else. I suppose the incident with the Reverend Hunter and Cathy had delivered a body blow. For a week or so I really had believed I was a plant worker from Kansas City. It may be unfair to plant workers but I have to admit it was pretty bad for my self-esteem. I had something better in mind for me than that.

But I was getting clearer about it all. I realised I had wanted a past on my own terms. Maybe I was different now. Maybe what was riding in me was a real curiosity.

'Most of us are not totally proud of our pasts,' May said. 'Why should you be different? At least you'll know.'

I sort of agreed but the fear was there at the same time. Most of the world doesn't have that haunting sense that you pierce the curtain of memory at your peril. That curiosity could lead through the curtain of amnesia into an uncontrollable nightmare.

She crossed the room and put her arm round my waist. 'In any case,' she said, 'I can't see you being able to live a normal life with a woman until you've wiped the slate clean. Properly.'

'What does that mean?'

'It could mean a lot of things. It could mean for instance that you'll discover you really were an assistant plant manager in Kansas City or Springfield, Illinois or whatever, just as the con-artists set you up to be.'

I smiled. 'That would be tough to take.'

'Not very romantic,' she conceded. 'Or it could mean that your nightmares really were giving you some sort of glimpse of your past.'

She detached her arm from around my waist. 'Either way,' she turned her owlish, bespectacled eyes upon me, 'there's only one way for you to face the future, Dan.'

I nodded slowly.

I knew she meant by discovering my past.

· Ten ·

To be back in Munich filled me with excitement and trepidation in about equal quantities. Of course many things had changed. There was no longer an American zone. The British and Americans had merged their two zones into what was soon to become the Federal Republic of Germany. GIs were everywhere, in bars and cafés, strolling in civilian clothes in groups of five or six down the Leopoldstrasse, driving in seemingly endless convoys out to training fields beyond the town.

There had been some rebuilding but many areas of destruction still remained. Yet there was, I was soon aware, a sense of new hope about. The US had proposed the Marshall Plan, the greatest single piece of international generosity ever known. The Deutschmark offered the hope of a stable currency and Germans were already working for a new future.

But much of this was not yet evident. The people in the streets looked grey-faced, their clothes were mostly worn thin, there was acute over-crowding because of the bombing and the large numbers of German refugees who had been brutally driven out of their Sudeten homeland by the Czechs. Yet somehow, around me, I felt the real stirring of hope, the anticipation of a new Germany being born.

I checked in at a small hotel in Schwabbing, the more raffish area of Munich near the University, and took stock of my position. Strangely, having come all this way from California, I was uncertain what to do. I knew that now, in the changed circumstances, Elisabeth Oster would no longer watch me, cold and frightened. In all probability her husband would quite simply call the police and have me thrown out. I had no right to be there, no right to insist on being there. And yet I was drawn out along the Perlacher Forest road towards Lingfeld.

Six hours after my plane had landed at Munich Airport I had installed myself in my Schwabbing hotel, eaten lunch, hired a car and was on my way to Lingfeld. It was late afternoon on a mild spring day. I soon left the city behind me. Along the country roads there was little motor traffic.

Farmers in creased green Bavarian hats drove carts pulled by lean horses. On the tiny farms scattered across the hillsides women worked and sometimes waved as I passed. At the Lingfeld five kilometre sign I almost turned back. For a moment I experienced a return of that feeling which urged or perhaps warned me to seal off the past. I had come to believe there was more to me than my rational surface self, whatever May said about my not being a psychopath. I didn't, of course, think that I was, or had been. But when these waves of irrational fear rolled over me I flinched like a child.

At that five kilometre post I forced myself on. The curiosity to see what effect Lingfeld would *now* have on me was as strong or stronger than my fears. At the great stone gates I turned and stopped the car. The shrapnel holes in the stonework had been repaired. A neat white board read in black lettering *Haus Lingfeld*, replacing the warning against mines. I looked up the drive toward the house. It had been freshly regravelled and the gardens beyond the line of linden trees were well kept.

I had been staring so intently in the direction of the house that I hardly registered the movement to my right. When I turned my head I saw nothing but the darkening shadows of the bushes beside the drive. I made a move to put the car in gear and again something caught my eye, and with it there was a rustle of leaves and the crunch of a footstep.

I climbed out of the car, now keeping my eyes on the patch of bushes where the sound came from. This time I caught the movement. A head ducked into the bushes as I dived forward. My hand went out, broke through a curtain of leaves and caught the cloth of a sleeve. I pulled hard and a small, wizened man came bursting out of the shrubbery. Saliva dotted a grey stubble, small bright eyes blinked in alarm. He gurgled and began to cackle nervously.

I let him go. 'I'm sorry to frighten you, old man,' I apologised, half ashamed myself that I had been frightened of a crazy old man. 'Do the Osters still live here?'

He nodded. 'Wilhelm,' he said. 'I'm Wilhelm.' He dived back into the bushes and disappeared from view.

I got back into the car and drove slowly up the drive. The wide cobbled forecourt had not changed but the house had obviously undergone major repairs. The roof and upper floor window frames had been completely renovated. For some reason I particularly remembered the line of machine-gun bullet holes in the stonework of the lower façade. Today in the light of a setting sun I could see the bullet scars had gone.

I stopped the car and got out. A woman was walking down the long slope of the parkland to my right. Two young golden Labradors galloped and pranced in front of her.

It was, I saw immediately, a very different Elisabeth Oster to the woman I had last seen in the shell of this house four years ago. The clothes were clearly different, new, probably London-made country tweeds, the shoes equally expensive-looking. But it was the set of her head, the imperious look of enquiry, the immaculate make-up and perfectly cut hair that struck me most. She was a woman now of perhaps forty or a year or so less, remote, controlled, self-confident. But she nevertheless made one simple mistake: she pretended not to recognise me and, as one of the few thirty-year-old Americans with a healthy thatch of white hair, I am, if nothing else, pretty unforgettable.

She came down the stone steps from the terrace, the dogs romping around her. 'Good afternoon,' she said coolly in German. 'Can I help you?'

We stood looking at each other for a long moment. Like old lovers who had long ago ceased to amuse or attract each other.

'I asked you if I could help you.' She changed to English. 'You're American are you?' she said looking at my clothes. 'Perhaps you're lost?'

'No.' I shook my head. 'Not lost.' I paused and she now began to look uncomfortable. 'I think you remember me, Frau Oster.'

'No.'

'I think you remember at the very least a night just after the war when I came here.'

With a minute facial movement she indicated assent. 'What are you doing here?' she said.

'I'm taking a vacation in Europe.'

'Then why have you come here? To Lingfeld?'

I extended my hand. 'My name is Lingfield,' I said. 'Or rather my given name. You must understand that for me this house is a starting point.'

She shrugged irritably.

'I wondered if seeing the house again would jog my memory, some detail, however small.'

'And has it?'

'Not the house, no.' I was sure I saw relief in her expression. I timed it carefully. 'But seeing you again is different.'

The alarm showed clearly on her face now.

'Will you invite me in?'

She shook her head.

'Are we to stand out here talking?'

'We have nothing to speak about,' she said.

'I think we have.'

'Will you please leave now,' she said almost shrilly. 'Will you please leave before I call someone to escort you out.'

'The old man, Wilhelm?'

It was meant to be no more than a cheap jibe on my part. The effect on her was devastating. She stood for a few moments in obvious confusion, obvious distress.

'Perhaps we'd better go into the house after all,' I said.

It was a rough shot in the dark but she immediately nodded a sort of defeated agreement and turned to lead the way back up the terrace steps.

We entered through tall french doors which matched equally tall windows on either side. The main entrance hall was to the left and the servants' quarters where the Osters had lived in candlelight, with cold blasts from broken doors, were somewhere deeper into the house.

There were no broken doors now. No candlelight. She switched on a blazing candelabra and six or eight small table lamps from one switch. She stood in the middle of the room breathing heavily, making no attempt to ask me to sit down. Then she turned and quickly took a cigarette from a silver box and lit it with a snap of a table lighter. 'Go on,' she said.

But now I was at a loss. It was easy to see that she thought I knew more than I did. The wrong sentence could re-establish her confidence. 'I saw Wilhelm at the gate,' I said.

Again that expression of panic crossed her face. 'Wilhelm is half-witted,' she said. 'We keep him on as an act of charity.'

My mind was racing. She was implying Wilhelm had been at the house for some years. When he had stuttered his name I had taken it as a crazy old man's statement of introduction. 'Wilhelm, I'm Wilhelm.' But what if, in fact, it was a reminder? To me. I recast the words in my mind. 'Wilhelm, I'm Wilhelm.' Was the implication meant to be – 'Don't you recognise me?'

'He recognised me,' I said.

She nodded dumbly.

'From when I was here,' I added unnecessarily.

She puffed her cigarette and walked across to the mantel, leaning one hand against it and looking away from me, out through the long windows across the park. 'Yes, you were here,' she said.

I felt an incredible surge of triumph. 'When?' I said. 'When was I here?'

'Don't you remember?'

'No.'

'Then I've no intention of unnecessarily adding to my own embarrassment.'

I decided to go for broke. 'Shall I say it or will you? We slept together.'

She went pale but she didn't answer.

'If I have to ask all over the village of Lingfeld, I intend to find out,' I said. 'It's part of my life, God damn it. It's not something I'm going to let go because of your embarrassment.'

She turned toward me. 'It's not a story I enjoy retelling,' she said.

I looked around desperately. I needed a drink. I gestured to the decanters on a side table and she shrugged indifferently. I poured myself a large whisky. 'Will you have one?'

She shook her head.

I sat on the arm of a chair looking up at her. 'I knew I'd seen you before,' I said deliberately. 'More than that, I know that you and I . . .'

She waved her arm angrily. 'What else do you remember?' she said vehemently. 'Anything, anything at all?'

'I think you'd better tell me the story,' I said.

'You remember nothing of those last days of the war?' The words had an elusive ring.

I stayed silent.

'You don't remember the chaos when German women and children were ejected from their homes by the new Czech government and forced to march through the snows into Germany while the war still raged around them? You don't remember the thousands who died on the road from starvation or cold?'

I shook my head.

'No, you wouldn't,' she said bitterly. 'Nobody does. Because this time the victims were German.'

I remembered what Zorubin had said about the hundreds of thousands, millions even of Germans who had died on the forced trek from Poland and Czechoslovakia at the end of the war.

'When the roads became too clogged with carts or bodies or sometimes by the fighting that was still going on all around us, the Czech army police established vast camps for us in the woods or used old German army barracks. My accommodation,' she said, 'was rather special. I was taken to Theresienstadt.'

I knew the name.

'Yes, Captain. To the old concentration camp where the Nazis had murdered their last victims only a few days earlier. The camp was pressed into service again by America's allies, the gallant Czechs.'

'Who was in military control of the area?'

'We're talking about the last days of the war. Small pockets of German soldiers were still holding out. The SS, of course, were fighting for their lives. But the American army was in the area, General Patton's Third Army had advanced almost as far as Prague and, to their credit, Captain, they were shocked by what they saw. By what they saw being done to German women and children. Teams of American officers came to our camp.'

I walked over to the decanter and poured myself another drink.

'We began,' she said, 'to feel slightly less abandoned by the world, slightly more human. When the American officers came the women dressed themselves as best they could, they made the best of themselves, you understand?'

'I think so.'

'Will you let me spell it out for you, Captain? The word spread. An officer could take a few hours off from his unit and choose any woman out of ten thousand for a *chocolate bar*.'

'I see.'

'When *you* arrived at the camp, Captain, I had eaten half a cabbage in twelve days. You gave bread, some cheese – and of course a chocolate bar. I was your choice, Captain. And I counted myself very lucky.'

'My name,' I said. 'What was my name?'

'Do you think I cared? You wore a khaki uniform. You had the power of life and death over me because you were dressed in that uniform. Your pockets were stuffed with enough food to keep me alive. What did I care about your name?'

'And Lingfeld,' I said quietly. 'What was I doing here?'

She paused. 'I had begged you to help me get out of Theresienstadt. I told you that my husband had a house here not far from Munich. You promised to pull some strings as you put it. You made the price perfectly clear. Within a few days I was released, turned loose on the road again. I made for Lingfeld, of course. The war was falling apart. The German army unit at Lingfeld left warning of minefields. It was, as I later discovered, the last day of the war. I hourly expected soldiers to appear. Perhaps Americans, perhaps Russians, I didn't know. Then a single Jeep appeared and turned into the drive. You had come to collect, Captain. But you never got as far as the house.'

· Eleven ·

I left Lingfeld and drove back to Munich. So I had behaved like a million other soldiers, American, British, French, at the end of the war. Not so much rape by force and threats but sex for chocolate bars, sex for food, sex for a piece of paper which allows a girl to travel home. So all my nightmares were because I had induced Elisabeth Oster to sleep with me. Slightly less than rape, a good deal less than an act freely entered into. But then a world war was ending and civilised values were still a long way from being re-established.

I spent the rest of the year seeing Italy and Greece. Mostly alone. Christmas in the south of France. Mostly alone. By the spring I was in Paris and needing company. From my left bank hotel room I placed a call to London.

'Speaking,' the familiar voice said.

'This is Dan Lingfield,' I said, 'inviting you to Paris for the dirtiest weekend you can imagine.'

'I accept,' Dorothy Curtis's voice said. 'Be warned, I've learnt some frightful new tricks.'

Paris was wonderful. An escape from the world at war. Not like London, which I'd seen, still battling, fighting a war which they were barely aware had already ended. Not like Moscow or Leningrad or Kiev, licking wounds in silent resentment. Not like New York or Los Angeles with a trace of guilt that they had escaped the whirlwind. Paris didn't care. The war, they told me, was over. France, they said, with a little help from its friends, had triumphed again. The world struggle, which had just taken place, had eluded Parisians.

So I took a hotel room at the George V and ordered some flowers, a bottle of '28 Krug and some whisky to be sent up. It was a bright day with still a sparkling frost on the cobblestones of the Champs Elysées.

I took a taxi to Le Bourget Airport. It was still only a concrete strip next to a series of long prefabricated huts with only the warm, opulently fragrant duty-free shops looking and smelling like a modern airport.

The flight from London had just arrived. I walked quickly across the baggage room. Watching the porters deliver a mountain of leather cases onto the trestle tables was a group of very British-looking passengers. Among them an overweight, puffy eyed, close to fifty matron, her fur coat ridged across her heavy rump.

I hesitated in the entrance to the baggage room. I cannot imagine why it had not occurred to me that five years had passed since I last saw Dorothy. That even then, in 1945, she was teetering on the edge of middle age.

She had several items of luggage, matching pigskin Gladstones of a quality you no longer see, and was concentrating her efforts on recovering them from the pile of cases before her. She had already engaged a porter, a small one-armed man in a blue blouson. When she pointed imperiously to a piece of luggage, he jerked it off the table and tucked it under the stump of his amputated arm awaiting further orders.

From time to time she glanced vaguely in the direction of the crowd at the doorway. I was standing a little apart just inside the baggage room. Minutes passed and still no further luggage arrived. Her foot tapped impatiently, a high-heeled black suede shoe from which rose a thick ankle and a broad nyloned calf.

'I am not flattered,' an amused voice said next to me. 'I'm not flattered at all.'

I turned to see Dorothy standing next to me, Dorothy pretty much as I remembered her, a very sexy woman in her early forties.

'Jesus Christ,' I said. 'I'm sorry.'

She signalled the porter who carried her one suitcase and we walked together towards the line of taxis. I took her arm. 'How are you? No permanent man?'

'Nobody, darling,' she said, 'could possibly replace the awful Oliver Sutchley.'

We drove into Paris and across the almost empty Place de la Concorde. 'Do you know,' she said, 'I haven't been here since before the war. Strange how the French seem to have recovered more quickly than ourselves. Or perhaps their genius is just for burying things deeper . . .'

She was delighted by the hotel and we decided, since it was still mid-morning, to take a walk, have an aperitif and have lunch on the Champs Elysées. It was a soft spring morning and Paris is the easiest city in the world to walk. We came down the Champs Elysées, wandered through the Tuileries Gardens, skirted the Louvre and crossed the Seine at the Pont

Neuf. I had been here before. Perhaps I could not always remember the names of the Quais but nothing was unfamiliar. As we turned down the Boulevard St Michel, Dorothy looked at me quizzically. 'We're not, by chance, on some sentimental journey, are we?'

'No,' I assured her.

'Because I wouldn't like that.'

'I've been here before the war, I'm pretty sure of that. But I promise it's not a sentimental journey.'

She smiled. 'Before the war you would have been in knee pants, as I think you call them. A little young to be screwing some pretty little thing in Paris in the spring.'

We chose a restaurant on the Boulevard and ate mussels and chateaubriand and drank a bottle of wine each.

'I always wanted to apologise,' she said, 'for that dreadful party I took you to.'

'I enjoyed it,' I said.

'Did you? You know it was a time just at the end of the war and for a whole variety of reasons, not all of them connected with Oliver, I was in a dreadful mess. I felt very let down by life.'

'I guess a lot of women did. What about your family?' I asked carefully.

'I'll tell you a story,' she said. 'My father was a remote but totally admirable figure to me as I grew up. Even in my twenties he was a strong, authoritarian figure who believed England needed more discipline etc., etc. When the war began he was too old for the army so he volunteered for some ministry and was posted to India. At least that's what my mother told me. Only after the war did I discover that his "authoritarian" views had been taken a lot further than I had ever dreamed and that he was imprisoned during the war as a Nazi sympathiser.'

We stopped at a sidewalk café and ordered drinks.

'What are your father's feelings now?' I asked her. 'Regrets?'

'I don't know,' she said, hard as steel. 'I've never spoken to him again.'

I hesitated for a moment. 'Do you know,' I said carefully, 'who it was that got me taken off my boat and transferred to Roehampton Hospital?'

'At that time the lists were being altered all the time.'

'So there was nothing strange about my name being switched?'

She sat, very thoughtful. 'I don't know, Dan,' she said at last.

The waiter brought the Pernods and poured water. She watched his long white apron flapping in the breeze. 'I've often thought about it since,' she said.

'Why is that?'

'Because, frankly, I was quite pleased to have met you. Rather more than quite pleased, if I'm to be unmaidenly.'

I laughed. 'OK,' I said, 'I was pleased to meet you too. But I have the feeling there was still something strange about the way I was held up in London. Who exactly changed the list?'

'I don't know,' she said. 'Not me.'

'But you were in charge of the lists.'

'I came home one day,' she paused sipping her Pernod, 'and Oliver was in the flat.'

'You were already divorced?'

'Oh, yes. Had been for months. It was like him to have kept a key without telling me.'

'What was he doing in the flat?'

'He claimed he'd come for some cufflinks and silver that I still had of his. But I do remember my list was on the table. He'd been looking at it. The typewriter cover was off too. In the fearful row we had about him keeping a key I'm afraid I forgot about the list.'

'You're saying your ex-husband might have made the alteration?'

'Could have. But God knows why. When I met you, as I said, I was just rather pleased the change had been made. I didn't really care how it happened.'

I remembered that certainty, the night in the Pheasantry club, of having seen Sutchley's face before – and the disturbing feeling that his Bank of England connections gave me. 'Can you imagine,' I asked Dorothy carefully, 'how I could have seen Oliver Sutchley before?'

'He was in America on business fairly often. Once I even went with him. Do you know Long Island?'

'I know New York City, Kansas City.'

She shrugged. 'You thought you knew Oliver.'

'I guess so.'

'He's the face of the well-bred con-man the world over. Except he turned out to be a lot more than just a con-man.'

I hesitated. 'When you divorced him, was it really because of his depravity?'

'No,' she said deliberately, 'it was because I discovered that in Lisbon he had been, at the very least, a Nazi sympathiser.'

I thought of her father. 'You don't have much luck with the men in your life,' I said.

She smiled at me. 'Oh, I don't know,' she said, peering into the bottom of the empty Pernod glass. 'The tea leaves say my luck's getting better all the time.'

'How did you find out about Oliver?' I asked as we stood up.

I paid the bill and we walked back to the river. 'I had a big bust-up with my father,' she said, 'the last time I saw him. He was still half suggesting that some of Adolf Hitler's views were not entirely insane. There was a strong streak of anti-Semitism in the British upper classes before the war, you know.'

We leaned on the granite embankment and looked across the river. Barges with brightly painted wheel-houses chugged along before us. Fishermen fished. Booksellers sold books from their high-mounted wooden boxes.

'In the middle of this fight,' she said, 'as I was telling my father he ought to be ashamed of himself, that he was a disgrace to me, Oliver and every man and woman who'd fought in the war, he suddenly smiled. A nasty smile. Oliver, he said, was as pro-Hitler as any man in the country. He told me to ask him about his time in Lisbon.'

I took her arm and we walked on down the quay.

'I went mad after that. Crazy. I invented stories about Oliver's depraved tastes though in fact it was me that had them. I went through a period of intense self-disgust. A sort of guilt that I had been attached to two such men as Oliver and my father. Near suicidal self-disgust.' She shuddered. 'Let's go back to the hotel,' she said, 'and go to bed.'

We stayed in bed until the evening, dozing, talking and gently screwing. The frantic, lustful part of her had gone. She was warm, fond and friendly. I looked forward to an easy weekend of walks through Paris, lunches in the Bois de Boulogne and evenings at a show or a play. I was to be proven devastatingly wrong.

That evening we went to the Grand Guignol and watched with amusement and sometimes a *frisson* as the Gothic horror show exposed maidens to the sadism of old men, as girls were stripped and beaten and violated on stage with an extraordinary realism.

We left before the end, sated and laughing.

At a café on the Boulevard St Michel we drank a late aperitif and watched the mix of students, West Africans and parachutists with red berets drift past under the budding trees. After a few minutes I became aware that Dorothy was looking at me closely. 'No special girl in California?' she said.

I shook my head. 'Not really,' I said.

She was still watching me with a slightly disturbing concentration. 'When I was a young woman,' she said at length, 'twenty-one or twenty-two, back in 1927, I was taken by my father to New York. Oliver was there too, we had just become engaged. My father had business there with an associate who lived in a very grand style on Long Island. This man, Pierre, was quite dreadful, screwing every elegible woman in sight, *including*, rumour had it, his daughter-in-law. Well, I was a demure little English girl and all I can really say is that I came completely under his spell. We were staying at his house at the time . . .'

'Why are you telling me all this?'

'You'll see in a moment. Just remember, I was newly engaged, most certainly a virgin, and considered men of forty-five or more to be far too old to raise trouble. I was in fact completely wrong.'

'He seduced you.'

'Yes. Quite openly he set about flattering me out of my wits. He sat me next to him at table. He talked to me with his hand on my thigh, paying me compliments as he worked his fingers up my skirt. The sheer outrageousness of it left my father and Oliver speechless.'

'Didn't they object?'

'They never actually *saw* anything, I suppose. And in any case Pierre was a terribly important client, his business was banknote printing for countries all round the world and he bought massive quantities of special paper from Oliver's family firm.'

'So Pierre used his position to take you to bed?'

'I was very willing to be taken. I don't think he was an evil man, but he was certainly a bad man. And a dramatically good-looking man. One afternoon while we were all sitting round the tennis court he simply took my arm and walked me straight up to his bedroom, put me on the bed and screwed me in my tennis whites.'

I laughed. 'Did you enjoy it?'

'I thought it was super,' she said, reverting to a schoolgirl terminology. 'The best thing since one man one vote.'

'Did Oliver know what happened?'

'God knows. He was certainly dreadfully sulky but Pierre wasn't having any of that and Oliver soon had to behave. So did my father. While *I* misbehaved every afternoon in Pierre's suite. Marvellous!'

Her enjoyment of the memory was so uncomplicated, so perfectly unalloyed.

'What,' I asked her again, 'made you tell me all this?'

'Something about you,' she said, suddenly serious. 'Perhaps it's just your white hair on a very young face. Pierre was white-haired too and his face was very young for his age. And he was a big man like you. It just reminded me, that's all.'

We skipped dinner and had sandwiches and coffee sent up to our room, made a little easy love and went to sleep.

She was awake before me the next morning and had ordered *café au lait* and croissants before I was really fully conscious. I struggled up on one elbow and stretched for the coffee, listening to the sound of splashing water in the bathroom. The sun slanted through a crack in the curtains with the promise of another fine spring day.

After a few moments she emerged from the bathroom fully dressed in a yellow dress and jacket. She pulled the curtains back and the sun now flooded in. She looked rounded and happy and she came over to the bed and gave me a good morning kiss. 'I could grow to endure this life,' she said.

'Me too.' I put my hands behind my head and lay back, eyes half closed, luxuriating in the warmth of the sun and soft opulence of her scent. Then I got out of bed and stood naked before her, my arms stretching towards her shoulders.

The boiling coffee hit me with the force of a fire hose. I fell back on the bed, my chest burning, to see the look of uncontrolled fury on her face.

'You disgusting bastard,' she said. She snatched up a heavy brass bedside lamp and swung the base at my head. I rolled across the bed as the lamp thumped the pillow. Then she stood back, breathing heavily. 'Loss of memory,' she snarled. 'God, you lying swine!'

She turned and crossed the room, jerking open the door. I scrambled into my clothes in total confusion. I ran outside into the corridor. The elevator had reached the ground floor. I re-called it and it stopped twice on the way. By the time I got down to the ornate, gilded lobby she had disappeared.

I was aware that people were staring at me but I was so dazed I just sat at one of the tables and looked blankly toward the door. After a few moments I ordered a black coffee and a large cognac and tried to make some sort of sense of what had happened.

Had she been saving up that moment for its maximum shock? Impossible. She had walked out leaving her luggage, even leaving her coat and purse. I drank the cognac and ordered another. What exactly had happened? She had come out of the bathroom and pulled the curtains. She had been relaxed, smiling, and she had leaned over and kissed me. I think then she must have picked up the coffee pot to pour herself some coffee. I wasn't one hundred per cent certain because I was lying back, my eyes half closed against the sun streaming in through the window. I had then got up and stood opposite her. Then what in God's name had happened to bring her to that stunning pitch of fury? Nothing.

I left the lobby and took the elevator up to our floor. As I emerged into the corridor a sudden thought struck me. She had ordered coffee and croissants while I was still asleep. She had ordered a newspaper too, a copy of *L'Aurore* was lying folded on the bedside table. Was there something she had seen in the paper? Something even about me?

The room door was still open. I crossed to the bed and snatched up the paper. The main front page story was of negotiations to form a new government. Below that was a story about the end of meat rationing in England. A long speech by the mayor of Lyon. Nothing that could possibly relate to me. I turned the pages and scanned every item but I knew by now it was hopeless. The single important fact was that Dorothy had not opened the newspaper between the time she came out of the bathroom dressed, relaxed and apparently perfectly happy and the time she had hurled the boiling coffee at me.

I sat on the edge of the bed looking at the things scattered about the room. Pieces of jewellery on the dressing table. Knickers, stockings and yesterday's blue dress thrown casually on the sofa, a pair of high-heeled shoes by the bathroom door. My eyes roamed the room desperately looking for an explanation. I picked up her purse. There was nothing unexpected. A little French money, twenty-five pounds in sterling. A neat leather case, scented with perfume, carrying calling cards. Keys, lipstick, that sort of thing. Her valise was equally unrevealing. Clothes, more make-up, all those female necessities for a dirty weekend.

I am not deeply intuitive. I can now recognise memories of the past trying to surface, but intuition plays no part in my life. Yet, that day, in my bafflement and frustration, I was taken with the image of Dorothy walking first down the Champs Elysées on the same route we had taken yesterday. I was suddenly energised. I left her a note in case she returned and another message with the concierge. Then I ran out onto the Avenue George V and down towards the Champs Elysées.

It was Sunday morning and the sidewalks and café tables were not crowded. In her striking yellow dress I was unlikely to miss her. Following yesterday's route I ran through the Tuileries Gardens almost certain I would see her sitting alone on a bench but the gardens were empty but for an old man sweeping the gravel and a busy flock of pigeons pecking at the areas he had just disturbed.

I skirted the Louvre. The traffic was thicker here along the quayside. I had slowed to a fast walk now. Crossing the river I reached the Boulevard St Michel and the small restaurant we had had lunch in yesterday. It was my last chance.

The tables were empty. The zinc bar inside was supported by three or four old Frenchmen in suits and plaid shirts. I turned away with a deep sense of shock.

I took a taxi back to the George V and hurried across to the concierge's desk. 'No messages but there is someone waiting for you upstairs, Monsieur.' I ran for the elevator, pressed the floor button, came out and turned toward my room. A gendarme was standing outside.

'What's happened?' I said. 'What's going on?'

'Monsieur Lingfield?'

'Yes.'

The gendarme opened the door of the room. Inside was a plainclothes policeman and another uniformed gendarme. The most awful sense of foreboding kept me quiet.

The inspector held Dorothy's stiff-covered British passport in one hand. 'Lady Dorothy Curtis has been staying here with you?'

'Yes.'

'We hear she left the hotel about 9 a.m. this morning in a state of some agitation.'

'Yes. What's happened, for God's sake?'

'A woman in a yellow dress was seen to wade into the Seine this morning by two small boys. By the time they persuaded anyone to believe them, the woman had disappeared.'

'Why,' I said slowly, 'apart from the yellow dress, do you think it's Lady Curtis?'

'We found this on the quayside, Monsieur.'

He held up a crumpled George V napkin. It was stained with lipstick, mascara and perhaps tears. She must have snatched it up as she left the hotel, dabbing at her eyes as she walked down to the Seine.

'You haven't found her?' I asked quietly.

'No.' The inspector shook his head. 'Many people have jumped into the river from the Pont Neuf in the last few years. They usually turn up within six to eight hours at the bend of the river at the Pont d'Iéna,' he smiled bleakly, 'the Eiffel Tower, Monsieur.'

As we drove across Paris to the Pont d'Iéna the weather changed. Cloud covered the sun not in wispy puffs of white but in great thick slabs of grey. Once there I passed the most melancholic hours imaginable. With a young gendarme and a pair of binoculars between us we stood at the rail of the first stage of the Eiffel Tower and searched the water between the Pont d'Iéna and the iron-framed bridge a few dozen yards to the east. At about four o'clock in the afternoon the gendarme nudged my arm and handed me the binoculars. A brief shaft of sunlight played on the surface of the river.

Below the sheen of the water the yellow dress billowed gently. 'La voilà,' the gendarme said. And we went down to ground level to inform the river police.

I came back to the hotel and ordered a bottle of brandy to be sent up to my room. I would take a shower, go to bed and drink myself to sleep. I took off my clothes and stumbled into the shower. There was an angry red patch of skin on the left of my chest and when the shower water hit it I flinched in pain. When I had finished I dried myself carefully but the skin was still stinging. Then I remembered that Dorothy had some moisturising cream in her night bag and I rummaged about until I found it. Carrying the pot back into the bathroom I opened it and began to apply some of the scented cream to the reddened skin on my chest. The burn extended across from above my left nipple and continued round under my arm. I took a glob on my right finger and lifted my left arm. The burn was worst in my armpit. I examined it carefully. I held up my arm until it caught the light from the shower – and I fell back in thunderstruck dismay. Deep in the armpit, hidden but for a trick of the light, was a tattoo. Even backwards in the mirror I could read it: SS 79461.

I dropped the pot of cream. For five years those tiny inked SS runes had remained hidden from surgeons, from lovers, from myself. And then in that angle of sunlight as I stretched back in the bed this morning, hands behind my head, in that blaze of sunlight the SS soldier's marking had been visible to Dorothy. So her lover had followed the same Hitlerite path her husband and her father had chosen . . . My heart was thudding like wild, uncoordinated drums. Hideous images of myself filled my mind. Elisabeth Oster's story was, as I had come to believe, a pure invention. When my body was picked up, far from being a US soldier who spoke fluent German I was a German SS man who spoke fluent English!

· Twelve ·

I flew to Berlin as soon as I had completed formalities with the French police in the morning. I now saw myself as a hunted man. I did not dwell too long on why Elisabeth Oster had lied. I assumed it was some attempt to protect her husband. Had Herr Oster and I been associated in the past? Had we been SS comrades? If so I could understand that he, having somehow acquired his denazification clearance, certainly didn't want me around. Any story, I could imagine Elisabeth Oster saying, was better than the truth. So what had Oster been involved in? What had I been involved in *with him*? What was the truth?

In Berlin it was the days of the Anglo-American airlift. Five thousand airmen had kept a whole city supplied with food and fuel and medicines. Every two minutes airplanes from the airfields of southern England were landing, every ten minutes they were unloaded by Germans working round-the-clock shifts. It was the first time since 1945 that the Anglo-American Alliance and the Germans had really worked together.

In the climate of anti-Stalinist feeling it was easier for small SS self-help offices to open up. Some, like the one near the Spandau prison, dealt mostly with claims for injury pensions and stayed clear of politics. I got the address by posing as a free-lance journalist at the press centre at the airport and took a taxi straight to the seedy bomb-damaged building which gave away no more than the name of the occupant of the upstairs rooms: Herr Peter Helm. It was the name I had been given at the press centre.

I mounted a dusty stairway and entered an office with a two-inch bombing crack down one wall and a small torn carpet on bare boards.

Behind a desk sat a large man with a badly scarred face. He had no right arm and the sleeve of his jacket was tucked into the pocket. He shook hands with his left. 'Sit down, Herr Lingfield,' Helm said, his smile restrained by suspicion. 'You are a journalist?'

'A free-lance journalist.'

He complimented me on my German and gestured me to a seat. He plunged into the problem, as he saw it, straight away. 'Do you understand the position of the former SS soldier?'

'You tell me.'

'The problem is simple,' he said. 'The SS was declared a criminal organisation at the end of the war. Membership was a criminal act. But what the Allied authorities assumed is that membership was a *voluntary* act. But in fact by far the majority of Waffen SS soldiers were ordinary conscripts. Soldiers like any other.'

I listened in silence.

'Of course you have come here to write yet another article about the SS. Is it too much to ask, Herr Lingfield, that you discover the facts first?'

'No,' I said. 'I'm here to discover the facts, at least to discover the facts about one particular SS man.'

He looked at me and sighed. 'You are a Nazi-hunter, am I right? You work for a Jewish organisation in New York or London and you have an assignment to trace Oberscharführer Braun or SS-Mann Schmidt. How can you expect me to help you find the real criminals who no doubt existed in our ranks, if the organisation you represent refuses to listen to the truth?'

I took out a pack of cigarettes and lit one. As an afterthought I offered one to Helm. He shook his head contemptuously.

I had hoped to get somewhere without revealing that it was I myself I was asking questions about but I saw now that that was a naive hope. This man would give nothing except a defence of the SS.

I stood up and took off my jacket while he looked at me in surprise. I unbuttoned my shirt and he waited knowing what was coming. I pulled aside my shirt and he rounded the desk and peered for a moment at the number printed in my armpit.

He smiled and clapped me on the shoulder. 'You know,' he said, 'there was something I liked about you from the beginning.'

I left the office, escorted down the narrow stairs by Helm. He had been a major in the Totenkopf, the Death's Head division, and had lost his arm in the fierce fighting around Demiansk, on the Russian Front. He told me that my story was safe with him but before taking action himself he required me to go to ex-SS Doctor Lutze who would examine my tattoo and confirm that it was genuine.

I crossed Berlin for a brief but careful examination and I was phoning Helm's office a couple of hours later.

'Don't come over now, comrade,' he said. 'Wait until dark. I'll meet you at the Gasthaus Beck.'

'Has Lutze been in touch with you?'

'Doctor Lutze has confirmed that it is genuine.'

My heart sank. It was as if I had been told that tests on an incurable disease had proved positive. 'Why wait until dark?' I pressed him.

'Be patient,' he said. 'It is better this way.'

I walked through the still shattered back streets of Spandau Old Town until the light began to fade. It was easy to see that Berliners felt themselves to be in the centre of international tension, the frontline against the Russians. They were tough, shabbily dressed but immensely determined. They were mostly Berliners but I could hear, from their accents, easterners among them from way out, from what was now called Poland. All that stood between them and the new horrors of Stalinism was President Harry Truman's will to resist. I sat in a small garden before a ruined church. Germans hurried past me home from work and I felt some distinct, moving affinity with them. But I still had to repeat, softly to myself: *I am a German. I am a German.* I did this but found to my bitter amusement that I was whispering in *English*.

I reached the Gasthaus Beck as darkness fell. It was no more than a long room with an oak bar and a few tables along the far wall. The *Wirt* was a big man who was very definitely in charge of things behind the bar. The ten or a dozen customers were all men of about twenty-seven to thirty-five years of age. I wondered if they too were former SS men.

When Peter Helm came in a few moments later he was greeted by customers and *Wirt* alike with marked respect. I had no longer any doubt that nestling under the left armpits of most of the men in this bar were the tiny SS runes and service numbers.

Helm ordered two beers and the *Wirt* hurried across to take them to a corner table. A sign passed between them which concerned me. It was a movement of eyebrow and mouth but it said not to worry, the stranger is one of us. The *Wirt* extended his hand to me and shook mine vigorously. 'I can offer you hot sausage, bacon, cabbage and the best dumplings in Berlin. Yes?'

'Why not?' Helm said. 'My young friend and I have a lot to talk about. And some more beer, Franz.'

'Coming, Herr Oberst.'

I watched Helm as he drank two long draughts of his beer and set the glass down on the scarred oil-cloth-covered table. With his index finger he traced the black marks on the cloth. 'It won't always be so,' he said. 'I give it a year before we can crawl out from under cover. Two million trained men linked by an indissoluble sense of comradeship, the Allies are going to *have* to call on us very soon.'

I said nothing and he took my silence for respectful agreement. 'First, let's get down to work,' he said. 'Where are my notes?' He fumbled in his inside pocket, glancing up in the mirror above my head, a mirror I suddenly realised gave him sight of the door. 'There are several cafés like this in the district. Strangers aren't welcome,' he said. 'Especially strangers asking questions about old comrades.'

He laid his notes on the table and the tension in my body became close to unbearable. 'My name,' I said.

'Martin Johann Coburg.'

I drank some beer and sat back. *Martin Johann Coburg*. Martin Coburg.

The *Wirt* brought a great pot of hot sausage, cabbage and dumplings. He set out plates and knives and forks.

'Martin Coburg of Lingfeld, Bavaria,' Helm said, 'born in March 1921.' He smiled. 'I assume the name you gave me, Mr Lingfield, was not a coincidence.'

'Not as it turns out,' I said.

The *Wirt* replaced our beers. 'There is a suggestion in your record that your mother was American. I can get you your Family History certificate if you wish. Details of your racial purity back to 1715.'

I shook my head.

'Yes,' he said. 'What difference does it make now?' He consulted his notes. 'You enlisted in Munich as a Freiwillige, a volunteer, in June 1940. You passed three As in preliminary training and were sent to Bad Tolz, the SS officer training school near Munich. From there we have no record of service.'

'Is that unusual?'

'Very. We take a pride in the fullness of our files.'

Waves of despair passed over me. I found it impossible to face the fact that I was not American. After all I had been American all my remembered life. I finished my beer. 'So that's it,' I said.

Helm looked at me strangely. 'No, not quite it. There's something else. I was told this afternoon that in our file your name has a green star beside it.'

'A green star. What does that mean?'

'A green star in our records means that at one time you must have made an application to serve on the SS guard detachment of one of the concentration camps.'

I was beaten. It wasn't difficult to guess now what I wanted to forget. Sickening images of myself as a camp guard churned my stomach. I could no longer deny the truth. My damaged memory could no longer hide it from me.

Helms had taken a thick brown envelope from the side pocket of his jacket. 'You don't appear to feature on any of the Allied wanted lists. But they are still incomplete.'

'I see.' I was watching the brown envelope.

He placed it on the table and pushed it towards me. 'These papers are the only record of your service in the SS.'

I took the envelope. I couldn't bear the thought of opening it in front of Helms. I'm not sure that at that moment I could bear the thought of opening it at all. I felt I knew more than enough about my past.

After that I bought a few drinks and heard a few stories of the mud of the Rasputitza and the bitterness of the Russian winter. By nine o'clock they were singing songs and I shook hands with my new comrades and slipped away into the night.

I was miserable beyond belief. It was raining and, as an economy measure, there were only streetlights at the intersections. Among these gaunt, dark streets there was no chance of a taxi. But I remembered an S-bahn station just across the gardens and I made my way in rain and deep despair toward it.

I stumbled into the lighted station. I caught a glimpse of myself in a mirror and recoiled. I was already the hunted man, my hair stuck down with rain, mud on my coat, my collar turned up, a furtive uneasy look on my face.

I bought a ticket and went onto the platform. There were few people waiting. I sat on a bench, my legs shaking. In my pocket was the brown envelope. I knew I must burn it without opening it.

A few more people came onto the platform. I sat staring at the sign on the arched brickwork across the tracks, Spandau. I thought of the Nazi war prisoners in the prison somewhere close to here. I thought about war-guilt and pleas of *Befehl ist Befehl*, orders are orders. I thought of that brown envelope in my pocket.

I pulled it out and tore at the adhesive flap. Nobody was paying any attention to me. Somehow, I thanked God, there were no letters. The top item was an SS paybook, green with worn silver lettering: SS Unterform M. J. Coburg. I opened it. I was staring down at a picture of myself, or at least of a very young man who was unmistakably myself. You could almost feel the pride in those black SS collar tabs. Born March 1921. Issued January 1941. The boy in front of my eyes was still less than twenty years old. I turned to the next item. A recommendation by someone named SS Brigade-Führer Holz for a cadet award Second Class, dated January 1941. Presumably the award was never confirmed.

Underneath that a photograph. Six uniformed young men outside a café, smiling, waving at the camera, and myself, or the young boy I was trying hard to accept was myself. Still fresh faced, but not smiling.

I pushed the photograph and papers back into the envelope and put it in my jacket. A train roared into the station and stopped on worn squealing brakes. I stepped through its open doors without even asking where it would take me.

The train was crowded and hot with the dampness rising from everybody's coats. I took a strap and stood swaying like a drunk to the movement of the train. My eyes wandered across the torn and disfigured advertisements from another age. The train rattled round a bend and the carriages straightened themselves into line as we approached a station. I could see the next carriage was equally crowded with straphangers. I saw an old man with a brown parcel under his arm; I saw a young girl with a long pretty face. And I saw, looking straight at me, Vik Zorubin.

I turned my face from him. Without thinking I pushed my way through the press of people. At the next station I got out and ran for the stairs. I heard a shout behind me. Or maybe I thought I heard a shout. I was not thinking clearly, only that he was the bounty hunter and I was his prey. I was in a more brightly lit part of Berlin. There were a lot of American and British soldiers on the sidewalks. Cafés shed their warm glow onto the street. A club advertised non-stop jazz.

I looked behind me several times. There was no sign of Vik Zorubin. I entered a café and ordered schnapps and beer. Had I really seen Zorubin? I began to be less certain, I began to think that when the mind gets as tortured as my mind had been it is capable of seeing anything, feared or loved makes no difference. And my mind was tortured, close, I would guess, to the limit of what I could take. I must go back to California, I knew that. I must remake my life as Dan Lingfield. I must forget Martin Coburg. I must build up enough life to expunge him from my mind. At a movement next to me I turned.

Zorubin was standing at the bar beside me. I kept my hands deep in my pockets. His huge hands were flat on the bar in front of him. 'It's been a long time,' he said.

'It has.'

'You don't seem pleased to see me, Captain.'

'I'm not sure,' I said. 'I'm not sure what sort of terms we left on.'

'If I remember,' Zorubin said, 'I still had an open mind.' He smiled that enigmatic, alarming smile. A man easy to like, easy to fear. 'What happened to *you*, Captain?' He was looking at my hair and mud-spattered coat.

'I went back with a girl,' I said. 'She and some guy tried to roll me in a park.'

He smiled totally without sympathy. 'You got enough left to buy me a drink?'

'Sure. Schnapps?'

'If it's as close to vodka as I'm going to get.'

I ordered drinks for both of us. 'What took you over to that part of town?' I asked carefully.

'I do a lot of work there, Captain,' he said. 'There are a lot of SS joints there, little clubs, hangouts, that sort of thing. Sort of an SS final redoubt.' I didn't look at him as I fumbled out the money for the drinks. 'I've been trying to hunt you down, Captain. But after Eastlake Vets Hospital you just disappeared.'

'I moved out west,' I said.

'Happy enough not to know who you really were?'

'Yes.'

'You still don't know?'

I shook my head. 'I told you a long time ago, Zorubin, that I'd no wish to know who I was. I'm just me. Whoever I was, whatever I said, whatever I did, it wasn't me, get it?'

He smiled that strange stretching of his dark, rubbery face. 'OK,' he said, shrugging. 'So you mean you don't want me to tell you who you really are?'

I froze. Very slowly I turned towards him. 'You think you know who I really am?'

'I'm sure.' He finished his drink and snapped a heavy finger and thumb at the barman. The man came running with the schnapps bottle.

I stood at the bar, my mind too confused to think straight.

'Your name's Coburg,' Zorubin said. 'Martin Coburg.'

Quite suddenly my head cleared. I knew there was every chance that I was fighting for my life. 'Martin Coburg,' I said, repeating the name as if I was hearing it for the first time.

'Suits you, uh?'

I looked into those unfathomable dark eyes. 'What makes you think my name is Martin Coburg?'

'It was simple,' Zorubin said. 'The way my investigations often work out. I was in Munich a couple of years ago, working on a completely different trace. My client was a rich French girl who was trying to trace a friend, a German girl from the Munich area. The two girls had become best friends at their school in Switzerland before the war.'

I couldn't see where this was leading but I drained my schnapps and nodded for Zorubin to go on.

'Now get this,' Zorubin said. 'My French client gives me the name and address. The German girl's name was Coburg. She lived in a mansion called Haus Lingfeld outside Munich! With her parents and her mother's younger sister, Elisabeth.'

'Elisabeth. Elisabeth Oster?'

'She lived there. But Haus Lingfeld was owned by her brother-in-law, Herr Emil Coburg.'

'So what took you to me?' I said hesitantly. 'What made you think *my* name was Coburg too?'

'The original list of guys killed or missing on the last day of the war. You saw the list.'

'The US Army list.'

'Sure. You don't remember the names but I did. There was a Coburg on it. Captain Martin Coburg. 327th Infantry. US Third Army.'

I gasped at him. 'US Third Army. I was a captain in the US Army!'

He grinned. 'My apologies, Dan. And my congratulations, Captain. I had come to think your story might be much more murky than that!'

I walked with Zorubin along the Ku'damm toward my hotel. My head was buzzing unmercifully. From time to time he glanced at me, then looked away, continuing his slow rolling walk. He was, I realised, giving me time to get accustomed to my new identity. He didn't, thank God, know how impossibly complicated that seemed to be.

It was me who reopened the wound. 'On the last day of the war parts of the Third Army were in the Munich area.'

'Parts of the Third Army were all over the goddamn place. I guess Captain Coburg took a couple of hours off from the war.'

'To drive to Lingfeld.'

'To find news of his cousins.'

'Elisabeth Oster was my cousin?'

'So was the missing German girl I was commissioned to find, Alexina Coburg.'

'What about this missing German girl?' I said carefully.

'Hell of a good-looking girl. I've seen pictures.'

'What do you know about her?'

'What do I know about her? Not much, I guess. She and the French girl, Andrée de Bretagne, were great friends pre-war. Used to visit with each other in France and Germany. The last time Andrée saw Alexina was in Paris in 1940. Alexina and her father, Emil Coburg, helped the de Bretagne family, who are Jewish, to get down to Spain.'

'And then?'

'And then I don't know.'

'You don't know what happened to her?'

'She vanished. Without trace.'

'What about her father?'

'Him too. The whole family.'

'Except Elisabeth Oster.'

'Except Elisabeth Oster, as she was by then.' Zorubin nodded.

'And what does she say?'

'She says it was wartime. She had been posted to the German embassy in Lisbon. She knew Emil Coburg was an anti-Nazi. Alexina even more so, it seems. Elisabeth says that when her letters starting coming back marked "Address Unknown" she went to Germany. Haus Lingfeld was shut up. The staff dismissed. Elisabeth's conclusion was that Alexina and her parents had gone underground.'

'And nothing else is known?'

Zorubin nodded. 'Yep,' he said. 'I traced the record through. Alexina and her parents were executed in a sub-camp of Mauthausen, Austria, August 2nd, 1940.'

PART TWO

· Martin ·

· Thirteen ·

When Martin Coburg was a young boy he believed all young boys lived as he did. He believed, first of all, that all young boys lived with their grandfather and although he wasn't absolutely sure he thought that all grandfathers were tall, suntanned, white-haired men who insisted that their grandchildren called them Pierre.

Martin knew many things for certain. He knew that Kansas City was the whole world which could be seen between the two rivers from the very top room of their house on Quality Hill. He knew that fathers and mothers were not half as important as grandfathers named Pierre and he knew that a twin sister was a great burden for a young boy to bear.

When he was five the family moved to Long Island and that confused him a great deal about the size of the world. He knew he was five and his twin sister was five which led him to believe that all children were five. So far so good. But he also knew, because he had asked him, that Pierre was 45. This led him to believe that all adults were 45. When he told his mother at a grown-up party that she must be 45 because she looked it, Pierre and the others burst out laughing but his mother slapped his face.

His mother often slapped Martin. She didn't seem to slap Celine, however naughty she was. His dad didn't slap anybody but that's because his mother said his father was as weak as water.

Martin's mother was named Rose. Everybody, especially the servants, was always saying that his mother was very beautiful. Certainly she was always buying new clothes but it didn't really matter how much they cost because the family business was printing banknotes. In his secret box under his bed Martin had saved up several dollar bills which had been made especially for him in the family's Kansas City printing plant.

The truth was that he kept the dollar bills in his secret box because he was planning to run away. He had four dollars and two French francs with holes in the middle and he was only waiting for the weather to get warmer before he ran away.

The problem was not so much that he was unhappy at home as things were, although he didn't love his mother as much as he should and his father was as weak as water, which left only Pierre whom he loved and who was big and suntanned and 45 . . . *no*, the problem was the German Coburgs were coming to stay for the summer and Martin couldn't stand the thought of that.

The German Coburgs spoke in German. Emil was the head of the German Coburgs. He was Pierre's twin brother and was tall and suntanned, and, like all other grown-ups, 45. His wife was a big fat lady in a red shiny dress who was always hugging Martin and trying to put his eye out with the sharp things she wore round her neck. Those things were known as stones but were more sparkly and shiny. Dorotta, as he was instructed to call her, was a very nice lady who didn't like his mother slapping him. Once she had spoken to Emil about it and Emil had gotten very angry with his mother. This only led to more slaps when Martin was in her bedroom.

No, the problem with the German Coburgs was not Dorotta's stones or the fact that they spoke in German. It was the two girls. These were Alexina, who, being a child, was also five. And her Aunt Elisabeth who was, mysteriously, said to be older.

The problem was that he and Celine and Alexina and Elisabeth were to go away on a special children's cruise for the whole summer and sail up to Canada and look at things and sail back. Him and three girls!

He had asked Pierre if something could be done about this but it was after lunch and Emil and Pierre were sitting at the table telling stories about when they were five-year-old children in the place they were born called the Waldviertel where everybody spoke German. Pierre had told him to have a word with his mother about it when she got back from New York City.

Pierre and Emil really did look alike. They had the same sort of loud voices and told jokes that everybody laughed at. Since the German Coburgs' visit Martin had been busily revising his view of the world. It seemed clear enough now that it was divided into two parts. One was called Europe and the other was called America. Emil, he was now certain, owned Europe and Pierre owned America.

This was a very comfortable cosmology for Martin until the table talk began to turn to places named China or Russia or England.

That afternoon he waited until his mother had returned to the house and he ran upstairs, into her bedroom and out onto the balcony where he liked to press himself among the ivy and look out over the gardens where the gardeners worked all day with their sleeves rolled up and their caps pushed back on their heads. There were a lot of things he liked about this house. He liked the swimming pool and he liked most of the servants. Especially the pool servant who gave him swimming lessons.

Below him now he could see his mother walking with her arm linked with his father's and a friend of theirs named Jack on the other. They came along the rose alley, which his mother loved because her name was Rose, and Martin tried to wave to them, but they turned onto the broad west lawn where his dad and Jack left his mother's side and started some horseplay, rolling about on the lawn with their city clothes. His mother soon got cross. He could see that even from where he was watching. He knew, when she walked with big long strides, she was angry.

For quite a while longer he stayed where he was until the two men stopped fooling about and got up brushing themselves down and came towards the house. As they disappeared into the main hall under the balcony he was standing on, he tried to wave and call to them again but he wasn't quite tall enough to make himself seen over the stone balustrade.

If he asked his mother and she said he didn't have to go on the ship to Canada he would try to love her more. He sat down and thought about it. If he made her a real promise perhaps she would say the girls could go alone.

Below him there was movement on the drive. He stood up again and strained to see over the top of the balcony. Martin's father was at the wheel of his sports car. 'Be back in an hour,' he said, waving to his friend Jack. The white car screeched away and Jack walked back into the house brushing himself down.

Only a few minutes later he heard voices behind him in the bedroom. He tried to remember the promise he was going to make. His mother's french window onto the balcony was ajar and he could hear her voice.

Martin frowned. His mother was putting on a silly, baby voice, which she sometimes did for Celine. 'You lamb,' she said, 'just come here and let me kiss it better.' He heard a deep man's voice say something and he edged forward to look round the edge of the French door. His mother was certainly kissing it better. Red-faced she was kneeling in front of Pierre gobbling away like a turkey!

Along the drive he could hear the Coburg girls coming back from their horse-back riding. Sometimes they took Celine with them but today they were alone. What was the promise? He couldn't go into the bedroom without having his promise ready. To love her more. Prepared, he stepped forward and flung open the french door. Pierre and his mother were under the silk cover having a wrestling match. All the grown-ups were having wrestling matches today! Then his mother started screaming at him, calling him nasty names and yelling at him to get out. After that he never dared to ask her if he could stay at home when the girls went sailing to Canada.

When Martin Coburg was sixteen Pierre decreed that he should accompany him to Kansas City. It was the spring of 1937 and Martin was the heir to Coburg Banknote. Nobody troubled to enquire why. John Coburg, Martin's father, was not in the line of succession. He was not interested. He painted, he played the violin and was interested in nigger music. Celine was a girl. Nobody but her mother Rose even considered her for the succession.

By then Martin had already received instructions in the US side of Coburg's, or Coburg Banknote Inc., as the company name was registered in the United States. He had never been back to Kansas City since the family had moved offices to New York and Pierre had bought the mansion on Long Island.

Martin Coburg stood in total awe of his huge, dominant grandfather, in awe of him when they visited the Governor of Missouri, in awe when he starved his striking workers into submission at the Coburg Banknote plant on the Kaw River, in awe when he drank whisky and hammered the table with Tom Prendergast, the acknowledged boss of Kansas City. Pierre Coburg was a rich and powerful figure in Kansas City and he had no plans to let anyone forget it.

It had not always been so. Pierre Coburg had left his homeland, an area in the middle of the old Austrian Empire, in the spring of 1900 to seek his fortune in America. He was twenty years old and his only real regret was that he could not persuade his twin brother, Emil, to come with him. The two boys were tall, powerfully built young men with big faces and thick blond hair. They spoke the languages of central Europe, German, Hungarian, Czech, and although their parents had been peasants they themselves had been apprenticed to a master printer in Budapest. The company's speciality had been the printing of bonds and banknotes. A Russian fifty-rouble note with the Tsar's head in the righthand corner excited their craftsman's pride. But one day Pierre sneaked a look at the company's accounts and discovered how the Tsar was paying for his fifty-rouble notes, and how much the Serbian Central Bank paid for its annual order of one million five-dinar notes. Thereafter it had been the brothers' ambition to own the finest, most specialised printing business in the world. Their views were split on how to do this. Pierre favoured taking their talents to America; Emil was convinced that Vienna could prove the foundation for their fortune.

In 1900 Pierre left for America. Both brothers were to work to establish a Coburg Banknote Printing Company. The two companies were to be independent yet linked in their division of orders received. There was to be no poaching; there were to be annual open examinations of the books; technical advances were to be made available to each other. Both companies, although carrying different names, Imprimerie Coburg in Europe and Coburg Banknote Inc. in America, were to share as their company symbol the head of Janus, the Roman god with two faces, separate yet linked, looking, the boys told each other, two ways, a vigilant guardian of both Coburg enterprises, the one in Europe, the other in America.

It was a dream. A dream of two boys, barely more than peasants themselves. But it was a dream backed by the Coburg will to succeed.

Pierre arrived in New York City in the bleak winter of 1900. The tenement he lived in on the few dollars he had left bubbled and fermented with ideas for becoming rich. When he talked of printing banknotes fellow immigrants sat back and laughed. The big German had a sense of humour. But Pierre was not interested in schemes to roast chestnuts or sell worn boots. He was looking for bigger money. One day an old drunk came to the tenement and rambled on half the night about life in the heart of America, about the prize-fighting and gambling and spending money. For four hours Pierre listened in the communal kitchen of the tenement until long after the fire had burnt out. By dawn he had decided that the free and easy life of the new America was where a man like him could make his first fortune.

Chance and odd jobs as railman and carter took him to Kansas City.

In 1900 Kansas City was still barely half a century removed from its foundation and a whole lot closer to the significance of its name. The Kansas or Kaw Indians were known for their roistering, feasting, dancing, speechmaking, gambling and drinking. By 1900 Union Avenue greeted visitors with cappers whose task was to part the newcomer from his money in the shortest time possible. Painted women swung their hips as they roamed the short thoroughfare. Cattlemen in high boots and gamblers in high hats joined ticket scalpers, bunco artists and ballyhoo men. Runners, barkers and cappers sought out a face to drag him into a saloon, barbershop or burlesque show along the way. Music, gambling, women and drinking were Union Avenue's specialities.

Calls for a clean-up of Union Avenue and the whole of the West

Bottoms district of Kansas City were frequent and ineffective. But another Kansas City was already in existence. Up on Quality Hill, Colonel Kersey Coates had established an area of exclusive residences, the Coates House hotel, with copper-roofed towers and a white marbled swimming pool, and a large and ornate Grand Opera House.

It was on Union Avenue that Pierre Coburg began his career but it was always to Quality Hill that he aspired.

Just down from the old Union depot as the New Year of 1901 approached, Doyle's cat house needed a capper. He needed to be big and fearless. 'You bring 'em in,' Mrs Doyle said, 'you make 'em pay, and you carry them out.' When she saw Pierre Coburg she decided he was the man for the job.

She decided within a short time that there were other jobs he, the big German, could usefully be put to carry out as well. He showed himself to be an inspired bookkeeper, a part-time runner and then a friend of Boss Jim Prendergast. And he kept his hands off the girls, at least as far as Mrs Doyle could see.

She married him in 1901 and died in childbirth at the age of 42 just nine months later. Pierre Coburg sold the cat house he had inherited and moved in with his baby son and a nurse above a small new printing plant in the West Bottoms. The American side of the House of Janus was in existence.

To celebrate his American citizenship in 1908 Pierre held an enormous party in the banqueting room above Jim Prendergast's Main Street saloon. Every member of Prendergast's Democratic Club was there. The food was wild boar and the wine was the best imported. The women, Pierre claimed, had been brought in from New York.

That party took Pierre to the edge of bankruptcy but in the following years it never ceased to pay dividends. The Prendergasts liked a man who made clear which side of the fence he stood on. Printing work came Pierre's way from politics and business. In 1910 Coburg Banknote printed its first currency bill, a Haitian ten-franc note, from an introduction by a former US senator for Missouri.

Pierre Coburg by now fitted perfectly the dual role of banknote printer. A tall, well-dressed, distinguished-looking young man with prematurely grey hair, he inspired confidence in his discretion and the utter reliability of Coburg banknotes. At the same time he was a ruthless fighter for a foreign currency contract, prepared to lie, bribe or menace.

By 1917 the House of Janus in both Europe and America was uniquely positioned to seize the opportunities of war and the even greater opportunities brought by the peace. The Treaty of Versailles had created some ten new states in central and southern Europe and almost every currency contract was for the taking. While Emil gained contracts for the new Czechoslovakian crown or marks of the Kaiserless new Germany, Pierre specialised in the phenomenally profitable China trade. Here the grand names of European and American currency trading, De la Rue of London, Banque de France, American Banknote, all engaged in a vicious cutthroat scramble under the veil of dignity and discretion. Often enough Pierre's Coburg Banknote came away with the order for Macao dollars or Shanghai bank bonds.

But not all elements of the boyhood dream had survived for Pierre and Emil. They remained as close as ever, the greatest of friends. But also the greatest of rivals. Within ten years of the end of the Great War, Emil had infiltrated the immensely profitable China trade; Pierre was dabbling in the Balkan lands of south-eastern Europe. Sometimes, rarely, they co-operated as when they snatched twenty per cent of the huge secret Soviet Union rouble contract from under the noses of American Banknote and De la Rue. But co-operation was not the name of the Coburg game. They had, both of them, in their different ways, qualities to bring to the House of Janus. Pierre was a master-salesman; Emil was a brilliant administrator and printing technician. They should have combined. They chose to compete.

For Coburg Banknote and Pierre, the years on either side of the Great Crash were spectacularly successful. His personal life was a scatter of affairs with some of the greatest beauties of the day. He seduced the Duchess of Manneringham on a *Queen Mary* voyage from London to New York. On the same voyage he seduced the brilliant new Swedish film star Karen Targa. He was completely ruthless in taking to bed the wives of his subordinates or the stenographers in the New York headquarters building. He still had a slight accent, but to women there was something rich and raffish about it. He was a world-travelled captain of commerce, a man of steadily increasing wealth.

Yet Pierre Coburg still retained much of his central European peasant upbringing. He was careful to disguise the fact but he was highly superstitious. He furtively crossed himself whenever a wolf-dog as he called it, a German shepherd crossed his path. It was an acute reminder of the werewolf myths of the old Waldviertel hills, and after all you never knew whether it was just a simple dog. Full moons affected him too, not inducing madness, but by making him uncomfortable, extra watchful in family and business matters. A Sunday falling on the seventh of the month was especially dangerous.

His son, John Doyle Coburg, was in every way overshadowed by the man. At the age of eighteen he had been sent to Oxford in England and had there met and made pregnant a young American girl of good but poor family. From the day John brought Rose back to meet his father their marriage, if it had ever had a chance, was doomed.

· Fourteen ·

For Rose Coburg life in Kansas City was as close to perfect as she could imagine. She had grown up in Boston, the third daughter of a former Beacon Hill family which had long ago fallen on hard times. They were not really poor. Her father who was an effete and unsuccessful lawyer received an annual sum from a family trust which barely enabled him to maintain what he considered the necessities of gentility. He drank vintage port, rode to hounds and he travelled once a year with his wife to London to stay with a cousin in Wimbledon. Each of the three daughters was given one chance in life as their parents saw it. At eighteen years of age they were sent to London to find a gentleman husband. The first daughter had sadly miscalculated and become engaged to a draper on Wimbledon Hill. The second daughter had been unsuccessful in her quest and had received no offers at all. Rose, a striking rather than beautiful girl, had met John Doyle Coburg at her one Commem ball in Oxford. Getting herself pregnant by him was not easy but marrying him in his college chapel a week after the 'discovery' had been a pushover.

He was, she decided, almost certainly happier with men than with women. And that too suited her plans. But most importantly his family was extremely rich. It's true that she had little more than his word to go on but he gave the information so casually that she became convinced that his word was worth more than the Wimbledon draper's.

Her return to America as a pregnant bride and her forthcoming meeting with her new husband's father, she believed, would be a massive ordeal. But from the day she met Pierre Coburg at the wedding breakfast he gave for them at Coates hotel in Kansas City, she began to formulate her plans.

She intended to seduce him. In the event, he seduced her. Or perhaps, she thought, they seduced each other, if that were possible.

It was little more than a week after her arrival in the big house on Kansas City's Quality Hill. At first Pierre had behaved coldly towards her, making no attempt to disguise his disapproval at the haste in which the marriage had taken place. Then one day two men arrived at the house wearing collars too tight for their bulky frames, brown tweed suits and brown derbys, proclaiming themselves to be detectives or, at most, Pinkerton men. Pierre was closeted with them for an hour. When they had gone he took Rose's arm and told her he wanted a walk in the garden. 'I hope,' he said, 'your father can be persuaded to come out to Kansas City for a visit. I'm planning a belated wedding breakfast for you at the Coates hotel. Everybody in Kansas will be there.'

'What did your two detectives have to report?' she said, looking up at him. 'That we were a not very wealthy, but respectable Boston family, I trust.'

He smiled. 'That's about what they said.'

'Just as I said.'

He squeezed her arm. 'Just as *you* said, honey.'

That first wedding breakfast had seen the beginning of a conspiracy between Pierre and his daughter-in-law. At the age of forty Pierre was still a young man; grey, certainly, but supple enough despite his powerful build. He was accustomed to absolute obedience from his son and from the members of his company who came to the house. His servants trembled before him. But he treated them with a rough kindness. Few had ever been dismissed from the Coburg household. Few had ever chosen to leave. Women who had become old women in his service were kept on. The large stable block contained small apartments for Coburg pensioners.

The girl who now entered this household was completely unprotected by her husband. From the first she knew that her choice was to fight Pierre or to join him. She was enough of a realist to understand that she could not fight him.

Her weapons were her youth and good looks. Her problem was the pregnancy. By her own calculation Rose had less than a month to get him into bed before the swelling distorted her shape too much.

She knew enough about the world to realise that this man who brooked no opposition would nevertheless be titillated by a display of spirit. At the wedding breakfast her husband, John, made a six-line speech of hesitant thanks to his father. It was not the custom for the bride to speak and when she rose a wave of whispering rolled through the banqueting room.

'Kansas City, as we all know,' she began with an air of shyness, 'is named from the Kaw or Kansas Indian tribe that hunted the Blue Hills and fished in the old Blue Muddy since time began. These Kaw Indians, it seems, were renowned for their festivals of speech-making and, I believe, several less mentionable enjoyments.'

The men at the wedding breakfast let out a loud cheer. Pierre's set face softened.

'As a newly married Kansas squaw,' Rose said, 'I knew enough to know I couldn't duck my speech-making obligations.'

Pierre smiled in response to the mutters of encouragement all around him.

'This is the Heartland of America,' she said firmly. 'The East can talk about its big cities, its big schools. Texas can talk about its size and the West Coast can talk about its opportunities which are always, *always* around the corner. But here in Kansas City the opportunities are here today. And I'm telling you, I may have been born in the east, I may have even been to Europe, but my place is right here in the Heartland of America.' She paused for effect. 'Beside my husband.' Then she slowly transferred her glance to Pierre: from that day some sort of pact was forged between her and Pierre. Friendship was no part of it, but an alliance had been forged. How far that alliance would take them neither knew exactly, but both knew how the alliance had to be sealed.

Of the two, Rose, already more than three months pregnant, had the greater sense of urgency. When her husband John went to New York for a week, Pierre was mostly busy away from the house. She had no wish to be too open about her intentions but she made efforts to send all those messages which she knew she had to send. When they were alone she would carefully arrange and then rearrange her slim legs for his pleasure. Leaving the pool she would let her wrap slip negligently from her shoulders. He acknowledged all this with a hard, wry smile. More than two weeks after the wedding breakfast she was still far from sure that she could have him.

Then one afternoon John left to visit a friend who had just bought a farm down the Raytown Road. The friend, Jack Aston, was a wealthy young man who had, like John Coburg, yet to do a day's work in his life. But the early death of both parents had enabled Jack to draw up plans for a house with English gardens, once the farm was demolished and the land resculpted.

Rose declined her husband's offer to take her for a drive. 'My dear John,' she said in that superior manner she had now decided to use in distancing herself from him, 'have you no idea at all what this heat does to a girl from the East?'

'I'm sorry, Rose,' John said hurriedly. 'Of course you must rest. Nothing energetic. I'll explain to Jack.'

He set off in his Lagonda, happy to get away for a few hours from the pressures his wife was able to exert. John Doyle Coburg was one of those men who had absorbed a sense of personal failure from his father's success. At school he had done averagely well and pursued archaeology to a respectable level at Harvard. But in the life of Kansas City politics and business he was completely lost. People like the rough-neck Prendergasts who ruled Kansas City shook his hand and turned away. Everybody knew there was no route to Pierre Coburg through his son. Nevertheless this tall slender young man, shy at parties and particularly before women, had one ambition, to please his father. To this end he had dabbled in the business but he had been shocked on his first selling trip to Peking to see how bribes were distributed or perhaps a reluctant official beaten on his way home. He would never, he knew, make a banknote salesman. And after his first month in the central printing plant in Kansas City he also knew that he would never be able to control the tough Irish overseers that security printing demanded in the wild post-war days.

He was barely nineteen when he left Oxford, cloaked in his sense of failure. Then he had met Rose, a beautiful American girl from the East. After a ball at his college they had taken a punt on the river. It was a warm June night an hour or so before dawn and they had allowed the flat bottomed boat to drift and nestle among the reeds on the bank. Punts full of other revellers moved past them as Rose undid the buttons on his fly. He was deeply shocked but he lay back, helpless on the broad corduroy cushions. It seemed to him that she was possessed as she knelt above him, pulling off her English knickers. When she straddled him the folds of her ball gown obscured his vision. He struggled to pull it from his face and when he was once again looking straight up at the chequerwork of black leaves against the lightening sky, he was aware that his penis felt enjoyably warm. She had enclosed him for fully two minutes before he realised that for the first time in his life he was experiencing sexual intercourse. His spasm coincided with the realisation. Rose rolled off him and lay beside him on the corduroy cushions. As a pink dawn rose behind Magdalen Tower, she snuggled closer to him. 'Wasn't that just wonderful, darling?' she urged him awake. 'When we're married,' she said happily, 'we'll be able to do it just whenever we like.'

Back in Kansas City his father's anger had at first been terrible. He had raged up and down the room like a bull, swiping at ornaments and kicking at oriental carpets. But he was faced with a *fait accompli* and he knew it. Whether he would accept it waited on the Pinkerton men and the brazen offer of alliance contained in Rose's wedding breakfast speech.

On the afternoon that John Coburg left to look at the plans for the conversion of Jack Aston's farm property, Rose took the gravel path that would bring her past the open garden doors of the room where she knew Pierre was working. Before she rounded the corner of the house she stopped in the shadow of a great wistaria and arranged her broad-brimmed sun hat and smoothed her hands down over the swelling in her belly. Then she walked slowly on.

She knew he was there in the deep shadow of the room. Her heels crunched on the gravel. She stopped and picked at an imaginary snag in her stocking but still he didn't call.

Continuing as slowly as she dared she passed the garden room and reached the main entrance to the house. Still he didn't call.

She felt furious. Humiliated. She had offered herself to an old man and he had *refused*. She stood indecisively before the vast front door, then let herself in.

Pierre was standing in the doorway of his work room, cigar in hand. He smiled at her and she swallowed hard and smiled back. 'I think I drank a little too much wine at luncheon,' she said. 'I feel quite light-headed.'

He drew on his cigar without speaking. His eyes, roving over her body, infuriated her. She was on the very edge of turning, flouncing out, when, with his free hand, he reached for a servant's bell and pushed it. She heard the ringing in the rear of the house. Then again and again as he pushed on the button.

They heard hurried steps on the servants' stairs and Jacob, one of the younger footmen, raced into the hall and stopped.

Pierre turned towards him. 'Ask Henry for me,' he said, 'to take a bottle of champagne up to Mrs Coburg's bedroom.'

Jacob half bowed and turned quickly away.

'Come in,' Pierre said.

She walked ahead of him into the room. 'And just why,' she said as he closed the door after him, 'have you had champagne sent up to my room?'

'If you feel a little light-headed, Rose,' he said nonchalantly, 'an hour's sleep in a cool room and a glass of good champagne upon waking, will do wonders for you. I'm sure your dear mother would agree.'

He had dropped into one of the armchairs.

'You've assumed, of course, that I don't enjoy this state of light-headedness. On the contrary I find it refreshing, liberating even.' She sat on the arm of his chair. It was a perfectly open invitation. Again he did nothing and again her anger began to rise. Then he placed one enormous hand on her thigh and began to caress upwards. She shifted her legs a fraction, opening them. His hand moved down the inside of her thigh and she felt his thumb between her legs.

'I think perhaps we should go and drink that champagne together,' she said.

He smiled. 'What a pleasurable daughter-in-law my son has presented me with,' he said, rising to his feet and offering his hand.

For a long time afterwards she wondered about his use of the word pleasurable. Did his English not quite extend to the knowledge that *pleasurable* was used not of a person, but rather of an event, an occurrence, even of a *thing*.

Rose Coburg's twins were born five months later.

· Fifteen ·

The family which Pierre Coburg transferred to Long Island in 1926 consisted of himself, his son John Doyle Coburg, his daughter-in-law Rose and his grandchildren, the twins Martin and Celine.

It was a privileged existence. Through the 1930s Martin grew up unaware of the grimness of the depression years. An athletic boy, comfortable in his body, he was devoted to tennis, swimming and especially boxing. At the Long Island sports club, by the time he reached his teens, his looks and his easy manner ensured a ready acceptance.

But there was a darker side. Surrounded by friends of his own age, he could avoid the problems of his home, the problems of family love and affection and the sources of authority. If he hated anybody it was his mother. If he admired anybody it was his grandfather; if he loved anybody it was his sad, nervous father.

Yet they had little or nothing in common. John Coburg played the cello to performance standard, but he played for himself alone in his rooms. As Martin got older he came to realise that music and whisky were his father's main supports in life. Music and whisky and Jack Aston.

They had made, over the years, clumsy efforts to come together. At family dinner each evening Martin would pretend not to hear the jeering note Pierre's voice naturally adopted when he spoke to his son John. As he grew older each evening became an excruciating exercise in speaking politely to his father without offending his mother or his grandfather. Celine, of course, sided openly with her mother. The many business friends of Pierre or Boston relatives of Rose who came for dinner or the weekend always gravitated toward the strong. Evening after evening Martin would watch in misery as his father sat at the table, totally ignored by all the adults.

It was music which opened up a tenuous line of communication between them. On his phonograph Martin often played the newly available records of the jazz bands of Chicago and St Louis. He had none of his father's formal understanding of music but something in him responded to this negro music with its humorous, liberating rhythms.

One day passing each other on the wide staircase of the house they both stopped, more than anything in the realisation that they could not really pass each other without speaking.

'I heard your phonograph all morning,' John Coburg said.

'Sorry, Dad.'

'No, no, that's not what I meant, son. I like the music. Least I find it more interesting than I at first thought.'

'You like jazz music?' Martin had looked at him in surprise.

'I think I might just grow to like it,' his father said cautiously. 'I might just grow to like it quite a lot,' he added desperate not to break the slender thread between them.

There was a long pause. 'Bix Beiderbecke is playing in New York,' Martin said. One hand was rubbing up and down the bannister rail. He was ready for rejection.

'In New York, you say?'

'At the Honey club. I couldn't get in by myself.'

John Coburg felt a throb of excitement. 'You wouldn't like me to take you?'

'Would you?'

'Why . . . sure I would. The Honey club, you say?'

Two days later they had sat at a table not twenty feet from Bix Beiderbecke himself. Martin was transported. His father, who had begun the evening smiling wryly, ended it with foot-tapping enthusiasm. 'I think I might be beginning to see,' he said in the back of the limousine home, 'what a young fellow like you sees in this music. I think this is something we ought to explore a little more together.'

Martin felt a warm glow of gratitude, a sense that he had been able to give something to his father. 'Next week at the Honey club,' he said, 'Armstrong's playing with Ella Fitzgerald.'

'Then we must go, old chap,' his father said. 'Let's see,' he said gaily. 'Tuesday before Christmas, marvellous. We'll have dinner at the Harvard club and go to hear ourselves some jazz.'

The feeling for his father generated by their visit to the Honey club remained throughout the preparations for Christmas. There was between them for the first time a certain complicit warmth.

Shortly after Pierre had moved the Coburg family to Long Island Jack Aston, Martin's father's friend, had turned up there with a shoreline property near Montauk Point.

He now came to the house quite often and Martin began for the first time to get to know him. A slender man of medium height with light brown hair which fell across his forehead, Aston wore quite different clothes from Pierre or most of the men Martin knew. He never wore heavy dark suits. In summer he wore cream linen with large red or deep green handkerchiefs that cascaded from his top pocket.

Martin had grown up with the sense that there was something undesirable about Jack Aston. His mother and Pierre were always scathing about him. At times, having drunk a little too much Armagnac after dinner, Pierre would begin a strange prancing imitation of Jack Aston which was not like him at all but which made Martin's mother shriek with laughter, and sometimes made his father rush from the room.

When Martin was younger there had been a proposal that Jack Aston should tutor him in Latin, but Pierre, Martin knew, had forbidden it and instead some seedy English clergyman would arrive twice a week to torture him with the dreadful complexities of *Bradley's Arnold*.

Only at prep school in Westchester had Martin come to understand, however vaguely, the charge against Jack Aston and his father. They were pansies, one of the older boys said, and began to pounce and mince around much as Pierre did on some nights.

At that moment Martin was still ignorant of what his father was being accused of. The bigger boy, Barrington, had nudged others in the group gathered round Martin. 'Well, Coburg,' he said, 'what do you say about that?'

'My father isn't a pansy,' Martin had said, defending himself desperately from the pushing group of boys. 'He used to run the hundred yards dash for Oxford.'

'He's a pansy,' Barrington said menacingly. 'What's he do, Knight?'

Eric Knight sucked in his lips. 'He goes kiss kiss with other men.'

'He doesn't. He isn't a pansy,' Martin had shouted in Knight's face. But Barrington had seized him from behind and with Knight's help had twisted Martin's arm until he screamed with pain.

'What does your dad do, Coburg?' The boys twisted Martin's arm. 'Kiss kiss with other men. What does he do?'

Martin clenched his teeth, throwing his head back from side to side.

'What does he do?' Barrington leaned harder on his arm.

Intense loyalty to his father rose like a spurt of anger. Struggling violently, he kicked backwards, his heel rising between Barrington's legs. As the boy screamed, the armlock broke. The games master, attracted by the shouts, came into the locker room. 'Stop that horseplay,' he said. 'I want you all outside, changed, in two minutes.'

A few days after their first visit to listen to jazz music in New York, John Coburg had come up to his son's room. Outside it was snowing heavily and Martin was sitting in the window seat, reading.

'Martin, I've got a great idea. Jack Aston says that Fats Waller's playing at the Courtesy Club right until Christmas. You like to go?'

Martin put down the book. 'Fats Waller? Sure I'd like to go.'

'These tickets are like gold dust,' John Coburg said. 'But I have influence in high places.'

'I'd really like to go, Dad.'

John Coburg watched with pleasure one of his son's rare expressions of commitment. 'OK. Dinner jacket. We eat at the Harvard Club and go on to catch the midnight show at the Courtesy. How does that sound to you?'

'Really great.'

Martin's father smiled as he moved back towards the door. 'Just one thing, Martin. Perhaps there's no need to mention to your mother or Pierre that Jack's coming with us. Jack's not their favourite man.'

On the night they were to go to see Fats Waller, Martin dressed in his first dinner jacket. Pierre had insisted that now that he was just fifteen he should be properly dressed for this night and for the huge Christmas night dinner Pierre always gave. A dinner jacket for the young Coburg boy was now essential.

Standing in front of the mirror in his bedroom Martin looked himself over with pleasure. Thrusting one hand deep into his trouser pocket he left his room on the second landing and came slowly down the staircase into the hall. The butler was helping his father on with his blue overcoat. John Coburg looked up and smiled approval at his son. 'Looks good, doesn't he, Frank?'

The butler, an ally of Martin's mother, looked at Martin without a word. 'Impeccable, sir,' he said, after a perfectly timed moment of insolence.

From the drawing room came the sound of voices as the door opened. Pierre, Rose and her sister Bette came out into the hall.

Rose stopped, staring angrily at Martin. 'That dinner jacket is for Christmas day,' she snapped. 'Who gave you permission to wear it tonight?'

Martin looked towards his father whose lips were pressed tight together, unable to speak.

'Dad said you have to wear dinner jackets at the Courtesy Club.'

'We're going to listen to some jazz music,' John Coburg blurted.

'I'm not having the boy wear that dinner jacket before Christmas day,' Rose said coldly.

Pierre stood with Bette a few steps behind Rose. He was smoking a cigar, content to let Rose exert her authority.

'Rose,' John Coburg's voice took on a note of pleading, 'I can't take him without the right clothes. You know the Courtesy Club.'

'Go and get out of that dinner jacket,' Rose said quickly.

Martin hesitated as his father struggled to protest. 'Listen, Rose,' her husband said. 'Just this once.'

She turned away.

'OK, Dad,' Martin said. 'OK. You two go on alone.'

Rose swung round. 'You two? Who else was going? You, Martin and who else?'

The butler smiled down at the black and white tiled floor. Pierre waved his cigar under his nose and inhaled the smoke. Bette's eyebrows lifted enquiringly.

'Jack Aston,' John Coburg said. 'Jack was coming with us.'

Rose took a step towards him. 'You were allowing my son to go with *Jack Aston*? A fifteen-year-old boy going with that pederast? Are you off your head?' She hurled the drink she was carrying to the floor. The glass shattered on the tiles. 'Are you out of what passes for a mind? My good God,' she exploded, 'it's bad enough having a nancy boy for a husband. Do I *have* to put up with him taking my son off to his nancy friend?'

Martin turned and blundered wildly up the stairs.

Barely checked, a violence roamed Rose Coburg's spirit. It was not directly sexual, she did not demand her lovers should be abased and certainly Pierre with his huge masculinity left her no choice. But she enjoyed suffering, she enjoyed the helplessness of the sufferer, she enjoyed most of all her part in inflicting suffering. It was, of course, not that clear cut even to Rose herself. She was fully aware of the extent of her harboured resentments against others. She was equally aware of that strange, exhilarating tingle of satisfaction she received when she reduced a maid to tears.

Most of her anger was directed towards her husband. The high points of her satisfaction could be gained from inflicting pain on him. Yet it was rare that he left himself vulnerable. He had learned, over several years, to protect himself. He never took part in family discussions; he accepted Rose's decisions without comment. But his relationship with Jack Aston was, everybody in the family knew, his Achilles heel.

The Christmas of 1936 was, as usual, to be spent at Island House. Apart from the immediate family, Rose had invited her unmarried sister Bette (who arrived in mid-November for the celebrations) and her married sister Zoe and her husband, a Boston lawyer named George Ackroyd. They brought with them three colourless teenage girls whose presence embarrassed, bored and irritated Martin in turn.

Pierre's guests were all men of political or business importance and their wives and children. There was a British ambassador and his wife, two governors of the Federal Reserve Bank, half a dozen politicians from Kansas City, a senator from New York State, and, as a special sign of Pierre's favour, Merril Soames, the young up-and-coming contracts vice-president from Coburg Banknote.

Notably absent from the list was Jack Aston. Rose had by now made it clear that he was not welcome at Island House. In answer to her husband's protests she had laconically invited him to ask Pierre himself. Everybody knew that he was unlikely to do that.

The Christmas programme had been settled over many years and dated back to Kansas City days. Christmas Eve was the high point of the holiday when the family and guests would gather in the long library at about five o'clock and drinks and canapés would be served. Martin in his new dinner jacket and Celine in a superb dress from Contrain-Laffont were for the first time to be invited to join the adult guests. The children were meanwhile entertained to a lavish party in the east kitchen.

The scene was etched as if with acid in Martin's memory. Rose, his mother, floated from one group of guests to another, talking of business, politics or clothes as seemed appropriate. Young Merril Soames flirted cautiously with her, one eye on the Coburg Banknote president. Pierre and Celine held court before the great fireplace where huge logs of silver birch burned with bright blue and white flames. Champagne and Martinis were offered from silver trays by waiters in white gloves. Christmas music played on a new, unending phonograph gadget which Pierre had acquired during the summer.

Waves of talk and laughter swelled through the room as the drinks began to have their effect. At seven o'clock Pierre would call for silence, would bow his head and briefly ask for the Lord's blessing on their Christmas. He would then offer Rose his arm, the double doors would open and Pierre would lead his family and guests across the great hall with the lighted Christmas tree and into the dining room for a dinner, the centre-piece of which was an enormous three-foot-long stuffed carp.

Martin was fretting. His girl cousins fluttered around him, all slightly older than he was, all anxious to please. Barrington, the boy from his Westchester prep school, was there with his parents. Now a young man with dark smoothed hair, he cultivated a disdainful manner. 'You ever run into Eric Knight these days?' Barrington asked. 'Remember him?'

'Oh, I remember him,' Martin said. 'Is it true he failed law school again?'

'He was never much of a brain,' Barrington conceded.

'He was never much of anything,' Martin said, looking over Barrington's head from the extra three inches he had over the older boy.

His mother touched his arm, indicating he should come closer. 'Where in God's name is your father?' she hissed.

'I haven't seen him,' Martin said.

'For God's sake drop your lifetime habit of telling lies. You saw him after lunch.'

'I meant I hadn't seen him since. I'm sorry, I don't know,' he muttered. 'I don't know where he is.'

Her head came up, nostrils flaring.

'I want the truth,' she said. 'Or you go down now in your smart new dinner jacket and you eat Christmas jello and ice cream with the kiddies in the kitchen.'

Pierre came sauntering over to her side. He stood opposite Martin, not more than an inch or two taller now. 'What's the trouble?' he said in a low voice.

'Martin refuses to tell me where his father is.'

Pierre's deep blue eyes narrowed. 'You want to celebrate Christmas with a whipping, boy?' His voice was loud now. In his anger he didn't care who heard.

'I promise, Pierre,' Martin said desperately, 'I don't know where Dad is.'

'Is he in his room?' Pierre asked Rose.

She shook her head. 'I just sent someone up to look,' she said.

'He won't be far away,' Pierre said. 'I told Dawson to lock his car in the garage.' He smiled grimly. 'And to make sure he didn't get the keys to any of the others. In this weather he's not going to walk to Aston's place.'

Rose frowned. She turned to her son reluctant to believe he knew nothing about his father's whereabouts. 'And he said nothing to you? Nothing about what he was going to do this afternoon?'

Martin shook his head.

She stared at him in frustrated anger. 'I just know you're lying.' Then a thought struck her. 'Your motorbike,' she said.

Martin paled.

'That's it, of course,' she hissed triumphantly. 'You gave him the keys to your motorbike.'

The children's excited screams were deafening. Jello and lemonade mixed with cake crumbs. Paper hats wagged on once well-brushed heads. Balloons rose and were popped by jabbing forks.

'Sit down,' Rose ordered, pushing two children aside to open a place on the bench. 'Sit down there. If you're not to be trusted to behave like an adult, you get treated as a child. Understand?'

For a moment he contemplated rebellion. For just one moment. Then he put one leg over the bench and slid down between the two little girls.

When his mother left he sat red-faced with pointless fury. If only he'd said no. Just no.

'Anything I can get you, Mr Martin?' one of the coloured maids said. The concern on her face was almost too much for him.

'No,' he said. 'No, for Christ's sake.'

From the direction of the open staircase he heard laughter.

Harry Barrington and one of the Ackroyd cousins were leaning on the stair rail. Barrington raised his champagne glass to Martin. 'Sorry we're not staying, old fellow,' he said laughing, 'but I think we're just about to go in to dine.'

Martin pulled himself from the bench. 'If my mother wants to know where I am,' he said to the maid, 'I'm in my room.'

The girl nodded expressionlessly.

He walked slowly to the bottom of the stairs. His head lurched with the humiliation of being made to sit with the children while his stomach churned with guilt at having given his motorbike keys to his father. He stood at the bottom of the stairs. Pierre was right. He knew where his father was going and he knew it meant he would not be back or if he did return it would be incoherent with drink.

He started up the stairs to the main hall. He could hear sounds up there, strange scuffling sounds. He took two more steps up. His father and Jack Aston were reeling together in the middle of the hall, their mouths locked together.

At that moment the double doors opened from the long library. Pierre stood there with Rose on his arm. Celine screamed, guests surged forward and Martin stared with horror at his father's white face.

· Sixteen ·

The news arrived by cable as a shattering blow from Shanghai. The Coburg Banknote agent there had changed sides, been bought by another company just as he was negotiating what would have been a fatly profitable contract for Pierre.

In the head office in New York confusion reigned for several hours. Desperate telephone calls were placed to everyone who knew anything in the world banknote community. De la Rue in London denied the company would ever descend to such an ungentlemanly level. Pierre snorted and put in a call to American Banknote. Again, a similar response. Contacts in Mexico were cabled but claimed to know nothing. The French payee of Coburg Banknote inside Imprimerie d'Orient knew nothing. For ten minutes Pierre raged at him while the board of Coburg's sat watching.

'We pay you a fat bribe you know,' Pierre shouted down the transatlantic telephone line. 'So goddamn find out.'

Merril Soames, Pierre's vice-president responsible for contracts, suggested he fly to China immediately. He knew the key man in the deal, Pan Ku-Yan, well. The great advantage of dealing with him was that he was endlessly shifty and totally on the make. It would need a water-tight deal but Pierre must be prepared to go high.

Pierre calmed slightly as he was inclined to do when money was mentioned. 'I'll stake a million to win eight,' he said. 'You leave for China right away, Merril. I'll join you as soon as I can discover who the hell bought our man.'

The call came late that afternoon. 'To the victor, the spoils,' a familiar voice said in German.

Pierre flushed with anger. 'Emil, you bastard. It was you? You'd undercut your own brother?'

'Why not?' Emil said easily. 'You've done the same enough times to me. Or worse.'

'I have eight million dollars riding on this deal.' Pierre's voice rose in fury.

'Had,' Emil corrected him. 'Now I have.'

'What the hell are you doing, Emil?'

'I'm trying to bring you to your senses.'

'You want me to throw money away on your new machine.'

'You've got more capital than I have. Spend some of it, for God's sake.'

'Waste it on you tinkering with new machines? Listen, the presses we use have not changed in fifty years and they'll go on for another fifty.'

'You're a pig-headed fool!' Emil yelled down the transatlantic line. 'Do you know what the fattest contract in the whole of Europe will be next year? Spain.'

'Perhaps.'

'If Franco wins,' Emil said, 'he has promised the contract for a complete new Spanish currency to the Italians. A contract worth millions of dollars to a small printing house in Milan. And why? Because they have a young engineer improving on the old Serge Beaune machines. This young man is the future, you dolt. He's the future unless we put money into development.'

'I'm not changing my mind,' Pierre growled. 'And I'm reminding you that you're breaking our solemn agreement on China.'

'You're breaking an equally solemn agreement on technical co-operation. So as far as I'm concerned that leaves China up for grabs, unless you change your mind. How are Martin and Celine?' He changed the subject abruptly, provocatively, as if now turning to more important matters.

'They're not so bad,' Pierre said sulkily. 'Martin's turning into a businesslike young fellow. Bit on the serious side sometimes. Needs a woman, I expect. Celine follows the family tradition. Or *part* of it,' he said, heavily. 'She'd double-cross her own grandmother if she had one. How're the girls?'

'Elisabeth's entering the marriage stakes. She's set her sights on a young man named Rolf Oster. Fairly bright, but a bit too Englishified, you know.'

'I know,' Pierre grunted, thinking of the types from De la Rue. 'And Alex?'

'She's become quite a serious young lady, too. Politics has got his hand in her knickers. She likes it there.'

Pierre grunted. He would leave for Shanghai now. It was going to be tough. Perhaps he should take young Martin to show him something of the sharp end of the business.

'No hard feelings,' Emil was saying.

'You treacherous sonofabitch,' Pierre said.

'See you in Vienna this summer?'

'Doubt it. Try to make Long Island in the fall. Give my love to Dorotta.'

'Auf Wiedersehen, Pierre.'

'Auf Wiedersehen, you cheating bastard.'

Hung with candle lanterns, the two painted barges were poled across the glistening darkness of the imperial city's lake, Pei Hai. In the leading boat His Excellency the British Ambassador sat with Sir Neville Hatton, the British Naval Attaché, and an American who was later to become famous as 'Vinegar Joe', Colonel Joseph Stilwell, the United States Military Attaché, and his wife.

In the second boat, lagging now some thirty yards behind, Martin sat next to Joe Stilwell's daughter Nance. He was in a state of acute embarrassment. His embarrassment was not occasioned by Nance, a friendly, easy American girl. It was because of the necessity he felt to shift his body unceasingly, moving from one direction to another, in an attempt to keep the group of adults in the prow of the barge from seeing his grandfather Pierre and Sir Neville Hatton's wife in the deep, cushioned stern.

The French couple and the English woman in the prow noisily admired the fall of moonlight on the white marble tower of the Dagoba. For Martin the fall of moonlight was to be welcomed less. To his anguished senses it showed clearly Pierre's hand, pale against the dark material of Lady Hatton's dress, undoing buttons until it slipped out of sight under the ruched material of the bodice of the evening gown.

He could even hear Mollie Hatton gasping and saw her slide further down on the brown velvet cushions. From across the lake came the sound of a guitar and the faint yellowness of a string of lanterns announced another barge. The attention of the group in the prow was diverted. They called in English to the other barge and American voices answered.

'You can't leave yet,' Lady Hatton whispered urgently in Pierre's ear.

Martin turned his head away trying to stop his ears to everything but the greetings exchanged across the water and the inexpert twanging of the guitar.

'I have to go, Mollie,' Pierre said in what seemed to Martin like a recklessly booming voice. 'Unless the British government is prepared to sell me those rust buckets in Shanghai, I've no excuse to remain in China.'

'I'll do something,' she said firmly. 'I promise you I'll talk to Neville. They're not his boats. Why should he care who buys them?'

China in 1937 was the land of opportunity for the tens of thousands of foreigners who fought, lied and bribed their way to concessions, franchises and rights to fulfil almost any function in the Chinese economy.

The country was disintegrating. The Japanese had invaded Manchuria. The principal port of Shanghai was a British concession with its own army and police force, currency and laws. Bandit warlords controlled large tracts of land, recruiting peasants into their private armies. An American regiment was permanently stationed in the imperial capital of Peking. British gunships patrolled Chinese rivers. Japanese planes shot down commercial airliners and confiscated Chinese merchant shipping.

Almost without exception banknote printing contracts were bought, that is to say Chinese officials were bribed. But this was not by any means a simple, crude process. Only those salesmen who could tread the delicate path between offending and satisfying Chinese pride would succeed. There were recognised experts like the Bulgarian Avramov of De la Rue and there were plainly gifted salesmen like Pierre Coburg of New York. Sometimes they divided the spoils, sometimes they double-crossed each other, sometimes, but not often, they conceded defeat. Not often because the stakes were too high.

To Martin the trip to China was the strangest experience of his life. A dozen things disturbed him. Most of all the Chinese girls strutting the Bund in their tight black skirts and flowery blouses, emitting their strange and frightening shriek of laughter when they saw a potential customer like himself. But even these girls who made his penis harden as he sat at a sidewalk café and drank a *citron pressé*, even these girls were made more strange and alien by the smells of shredded duck, the shouts of merchants, the shuffling old ladies, the screams of the rickshaw boys, the constant tinkling of bells and the blaring horns of ancient delivery trucks or shining Western limousines.

Sitting in one of the big window alcoves of the Hotel Woodrow Wilson on the Bund, looking down on the endless stream of vegetable sellers pushing bicycles, old mandarins, rickshaws and bakery boys, Merril Soames watched with amusement as Martin picked out the street girls' slow, purse-swinging strut amid the mercantile hustle on the sidewalks.

'Pretty, some of them.' He nodded towards two girls passing.

'I guess so,' Martin said.

Soames drank his *café au lait*. 'But if you start getting hot about them you ought to know the score.'

'The score? You mean how much they charge?' Martin said tentatively.

Soames brushed the question aside. 'That's not the score. A dollar will take you where you want. I mean risks.'

'Risks?'

Soamed nodded. 'Less than half of them are girls.' He smiled as he saw the flush rise on Martin's cheeks. 'So, unless you like the idea of finding yourself in bed with another boy, feel first.'

Martin's eyes opened. 'First?'

'Before you buy.'

It was at that moment that Martin knew that his sex life would not begin in Shanghai.

Behind the façade of street energy the hotels and private houses of the rich were sunk in an oppressively dignified silence. To Martin it seemed a metaphor for the banknote printing business itself. Out on the street where the contracts were won and lost it was the most persistent, the most cunning, the fastest tongue that triumphed. Once gained the contract was carried on a silver plate back to the banknote printing houses of America and Europe where men in wing collars genteelly toasted their success.

Martin and Pierre had arrived in Shanghai in the early summer of 1937 by the cruise ship *Voltaire*. They had rented a house on the Avenue Pétain in the French concession. Within a week Merril Soames had arranged a meeting with Pan Ku-Yan, a senior official of the Bank of China, the man targeted by both Coburg brothers.

'Now I'm going to show you, Martin, what doing business is about in China today,' Pierre had said minutes before the door opened to show Pan Ku-Yan into the salon.

Martin sat as far from the centre of the room as he could while first Pierre and then Soames greeted the tall round-faced Chinese in the long embroidered robe who had entered the room. It seemed to Martin that the smiles, the many small jokes, the enquiries after the health of families was all, on both sides, utterly insincere.

When tea had been served the smiles faded as Pierre began talking. 'We in New York have taken a great interest in your rise to deserved prominence in the banking world of China,' Pierre began. 'We have looked with pleasure as you were appointed first to the office of the Minister of Finance, Mr H. H. Kung, and then to the post of representative of the Central Bank here in Shanghai.'

'Only time itself can limit the possibilities for Pan Ku-Yan,' Soames said politely.

The Chinese gravely inclined his head in agreement.

'From Washington I am able, personally, to bring the congratulations of the US Secretary of the Treasury.'

Again Pan Ku-Yan inclined his head. Martin, watching from the far end of the salon, wondered if the Chinese actually believed Pierre. Or perhaps decided it didn't matter because this gross flattery was all part of the game.

'Secretary Morgenthau offers his best wishes on the marriage of your daughter Ping.'

Did the Chinese stiffen slightly? Martin watched his eyes rest on Pierre over the raised teacup.

'The Secretary consulted me on the subject of a suitable gift to your daughter and her new husband.'

Silence.

'Mr Merril Soames informed me of the interest of your son-in-law's family in merchant shipping.'

'His family is prominent in this area,' Pan conceded.

'Let us all hope,' Pierre said piously, 'that the new Tokyo demands will not transfer all China's commercial shipping to the Japanese merchant fleet.'

Pan's eyes fluttered.

'My advice to Secretary Morgenthau,' Pierre said carefully, 'was that in normal circumstances an appropriate gift to the young couple might be an addition, or perhaps two, to the shipping interests of the Li family.'

Again the hooded eyes fluttered.

'But Secretary Morgenthau considered this might not be wise.'

'Ah . . .'

'His question was how to ensure that the ship or ships might remain in the possession of your daughter's new husband now that Japan and China are at war.'

'Ah . . .'

'I therefore offered to have the tonnage registered in my name, thus giving the protection of US ownership to the ship or ships. In practice of course the gift is a gift like any other. Your son-in-law will be free to use the tonnage as he wishes.'

The Chinese breathed in deeply to indicate a change of subject. 'I understand there was an attractive tender from your sister company, Imprimerie Coburg.'

Merril Soames was watching Pan closely. Pierre's face was set, waiting. Was the gift of two merchant ships a higher bribe than Emil's?

'At a time when China's fortunes seem cast on a turbulent sea,' Pan said, 'it is good to have trustworthy friends.'

'We can count on the Central Bank's endorsement, then?' Merril Soames said.

'I am sure so.' Pan rose to go. 'Allow me to convey to the US Secretary my daughter's gratitude for a handsome gift.'

The men shook hands. The Chinese bowed briefly to them all and Soames opened the door.

'I will arrange for a signed copy of the provisional endorsement to be delivered this very afternoon, Mr Coburg.'

The door closed behind him. For a moment Pierre stood, smiling to himself. Then he took a cigar from a box and offered one to Soames as he re-entered. 'So we made it, Merril.'

'It's only provisional,' Soames said.

'A perfectly balanced deal,' Pierre smiled. 'The ships are his but in my name. The contracts are mine – but only as long as *his* name remains on the endorsement. This way neither of us can double-cross the other.'

'And the ships that we're presenting to Pan Ku-Yan? Where do we get them from?'

Pierre grinned. 'That might be the most difficult part of the deal.'

Martin Coburg spent his sixteenth birthday with a notebook on Shanghai's waterfront. He had never seen such a confusion of ships, Chinese red-sailed junks unloading into sampans, old tubs from the last century that listed and belched black smoke. Between anchored cargo ships registered in Liverpool and San Diego and Hamburg, the slow sea sucked and fell, heavy as the oil that glistened on it.

He had talked to grizzled skippers in bars, to the sad patient rickshaw boys, to sampan loaders and to street girls. 'We need two old coasters,' Pierre had said. 'Three or four thousand tons each. Go out and find 'em, Martin. But don't go to any shipping office, or regular official. You just find them and let me know where they are. We've hooked this fish and we've got to keep it on the line. Emil is here with a bunch of German salesmen. I don't want anybody to know you're sniffing round the old freighters in the port.'

On the second day he struck lucky. A sampan boy had told him that two rusting freighters, one with its smoke-stack collapsed, the other with part of its bridge eaten away, had been moored there since the end of the Great War. Careful enquiries with a port-hand had revealed they belonged to the British Admiralty. Martin sat on a stone wall amid the frantic bustle of the Chinese port flowing past him and began to sketch the two ships.

Surrounded by the screech of laughter from the shop women, the clank of anchor lines, the shouts of Europeans and the rattle of provision carts, Martin was unaware that someone was standing over him until a girl's voice said, in English: 'I didn't know you were an artist.'

He looked up in surprise to see a very tall, slightly angular European girl of about sixteen, her face shaded by a wide-brimmed sun-hat. She wore a pale yellow silk dress belted with a white sash to show a figure still barely poised on the edge of adulthood. In the way she stood, looking down at him, he could feel an adolescent uncertainty in her.

'You remember me,' she said. 'I'm Alexina, your cousin.'

He snapped shut the notebook and stood up. He wasn't thinking how pretty she was, although she certainly was that. He was wondering just how much of his sketch Emil's daughter had seen.

Alexina turned to a young Chinese behind her. 'You can go now, Lee,' she said, giving him a coin from her purse. 'Mr Coburg will escort me back to the hotel.'

'What are you doing in Shanghai?' he asked as they walked along the waterfront.

She laughed, taking off her straw hat and letting tawny blonde hair billow in the offshore breeze. 'You know perfectly well what we're doing in Shanghai. And I for one think it's utterly ridiculous.'

'Ridiculous?' he echoed carefully.

'Two brothers with the whole world to divide up between them and they can't agree which market belongs to whom . . .' She had lost any uncertainty she might have had. She was telling him, now, firmly, her forehead lined in concentration, her eyebrows pressed down over her dark blue eyes. Physically he could see the resemblance to Celine, although his sister's mouth was different, usually set in a thinner, more self-absorbed line. If one thing was totally absent in the face of Alex and dominant in Celine's, it was calculation.

They turned into the narrow Imperial Boulevard and Martin asked her if she wanted to stop at a tea house. She nodded briskly. 'But don't *you* think it's stupid, this rivalry?'

He found his deep sense of loyalty to Pierre touched at a sensitive point. 'Emil started it,' he said. 'China has always been recognised as Coburg Banknote territory.'

They sat down and ordered tea from the wraith-like girl who appeared from behind a screen of tinkling bamboo.

'You believe it was Emil who first stepped out of line? What about Pierre's bid for the Luxemburg contract. And the Kroner contract from Norway?'

'They were nothing contracts, a few thousand dollars' profit in each,' Martin said. 'You know why Pierre tendered for Luxemburg and Norway?'

'Because they couldn't agree about a joint research budget.'

Martin nodded. 'Pierre believes printing presses have remained basic-ally the same for a hundred years. Who wants new ones?'

Her young face tightened in concentration. 'I think my father's right,' she said. 'We can't afford to be left behind. De la Rue in England, the Italians, the Dutch, they're all working on new machines.'

Martin shifted uncomfortably. The truth was he had never agreed with Pierre's refusal to create a Coburg research fund. And when Pierre had lunged into Emil's territory and snipped off two small contracts he had thought it childish.

'But don't you see the way it's going?' she said earnestly. 'Whoever's right about developing new machines, the important thing is that sooner or later Emil and Pierre will fall out. Seriously. And that's the end of the House of Janus.'

Martin looked at her uneasily. This was territory that Pierre would not appreciate him getting into. 'I can't see Emil and Pierre ever seriously falling out,' he said. 'They're brothers. Twins.'

'You'll never fall out with Celine? Is that what you're saying?'

He looked at Alexina in surprise. For a sixteen-year-old she knew how to hit below the belt.

The tea arrived and the ceremony of pouring saved him from having to make an answer.

'You know that one day,' Alexina said, sipping the hot tea, looking at Martin over the edge of her cup, 'you and I will own the House of Janus. Me because I'm the only child; you because you're the male heir.'

Neither of them mentioned Martin's father.

'Perhaps we'll hate each other,' he said grinning.

Her face was totally composed, totally regular in that slightly rounded bloom of extreme youth. Her tongue searched her top lip. 'Perhaps we won't,' she said.

Leaving the teashop they walked back to her hotel.

He felt her eyes boring through the covers of the notebook, exposing the sketches of the two British freighters.

She smiled. 'When Pan Ku-Yan finished his meeting with Pierre,' she said, 'he came straight to Emil.'

'Jesus! So Emil's upped the offer?'

'Not yet.'

'Is he looking for ships?'

She stood silent, looking down at the notebook. 'Those are your two ships,' she said. 'You saw them first.'

He stared at her unbelievingly. 'You mean you're not going to mention the ships to your father?'

'I'm not even going to mention that we met. Between the two sides of the House of Janus there must be no competition. If Pierre and Emil are too stupid to see that, it's up to us. Do you agree?'

'I guess so,' he said.

She gave him her hand. 'And don't do anything silly like getting engaged to some American girl before you next come to Germany, will you?'

'No,' he said as she turned briskly away. 'No,' he said to the retreating back of her pale yellow dress.

· Seventeen ·

Celine Coburg was always going to grow up beautiful. Her mother told her so, the servants told her so, but most of all her grandfather Pierre told her so. 'When you're a full-grown woman,' he had said, 'you'll drive men wild.'

At the age of twelve she had desperately wanted to know when that would be. Her mother had not helped much with talk of tufts of hair between her legs and under her arms. She already knew about monthly periods; it was, beyond anything, breasts she was interested in.

And then, it seemed almost suddenly, one day they had arrived. No longer just a faint plumpness on either side of her breastbone but now something definite, shaped, almost pendulous.

The phonograph was playing a new piece by the Harry James band. A new singer named Frank Sinatra was crooning 'Once upon a Time'. Even on the balcony of her bedroom looking out over Montauk Point Celine Coburg had felt the summer of 1933 was proving horribly hot and humid. She had danced about in her shift, her new breasts jumping against the light material of her nightdress.

She could see, almost on the shoreline, that the pickup truck used by Culver, the sour-faced head gardener, had turned and was making its way up to the house.

God it was hot! She lifted her nightgown up above her knees and kicked out her legs like a show girl. At twelve years of age she was already tall, with Coburg features and tawny blonde hair.

Culver, she noticed, had stopped the pickup in the main garden aisle and had got out. No more than fifty yards separated them and he looked up at her with his usual sour-faced disapproving expression. Then he smiled. She stopped dancing.

'Good morning, Miss,' Culver said, still staring unblinkingly up at her. His hand was rubbing slowly at his groin.

This she could not understand. Culver never called her Miss unless

Pierre or her mother were present. She came to the balcony rail, leaned on it, and looked down at him. 'Good morning, Culver,' she said in the most haughty accent she could remember from the movies.

She expected him to get back in the pickup, or tie his shoe or roll himself a cigarette but he did nothing. Just stood there. And still rubbed slowly at his groin. She began to feel uncomfortable. 'Why are you looking at me like that, Culver?' she said sharply.

'I was just thinking, Miss,' he said slowly, 'that you look mighty pretty, dancing away like that.' Again he smiled.

In her room behind her the phonograph clicked off. She stood up, stretched her arms above her head, and pretended to yawn. She knew that was the best way of showing off her breasts because she'd stood in front of her mirror a thousand times trying to assure herself they were not shrinking back into her chest.

There were voices somewhere along the front of the house. Culver turned abruptly back to the door of the pickup. 'If there's anything you want, Miss.' He was looking up at her again. 'Anything you want me to do for you, you just come down to my cottage and tell me. OK?'

She shrugged and turned back into her room but she could feel the flush of excitement in her cheeks. Culver was over *twenty*. Maybe even *thirty*. And he liked her. Suddenly he liked her.

After that she did it to amuse herself. She would stand at the top of the garden steps when Culver was working below. She knew that with the sun behind her he could see the shape of her body through the muslin dress. Or in Shoreline Wood she would stop before him when he was pruning and command him haughtily to help her onto a tree trunk. To give her a better view over the ocean, she said. But she would turn her back to the sea, and to him, and enjoy the awareness of him standing there, beside her, sweating.

By the end of the summer Rose Coburg had begun to organise a few parties of selected friends of Celine. The boys would arrive in ties and white trousers and would stand one hand in their pockets trying to imitate their fathers. The girls would gather at a separate end of the garden and giggle together while Culver prepared the grill for the hamburgers and one of the maids served fresh lemonade into which the boys poured moonshine they bought in Montauk. The parties usually ended in disaster, with fourteen-year-old boys reeling sickly around the garden and the girls shrieking in alarm or an imitation of alarm.

On one evening when it seemed to her that not one of the boys was sober and the girls were all exceptionally stupid, Celine watched Culver clear up the barbecue, then stand wiping his hands on a rag. He said nothing. But there was a very faint smile on his face, contempt perhaps for the behaviour of the rich kids reeling and vomiting around him.

She watched him turn away and walk slowly toward the garden aisle where he had left his truck. It was not yet dark, though the shrubbery was a thick mass of shadow as she followed Culver along the twisting path. He walked fifty, sixty yards before he stopped and turned toward her. 'You ain't enjoying your party, Miss?' he said. She saw he was rolling a cigarette.

'The boys are drunk and the girls are too young.'

He nodded, tongued the paper and stuck the cigarette into his mouth. With a brass petrol-lighter he lit the wisps of tobacco hanging from the paper and inhaled.

'Don't you think they're all appalling?' she pressed him.

'Not for me to say, Miss. Anyways, they're your guests. Not mine.'

'Do you like my dress?' she said suddenly, swirling around until it lifted above her knees.

'Sure,' he said. She saw that he was again rubbing slowly at his groin.

'Why do you do that?' She pointed.

'Because it makes me feel good, Miss.'

She nodded. 'Would it make you feel better if I did it?'

He threw the cigarette away. 'It might at that,' he said.

She had never as much as petted with a boy before and now she had done things with a grown man. She had reached out to rub his groin and been surprised at the hardness pressing against his blue jeans. His hands, the fingers wide, had engulfed her breasts. She recoiled, slapping his hands away. 'You take your hands off my dress,' she said. 'Stand there against the tree.'

She had watched the anger in his face. He hesitated, half turning.

'If you go now, Culver,' she said in her movie voice, 'don't ever come back for more.'

He swung back towards her, then leaned against the tree. Very calmly, though her heart was beating wildly, she unbuttoned his fly. Slipping her hand inside she began to caress the heat and hardness, her eyes on his face as he threw back his head and gulped great mouthfuls of air. Then she smiled, withdrew her hand and turned away. Before he was fully aware of what was happening she was several yards down the path.

He came blundering after her. 'For Christ's sake,' he said, grabbing her arm, 'you're not going to leave me like that.'

'I'm not?' She peeled his fingers from her arm and walked back down the darkened path to where the girls were dancing to the phonograph while the boys looked on, their ties askew, their eyes barely focusing.

For a few moments Celine stood hugging herself, encompassed in an utter feeling of triumph. Only when the high tide of her feelings began to recede did she leave the party in the garden and walk rapidly back to the house.

In the days that followed Culver pursued her with an expression of yearning. The cool superiority of just a few weeks before had gone. If she played tennis he contrived a gardening job near the courts. If she went riding he tried to follow her in the pickup. Within less than a month first the coloured maids and then Rose herself noticed it. 'That man Culver,' she said to Celine, 'has got to go.'

'Go?' Celine said innocently. 'Go where?'

'He's got to go,' Rose snapped. 'Leave. I'll tell Pierre to fire him tomorrow.'

'What's Culver done?' Celine asked smiling. 'I thought you always said he was the best gardener we had.'

Rose put her arm round her daughter's shoulder. 'What a little bitch you are,' she said affectionately. 'What a little bitch!'

Ambition seemed to Celine as if it had been with her all her life. As she entered her sixteenth year she would have been hard put to describe it in specific, comprehensive terms, but she knew beyond doubt that it was part of her, just as, she recognised, it was part of her mother.

She was not afraid of Pierre. Why, exactly, she did not know. Her grandfather was capable of towering rages, of striking servants or even once attacking her father last Christmas when they had all walked into the hall to find her dad kissing Jack Astor under the mistletoe. She wasn't sure how shocked she'd been herself. She had pretended to cry and her mother had started to scream or something and Pierre had barged his huge shoulders between the two men, striking his son to the ground.

'Weak as water,' her mother always said about her father. Weak as water she said about Martin too. Celine wasn't by any means so sure. Inadvertently it was Martin who had introduced Celine to Harlem. Long Island Mission was a clapboard building off Lexington founded in 1930 by a group of Long Island businessmen (among them Pierre Coburg) as a sports club and boxing hall for the children of Harlem. As the grandson of one of the founders and himself developing into a useful amateur boxer, Martin spent an evening or two a month at the Mission, teaching some of the younger boys, sparring with those of his own age.

His coach most nights there was Joe Williams, a young negro not more than two or three years older than Martin himself; a strongly built boy whose ambition, stated candidly and without boastfulness, was to become cruiser-weight champion of the world. He had already performed brilliantly in last year's Golden Gloves and his first professional fight had already been arranged for him at the old Masonic hall in Queens. He was a quiet, self-contained youngster who knew that boxing, even moderately successfully, was one of the few and quickest ways out of Harlem for a coloured boy.

They became friends. Awkwardly, and within the limitations of a rich white boy and a poor negro, they arrived at some sort of friendship. Some nights Joe would take Martin down to Henry O's where you could hear some of the best musicians in New York.

To Celine her brother's forays into Harlem were intriguing and spiced with danger. Her friends at school, Suzie van Meegren in particular, claimed negroes were naturally more virile than white men and that every girl should try it at least once. Her dreams were stimulated further by the photographs of black boxers Martin kept in his room. Joe Louis was appealing but too dome-headed; he had nothing of the svelte blackness of a middle-weight named Steve Bomber Hartley, who posed with a great swelling in his boxer shorts and an expression that was somehow both haughty and humble. Sometimes she would remove the picture and take it to her room.

During the spring in which she was to be seventeen Celine had begun to go into New York to visit her friend Suzie van Meegren. She would be driven into Manhattan by the chauffeur, Oates, and dropped on Madison Avenue at Suzie's apartment block. At around nine o'clock Oates would return, collect Celine and drive her back.

All Suzie's mother knew, since the family spent the summers out of New York City, was that *their* chauffeur also deposited his charge at the same Manhattan apartment building. The only difference was that the address was thought by Suzie's mother to be the Coburgs' town apartment. It required no more than an occasional ten dollars to the hall porter for the whole thing to operate like clockwork.

Free now for the afternoon and early evening, the two girls would make for Harlem. Henry O's was called a lunch club. Occupying the whole of a faded but elegant building on Lennox Avenue the lunch club welcomed guests, or at least some guests, from about midday until the small hours of the morning. Lunch was served, of course, all day and most of the night and accompanied by a dazzling selection of liquor. In the rear rooms you could relax with a drink on large comfortable sofas and back horses running anywhere from Belmont to Florida. It was Suzie van Meegren who had found the name of the club after overhearing Martin talking about it at a cocktail party. Since then, having used Martin's name when he was on a junior club tennis tour, the two free-spending girls were welcomed guests. Henry O, a big light-skinned negro, even kept a mostly benevolent eye on them.

Joe Williams was Saturday waiter at the club. After the first two visits to Henry O's, Celine, in her best movie voice, insisted she would be served by nobody other than Joe. By mid-afternoon Henry had called Joe into the kitchen. There were only the Chinese cook and a couple of women washing dishes there. 'You know what she's doing, don't you, Joe?'

Joe shrugged uncertainly.

'She's prick-teasing a coloured boy. It's one of the least edifying sights I know.'

Joe didn't answer.

'Stick to your boxing, son, you're a good fighter. If you're going to get your head scrambled, get it scrambled by a left hook, not by some white girl.' He flicked Joe lightly under the nose. 'And for this advice *I'm* paying *you* sixty-five cents an hour!'

The week after Henry O had delivered his advice Suzie and Celine had arrived for lunch to find their table waited on by an apologetic regular waiter. 'Joe don't come in till afternoon now, Miss,' he said in answer to Celine's questions. 'Henry O's moved him into the gaming room.'

At six o'clock that evening Celine watched Joe come out of Henry O's and look hurriedly both ways down the street. She pressed herself back into the shadow and watched as, after a few moments, he began to walk north on Lennox Avenue towards 134th Street. When he had almost reached the corner she ran quickly across the road calling to him.

He turned quickly, stopped and moved his shoulders inside his jacket like a boxer loosening up. She stopped in front of him. 'Are you going to show me where you live, Joe?' she said.

The boy shook his head. 'I can't do that.'

'Why not, Joe?'

'You know why not, Miss.'

'Call me Celine,' she said. 'So why not, Joe? You live with your family?'

'No.'

'What do you have, an apartment? Or a room?'

'It's a room,' he said. 'Just a small room. The house isn't that clean.'

'This way, is it, Joe?' She started down 134th Street. 'I don't think I've ever been in just a room before.'

He had stopped before a bakery now closed with wooden shutters. Through an open doorway beside the shop Celine could see a tobacco-brown plaster wall with a haphazard pattern of deep scratches. There seemed to be no front door.

'Please,' he said desperately, 'you can't go up here.'

'This is it, is it?' She looked past his shoulder. She felt totally confident, unworried by the stares of passers-by as she stood with Joe outside the bakery.

'Listen,' the boy said, 'if a cop comes along now, I could be in trouble.'

'Nonsense,' she said.

'Believe me, it's not nonsense.'

'If a cop comes along now, Joe, I shall tell him to mind his own business.' She walked past him and entered the hallway. The sweet smell of poverty floated around her. It was the first time she had smelt it.

He had run after her.

'Which floor?' Celine said, plunging up the oil-cloth-covered stairs. He caught her at the first landing, angry now. 'Look I don't have to show you where I live,' he said. 'In the restaurant it's "bring me this, bring me that" and I have to do it. But this is where I live, this is different.'

'Why is it different, Joe?'

A door opened before he could answer and a thin black woman in a flowered apron stopped in astonishment, then stepped back, slamming the door.

'I'm not here to be laughed at,' Joe said. 'I'm a poor man but I'm a fighter and a good one. When I get me my own apartment in Jersey somewhere, then you can come. If you want to, that is.'

Ducking quickly under his arm she was in the room before he could react.

'You'll have to be faster than that at the Masonic Hall on the twenty-third, Joe.'

He followed her through the door. 'You certainly know how to get what you want,' he said grudgingly.

She stood in the middle of the room. It was small with one long well-shaped window looking down into the bakery yard. The ceiling was high and the walls were plain green, newly painted.

'I did it when I took the room,' Joe said. 'I said to myself: does this place need a paint job! And I did it right off.'

She nodded, letting her eyes wander over the single bed with a fresh clean pillow in evidence, the two straight-backed chairs, the old brown-painted chest of drawers and the dark green oil-cloth-covered floor.

'It's a nice place, Joe,' she said at length. 'You got one of those rubber things here?'

'What rubber things?' He stared at her.

'Rubber things you put on you?'

'Oh . . .' he said.

'Yes or no? You know what I mean.'

'Yes,' he said. 'Yes.'

She began taking her clothes off. 'I've chosen you, boy,' she said with deliberate offence, 'to be the first one.'

When Martin returned from the tennis tour he rang the Mission to speak to Joe Williams.

'Joe's not here,' the gym manager said.

'When can I reach him there?'

'You can't, Mr Coburg. Joe wouldn't want that.'

That same evening Martin took his father's car and drove into Harlem. At Henry O's his reception was brief, short of welcoming.

'Henry,' Martin said as he ordered a bootleg scotch and water at the bar, 'where's Joe?'

'He doesn't work here any more.'

'What?'

'I dismissed him. OK with you, Mr Coburg?'

'You dismissed him?' Martin echoed.

'On account he couldn't do his job, I let him go.' He pushed Martin's money across the counter. 'No cause for you to be coming round any more. OK with you, Mr Coburg?'

'Where is Joe?' Martin asked desperately.

'I think he's taken off for Chicago. OK with you, Mr Coburg?'

Martin got off the bar stool and walked toward the door.

'You like Joe, right?'

Martin turned at the door. 'You know I do. He's a friend.'

'If you're a friend don't go looking for him at his rooming house. Joe's got the message.'

Martin shook his head. 'Message, what message?'

'The message was loud and clear: you stay away from the white folk.' Henry big-mouthed the words parodying his own accent.

'Who sent the message?'

'I don't know and Joe doesn't care. Goodbye, Mr Coburg.'

*

The day Martin returned from his tennis tour Joe Williams had been found badly beaten up in the hallway next to the bakery on 134th Street. It had happened, an unnamed witness reported, at about ten o'clock in the evening as Joe was getting back from the training run he put in every night. A car full of white men had pulled up outside the bakery. The witness wasn't sure but she thought there may have been another car behind the first. Four men had got out as Joe came running towards them. The first had hit him with something without speaking. The others had baseball bats and they hit him too. Joe had managed to get into the doorway before he went down and stayed down. The doctor called by Henry O reported that Joe's right arm was broken in four places between the elbow and the wrist. Most serious was the broken elbow. There was no chance he'd fight in the Masonic Hall or any other place after this.

The morning after Joe Williams was beaten in Harlem, Pierre Coburg called Celine to the library. She took her time after her maid told her, dressing in a leisurely way, rubbing rouge into her cheeks and reddening her lips. When she was ready she went down to the library.

Pierre was sitting behind his desk. When he looked up she felt a spasm of alarm. She should have got down here more quickly. His face was dark and rigid with anger. 'If that girl can't deliver a message from me more quickly than that, I'm going to have to fire her,' he said.

It seemed best to say nothing.

He got up and began to prowl the length of the library. She stood watching the broad shoulders as he moved away from her and then the mass of grey-white hair turned and his face had a ferocity she could not remember seeing before. 'Why, in the name of God?' he said, stopping five yards from her.

'Why?'

'Why, in the name of God, do you choose a coloured man for your paramour?'

Her principle was to admit nothing until it was proved against her. 'What coloured man?' she said. 'What paramour?'

He took two enormous strides and hit her.

She fell backwards against a table and dropped painfully onto a pair of library steps. Her face was stinging, her head thumping with pain and anger.

'You're seventeen years old,' Pierre roared, 'and you don't have the common sense to realise that a Coburg girl *cannot* be seen screwing a coloured man. Don't you understand that? Don't you see you can bribe, steal, even arrange murder, but you cannot be known to be screwing a coloured man in Harlem. Oh, my good God,' he shouted. 'Thank the Lord you were seen by someone close to me. Thank the Lord you weren't seen by anyone else. Don't you know that if the muckrakers had got onto what you were doing half our business connections would have faded away before our eyes?'

The pain was changing now, deepening. She had half risen onto one knee, still afraid that he would strike her again. A silence fell in the long room. He reached out a hand and pulled her to her feet. They stood close together, he with his arms round her. 'I've dealt with the situation,' he said. 'There'll be no blackmail. You just keep away from Harlem from now on,' he slid his hand down across the curve of her hip, 'or I'll have your beautiful ass.'

'What happened to Joe?' she said, although she thought she could guess.

'Taken care of,' he said, 'by a few friends of friends from the Kansas City days. Remember, you talk to no one. Not to your mother. Not to Martin. No one.'

She felt his arm tighten round her. 'A girl like you,' he said slowly, 'can have just about any man she wants.' His hand came up and brushed her breast. Deliberately she relaxed into it. 'As long as it's not a coloured man,' he added softly.

Martin left the hospital with anger boiling inside him. Running along the tattered corridors he burst through the swing doors out into the afternoon sunlight. There was too much for him to absorb: Celine and her friend at Henry O's; Celine making up to Joe; the appalling sight of Joe in splints and bandages; and most of all the recurring thought that it was all connected, that Pierre had paid for Joe Williams to be given a hard warning.

He got into his car and drove back to Long Island. Afterwards he could remember nothing but the whining of the car engine and the screech of tyres and the wind plucking at his face. But somehow, passing along the familiar coast road, seeing the house up in the distance, his earlier certainty that Pierre was involved began to decrease. He thought of his grandfather at the centre of jostling friendly crowds, joking at dinner tables, drunk and mellow after a big family evening, and he could not believe he had stooped to ordering a vicious beating for a young coloured boy in Harlem. And then he thought of China and the double dealing he had seen, had even been part of, and he had to recognise that for Pierre none of the normal limits seemed to apply. He was larger than life.

So why stoop to having a young man beaten half to death?

The certainty that Pierre was responsible abated. Could Pierre do that?

Martin turned into the drive and pulled up outside the house. Through the corner of his eye he saw his father gardening among the rose bushes. Briefly it crossed his mind to ask his help. But he dismissed the thought. On this he would have to face Pierre alone.

As he crossed the hall, his anger rose. Usually he knocked before entering Pierre's domain but this time he twisted the handle and walked straight in. Pierre, standing alone next to his desk, looked up, irritated.

His face lightened when he saw Martin. 'Come in, boy,' he said. 'You haven't really told me how the tour went. You did pretty well, I hear.'

Martin walked slowly down the length of the library. Why hadn't Pierre been angry that he hadn't knocked?

'What is it, Martin?' Pierre asked. 'Face as black as thunder.' His hand rested on the servants' bell. 'Want some tea?'

Martin shook his head. 'A friend of mine from the Project, a boxer named Joe Williams . . .'

'You talked about him,' Pierre said, nodding. 'Very promising fighter.'

'Not any longer.'

'No? Why so?'

'He was beaten up outside his apartment last night. Beaten with pick handles.'

'Sorry to hear that, Martin. It's a hard neighbourhood. Arrange with my secretary to send him something. Whatever you think's right in the circumstances.'

'That depends on what the circumstances are.'

Pierre sat on the edge of his desk looking at the young man in front of him. 'What's on your mind?' he said. 'Something about your tone I don't like much.'

'Did you know that Celine was seeing Joe Williams?'

'What does that mean?'

'I'm not here to tell tales, or even home truths about Celine. I'm just asking if you knew she had been seeing Joe Williams.'

'The little bitch,' Pierre said tonelessly. 'I'll have a word with her. That's what was bothering you?'

'I'm still looking for an answer to the question, Pierre.' Martin stood in front of his grandfather, his fists clenched in an effort of self-control.

Pierre came off the edge of the desk. 'What are you asking me?' he said, an edge of menace in his voice.

It would have been easy to capitulate. Very easy. Instead Martin took a deep breath. He knew he could not live with himself if he didn't speak up.

'I'm asking you if you paid someone to have Joe beaten,' he said.

They stood in silence.

'And if I did?'

Martin hesitated. 'If you did,' he said slowly, 'then I'm going to call in the police.'

'I didn't.' There was no attempt to persuade him. Pierre's face was flushed with anger.

'How can I know that?'

'You know it, boy, because your grandfather tells you. Understand?'

Martin shook his head. 'I'm sorry, Pierre,' he said. 'Not good enough.'

'I did *not* arrange for your boxer friend to be beaten up. Is *that* good enough?'

There was a taste of ashes in Martin's mouth. He knew he would never be certain, and because of that would never again be certain about his grandfather.

'A professional boxer getting a street-beating is common enough stuff when so much money rides on even small fights. You got the picture, Martin?'

Martin nodded stonily. 'OK . . .'

Pierre broke into a broad smile. 'OK. Now you come in here handing out accusations again,' he said jovially, 'I'll have to give you a whipping.'

Martin shook his head. 'Either way, I think you know, Pierre, the time for that has passed.'

· Eighteen ·

Until he met Jack Aston, John Doyle Coburg's life had been devastatingly unfulfilled. He did not love his wife; he feared his father; he could not talk to his children; he hated being a member of the powerful Coburg family. He had never worked in the family business since his marriage and had no expectations of a major inheritance from his father. For tax reasons Pierre had transferred a hundred thousand dollars to him at the age of twenty-one and he knew that was a sufficient bulwark against the poverty people spoke of after the Great Crash of a few years before.

He had thought many times of leaving his father's house. It was not the long-running affair with Rose that troubled him. He knew of his father's greedy sexuality and it did not concern him even when it was directed towards Rose. But he also knew that Pierre's existence as an American business tycoon was only skin deep. He felt his father to be still a man of the woods and hills of the Waldviertel. He had never forgotten a story Emil had once told him of a farmer from a small Waldviertel hamlet whose wife had died leaving him with a daughter in her early teens. Within a year or two, Emil claimed, the village generally acknowledged that the farmer and the girl were sharing the same bed. Within two years the girl was pregnant. Within days of the birth the girl was addressed as Frau rather than Fräulein and as other children were produced the original relationships dropped to the background as a folk memory. The girl became, to all intents and purposes, the farmer's wife.

John was afraid for Celine. He was ashamed for himself when he did not have the courage years ago to intervene when Pierre had whipped his son Martin with the leather cords. He was ashamed of many things. But he was afraid for Celine.

For many years now the most stable element in his life had been his relationship with Jack Aston. The relationship had undergone and survived strains, it is true. When Rose's sister Bette had come to live at the Coburg house on Long Island she had set her cap at Jack . . . And Jack had for a month seriously considered marriage. His desperate anxiety was that his home was without children. The single disadvantage, as Jack Aston saw it, was that he would have to have a wife too.

The crisis had passed. John Coburg and Jack had resumed their relationship which was only occasionally physical and was mostly a calm, companionate friendship. Whisky heightened their feelings for each other and sobriety keyed it down to what they both regarded as a respectable level.

There had been only one public error, that Christmas night when they had seized each other like teenagers kissing under the mistletoe at the very moment Pierre had been leading the family out of the dining room. It was an incident he had since paid deeply for in sneers and contemptuous glances. It had made it impossible for him to play any real role in his children's upbringing. The mere presence of Jack Aston in his life had debarred him in the eyes of Rose and Pierre and the children themselves.

Even so he had refused to end his relationship with Jack. Apart from anything else Jack Aston was the only one he could talk to about what was becoming an obsession with him. When he had first told Jack, they had been walking along the shore, shoes tied by laces round their necks, bare feet splashing through the shallows.

'I'd believe a lot of things about your father, Johnny,' Jack Aston said. 'But not that he was having some sort of sex with his own granddaughter.'

'I'm not saying that yet,' John Coburg said in an agitated voice. 'I've no evidence, Jack. But the way he looks at her, the way he touches her is bad. And she responds. The girl responds, Jack. For all I know she could be leading *him*.'

They splashed on for a few moments in silence.

'I suppose I gave up my right to protest,' John Coburg said bitterly, 'when I acquiesced in his affair with Rose. He got away with that. People knew, business people, politicians that came here, they all knew he was sleeping with Rose. Just nobody ever mentioned it – to his face.'

'Celine would be different,' Jack said. 'With Rose it wasn't against the law.'

'He believes he makes his own rules, Jack. You know him. He's devious and clever behind the hail-fellow-well-met appearance. He won't flaunt it, Jack. The way he'll behave in public anybody could put him down as a doting grandfather, nothing more.'

'And are you sure there's something more?'

'I don't know,' John Coburg said in anguish. 'I just don't know.'

When later he was trudging up alone in the woods towards the house, John Coburg's sense of self-esteem, never high, had reached the lowest point he could remember. He knew what he should do, but he wasn't sure, absolutely sure, that anything was really happening. And within the family he was isolated.

There was Rose, of course. But she would respond with utter contempt. A prurient old fool, she had called him after that incident at Christmas.

If he had one glimmer of hope it was with Martin. Especially now since Martin was so obviously the Coburg heir. It had happened slowly over the last year or two. Gradually he had seen that Pierre was changing his views of Martin, if not consulting him about the business at least confiding in him. And Martin, as curious and complex a person as he was, could respond to Pierre, at least with some of his concentration and commitment. They could talk of contracts and delivery dates over drinks in the garden. One day a week Martin would travel to New York City and attend board and sales meetings at the Madison Avenue offices. Yet he seemed to maintain a central position in the family. Most important he had never included himself in the family coldness which was extended to his father. John Coburg was infinitely grateful for this, touched, because he didn't understand how his son seemed able to maintain a core of independence among people like Pierre and Rose and Celine.

If Celine was completely unapproachable, if, rather, he had forfeited all right to take part in her life, he still saw the faintest possibility of talking to Martin. After a rare game of tennis with his son they sat one day in the arbour next to the tennis court overlooking the ocean.

'Rose tells me that Pierre is sending you to Europe this summer,' John said hesitantly.

'I'm representing the family at Elisabeth's wedding.'

'Of course,' John said. 'Europe is a strange place right at this moment for a young man like you, Martin.'

Martin waited. He had an awful feeling that his father was about to try to give him some advice about life. Or women. But from the earliest days he could remember his father had shied away from facing up to Pierre.

'You know there could be war this year.'

Martin shrugged, relieved.

'I just don't want you getting tied up in Europe, son,' John said heavily. 'The place is a mess. Everywhere. England as much as France or Germany or Italy. You're an American boy.'

What *was* his father talking about?

'I'd just as soon you didn't go,' John Coburg blurted out, then towelled his face furiously.

'Pierre says I'm to go,' Martin said with the brutal finality of youth.

'And that clinches the matter?'

Martin got up. 'Can you manage another set?'

John Coburg stood up, dropping his towel on the bench. 'I guess so,' he said and followed his son back onto the court having said not a word about Celine. He was, he acknowledged, as Rose always said, *as weak as water*. Was Martin? Would Martin be able to stand up to Pierre? Ever?

Martin placed his feet carefully just outside the baseline, bounced the ball once or twice, then came up with a smooth movement as he tossed the ball high above his head. At the economic moment the racquet struck the ball with an explosive *pock*. The ball cleared the net with an inch to spare and struck deep and perfectly placed way outside his father's reach. But his father had in any case turned away, his arms hugging his ribs, his racquet on the court at his feet.

Martin walked to the net. The ball had not hit him. 'What is it, Dad?' he called. 'You OK?'

His father walked on to a shaded corner of the tennis court and Martin rounded the net and came quickly across to where his father was standing, arms still hugging his ribs, his back towards Martin.

A yard or two away Martin stopped. He could see from his heaving shoulders that his father was weeping.

'Dad,' he said tentatively. 'You OK? You want me to go?'

His father turned and used the back of his hand to wipe tears from his eyes. 'No, don't go, Martin,' he said. 'I can't imagine I'll lose anything in your estimation by a few tears.'

'What is it, Dad?' Martin asked, desperately hoping at the same time that his father would not say. What he did say baffled Martin completely: 'I'm sending Celine away to college,' he said. 'There's nothing else for it. You're going to Yale this year, Celine can go to Sarah Lawrence.'

'Celine doesn't want to go to Sarah Lawrence, Dad. She's doing her accountancy and working in the business. That's what she wants.'

'I insist she goes to college this year, Martin.'

They stood facing each other locked in a tension Martin could not understand.

'I want your support, Martin.'

'My support?'

'Your grandfather is not a good influence on Celine.'

Martin looked at his father in astonishment. Nobody in the Coburg household had ever said anything like that before.

'I don't know why you say that, Dad,' Martin said carefully.

Did he know? Was his father really talking about the way Pierre always seemed to be touching Celine these days? All during the summer months, he would reach for her, she would laugh and duck away from him. Rose ignored it. Did it mean anything? Martin's stomach lurched. 'I tell you, Dad,' he said, 'I don't know what you're talking about. If you think Celine ought to go to college why don't you take it up with Pierre yourself?'

The boy picked up a ball and bounced it. 'You want to play, Dad? Or do you want to call it a day?'

John Coburg looked at his son for a few moments. He was trying to decide whether he was strong or weak. It had become an obsession trying to understand the terms. He knew they were easily confused. Weak people sometimes seemed to behave like the strong, but that was just in panic or perhaps an outburst of viciousness. Why don't you take it up with Pierre yourself, Martin had said. Was that strength or weakness? The strength to reject his father's pathetic appeal for an ally. Or the weakness which paralysed so many men faced by Pierre Coburg.

'What's it to be, Dad? Do we play or not?'

His father shook his head. 'I guess not,' he said. 'It's late. I'd better get over to Jack Aston's place. We have some things to talk over.'

· Nineteen ·

In the spring of 1939 Martin Coburg was pleased to be going to Germany. He was pleased to be getting away from his mother who now bored rather than frightened him. He was pleased to be getting away from his sister Celine who was rapidly becoming as assertive as his mother had been. He was pleased, too, to be getting away from the Long Island gossip about Jack Astor and his father. But most of all he was pleased to go to Germany because Alexina would be there. And because she had said those words outside the hotel in Shanghai: don't do anything silly like getting engaged to an American girl before you come to Germany.

The accepted family reason for Martin's visit was that he was going to Germany to represent Pierre at the marriage of Emil's young sister-in-law, Elisabeth. But the visit to Germany had a deeper significance. It was the visit which would finally announce that Martin, not Celine, not their father John, but Martin Coburg alone would be the heir to his grandfather's place in the Coburg Banknote Corporation.

From the time Martin and Celine were fourteen Pierre had made it clear to both of them that Martin alone would inherit Coburg Banknote. Celine had screamed in a tantrum of envy and injustice. She had done what she had never done since. She had begged and sobbed and fallen to her knees, pleading to be allowed to be a real part of the Coburg family. But the ancestral lines of Pierre Coburg were stronger than his granddaughter's grief. If there was a son, or a grandson, he must inherit. It had been that way with the sparse farmland of the Waldviertel; it was deep in Pierre's blood.

Pierre talked openly about such things. The problem, Pierre said as they sat in his study the week before his grandson was due to leave for Germany, was that Martin was still unproven.

'You're a good young fellow,' Pierre had said. 'You're loyal, discreet, hard-working and intelligent. Now if I wrote that recommendation for one of my employees most employers would think it was all there. But it isn't. It never is. The question is, Martin, one of *will*. You understand me?'

'I think so.'

He hammered his fist on the table. 'Your father,' he said, 'was once a good young fellow too. But now he is as weak as water. Are you?'

'No, sir.'

'Celine isn't.'

'I know that.'

'Your mother isn't.'

'I know that too, Pierre.'

'But are you?' Pierre had sat back watching the boy. 'You remember our troubles in China with Emil poaching our Shanghai contract?'

Martin stayed silent.

'Things aren't the way they were with Emil. You remember his idea of a Coburg research fund? I didn't go along with the idea.'

'I remember.'

For a moment Pierre remained silent, watching Martin across the library table. 'I was wrong. Emil is developing a printing press,' he said suddenly. 'A press which could print the rest of us out of business.'

'Emil wouldn't do that,' Martin said. 'He wouldn't put *us* out of business.'

Pierre looked at his grandson, irritated that he had been taken so literally. 'I'll never give him the chance,' Pierre grunted. 'In any case the full development of Emil's press could be years away.'

'Did he tell you about it himself?'

'Yes. Mockingly. He told me last month that in two years he will have a press which other companies will have to adopt. Or they will fade away.'

'You think it's true?'

Pierre nodded. 'Several people have been working on a fast multi-colour press of this type. The original work was done by a French engineer named Serge Beaune. His patents have now lapsed, but he showed the road ahead. He showed people like Emil what is possible.'

Pierre got up and walked the length of the room. To Martin he seemed more agitated than he had ever seen him. More agitated even than when he had ordered the pickets on the Kansas City plant to be beaten up at the plant gates.

'Germany's growing fast,' Pierre said. 'Not just adding territories like Austria and the Sudetenland but growing fast in influence. Influence on markets like Bulgaria, Romania, Hungary, Spain. Influence on countries much further afield, like Argentina, Ecuador, Peru. Germany's influence is spreading right into our backyard, Martin. And in our business that mostly means Emil's influence. Especially if he *has* developed the Serge Beaune press.'

Suddenly Martin knew why he was going to Germany. He was going as a spy. He was to report back on the new presses. He was to report back on Emil's new position as a leading banknote printer in the newly powerful Reich.

'Listen, Martin.' Pierre leaned across his desk. 'Isolation might be the best war policy for America, but it is definitely not the best commercial policy for the Coburg Banknote Corporation. Our markets are mostly overseas, and they are threatened by the political punch Germany can deliver. If Hitler ever delivers that punch to France and England we could be done for. Get over to Europe and find out all you can. You've got to grow up quickly, boy. Or your sister takes the prizes.' It was the first time he had put the threat into words.

The Martin Coburg who left for Europe in the spring of 1939 was a tall, well-formed young man of just eighteen. Fair-haired and good-looking in a long-headed Germanic way, he had eyes of a strong blue colour and a smile that when it came, not too infrequently, was disarming. He was unaware that his manner might have been described as charming and would have been fearful of the word if it had been applied to him. Fearful because it evoked his father and all the softness which Pierre despised.

He had never slept with a woman although he was wracked by periodic lusts. On this trip to Europe he had promised himself the experience he lacked. He lacked knowledge too. Mostly because his father was in no position to give him advice and his mother had no inclination. Pierre, in a straightforward peasant way, assumed that the barrier had been long surmounted.

But Europe beckoned. As full of hope to Martin Coburg as America had been to his grandfather.

· Twenty ·

As the train steamed into the Vienna Hochbahnhof, Martin shook hands formally with his fellow passengers, took his single travelling grip and swung himself down onto the platform. The noise struck him first, the hissing of the locomotive, the shouts of porters and railwaymen, the clash of cymbals from the brass band on a podium in a crowded concourse.

He was almost at the ticket barrier when he heard his name shouted. He had played with the hope that Alexina would be there to meet him – or at least that she would be with her father. Turning he saw Emil pushing his way through the crowd towards him. But it was a different Emil. Instead of one of his usual English tweed suits Martin saw to his surprise that his grandfather's twin brother was wearing what at first looked like the outfit of a stormtrooper. Under an open brown leather overcoat he wore high laced boots, corduroy breeches and a short brown jacket. In his hand he carried what appeared to be a flying helmet of soft brown leather.

A waiting porter took Martin's bag as Emil embraced him. 'I've given instructions for your travelling trunk to be sent on to us,' he said. 'Martin, it's good of you to come all this way.'

'I have been looking forward to it,' Martin said uncertainly.

'But a family wedding. What young man of your age wants to attend a wedding? Unless he could find his own bride there.'

They were following the porter past a line of automobiles. Martin was looking for something open-topped. A Mercedes, super-charged, like the car Adolf Hitler rode in on newsreels. But instead the porter reached the end of the line of cars and stopped. He was standing beside a BMW motor-cycle with a large bullet-shaped side-car.

'Your grandfather Pierre insisted,' Emil said mysteriously. 'There's a leather coat in there. Put it on and we'll go for a drive.'

The drive took them out of Vienna to the west toward that little known region of Austria between the Danube and the old Bohemian border. Head down against the wind, knitted scarf flying, Emil Coburg drove at seventy miles per hour taking bends at a speed which made the side-car rise in the air to descend with a thump and screech of tyres as the road straightened.

To Martin, crouched in the side-car wearing goggles but no helmet, his grandfather's brother was driving like someone possessed, laughing, shouting into the wind, accelerating past farm carts and ancient, listing trucks loaded with hay.

They met the Danube at Melk before lunch and stopped for beer and sausage at a simple *Gasthaus* on the Danube at Pochlarn. It was the first time Martin had had an opportunity to speak. Or at least to be heard. Stretching his cramped legs and pulling off his goggles he followed Emil toward the half-timbered *Gasthaus*. It was still a fine morning although dark clouds piled up above the hills to the north.

Emil was in good spirits. 'A sausage,' he said, 'some black bread and a stein of beer, that's the standard fare of this part of the world. Nothing French, nothing fancy here. Good?' Without waiting for an answer he ducked under the low doorway and entered the *Gasthaus*.

Martin could sense in Emil something not quite secretive but not yet revealed. When the plates of steaming sausage and sauerkraut were put before them, Emil plunged into questions about the family in New York. He had not seen Pierre since they had met almost a year ago at a banknote conference in Mexico City. There, he said, the Coburgs had seen off the competition, the American Banknote Company, Givierke & Devrient and the British from De la Rue in London. He plied Martin with questions about Pierre, his health, how hard he worked and about Martin's mother Rose and twin sister Celine. Never once did he mention Martin's father. It was clear to Martin that John Doyle Coburg had been consigned to the abyss.

Martin looked out across the river to the country beyond. 'I was surprised to see that you are still a motor-cycle fiend, Emil.' He addressed his grandfather's brother respectfully despite using his forename.

'Anything technical, my boy. Motor-cycles, cars but most of all printing presses. They have a beauty, you know, beyond many paintings. Some of them approach a work of art.' He stopped, a forkful of sauerkraut in mid-air. 'But you're asking me of course why I didn't collect you by car. Why this mad drive along the Danube with a geriatric road hog?'

'It's true I wondered about the car,' Martin said carefully. 'How far are we from Lingfeld?'

'It's fifty kilometres or so to the border.' He stopped. 'Ah, a common error.' He lifted the fork, this time carrying a fat slice of sausage. 'Until last year, you understand, there was a border between Austria and Germany.

Now, since the Anschluss, since Herr Hitler brought the two countries together, there is none.'

'You don't approve of the Anschluss?'

Emil leaned forward and tapped Martin's nose with the end of his now empty fork. 'You were asking me how far it was to Lingfeld?'

'Yes.' Martin took the rebuke without clearly understanding the reason for it. If his uncle didn't approve of the joining of Austria and Germany, why not say so?

'If we were going direct to Lingfeld, which is just this side of Munich, it would take an hour or two more.'

'We're not going direct?'

Emil shook his head. 'First there is somewhere you must see.'

They left the *Gasthaus* and drove north across the Danube toward the old Bohemian border. They now entered an area of wild and desolate country where peaks rose toward low cloud from a high plateau of rock. Great slopes of pine forest led the eye up to tiny isolated villages or to even smaller farmhouses, the grim enclosed stone bastions of the area.

After half an hour or so it had begun to rain, cold, slanting and wind-driven. In the side-car, the chill air swirling round his shoulders, the rain flattening his hair, Martin could see that Emil was indifferent to the cold. He drove the motor-cycle combination like a young man, swooping down roads which were now no longer metalled, hurling gravel from under the wheels as he took a bend. On the top of a hill he brought the machine to a skidding halt. Climbing off the saddle he motioned to Martin to get out of the side-car.

'Here, Martin,' he said when they stood together, 'is where you hail from.' He swept a huge hand outwards encompassing the thick wooded hillsides, the narrow ribbon of road and the stone villages under a brooding sky. 'This is the Waldviertel,' Emil said. 'The people here believe it's closer to the Mist-Life than anywhere in the world.'

Rain slashed their faces. Martin only wanted to get back into the minimal cover of the side-car, but he felt he ought to ask. 'The Mist-Life,' he said, 'what's that?'

'It's the land of evil,' Emil said. 'It's a land of perpetual rain and mist, deep, impenetrable forests and unfished streams. It's the land of the dead, the domain of the goddess Hel, its entrance is guarded by the monstrous wolf-dog, Garm.'

Emil walked back to the machine. 'You will see,' he said, 'that even now, every crossroads is provided with a wolf spear. Of course now it's just a staff of ashwood tied across a tree. Nowadays they call it a cross.'

Martin climbed back into the side-car. Emil stood for a moment, one gloved hand on the handle-bars. 'Living so close to the Mists the people of these parts *know* evil. Their Christianity is mixed with pagan tales. When we were boys, Pierre and myself, our great-grandfather was the storyteller of our village. He was born in 1775, Martin. More than a decade before the French Revolution. A year, even, before America began to struggle for its freedom.'

Emil climbed onto the saddle. 'The people of these villages have an enormous potential for good, Martin. The stories tell us so. But they also have a great potential for evil.' He looked down at Martin, his face hard. 'You laugh at me, Martin. You laugh at Pierre and myself as old men unable to throw off the shadows of the past.'

'Of course not,' Martin said hurriedly.

'That village below us,' he pointed to a miserable straggle of stone houses, 'Strones, it's called. From October to May it lies deep in the mists and mountain fogs. A man was born there in the last century, at house 13, the father of Adolf Hitler.'

For the first time Martin felt a chill, unconnected with the blasts of rain, pass down his back. Good or evil? It wasn't difficult to see where Emil stood.

They stayed that night in a farmhouse outside the village of Weitra. It was a farm occupied by Coburgs still, the males huge hulking men, the women big, broad-faced and dour. Generations of inbreeding had given them all a familiarity of feature. Martin saw, uncomfortably, how much he resembled the males of the family, how much his sister Celine shared the dark blue eyes, the broad shoulders and narrow waists of the Coburg women.

There were six members of the family at the farmhouse and other Coburgs came in to see Emil and Martin during the evening. When they sat down at the planked table for dinner they were fourteen or fifteen, all Coburgs and those married to Coburgs.

The evening passed in much drinking and a harsh sort of jollity rather than gaiety. Emil and Pierre were held in almost god-like respect and the women, Martin noticed, lowered their eyes respectfully when they passed even him.

The farmhouse itself was astonishingly primitive. In the one large, flagged room a log fire roared. Blackened cooking pots swung over it. Through the rough-hewn panelled walls cattle and horses shifted and stamped in the barn. In a stone chamber off the main room was an enormous brass bed. For the six members of the family it was the only bed he saw.

When the soup and sauerkraut were consumed the family sat round the fire talking of the late snow this spring, the loss of lambs to a pack of wolves which had crossed from the Bohemian hills, the death of this or that member of the commune. But as the schnapps was passed around and one by one the older women slipped away, the men began to recount stories of the past. Of apparitions seen at crossroads, of a company of dwarfs seen feasting in a ruined castle hall, of the disappearance of a young girl, selected for her pleasure by the demon-goddess, Hel.

Bemused by the fumes of the schnapps Martin found it impossible to guess whether or not they believed these tales. Certainly they believed accounts of betrayal and treachery in families or villages and certainly they believed in retribution demanded by God or spirits.

By midnight the talk became bawdy. Martin's neighbour on one side was a big Coburg girl with a flat ugly face. She nudged him. 'I wouldn't mind,' she said to the room at large, 'if this one was my wedding guest, my first invited.'

The assembly round the fire roared with laughter. Martin frowned. 'I didn't know you were getting married,' he said politely. This time the assembled Coburgs could hardly contain themselves, slapping their great knees and shaking with laughter. 'Tell him, Traudi, *show* him!'

Taking pity on him Emil came over to where Martin sat. Pouring them both another glass of schnapps he said, in English, 'In Waldviertel the custom is for the first invited to arrive early. He will always be a member of the family. It is his responsibility to take the bride's virginity. You've heard of the old *droit de seigneur* when the local lord or sometimes priest assumed the pleasant duty of deflowering the brides?'

Martin nodded, dry-mouthed from the bite of the raw schnapps.

'Then this is simply the *droit de famille*. Until recently it was practised by every peasant family in the Waldviertel.' He smiled. 'For all I know it still is.'

The talk around the fire swept on. Out of it Martin saw arising the shape of a strange semi-pagan world. They told stories of the end of the earth when the Valkyries, young women in silver armour, rode their steeds across the sky to take part in the last great battle, the *Götterdämmerung*, the twilight of the gods.

How much of this they believed Martin did not know. Most certainly they believed in wood spirits and their ability to create natural disasters.

'Up on the Waltersberg,' a young man, Martin's neighbour, said, 'the earth was split open, throwing hot rocks up to the sky.'

One of the girls pulled a face. 'Burning rocks,' she said dubiously.

The young Coburg farmer bridled. 'Haven't they sent the soldiers up there to warn off farmers and passers-by?'

The girl shrugged. 'Perhaps,' she said.

Emil leaned across to where Martin was sitting. 'You don't have to believe all the Coburgs say.' He spoke in English. 'It's a camp the government is building up there. One of the new prison camps.'

Emil and Martin slept in the hayloft above the barn. In another section of the loft, as Martin drifted into sleep, he heard women's voices, and the deeper voices of men demanding, and scuffling, and laughter and long grunts of pleasure.

It was almost mid-morning the next day when he and Emil arrived, crumpled, unshaven, smelling of hay and wood smoke, at the newly acquired family house at Lingfeld just inside the old German–Austrian border. The contrast with the stone farmhouses of the Waldviertel could hardly have been greater. As the motor-cycle swept up the drive and past the house, Martin saw gardeners straighten and touch their hats, maids at the long curtained windows peer out at the newcomers' arrival and Emil's wife, Dorotta, in a peach-coloured dress, come out on the terrace to wave a welcome.

With Dorotta, greetings were always effusive. As Martin came forward she ran down the terrace steps, threw her arms around his neck and placed two or three loud smacking kisses on each cheek.

'What a man he's become,' Dorotta burbled to Emil as she held Martin at arm's length.

'In Waldviertel,' Emil said proudly, 'he couldn't walk down a village street without being recognised as a Coburg.'

'That wicked man my husband took you off to Waldviertel when you should have been here in comfort after your long journey?' She punched ineffectually at Emil's huge chest.

'But he insisted, you know. "A Coburg," he said, "should see Coburg country first." He loves all these great shambling peasant oafs.'

Martin laughed. It was some years since he had seen Dorotta but he always felt the same ease in her ebullient company.

'And how are you, Dorotta?' Martin said. 'Winning the battle against the pastries and chocolates, I see.'

'The boy is a born flatterer,' she laughed, smoothing her muslin dress over the amplitude of her hips.

A movement above them behind the windows of the long terrace room caught Martin's eye. He turned as Alexina came out on the terrace, shielding her eyes against the sunlight.

'Alexina,' Emil boomed, 'come out and say hallo to Martin!'

She stood for a moment, then dropped her hand from her eyes. She was no longer the slightly angular adolescent he had met in Shanghai. She moved forward with a sensuality which was not quite conscious. Her dramatic tawny gold hair framed a face dominated by cobalt-blue eyes and a wide, almost Slavic mouth.

Her impact upon him was immediate and engulfing. He was suddenly aware of a level of perception he had never experienced before: the movement of the folds of her yellow dress, the flare of the skirt as she came down the steps, the ferfoils of golden hair on her brown arm as she stretched out a hand to him. Martin Coburg had read that some girls possessed an improbable beauty but he had never before felt himself in its presence.

· Twenty-one ·

Alexina Coburg was an adopted child. Like the Coburgs themselves she had origins in the desolate forests of the Waldviertel. Her mother, Hanna, was a Coburg girl from Weitra who had travelled to Vienna for a domestic post arranged by one of the agencies which recruited girls from some of the more remote areas of Upper Austria. In Vienna there was a perpetual shortage of what were described as reliable servants and country girls were favoured as being more readily teachable. To the master or son of the house this might often have been translated as beddable. But Hanna was not beddable. In her first week at the magnificent merchant town house in Vienna she had refused the eldest son's advances. She had even stayed awake until she knew he was safe in bed two floors below. Then, in her second week as a parlourmaid, the son of the house had left for a week hunting wild boar in Czechoslovakia and Hanna had finished her duties and retired to her room exhausted but relieved.

The turning of the door knob ten minutes later had at first terrified her. When the master of the house had stood in the doorway, a lighted candle in one hand, his nightshirt at the front draped over his erection, she had burst into nervous laughter. She was not afraid of men – no girl from the Waldviertel was – but she liked to choose her own man. At first she begged the master to return downstairs but he refused. He was not yet an old man and he still possessed that steely determination which made him a successful merchant. She succumbed twice, succeeded in blackmailing from him a respectable reference and left to take another post in Vienna. But she was already pregnant.

Her daughter, Alexina, was born in 1921. For the first three years of her life she lived with her grandmother in Weitra. When the old lady died Hanna Coburg was desperate. She could not support the child herself; her work as a domestic in Vienna made it out of the question for Alexina to come to live with her. Hanna took her problem to an old lady they called old Grandmother Coburg. Within a week the little girl had been adopted. Within a year her mother had died in a second childbirth.

Many times in the years following, Emil asked himself why he had agreed to the adoption. If he wanted an heir he might have adopted his wife's young sister Elisabeth, still a child when he and Dorotta were married. His own war service had resulted in a piece of flying shrapnel severing a vital duct and achieving its own crude form of vasectomy. Thus a son was out of the question. Perhaps he might have adopted a boy. But he didn't. In the end he accepted what was in fact the truth of the matter, that he had adopted Alexina because she was a child of the Waldviertel in need.

She had grown up in many ways as much of a Coburg as Emil himself. She was tall and well-shaped as she came into adolescence. Her eyes were of that same dark blue which so many people of Waldviertel shared and her hair was a dark tawny blonde, again a common enough colour in Upper Austria but rarer further north-west where the Coburg family had now settled.

She no longer remembered her mother, though both Emil and Dorotta were careful at first to try to keep the memory alive. But by the time she began to emerge from childhood both the Coburgs had given up the uneven struggle and come to regard her as a daughter of their own. Certainly the physical resemblance between Emil and Dorotta and Alexina was striking. Dorotta herself had come from the Paukers, a Waldviertel family as large as the Coburgs so that Alexina's own stature might equally have derived from a Coburg father or a Pauker mother. Elisabeth, less tall, less imposing, seemed strangely to have missed some of the essentially Pauker characteristics. As a young woman she was attractive rather than spectacular, formal and distanced from the world with no part of the energy that Alexina exuded, with none of that physical candour which was part of everything Alexina did.

Alexina had first visited the United States when she was five years old and again every three or four years until she was sixteen. Though easy and outgoing in her manner she was a young woman capable of making her own judgements on the circumstances she found herself in. She liked but was wary of Pierre. She felt with that subcutaneous instinct of women that there was something beyond friendliness in his touch. She felt uncomfortable with his arm draped round her shoulder, the huge hand covering, but not touching, her breast. She did not like Rose, Martin's mother. And she reacted with adolescent shock to the discovery that Pierre and Rose, from time to time, slept together. She did not like Celine. Though girls of the same age, similarly formed, sharing the interests of their age group, they did not get on together. Alexina usually felt this was mostly her own fault.

Celine had made the advances, the offers of friendship, several times, but Alexina had politely rejected them. The reason probably was because she felt that to side with Celine was to take sides against Martin and his father.

It was a standing joke among the Coburg adults that at the age of five Alexina had decided to marry Martin. It was not a joke which either of them found easy to endure in their early adolescence. To Martin it created simply an acute sense of discomfort when the idea was bandied around the dinner table. Alexina dealt with it more firmly, telling Pierre and Emil that she was capable of making up her own mind.

Was Martin? She had never been able to talk to him. At fifteen she felt things stir in her when she saw the tall young man loping across the tennis court to drive the ball down the line. Even she recognised that at fifteen he was a little overgrown, too tall, a little gangly perhaps, but she knew he interested her.

The difficulty was that he was a boy of few words, someone difficult to get close to, someone impossible to talk to about Emil or Dorotta, or Pierre or his father. About the things, in short, which concerned her most in life, that is being a Coburg, coming from the Waldviertel forests with all their history and myth.

On her last visit, in the spring of 1936, she had been fifteen. Like her aunt Elisabeth, now aged 25, her interests lay in the romance and hope and ambition for a better future that the Nazi Party had inspired in the young. She knew Emil and Dorotta did not share these hopes or ideals and she found it difficult to accept in someone she so much trusted. But she was much more baffled by the fact that Martin appeared to have no views on the future *whatsoever*. He was neither for nor against Adolf Hitler. He seemed to understand nothing of the desperate plight of Germany from which Adolf Hitler was raising the nation. He seemed to know nothing of the depradations of the Zionists and their secret plans contained in the *Protocols of the Elders of Zion* to dominate and plunder the Aryan race. At the end of that visit she had sadly concluded that he was big, beautiful and completely empty-headed.

They had had one conversation which impressed her. They were sitting on the great trunk of a fallen elm drinking the cook's own lemonade. They had just completed a game of tennis in which he had beaten her by a humiliatingly vast margin. 'You should become a tennis player,' she said, mostly to cover her own loss. 'You know, travel round the world. Go to Paris, Wimbledon, that sort of thing.'

'Oh, I'm not good enough, I know that. Pierre says I'm a long way from that standard.'

'What does Pierre know about it?' she had asked casually.

'I guess he just knows about sports.'

'You think Pierre knows everything. He doesn't.'

'What do you mean?'

'He doesn't know for example,' she said with icy fifteen-year-old female deliberateness, 'how to keep his hands to himself.'

During the summer of 1938, Alexina was called for her Hitler Youth, or rather League of German Girls, training. She had worked on a farm and met other girls from the poorer districts of the port of Hamburg and Berlin, as well as the young women from the Junker class of the eastern Prussian Marches.

With eight hours' work a day in the fields she had grown trimmer and fitter. With the sun her body had grown browner and her hair a deep gold. But most important to her were the evenings when everybody gathered in a meeting hut and sang songs and talked about Germany and its future and Adolf Hitler's gift of pride to the German people.

On these occasions the group would be mixed. Boys from the Hitler Youth camp in the mountains would come down to attend the talks and lectures. There was strict supervision but some fraternisation was allowed, under the eye of the Party supervisor.

Hans Emden was from the north, from Bremen. He was a medium-sized, dark-eyed boy who failed in every way Alexina succeeded, in living up to the physical standards of a Nordic master race. But he had a fast, irreverent wit. He sang different words to Party songs and had scurrilous jokes about Party officials. And he was of a temperament to help anybody out at any time.

Some of the young people were wary of him, but Alexina took to him instinctively. She liked to listen to his stories of life in the industrial suburb of Bremen and the grinding poverty of life there even now. To a girl brought up in the luxury of the Coburg household the stories of Hans's mother dividing the bread every day between the four children was infinitely moving. It was a window on life that neither home, nor school, nor tutors had given her.

Sometimes he went further. He would take a lecture or a piece of Party literature they were learning and invert its meaning, make fun of it or simply deny that it was true. One day they left a lecture together and he walked with Alexina to the corner of the clubhouse. The subject of the lecture had been those same *Protocols of the Elders of Zion* that she had talked to Martin about in America the year before.

'What do you think?' he said, inexpertly lighting his pipe.

'About what?' She was swinging her satchel of lecture notebooks looking up towards the great peaks of the distant Swiss mountains. She felt she had not a worry in the world.

'About the lecture,' he said deliberately.

'Excellent.'

'Just that? Excellent?'

She turned to him, surprised. She was wearing her brown uniform jacket, white shirt and tie, and her tawny hair was restrained by the regulation two pigtails. She looked infinitely innocent to him. 'What would you say the lecture was about, Alex?'

'You know what it was about, the *Protocols*, the document that proves conclusively that the Jews . . . Oh, you were there, why do you ask?'

'If I told you it was about a cheap forgery,' he said quietly, 'what then?'

'How can it be?' She looked at him. 'It's in the Führer's book, *Mein Kampf*.'

'We are to believe that these documents were recently discovered and show evidence that the Jews are determined to destroy the Nordic race.'

'Why not?'

'To begin with,' he said casually, 'they're pretty old documents, even if you believe they're genuine.'

'Of course they're genuine,' she snorted.

'They were first known of over seventy years ago. In France. That's where the forgery originated,' he said. 'A false document written by anti-Semites. The Tsar's secret police found this trash useful to stir up further anti-Jewish feeling. The Gestapo finds the so-called *Protocols* equally useful.'

'You don't believe all this, Hans?'

'I believe it. The London *Times* believes it and most eminent historians in the world believe that your precious *Protocols* are what I said they are. A cheap and vicious forgery.'

Alexina heard her supervisor's voice calling through a mist of tears and panic. How could Hans say such things? She turned back to where her supervisor stood, tapping her foot, at the entrance to the clubhouse.

'Alexina,' Frau Busch said severely. 'I want you to stay away from that young man.'

'Stay away from Hans?'

'Yes. What was he talking to you about so earnestly just then?'

'He was discussing the lecture, Frau Busch,' she said, dry lipped. 'He was saying that he thought it was . . . excellent. Excellent in every way.'

The supervisor frowned. 'Stay with your own group,' she said. 'There's something I don't like about that young man Emden. Something unclean about his thoughts, I suspect.'

One late-summer morning as her period of service was coming to an end, Alexina was sent by an organiser to gather kindling in the woods by the stream. The main group of girls had gone for an all-day ramble and her own supervisor had gone with them. She knew she had all morning if she wanted to wander by the stream or sit and read in the clubroom.

She had chosen to collect her kindling first and was making her way down the steep path, the mountains rising distantly from a pale-blue haze of heat, when she thought she heard something in the thicker part of the wood ahead. She knew that some caution was necessary. Wild boar were common enough in these woods and if a sow was leading her young down to drink in the stream it was dangerous to get in their way. She stopped and listened again. Without doubt there was something moving there. She could hear the shuffle of leaves and the crackle of twigs. She called out in order to warn the boar of her presence, if indeed it was a wild boar. 'Hey! Hey! Hola!' using the calls she had heard on her visits with Emil to the Waldviertel. 'Hola, hola! Hey, hey, hola!' the peasants there called as they rounded up their cattle.

She moved forward cautiously. She was about to call out again when she heard a voice whispering her name and Hans Emden stepped onto the path in front of her. For a moment she looked at him in alarm. She could see an ugly tension in his face, his mouth set, the brow furrowed.

'Hans,' she said. 'What is it, Hans?'

He seemed to relax a little at the sound of her voice. He stepped forward, no taller than she was, his hands coming out to rest on her shoulders. 'I shouldn't do this to you,' he said. 'I know that. But I've no one else to come to. I'm on the run.'

'On the run?' she said. 'Who from?'

He shrugged. 'Supervisors, police, local Gestapo.'

'Police? Gestapo? What have you done, for God's sake?'

He smiled. 'You still think it's necessary to *do* something to be on the run in the new Germany?'

'You're splitting hairs, Hans,' she said shortly. 'All right, what *haven't* you done? You missed out on a duty or what?'

He shook his head. Then he glanced up the path to where the outline of the girls' clubroom was visible through the trees.

'They're on an all-day ramble,' Alexina said. 'Nobody can see you from here.'

'All the same, let's go down to the stream. It's safer there.'

They walked quickly on down the path to the stream, he slightly ahead of her making it impossible for her to press her questions. At the water's edge he stopped, turned towards her and opened his arms wide as if exposing his chest. 'Last night they found out,' he said. 'They found out I'm a Jew.'

Alexina stood in front of him in shock. He smiled his crooked smile and, reaching forward with one index finger, pushed up the jaw of her gaping mouth.

'Oh, Hans,' she said. 'I'm so sorry.'

He burst out laughing. 'You're so sorry I'm a Jew, uh?'

The laughter cleared her head. 'You know what I mean,' she said. 'You know what I mean.'

He sat down on the grass by the bank of the stream and looked up at her. She was wearing a white blouse, a dirndl skirt and sandals. He thought, irrelevantly, that she was the most beautiful girl he had ever seen in his life.

'There's no one else I can ask,' Hans said. 'I need a little money and a little food. There's no one else.'

She crouched down beside him. 'What you told me, Hans, about the *Protocols of the Elders of Zion* being a forgery. That was true, was it? You didn't tell me that just because you're . . .'

'A Jew myself? No.' He looked into her extraordinary eyes. So dark a blue that he could see his own reflection there. 'No,' he said. 'I swear it.'

She nodded. 'Your sisters,' she said. 'Your mother. Can't they help?'

He laughed. 'Oh, my lovely Alexina,' he said. 'My parents were put in a camp somewhere early this year. A work camp. My mother bought the papers of a dead boy my age. It's good business now in Germany to have a dead son. I became Hans Emden. Until last night, when a new Hitler Youth section arrived from Bremen as luck would have it. One of the boys had been to school with the real Hans Emden. He was even present at the canal bridge when Hans drowned.'

For Alexina what she would do was never in question. Hans Emden, *this* Hans Emden, was a friend. She was too young for the belief in an ideological divide to have any influence on her. And she brushed aside the danger to herself. 'I'll get you money and food, Hans,' she said. 'Of course I will.'

'You know it's dangerous?' he said. 'You know *how* dangerous? German you may be, Nordic you may be, but there are hundreds of thousands of honest Germans, Nordics like you, already in concentration camps.'

'Is this true, Hans?'

'This and much more is true,' he said bitterly. 'Much, much more.'

She looked at him with a mounting sense of dread. 'But surely,' she said urgently, 'Germany has a *right* to be free.'

'Germans have a right to be free,' he said. 'If Germans are free, then Germany is free.'

The simple statement was a revelation to her. The stream trickled on through the woods. She thought of what he had said. Even then she knew it would be a burden to her. But it was a burden she would willingly bear.

'Where will you go?' she asked him.

'I'll make for Switzerland.'

She was on the edge of tears. 'But Switzerland is turning back Jews.'

He was standing looking down at her. 'We'll see,' he said simply. 'There's nowhere else to go.'

She gave him a sapphire ring, a necklace with three large diamonds, a hundred marks, and cheese and bread from the club foodstore. Then she walked with him through the woods. She reached out and held his hand. 'It's not far,' she said, 'to the border.'

He stopped. 'You must go back now.'

She nodded. 'When you get to Switzerland . . .' – tears were running down her cheeks – 'go to the Coburg Printing Company in Zurich. As soon as I get back home, I'll make sure they know who you are.'

'I'd like to kiss you,' he said.

She nodded. 'Kiss me.' She held her lips out to him and he kissed those puckered lips.

'So that's it,' he said. He smiled a smile close to tears and turned, climbing quickly through the forest towards Switzerland.

For Alexina it was an instant conversion.

· Twenty-two ·

She had watched from the terrace of the drawing room as the motor-cycle combination had drawn up and Wilhelm, the head mechanic, had come forward to take it round to the garages. Emil was looking up at the terrace where Dorotta waved. The American boy had clambered out of the side-car and was peeling the goggles from his eyes.

She had somehow not expected to find him greatly changed since she had last seen him in China. He was, if anything, taller but he was also much more obviously a Coburg. In the line of his jaw and in the high cheekbones he closely resembled Pierre. Except for a certain refining of the features, he seemed to have absorbed very little from his mother, Rose.

She came forward onto the terrace and watched Dorotta embrace Martin. She rested one hand on the balustrade and came slowly down the terrace steps. She could see his eyes were upon her, as she had intended. She had carefully chosen her frock for the occasion. In English did one say frock, or dress?

'Go and give Alexina a big kiss hallo.' Emil pushed Martin forward.

She held out her hand to him. 'Hallo, Martin.'

They shook hands formally. 'You've changed,' he said.

'I should hope so.'

'Now,' Dorotta said, coming to Martin's rescue. 'Now we shall send for Rolf and Elisabeth, the young lovers we call them, and have some tea served. No,' she corrected herself looking at Martin's crumpled clothes. 'First Alexina will show you your room. Your things are already here. You can bathe, change, then join us for tea in the terrace room. So much to show you, so much to talk about,' she said, excitedly raising her hands in the air.

Alexina showed him to the magnificent guest room overlooking a long slope of woodland and the mountains beyond. She stood in the middle of the room for a moment watching him. He moved easily for someone so big. Easily and confidently. Then, as she often did, she thought of Hans

Emden last year struggling through the mountains alone. In his pocket he had the ring and necklace she had given him and, in money, the two fifty-mark notes. She knew she did not love Hans, or even have any trace of that sort of feeling towards him, but he remained strongly in her consciousness as someone she respected, a yardstick against which to measure other boys.

For Martin Coburg that first tea taken with the family was one of the most uncomfortable experiences of his life. It had began well enough with Dorotta plying him with questions and Alexina offering cakes and comments on the edited versions of his trip via London to Vienna.

'I've never been to London,' she said. 'What sort of city is it, magnificent like Vienna or the pictures I've seen of Paris? Or fog-bound and grimy?'

Martin felt like the world traveller. 'No,' he said judiciously, 'not like Paris.'

Alexina waited.

He cast around for any sort of phrase which would fill the gap. 'More homely,' he said. 'Not as many public buildings in evidence.' He was enjoying this now. 'Of course you see a great deal of private affluence in Britain. But unemployment is high.'

'Here in Germany,' Dorotta said, 'the Führer has abolished that. And crime of course. We no longer have crime.'

Emil nodded briskly. Martin looked toward Alexina, her enthusiastic opinion about the new Germany he knew well from the last time he had seen her on Long Island. But this time she said nothing.

The door opened and Elisabeth Pauker entered with her fiancé. She was much as Martin had remembered her, much older than himself, attractive rather than flamboyant. Her husband-to-be wore a well-cut uniform with black collar tags. 'May I present my fiancé,' Elisabeth said as Martin rose from his chair, 'SS Standartenführer Doctor Rolf Oster.'

They shook hands. Oster was a tall, distinguished-looking officer with the faintest line of a scar at an angle across his cheekbone. Older than Elisabeth, perhaps in his mid-thirties or a few years more, he conducted himself in a totally relaxed manner, pouring tea for her and himself, praising the cakes set out on the silver tray. 'So, Martin, if I may call you that, have you had an opportunity yet to form an opinion of our new nation?'

'Not yet,' Martin said. It was not the last time he was to see that politics was the principal subject of conversation in Germany. 'I hope to while I'm here.'

'If there's anything I can help you with, any books I can lend you, don't hesitate to ask me. The SS library in Munich is particularly fine. It's said to contain the most comprehensive collection of the literature of racial matters in the world.'

'Thank you very much, Doctor.'

'You must call me Rolf,' he said amiably. 'We're about to become related after all. In any case,' he said, fixing Martin with a smile, 'it is generally accepted that SS Standartenführer is a title which takes precedence over doctor.'

'Will you live in this part of the country when you're married?' Martin asked as Elisabeth sat next to him.

'So much depends on Rolf's military posting,' she said. 'But in any case if there's war I am registered as a member of the Foreign Ministry. I should expect to be posted to a legation or embassy somewhere abroad.'

'War?' Martin said. 'You expect a war?'

'We do.'

'We don't,' Emil interjected flatly. 'That's to say, we don't *want* a war, Martin. That's the message to take back to the United States.'

'The message to take back, if you don't mind me saying so, Emil,' Elisabeth said, 'is that we hope we shall not be *forced* into war.'

'But that if we are . . .' Oster left the sentence hanging menacingly.

'I'm quite sure,' Dorotta said soothingly, 'there will be no war. I saw enough of the last one to last me a lifetime.'

Martin looked across at Alexina. She sat with her face composed, looking directly at him as if waiting for him to speak, to reveal himself.

'In America people are split two ways,' Martin said. 'A lot of people see Adolf Hitler as a man of his word. Others just don't trust what he seems to want for Germany.'

'And what do you think he wants for Germany?' Alexina asked.

Martin saw Elisabeth shoot an angry glance at her but the meaning of the look eluded him.

'I'm not ashamed to say I haven't made my mind up yet. I've just arrived. I don't feel qualified to come down on one side or the other.'

'There's no time for dithering,' Oster said with a broad unfriendly smile.

'I'm not dithering,' Martin said calmly. 'I'm making up my mind. Not surprisingly on as big a question as this one it's going to take some time.'

'Adolf Hitler is looking for justice for Germany,' Oster said with finality. 'For Germany and all Germans.'

'Including German Jews?' Alexina stared coldly at him. Emil stood up.

'Enough of all this political talk,' he said. 'Come with me, Martin, I want to show you Lingfeld. Like all self-made men,' he said, 'I'm inordinately proud of my property. It's different with an old family like the Osters, they've never known what it's like to be without a great mansion somewhere.' He clapped Rolf Oster on the shoulder as he passed him on the way to the door. 'Come along, Martin, let's leave Rolf and the ladies to get this wedding organised.'

That evening after dinner Martin found himself alone with Alexina for the first time. He was helping her water the plants in the conservatory which ran along one side of the house. Now in the light filtered through the leaves of plants he watched her moving along a row of cuttings giving each a cupful or two of water. She knew he was watching her.

She looked up at him. Light danced across her hair as she moved.

'I didn't get engaged to an American girl when I got back from China,' he said.

'No . . .' She smiled enigmatically and poured water on the cuttings. 'You asked me not to.'

'A silly joke,' she said moving behind a tall fern plant.

He waited until she reached the end of the line of cuttings. 'Pierre told me that Emil is working on a new machine, a new printing press.'

'Is Pierre afraid?'

'I think maybe he's concerned.'

She nodded, put the watering can on a shelf and brushed drops of water from her hands. 'I can see why he's worried,' she said. 'So much has changed even since we were in Shanghai: Germany has become so powerful.'

He frowned, not sure what that had to do with Pierre and Emil and the Janus printing press.

'If Germany is powerful, German industry is powerful,' she said. 'You know that of the two parts of the House of Janus, the American company, Pierre's company, has always been stronger, more successful.'

'I guess so. I guess there aren't as many opportunities in Europe.'

'With new machines and Germany's new position in the world there will be more opportunities in Europe than anywhere.'

'You think they could become out-and-out rivals?' Martin said. 'I can't see that myself.'

She began filling the watering can at the tap. 'You know what those Waldviertel peasant feuds can be like?'

'Emil and Pierre are not exactly peasants.'

'Sometimes I think they are, at heart,' she said watching the level of water in the can and turning off the tap. 'All my life I've heard stories of feuds over tiny strips of land. Fighting. Burying brothers or uncles at night.'

He stared at her baffled. 'Something I have to get right,' he said. 'You've no love for what we come from?'

'I hate it,' she said passionately.

'When you were in America it's all you wanted to talk about, blood and soil and that stuff.'

'It's evil,' she said stubbornly. 'It's what Hitler rants about all the time.'

'But it's the family's origins,' he said. 'Whether we like it or not.'

'We have a choice. A choice about whether or not we succumb to medieval ideas no civilised modern person would do anything but laugh at.' She hurled the half empty watering can into the corner and before Martin could stop her, ran past him into the house.

It was idyllic August weather. Throughout the month the sun shone, drawing out Alpine flowers and grasses over the high hills behind Lingfeld.

Much of the time during the first weeks after his arrival Alex and Martin spent together. They rode, swam, played tennis together. And throughout the time Alex struggled not to speak of what preoccupied her, of what, as the days passed, soon began to terrify her. She found it difficult to keep her eyes off him. She prayed that it wasn't obvious to everyone else. Most of all she prayed it wasn't obvious to him. If he was calming a horse in the stables, she watched him; while he swam or talked to Emil her eyes never left him. Once, as they played tennis, she had let the ball pass, unaware of it, mesmerised by the way he moved across the court.

That day he had noticed.

He walked slowly towards the net, towards her. 'I don't think that you're the best tennis player in the world,' he said. 'But you could easily be the best-looking one. That was a pretty wild shot of mine. I wasn't concentrating.'

She wanted to reach out and touch his hand across the net for saying that. Behind his head the hills rose to mountain height. For a moment she thought: he is going to kiss me. He has only to bend his head forward to kiss me. But the sound of laughter and Elisabeth's voice calling caused him to step back.

Alex watched Rolf Oster and Elisabeth come down the stone steps to the level of the sunken court. Dressed in a pale-blue top and a brief tennis skirt Elisabeth waved her racquet toward Martin. 'Will you give me a game?'

she said. 'Rolf's decided his wife-to-be is too good for him.' Elisabeth patted her fiancé on the backside of his tennis shorts with her racquet. 'Why don't you challenge Alex?'

'Alex?' Oster lifted his eyebrows to her.

'Love to.' Alex turned abruptly and walked toward the second court.

'You weren't playing a game?' Elisabeth's voice was husky with concern.

'No, I guess we'd abandoned it,' Martin said.

'I wouldn't want to upset Alex.'

'Let's play,' Martin said, uneasy at Elisabeth's tone.

'She's young, of course, and very headstrong. And she has this embarrassing crush on you. But you know that already, I'm sure.' She looked up at him, smiling. The smile died slowly. 'You're a very beautiful young man, Martin,' she said. 'I'm sure you're already turning the heads of all the young matrons of Long Island.'

'Hey, Elisabeth.' He jumped the net. 'Do you want to play tennis?'

'I want to play tennis,' she said, the smile again touching her lips.

It was a good game. She played fast and strongly enough to make him work at it. Losing six–four was no humiliation for her. She came over and shook his hand across the net. 'Excellent,' she said. 'Excellent game. Only your service is too strong for me.'

They walked toward the wooden hut at the far end of the court. Taking deck-chairs out onto the stone terrace in front of the hut, they watched Alex and Rolf finish their game. When the last ball crossed the net Alex thanked Oster briefly, waved towards Martin and Elisabeth outside the hut and walked quickly off the court.

As Alex disappeared along the wooden path that led to the house, Elisabeth leaned towards Martin's chair, a hand on his arm. 'My adoptive niece does not like to lose,' she said.

In her room Alexina struggled with the feeling of gnawing emptiness in her stomach. She paced back and forth between the door and the window. She hurled herself on her bed. She rolled into a sitting position and jumped to her feet taking breath until she was dizzy.

But still the dull gnawing inside her would not go away.

She knew it was jealousy. She knew that one look passing between Martin and Elisabeth could cause her hands to start shaking.

She was not sure when she had fallen in love. Perhaps when she and Martin were still children; perhaps in those few hours in Shanghai the year before last; perhaps she had simply fallen in love with the photographs

Pierre sent regularly of the American Coburgs; or perhaps it was that moment when he first arrived at Lingfeld. She had come out onto the terrace expecting to see him, yet never expecting to be dazzled by the way he looked up at her.

But no singer, no poet had described the feeling like this. No one had ever told her that it was a feeling that could take a balanced, confident, eighteen-year-old girl and tear at her like some clawed animal. Make her lie awake wracked by fear of what she was certain was about to happen. Wracked by doubt about how Martin would react when the moment came. The moment she knew would come.

At times she herself had doubts. Doubts about her own fears. This was usually when they were riding or swimming together, with the sun shining over the mountainsides.

But at night it was different. Then she felt certain that she knew what was planned. And that Elisabeth already knew. She had thought about going to Emil, telling him she knew what was going to happen, but her pride refused her.

She could do nothing. She could do nothing but wait . . . for the wilful destruction of all she had come to hope for.

During the week before the wedding Martin and Alexina never came as close to each other as they had just before Elisabeth had arrived at the tennis court. The tone between them was not cool, not really distant, but Martin could see that Alexina was deliberately maintaining some barrier between them, deliberately preventing things developing from that moment on the tennis court. In particular she refused to talk about the Waldviertel. Horseback riding through the woods on the estate, she blocked every attempt by Martin to find out what it was about the family's background in Upper Austria that upset her so much.

'I told you what I think,' she said finally. 'I think these old cults and customs, these old feuds and peasant obligations should be left to rot in the past.'

'Emil and Pierre don't believe that.'

'Too bad,' she said, kicking her horse into a canter. 'Perhaps one day they'll learn. In the meantime, what about you?'

Before he could answer she had turned the horse into a narrow path and was galloping through the woods ahead of him. It took nearly ten minutes of hard riding through narrow forest paths, under low-hanging branches and across rock-strewn streams, before he drew level with her and grabbed her horse's bridle hard enough to bring it down to a walk.

They were both breathing hard.

'Let me go!' she said fiercely.

'Not until you stop behaving like some ten-year-old kid. If you've got something to say, say it now.'

She looked furiously away from him.

'What is it, for God's sake?' he said. 'What happens to you when you talk about the family?'

'I reject the idea that that world is where I come from.' She swung off her horse and walked it through the woods.

'Listen.' He swung down beside her. 'You don't have to go along with it but it was their past, Pierre and Emil's. You can't take it away from them.'

'I'm not worried about them,' she said. 'I'm worried about you.'

'OK,' he said. 'I'll tell you. I'm an American, do you understand that?'

'Of course.'

'I don't think you begin to. I think it's *you* that's stuck in *fear* of the old ways. See me for what I am. These things are interesting to me, of course they are, but they're interesting at a distance. What's got into you? You think Emil's corrupting me? You think I'm going off to be a peasant farmer in Upper Austria?'

'Perhaps you're right,' she said. 'Perhaps I am just stuck in fear of the old ways. And I'm worried about you.'

'You're crazy,' he said angrily. 'I'm an American from Long Island. Does that give you my answer?'

She smiled. 'It's the answer I wanted. But it took a hell of a lot to provoke you into it.'

'There's still something you haven't told me.'

'True.'

'When will you tell me?'

She looked down at the path. 'When I'm no longer afraid,' she said.

Martin took her hand. 'You won't tell me more?'

She shook her head and he could see tears in her eyes.

'I also have some sort of feeling this is some sort of test.'

She shrugged, pulling her hand away.

'If it is,' he said quietly, 'if it's anything to do with the way I feel about you, I'm going to pass that test.'

She reached up a hand and rubbed at her eyes. When she looked up at him she was smiling. 'I feel better,' she said and putting a riding boot into her stirrup she swung up above him.

Most of the days of brilliant August sunshine before the wedding passed in large family picnics by mountain lakes, drives through deep forests, a lot of laughter, champagne and good food.

The only real flaw in Martin's view was Gregor Stot, a young neighbour of the Coburgs, newly commissioned in the Luftwaffe and undergoing pilot training at Augsburg Airfield.

His interest in Alex was obvious. On a good day Martin could persuade himself she only responded as a friend. On a bad day it seemed she encouraged him outrageously. Worse was the fact that Martin himself found Gregor a friendly and likeable young man. Two nights before Elisabeth's wedding it came as a shock to Martin to discover Gregor was to take Alexina to a Luftwaffe dance in Munich.

He had come to collect her in his English sports car and stood in the drawing room at Lingfeld, far too good-looking for Martin's taste, in his pale-blue Luftwaffe dress uniform. When Alexina came down the curving staircase in a low-cut ball gown everybody in the room stopped talking.

'I have a lovely daughter,' Emil said, advancing to the foot of the stairs to take her hand. 'Look after her, Gregor. And not too late, uh?'

After a strained dinner with Emil and Dorotta, Rolf and Elisabeth, Martin went up to his room with a large whisky. It was still only nine o'clock. He turned on the radio but it was mostly politics. Poland was mistreating some ethnic Germans in the Polish border areas. He changed stations. The Swedish singer Lale Anderson was singing a new German hit, 'Lili Marlene'.

For a few moments he walked about the room, sipping whisky, thinking of Alex, puzzling over the way she behaved. Sometimes she seemed interested, sometimes she seemed to be thinking about something else altogether. She was worried about Pierre and her father falling out? Well, so was he.

But most of all she was caught up in this Waldviertel thing. Why? Why not let Emil and Pierre sort out their own problems? They were brothers, twins even. Grown men. It couldn't get that serious.

He finished his whisky. It was just after ten. What time did Luftwaffe balls end? Midnight? He went downstairs and refilled his glass. No ice, no water.

His watch showed two-thirty as Gregor's car drew up and it was at least another half an hour before it rattled off down the drive.

Cool air streamed through the open window. His hand reached for the lamp switch. He hesitated. He could hear Alex coming up the stairs. The familiar creaks of the old floorboards.

Then silence. And a gentle tapping. The handle turned and the door opened.

He sat up in bed naked to the waist and switched on the light.

Alexina took a step into the room and closed the door behind her.

He began to ask if she had had a good evening but broke off at the look in her eyes.

'What is it?' he said.

She leaned back against the door. 'Gregor has asked me to become engaged to him,' she said.

Martin's mouth went instantly dry. He forced words rasping across his tongue. 'For Christ's sake, you didn't say yes?'

She half turned and reached for the door handle. 'I told him,' she said, deliberately, 'that I didn't know yet.'

'You told him you weren't sure?'

'I told him I didn't know.'

He grabbed his robe, got it round his shoulders and swung his legs out of bed. 'And when will you know, for God's sake?'

'He's invited to Elisabeth's wedding of course. The day after tomorrow.'

He stood up, wrapping the robe round him. 'You'll know the answer then? You'll have made up your mind?'

'I'll know by then.' She seemed to be correcting him. His mind was fuzzy with sleep. Did that mean she had made up her mind already?

He stood in the middle of the room. 'Listen,' he said. 'I'm just a straightforward American boy. I can't understand this double-talk.'

'If you're just a straightforward American boy, why not just be straightforward?'

'OK.' He walked towards her and put his arms round her waist. 'I love you, Alexina,' he said. 'I don't know when it happened. The first day I arrived here. Or maybe I always have.'

She lifted her head as if to kiss him, then suddenly broke away and reached for the door.

'Have I offended you, for God's sake?' he exploded.

He could see how close she was to saying something.

'Tell me that again when you've had time to think about it,' she said finally. 'After the wedding.'

She opened the door. Before he could reach her she was out into the corridor. He pulled open the door. As a clock struck the quarter somewhere in the house he watched her reach her room and, with a final glance at him, open the door and disappear inside.

The next morning, with the wedding now only one day away, Emil invited

Martin to go for a drive. 'We're not wanted here,' he said. 'I've something I want to show you.'

Emil took the wheel of the super-charged Mercedes himself and Martin sat next to him in the deep leather passenger seat.

'Let me tell you about making banknotes,' Emil said. 'Rag paper and Swiss inks we will put aside for the moment. When I talk about making a banknote I talk as a printer, I talk about *printing* banknotes. You know, Martin, a printing press which could print five colours with a hairline registration would sweep the competing banknote companies of the world into the sea.'

Martin looked at him. He knew of course that Emil was talking about the press he was working on himself. 'Has anybody developed such a machine?' he asked.

'For the most part the great banknote printing organisations of the world have not yet appreciated the possibilities of such a machine,' Emil said. 'Even giants like De la Rue in London have not yet appreciated the impact of this press. Should anyone ever succeed in building it . . .'

'Will they? Ever?' Martin said carefully.

Emil shrugged, clearly enjoying himself. 'A French printer-inventor named Serge Beaune has made some steps in the right direction. But at the moment, Martin, the field is open.'

The car swept through the wooded countryside. The signs read Augsburg.

'Are we going far?' Martin asked.

'A few miles. To Augsburg.'

'You have a factory there?'

'Not really.' Emil smiled enigmatically.

'Why are we going to Augsburg, Emil?' Martin asked at length.

'My old friend Willy Messerschmitt has a testing airfield there. This afternoon he's putting his new Me 109 through its paces. The sort of thing a young man likes to see, isn't it?'

To the young American the afternoon's low-flying test programme was riveting. Three of the new 109s made passes and rolls over the airfield then climbed steeply into the sun, banked and power-dived at what the commentator said was just over 600 kilometres per hour, 400 mph. Emil and the American boy stood among a group of civilians to the left of the main party which consisted of Goering and his wife, three Luftwaffe generals and one of the heroes of Martin's boyhood, Colonel Charles Lindbergh.

When the main party withdrew to the offices which made up three sides of a square behind the forecourt in which they were standing, Emil took Martin's arm and led him thoughtfully to the car. 'This is a time in German science and technology when enormous advances are being made. You saw the 109. Perhaps Britain's Spitfire and Hurricane are as good. Let us hope we never find out for sure. But the 109 is a fine piece of engineering.' He gestured Martin into the car and climbed into the driver's seat himself. 'I said I have something to show you. It is, in its way, as secret as the specification of the 109 we have just seen . . .' They drove across the airfield and pulled up in front of a small hangar. Leaving the car, they walked towards the small inset door.

'I've no doubt you have already guessed, Martin.' Emil knocked and they were admitted. 'My old friend Willy Messerschmitt has allowed me this hangar. It's guarded by Luftwaffe soldiers night and day.'

Martin looked into the depths of the windowless aircraft hangar. A row of half a dozen large lights hung from the ridge of the metal roof. In the middle of the concrete floor was a brightly lit wire cage twenty feet by twenty. Inside it ten men were working on a long low machine shining with steel fittings.

For some moments they stood reverently outside the cage. 'That press, Martin, will give the Coburgs the power to sweep aside every banknote printing company in the world. It is the most sophisticated printing press in existence. Tell Pierre that, in honour of the symbol of our family house, I have decided to call it *Janus*.'

They took a different route back, a road which climbed up above the Augsburg autobahn and turned and twisted through the high summer woods. They drove for over an hour towards the Austrian border until darkness fell and even the Mercedes' powerful headlights showed Martin no more than the shape of the road ahead.

They had not seen a light or any real sign of habitation for over twenty minutes when Martin realised they must be driving through some private estate. 'Where are we, Emil?' he asked, puzzled.

Emil laughed. 'You know how much I love a little mystery, my boy. Don't press me with questions.'

Martin sat back in his seat watching the tops of the trees fly by against the very faint luminosity of the summer sky. He thought of Alexina and the way she had ignored him this morning. He could not believe that it was politics. She'd found in Gregor someone else she liked better. What other answer could there be? The politics was an excuse. Anger began to overtake jealousy. When suddenly the car stopped before a long low wooden building with a string of lights along its veranda, Martin realised he was unaware even that they had turned off the road.

'I'm lost, Martin,' Emil said. 'Go and ask at the house where we are while I turn the car round.'

Martin got out and walked across the gravel towards the house. Behind him he heard Emil turning the car, the tyres crunching over the gravel.

Martin mounted the rough-board wooden steps. Behind him the engine note changed. He looked round to see the Mercedes moving swiftly away down the narrow track. For a few moments he stood, dumbfounded. The tail lights of the Mercedes twisted with the track – and disappeared. He stood uncertainly. What was Emil doing? He looked out across the woods to where he could pick up the lights of the Mercedes again. The faint glow of light fled along a bank of trees and continued on until it dissolved into complete darkness.

He walked along the veranda and tried to look into the windows but where there were lights the curtains were too thick to see anything inside. He walked back to the pine door. His footsteps on the veranda boards echoed loud on this silent summer evening.

Taking the brass lion-head knocker he hesitated a second, still baffled by the course of events, then let the lion head fall against the brass stud. The noise seemed to thunder along the veranda and out into the stands of fir trees. He waited.

After a few moments he knocked again and stood listening. Inside he could hear footsteps on bare boards approaching the door. There was a rattle of a bolt being drawn. The handle turned and the door was opened. Elisabeth Coburg stood in the doorway. 'I thought it would be you,' she said, 'the first wedding guest. To tell you the truth I'd rather hoped so.'

They sat in the main room of the chalet beside the log fire. 'Of course you have the right to say no,' Elisabeth said. 'It's not a duty, you know.'

Martin looked at her without answering. He could feel himself already responding. Elisabeth was older than him but full-figured and long-legged. What she was offering made fumes like brandy rise to his head. He was still absurdly unable to speak.

'Nobody knows, of course, who the guest is. Or even if there is one. This is the way it's done in the villages of the Waldviertel. Rolf will never know. Only the head of the family, the one who makes the choice.'

She got up and poured two large glasses of brandy. His eyes were on the shape of her body under the wine-coloured woollen dress. She turned, saw him looking at her and smiled. 'You'll be more relaxed in a moment,' she said. She handed him the glass.

'But what about you?' He drank some brandy. 'On the eve of your wedding . . .'

She acknowledged the thought crisply. 'Some modern girls find it hard perhaps,' she said. 'But I've never heard for certain of any woman from the five villages who has ever refused. They often claim afterwards that they ran away into the woods, but it's only for the benefit of their husbands.' She stood sipping her brandy. 'Yes,' she said reflectively, 'some modern girls find the custom distasteful.' She paused. 'I am not a very modern young woman. I'll not be running away into the woods.'

'You really believe this custom is important?'

Her eyes narrowed. 'All German customs are important,' she said. 'Even more so now when the Jew is trying to take them away from us.'

'The Jews are trying to destroy the old customs?'

'Of course,' Elisabeth said. 'There is an attempt to de-Germanise us until it is impossible to tell the difference between a German and a Greek. Our old customs are our shield against this attempt to de-tribalise our race.'

'Does Emil believe this?'

'He brought you here, didn't he?' She was aware that she had destroyed the warmth between them. She took his glass and refilled it. 'Don't you approve of our old customs, Martin?'

What in God's name was he doing here? Images of Alexina flashed across his mind. Alexina riding, Alexina standing in the ball gown in his bedroom. He let the brandy burn the roof of his mouth.

'Even in a practical sense it is often better that a woman is not introduced to physical relations by her husband,' Elisabeth was saying.

He found her words deeply disturbing.

'I'm not a very experienced woman,' she said.

He watched the movement of her body under the woollen dress.

'Of course,' she said, 'humiliating as it would be for me, you have every right to decline.'

He stood up. One single step toward the door would have been enough.

'I think you have to understand that this is not an infidelity on my part. Or on yours,' she added, watching him. 'This is part of a ritual. Don't confuse the two.'

One step toward the door.

She put a record on the phonograph, a slow Berlin night club piece. 'I've seen you watching me, I think, as I crossed the room.'

'Perhaps.'

'Even Rolf noticed that.'

'I'm sorry.'

'You don't have to apologise. Drink your brandy and come and dance with me. Like this we shall relax a little together.'

He was mad with lust as perhaps only a very young man can be. In bed he hurled himself at her, wrestling her down onto her back, forcing her legs apart with his knee. She laughed and sometimes squealed with pleasure as he plunged into her, hammering at her like a man-bullock.

Underneath him she rolled and swore and pulled his head down onto her breasts and bucked and shouted jeering obscenities until he drove deeper into her, sweat thrown from their bodies by the sheer vigour of their union.

Morning came to Martin as bright sunlight from the drawn curtains. Elisabeth stood beside the bed in a severe grey dress and heavy flat shoes. To Martin she looked so old. She gave him a cup of coffee but she did not sit on the bed.

'You'd better get up,' she said in a completely neutral tone. 'Emil will be here in a few moments. Neither of us will talk about this, ever.'

He struggled onto one elbow, his head swinging slowly from the effects of too little sleep and too much brandy.

'As far as the rest of the family is concerned,' she said, 'you and Emil took the wrong road back. You were forced to spend the night in a hotel. Emil has already telephoned Dorotta, of course.'

Martin stretched out a hand to touch her thigh but she backed away as his fingertips brushed the woollen dress.

'You do understand that from midday today I shall be a married woman?'

He fell back onto the bed. 'Of course.'

'It is not the custom to make reference to last night ever again. Even if we are alone.'

She walked across the room to the door. 'Now please get dressed, Martin,' she said in a hectoring tone. 'Emil will be here any moment.'

At that moment it hit him like a thunderclap.

Alexina knew. She had known from the beginning that he had been brought from America to be the first invited.

And now by his absence she knew that he had accepted.

· Twenty-three ·

When Emil and Martin got back Lingfeld had been transformed. Yellow and white striped awnings now shaded the long terrace. Lines of trestle tables with white cloths held silver dishes and nearly two hundred place settings. Maids and footmen hurried back and forth. Small crises developed: the smoked salmon flown in from Scotland had barely arrived in time; an eddy of wind was plucking at the long red swastika flag on the east corner of the house; the SS general who was to marry the couple according to the rites of the SS Black Order had not yet arrived.

Alexina, running at full pelt across the front lawn with an instruction for some part of the massive operation, stopped when she saw Martin.

'Hi,' he said. It was the first time he had talked to her since she had come into his bedroom.

They stood in the middle of the lawn, the activity of the house servants and caterers swirling around them. 'Where did you get to last night?' she asked casually.

'Last night?' His stomach twisted.

She knew.

'Emil got lost,' he said. 'We had to find a hotel.'

'I see.' She didn't move, kept her dark-blue-eyed stare upon him. 'Waldviertel,' she said. 'It won in the end.'

'I don't know what you mean.'

He did – clearly. He gasped as the meaning flooded him. She meant he had been suckered by the peasant fantasies – just like Emil and Pierre, and even Elisabeth too. It's what she had been telling him in the conservatory, in the forest, up in his bedroom. She *knew* why Pierre had sent him to Germany. To play the part. To be the first invited at Elisabeth's wedding. To reinforce for two old men the meaning of the House of Janus.

But it had lost him Alex.

'Alex,' he said, his heart pumping, 'I'm sorry. You understand what I mean?' he said desperately. 'I hate myself for it. For what I've done to you.'

She stood watching him, without speaking.

'Try to understand.'

He thought her face had been turned to stone. 'I understand,' she said. 'I'm sure you do, too. There's nothing to apologise for. You behaved as a young Coburg should.'

She turned and hurried towards the house. There was nothing for Martin to do. He watched while the SS guard of honour rehearsed the arch of rifles the bridal couple would emerge from. They seemed to be so utterly perfect that by the third rehearsal Martin moved on. Old Wilhelm, the mechanic, had been watching too. 'I wonder,' he said. 'I wonder, how those parade dummies would have done in Flanders mud?'

Martin went up to his room, showered and sat naked on the edge of the bed smoking a cigarette. He could make no sense of the emotions which flowed over him, confused and contradictory. One idea kept returning: she had known all along that he was to be the first invited. She had used it to put him to the test. If it were sex alone he wanted she had even offered to sleep with him.

And he had behaved as a jealous kid. Weak as water.

He got up from the bed and dressed in his morning suit and tail-coat and striped trousers, dove-grey vest and silk cravat. He looked in the mirror thinking about how he would congratulate Rolf Oster after the wedding. And what he would say to Elisabeth.

He was downstairs half an hour before time. The immense long-windowed room with its pale grey, swagged curtains was the ballroom of Haus Lingfeld. Stucco work graced the interior walls and four great chandeliers were suspended from the ornate ceiling. Guests swirled around, greeting each other; SS adjutants hurried back and forth, conspicuous in their formal black dress uniform. Looking around him, past the girls in their pale-coloured dresses and crimped blonde hair, Martin was surprised to see how many of the young men were in the uniforms of the army, navy or Luftwaffe.

Twenty minutes before the ceremony was due to begin the senior SS aide, an immensely tall young man named Gunsche, rapped his millboard for silence. 'Ladies and gentlemen,' he said, 'may I ask you to take up your positions. Herr Coburg has an announcement to make.'

The guests shuffled and bumped against each other to get to the position they had each been assigned, up on opposite sides of a long corridor between the door and a small table covered with a black and silver SS flag.

Martin was positioned quite close to the door. Gregor Stot, in Luftwaffe cadet officer's uniform, was beside him.

'Alexina tells me you've asked her to marry you,' Martin said.

'I thought I'd get in before you did. Was I right?'

'She said yes?'

'Not yet,' Gregor said. 'She wanted to wait until after the wedding.'

Martin stood there looking towards the exhalation of light around the long window in front of him. He was short of sleep and desperately in need of another glass of champagne. His thoughts drifted to last night. Perhaps he closed his eyes for a moment because he leaned against Gregor who pushed him upright. 'Don't go to sleep on me yet,' he said with his easy grin. Martin opened his eyes. Across the room Alexina was watching him.

'Ladies and gentlemen,' Emil said, 'dear friends and members of the family, I have an announcement to make to you. You will understand that for reasons of security, we were unable to tell you before.' He paused. 'The Führer has kindly consented to give Elisabeth away today.'

A shiver ran through the guests and a flutter of low excited conversation. In their enthusiasm no one had noted the flatness of Emil's statement.

The guests now stood like soldiers, silent and upright. Anyone who dared to speak received harsh, penetrating looks. At five minutes to midday the great oak doors opened and Rolf Oster and his escort walked stiffly down between the guests, his black uniform impeccable, his sword held tightly to his side. From somewhere among the guests near the table, the SS conducting general stood with one outstretched hand lightly grasping the flag.

The minutes ticked past. Now no one spoke. Then a small organ which had been positioned in the hall beyond the oak doors began to play softly. It was a piece that Martin did not know, sombre, heavy.

The doors opened. Adolf Hitler stood there in a simple brown jacket and black trousers with a silk stripe. On his arm, taller than he was, Elisabeth Coburg looked splendid in her ivory wedding dress. The music swelled. Adolf Hitler stepped forward with Elisabeth.

It was only then that Martin saw Alexina a few steps behind the bride. Her face was composed, set even. It seemed to Martin that she looked like a Greek goddess with a rope of pearls banding her forehead and her long cream dress cut deep between her breasts. Carrying Elisabeth's train she walked with long slow steps behind her aunt and the Führer of the Third Reich.

From his position near the door Martin was unable to see the progression of the SS wedding ceremony. Stretching his neck he was just able to see bread broken on the black flag and salt sprinkled on the hands of the bridal pair. The SS provided wedding rings and as they were placed on the third finger of the left hand of the bride and groom the presiding SS officer intoned an oath of mutual fidelity and respect.

Throughout the ceremony Adolf Hitler stood slightly to one side, staring fixedly at the proceedings. Next to him stood Alexina, and to Martin, with the knowledge of last night now a source of overwhelming guilt, she seemed more classically beautiful than he had ever realised.

At the end of the ceremony Adolf Hitler shook hands with the bride and groom. Then the room fell silent as the Führer took up a position at the far end of the room between the two lines of guests. For a moment it seemed possible that he would speak, then, seemingly deciding against it, his face grim, his hands clasped almost awkwardly in front of him, he began to pace slowly between the lines of guests towards the door at Martin's end of the room. From time to time he stopped in front of one of the guests and shook hands and his sombre expression would suddenly change so that the smile that illuminated his face seemed all the more friendly, more human, in contrast. As he approached, stopping to nod gravely to one guest, courteously shaking hands with another, Martin felt some sense of the unpredictable nature of his personality. When the set look and the unseeing blue eyes were suddenly replaced by an almost playful smile the whole room seemed to sigh with relief, to relax for a moment, before the Führer, turning abruptly, continued on towards the door, his thoughts seemingly far from Haus Lingfeld and the marriage ceremony that had just taken place.

At the door he stopped again and the smile and handshake for Oster and Elisabeth were brief and courteous. Then he was gone.

For a moment the whole room of some three hundred persons stood with bated breath, then, as if with one exhalation of tension released, everybody began to talk at once.

Suddenly Martin heard Alexina's voice. 'What an odious little man,' she said in a voice loud enough for three or four people around them to hear.

'For God's sake, Alex,' Gregor hissed in her ear. 'Are you mad?'

'I think we're all mad,' Alexina said. 'Have you heard the news?'

'No, what news?'

'One of the beast's aides whispered it to me as he passed. This morning the German army, *our* army, invaded Poland. You don't need to be a world statesman to know that this day is the beginning of another world war.' Alexina's eyes flashed fury toward Martin then she burst into tears and ran from the room.

*

Within an hour the chauffeur was loading Martin's cases into the car. Martin himself, pressed by Emil to hurry, had been able to say no more than a word or two of goodbye to Alexina while Dorotta had been present. When the chauffeur was ready Emil took Martin into a small office off the salon. His agitation was evident as he poured himself and Martin a glass of whisky.

'I have instructed the chauffeur to drive straight to Switzerland,' he said.

'Is that necessary, Emil? I could take a train from Munich.'

'Listen to me, Martin,' Emil said gently. 'You're a young man, you're learning all the time, but you haven't learnt enough yet. Within hours or days at the most Germany will be at war with France and England over the Polish issue. If President Roosevelt can bring in the United States, he will.'

Martin stepped back in shock, as if he had been struck with a blow. In all this talk of war in the last weeks he had never imagined the US having any part in it. It was a European affair, politics was a shady European business, it had nothing to do with America.

Emil was nodding slowly. 'Yes,' he said, 'it may take the President months or even years, but he is determined to enter this war on the side of the democracies. He will not stand on the sidelines for one second longer than he has to.'

'Do you know this, Emil? Do you know this is true?'

He nodded gravely. 'I am far from alone in thinking so. Listen to me, Martin. Chance has insisted that you play a part in these events.'

'Me? I play a part?'

'When I showed you the Janus machine, you saw it printing banknotes, but you didn't see of course what kind it was printing.'

'No, the whole conveyer was covered.'

Emil opened a drawer in his desk. 'The Janus press has received its first order, Martin.' He slid a green banknote across the desk.

It was a brand new twenty-dollar bill!

Martin stretched out a hand and touched it.

'Pick it up, Martin. You know banknotes. Feel it, smell it, run your thumbnail across it, look at it against the light.'

Martin's mind reeled. 'You've got an order to print twenty-dollar bills?'

Emil nodded grimly.

'But the American continent is agreed to be Pierre's area. In any case the Bureau of Engraving and Printing prints dollar bills for the US government.'

'The order for one million twenty-dollar bills did not come from the Federal Reserve Bank.'

'Where did it come from?'

'It came,' Emil said sombrely, 'from our own Reich government, in Berlin.'

From the wood beside the drive, Alexina watched the car carrying Martin sweep through the gates hurling dust and gravel from its wheels. He had played the part Pierre and her father had assigned to him. He had proved himself, in all ways, a Coburg.

And, his duty done, he had been sent home.

She was no longer sure what she felt. Everything that she feared most had happened. Last night confirmed that Martin had been sent to Germany as the first invited at Elisabeth's wedding. Worse, he had accepted the role. She stood among the scents of summer in the depths of the narrow wood. She knew she was indulging her misery but there was nothing she could do to stop herself. At the core of her sadness was the knowledge that Martin Coburg was the man she still wanted, that there were still some strands of the Coburg inheritance in her too.

She walked back to the house by the path through the woods. The noise of the guests on the terrace rose like the chatter of starlings. She had told Martin that she understood, but that was bravado. She knew the truth was that she understood nothing. She was certain he loved her. So how could he have done what he did?

Her wide-brimmed straw hat in her hand, her head held higher than was natural to her, she emerged from the wood and followed the path round the lake toward the house. She could see the guests now, packed brightly coloured on the long terrace. The women's dresses, the men's summer uniforms sparkled in the sunlight. She had not picked out Emil before she saw a figure in a cutaway coat, coming down the stone steps towards the drive.

He had seen her and she stopped by the side of the lake as he waved solemnly and walked across the cropped grass towards her.

At first last night, when Emil had phoned to say he and Martin would not be back, she had been overwhelmed with fury, with a black sense of betrayal. She could not contain it. She had screamed at her mother and run through the house sobbing. Maids who only knew her as warm and even-tempered recoiled as she ran past them. Only a few of the oldest servants, recruited in Waldviertel itself, guessed the significance of the master's telephone call that evening.

But now she felt numb.

She watched the huge figure, white-haired, broad-shouldered and now thick around the waist, cross the grass and stop in front of her. For a moment they stood like combatants in the ritual pause before the attack.

'I will never be able to tell you how sorry I am,' Emil said slowly. 'You might ask why I didn't realise what I was doing to the daughter I love, but I didn't. If I had told your mother in advance she would have known what my stupidity meant to you.'

Alexina looked down at the toe of her cream silk shoe, scuffed as she had run through the wood. 'I know why you did it, Papa,' she said, her lips barely moving. 'But why did he?'

Emil shrugged heavily. 'The instincts of men, especially young men, are not like those of women,' he said. 'There are sudden storms of lust, rapaciousness, which obliterate everything else.'

'Even love?'

'Even love,' he said. 'Men act with nobility, men are capable of self-sacrifice or altruism, but it is not in their *nature*. It has to be learned, my darling Alexina. In their nature lies their instinct, lustful, greedy, insolent of others' feelings. At this very moment, Martin is regretting last night more than anything he has ever done. But he'll learn, Alex. I promise you if you give him a chance, he'll learn.'

'And you, Papa, will *you* learn?'

He smiled. 'You're too bold, my darling. It will lead you into trouble. Two or three people have already had a word with me about your comments about the Führer this afternoon.'

'A lot of people feel as I do. In Munich at the university, we already have an organisation.'

'Alex,' he said, 'go to America. Marry Martin.'

She shook her head.

'Forgive him. He will not betray you again.'

· Twenty-four ·

By the time Martin arrived back in the US the first part of Emil's predictions had materialised: Germany was at war with Britain and France. The beginnings of another world conflict were there for all to see.

Yet on the surface there were few signs of the impending catastrophe. Travelling from Switzerland to Paris Martin saw French troops assembling at every station he passed but the atmosphere was festive, something approaching a holiday spirit prevailed. No one among the young conscripts marching up to the German border believed the war would last for more than three months. It was, in fact, all grimly reminiscent of August 1914.

From Paris Martin took a train from the Gare d'Austerlitz south through Limoges and on to Bordeaux. From there a Norwegian freighter took him to Lisbon and from Lisbon he caught the Pan American flight to New York. The whole journey took less than four days.

It was after midnight when the limousine pulled to a halt outside Island House. On the bedroom floors the lights were out. Only in the library where Pierre liked to sit over brandy and a cigar did the lights still burn behind the heavy silk curtains.

Inside the library Celine and Pierre heard the automobile pull up on the gravel forecourt. She was sitting, as she often did now, on the arm of his chair. She wore a robe and bell-bottomed satin pyjamas of the latest fashion; one foot resting lightly on the seat of the chair so that her leg was lifted to about the height of Pierre's shoulder. Absent-mindedly, it seemed, his hand stroked the inside of her knee.

Both of them knew the movement to be far from absent-minded. It was, rather, part of a complex process, infinitely slow, that had been building up each time Rose stayed the night with friends in New York. He had never yet touched her bare flesh but there were landmarks she remembered vividly. He had once stroked the inside of her thigh almost to the groin; once he had fondled her breast through no more than the satin pyjama jacket. And once, while they talked New York stock exchange and banknote contracts and new technical developments, she had allowed her hand to fall and rest, very lightly, in his crotch.

'Do you want to see Martin before he goes to bed?' Celine asked Pierre as they listened to doors opening and closing and the muffled sound of voices in the hall.

'I'm enjoying just sitting here with a glass of brandy,' Pierre said, smiling up at her. 'Anyway I guess Martin'll be tired after his long flight. I told Frank to say I'd see him in the morning.'

Her hand was now round the back of his collar, a finger curling the hair on the nape of his neck. Not for the first time in her life, she was astonished by men. However banal or 'Hollywood' the caress, they reacted immediately. 'No,' Pierre said firmly, 'I don't think we need Martin barging in here tonight.'

The knocking on the library door caused his expression to set with annoyance. He could hear Martin's voice calling.

'Shall I tell him?' Celine asked, half rising.

'You stay where you are,' Pierre said. 'Frank'll tell him.'

The knocking continued. The brass handle turned. The locked door was rattled.

Pierre stood up furiously. 'Goddamn, Martin,' he was shouting long before he reached the door. 'You heard what Frank said!'

Celine watched him with pleasure. She had been worried by this home-coming. Emil had cabled Pierre several times to say how well Martin was shaping up during the summer in Europe. She had watched Pierre nod his own confirmation to her twin brother's estimate and she did not like the implication for her own future, because she had decided that there was a chance, however slender, that she would inherit Coburg Banknote when Pierre died. Or at least part of it.

The knocking ceased. Pierre unlocked the door and threw it open. 'Did Frank tell you or not?' he demanded.

The butler was standing nervously behind Martin. 'I gave Mr Martin your message, sir.'

'Of course you did,' Pierre snarled. 'God damn it, of course you did.' He looked at Martin. 'So why did you choose to come knocking down the door when I'm having a quiet little talk with your sister Celine?'

Martin looked past his grandfather down the length of the library to where Celine was standing in her robe and satin pyjamas. She was lighting a cigarette, her eyes on him over the lighter's flame. For one second the memory of his father's concern crossed his mind and he thrust it aside immediately.

'Well . . . ?' Pierre was demanding.

'I have a message from Emil.'

'Can't it wait until the morning?'

'Emil says it couldn't be more important. He asked me to deliver it to you the moment I got back to Long Island.'

'Well, deliver it, then.' Pierre still blocked his way into the library.

'I have to speak to you alone. I gave Emil my word.'

With intense exasperation Pierre stepped back and gestured to Martin to enter. He turned and walked towards his chair. 'Shut the door behind you,' he growled over his shoulder.

Martin came into the room. 'Hello, Celine.' He nodded in her direction.

'Hi,' she said casually. 'How was Europe?'

'Europe was OK.'

'And the lovely Alexina?'

'Knock it off!' Pierre said crudely to Celine. 'He's got a message for me. He insisted on bursting in here because he has a message for me.'

'I heard,' Celine said. 'What's the message, Martin?'

'It's for Pierre. Alone.'

She looked at her brother and drew sharply on her cigarette. Then she swung round towards Pierre. 'Do I have to put up with that?' she asked icily. 'Am I a member of this family? Or not?'

Pierre lifted a hand to placate her. He still hoped that once Martin's message was delivered he would be able to persuade her to resume her place on the arm of his chair. 'I don't think it's very polite to your sister,' he said, 'to exclude her from a Coburg business matter. I take it that that's what it is.'

Martin reached inside his jacket and took out a pocket book. Celine watched him remove a twenty-dollar bill and place it on the corner of the long library table. Pierre looked down. As ever, he could not resist examining a newly printed banknote. This one was without even a single centre fold. Celine crossed to stand next to her grandfather. Below the peach shade of one of the library reading lamps she looked down at the Abraham Lincoln twenty-dollar bill and shrugged. It was a new twenty-dollar bill. So what?

Pierre raised his head slowly. He was, Celine noticed, breathing heavily. 'The serial number,' he said.

Martin nodded. 'Emil said you would see it, immediately.'

'Go to your room, Celine.' Pierre dismissed her with a wave of his hand. He had not even looked at her.

She straightened, unable to understand. She made the error of an attempt to protest. 'If it's Coburg business . . .'

'Go to bed, I said,' Pierre roared at her.

She stepped back in alarm, then threw her cigarette into the fire and ran angrily from the room.

As the door slammed after her, Pierre's eyes rose from the banknote. 'The serial number is my – and Emil's too of course – birthday, repeated three times. The Coburg Imprimerie in Germany printed this twenty-dollar bill? Is that the message?'

'Yes.'

'But printed the bill on a new intaglio machine. Is that the message from my goddamn brother?'

'The engineers in Germany, mostly Emil himself, have developed a new machine. Emil is naming it *Janus* in honour of the Coburg symbol.'

Pierre's expression suddenly lightened. 'Are we in New York to have full access to the machine then?'

'Emil says those are matters for discussion between you and him.'

Pierre's face flushed darkly. 'Discussion, is it? A diktat more like, with Emil calling all the shots.'

'Pierre,' Martin said, 'I don't believe Emil intends to call all the shots.'

His grandfather strode across the room and poured himself more brandy. As an afterthought he held up the decanter to Martin.

Martin shook his head. 'I'll get some coffee.' He moved towards the bell beside the telephone.

'Forget the goddamn coffee,' Pierre said. 'Either drink brandy or nothing.'

'Nothing,' Martin said. 'I guess I'll have nothing.'

'So Emil does not intend to call the shots, you say? Yet how does he send me a message?' he raged. 'He sends it on a twenty-dollar bill printed by his Janus, his new wonder machine. I get the message, you hear me? I get the message loud and clear.'

Martin stood stock-still. He had seen his grandfather in a rage before now but he had never seen him quite like this. He felt he wanted to do something, to help him over his anger so that he could hear the rest of Emil's message. 'Pierre,' he said. 'You haven't heard everything yet.'

Pierre stopped his restless pacing. 'There's something else?'

Strange emotions flooded through Martin. The eagerness in Pierre's voice made him feel a twinge of pity for his grandfather, for a man who had been so dominant a figure in his own life. Who still was. Yet the edge of pity was there for Martin to feel.

'What did Emil say to you? What else?' Pierre went to the fireplace and rang the bell. Lifting the ancient brass speaking-tube he blew into it and held it to his ear. A girl's voice said: 'Yes, Mr Coburg.'

'You got some coffee on down there?'

'Yes, Mr Coburg.'

'Bring a pot to the library for Mr Martin.'

He put down the speaking-tube. Martin found himself feeling a curious sense of elation, as if he'd won some struggle. And yet at the same time he wanted, passionately, that this man should not be defeated.

'Sit down, boy,' Pierre said. 'Let's hear from Emil in full.'

Martin crossed and sat on the arm of one of the big library chairs. 'Emil didn't just print one twenty-dollar bill just to demonstrate the Janus.'

'Go on.'

'Emil didn't intend to give me the twenty-dollar bill. His plan was to show it to you himself, but the outbreak of war in Europe changed that. Emil believes that it is essential that you take this bill to the President.'

'To Roosevelt?'

'Yes.'

'Why, in God's name?' He stopped. 'Because it's not the only one!'

Martin nodded. 'There are one million others,' he said.

'Jesus.' Pierre got up and went to the door in response to a hesitant knock. Opening the door he took the coffee tray and kicked closed the mahogany door. 'Twenty million dollars! What, in God's name, is happening to my brother?'

'The order for the counterfeits came from Berlin,' Martin said as he watched Pierre pour coffee for him. Again that mixture of elation and pity struck him as he reached forward and took the proffered cup.

'These false bills, where are they now?'

'On the high seas. Heading for the US.'

'Heading for who in the US?'

Martin leaned forward to give proper emphasis to the story, to savour the first moment in his life when he had Pierre's absolute and undivided attention. 'Emil believes that Franklyn D. Roosevelt will want to bring the United States into this war.'

Pierre nodded. 'He's left no one in doubt about what he thinks of Adolf Hitler. Sure, he'll want to bring in the US. But first he has to win next year's election. The way I see it, Martin, this will be America's most important election ever. Politically I've always been a Democrat. I just hope FDR knows what he's doing.'

'Emil also believes that this is America's most important election. He says *whoever* wins will alter the history of the world. Berlin knows this. Berlin wants a president who will not take America into the war. Any president but Roosevelt.'

'And the twenty million dollars?'

'Are to lose President Roosevelt the 1940 election.'

Pierre whistled through his teeth. 'And Emil, what does he want?'

'He wants Roosevelt to win.'

In the late evening of 15 March 1940 Pierre Coburg and his grandson, Martin, climbed into the back of a black limousine and were driven along the north shore of Long Island towards Queens Bridge. There was between them a shared sense of excitement, and for Martin it was that much sweeter since his mother Rose and Celine had been excluded from all knowledge of what was happening.

Both had protested violently. Rose, by now a mature woman with heavy shoulders and a thickening waistline, had been shaking with rage. Celine, more diplomatic, craftier, Martin would have said, had adopted a hurt, silent manner, but neither woman had succeeded in swaying Pierre.

'I refuse to accept,' Rose had said haughtily, 'that my son should have secrets from me.' She was angry too because she knew she was slipping back in the Coburg race for power. It was over a year since Pierre had shared her bed. She knew he had innumerable other women in New York City but lately an intrusive, frightening suspicion had been forming in her mind when she watched her daughter and Pierre together.

But this night the opposition was clearly and simply her son Martin. Since his return from Germany she had seen him move into a different relationship with Pierre. Celine claimed it was because Emil's Janus machine was about to change the balance between the two Coburg companies and Martin formed some sort of bridge. Bridge or not Rose could have screamed with fury when Pierre and Martin left for their unknown rendezvous.

She turned to her daughter. 'Sit down, Celine,' she said. 'It's time we had a talk.'

'What do you want to talk about?'

'Let's start with Martin,' Rose said. 'He's getting too uppity, too big for his boots.'

'What do you expect me to do about that?'

'I expect *us* to do something about it. Not just you, not just me.'

Celine shrugged. 'He's grown up at last, I guess. Don't they say boys grow up more slowly than girls?'

'You know it's more than that.'

Celine had seldom felt more in command of a situation when talking to her mother. She knew she wanted something, but as yet she still didn't know how far her mother was prepared to go. 'Let's have a drink,' she said to her mother.

Neither of them drank very much and Rose accepted the gesture as it was intended. 'Yes,' she said. 'Why shouldn't we have a drink together?'

Celine poured the drinks.

'You know,' Rose said, 'when I was a little girl, my mother's uncle died . . .'

'The one that owned the prosperous law firm that she *didn't* inherit?'

Rose's head came up. How much she disliked the sharpness under Celine's smile. 'I guess I already told you about it.'

'You did, Mother.'

'Did I ever tell you why my mother didn't inherit?'

Celine turned away.

'Listen. She didn't inherit because she was a woman. It all went to some distant cousin, a *male*. You know what I'm talking about now?'

'You're talking about me and Martin.'

'I'm talking about getting what's fairly yours. A half share in Coburg Banknote. A half share *at least*. I'm talking about your interest and mine.'

Celine recognised the proposal of alliance to be as far-reaching as Rose intended. She was by no means sure that an alliance was possible between them but she nodded and said: 'Go on. I'm interested.'

Rose stood in front of the mirror and looked at herself, a woman still capable of attracting men. But capable of attracting Pierre again? She doubted it. She had always been a realist. Since long before the night she had seduced John Coburg in a punt on some piddling river in England, she had been a realist. That's why she had got Pierre into bed and manoeuvred her husband onto the sidelines. But realism required that she look at herself as harshly as she might a rival, and she didn't like what she saw. Lines across her forehead; pouches of skin, soft and rather charming like a chipmunk's at the moment but clearly poised to droop and become jowly.

She was aware that her daughter was watching her as she smoothed her hands over her widening hips. Her daughter, whose hips were slender, whose legs were slender, whose neck was slender . . . She flushed with anger. If Pierre had died two years ago she, Rose, would have inherited the company, she was sure of that. Her husband was a despised nancy, her son still young enough to keep in a state of subjection, her daughter a flat-chested teenager desperate to seduce the gardener.

She swung away from the mirror. 'You know what I'm talking about?' She stretched out her hand for her glass.

'I'm not sure.'

'You know,' she said, her eyes glittering. 'I'm talking about Pierre.'

'Pierre?'

'Has he been playing around with you?'

'Mother!'

'He tries to touch you sometimes. I've seen it.'

Celine sat down. 'Do you realise what you're saying?' she said slowly.

'Of course I do. Don't play the high and mighty Miss with me. Pierre Coburg comes from a part of central Europe with different standards from ours.'

'I come from Kansas City, Missouri, or that's what you've always told me.'

'You're ambitious, Celine,' she said, a note of desperation in her voice. 'I don't mind admitting I am too.'

'Is that why you abandoned your husband and started sleeping with his father?'

There was a long pause. 'Yes,' Rose said. 'Yes.'

Celine nodded her head slowly. She recognised the moment. The jugular had been exposed.

'There's no reason in the world that Martin should inherit Coburg Banknote alone,' Rose said.

'It's the way Pierre wants it.'

'Don't be so goddamn demure. I know you want Coburg Banknote.'

'And I know I'm not going to get it,' Celine flared. 'Because I'm a *woman*.'

Rose stood stock-still, staring at her daughter. 'You know what to do,' she said.

Celine stiffened. 'Do I understand what you're saying?'

'I think you do.'

'You're suggesting I take over where you left off?'

Again Rose paused. 'Yes,' she said finally. 'I'm suggesting it.'

'You dirty-minded bitch.'

But Rose saw Celine was smiling. It was not the first time she had been called a bitch. Why should she care? 'Well,' she said. 'Will you?'

Celine stood up looking at her mother. Then she turned away. 'I don't know. I might,' she said. 'If only to find out what the two of them are up to tonight.'

*

The black limousine passed through the dock gates on the nod of the civilian standing next to the uniformed Port Authority cop. It swerved across the cobblestones and ran along the silent, lighted quays.

In the car, Martin turned to his grandfather. 'Where are we?' he said. 'I'm lost.'

'Hoboken, New Jersey,' Pierre answered.

A figure in front of them flashed a dimmed light and Pierre rapped on the window for the driver to stop. Then, opening the rear door, he got out, waiting while Martin joined him. They stood on the eerie waterfront for a moment, the shadow concealing the fact of Martin's youth, two big men in dark overcoats.

They walked forward as figures came towards them. Pierre extended his hand. 'Good evening, Inspector,' he said. 'Pierre Coburg of Coburg Banknote. This is my grandson, Martin Coburg. He's had a very great deal to do with us all being here tonight.'

'It's a pleasure to meet you, sir,' the FBI inspector said. Martin realised with a flush of pleasure that the inspector was talking to him.

They walked on, now further along the waterfront, their footsteps echoing on concrete slabs, cracked and puddled with dirty water. Mist caught the lights and swirled around them. It was not much past midnight. There seemed to Martin no sign of activity, no stevedores or longshoremen, no seamen on the high boat decks of the rusting freighters that lined the waterfront.

They had stopped now in shadow. The FBI man pointed at a small black freighter with a lighter band painted along its middle and a squat red funnel illuminated by a single light bulb.

'Five minutes,' the FBI man said looking at his watch.

The group of men stood in silence. By straining his eyes Martin could just detect movement further down the quay. Mist rolled in from the black water beyond the freighter. Could he see the outline of a port patrol boat, lights out, riding the choppy surface of the water? Mist and excitement played havoc with the senses.

The FBI man said: 'One minute.'

Martin waited while the long seconds ticked past, but even beyond the excitement of the moment Martin felt something else. Emil had stressed that the Coburg name must be kept out of this. Pierre had announced their names, though certainly only to the FBI. But could it go further?

'Now!' said the FBI man and simultaneously searchlights hit the freighter from the waterfront and three patrol boats in the mist beyond.

At the same time a group of about twenty men detached itself from the shadow and headed for the freighter's accommodation ladder. From below Martin watched them reach deck level and fan out around the ship.

There were already shouts coming from the seamen and deck lights began to flick on. Below, Pierre passed round cigars. The band of each Havana, Martin registered, carried the legend: *Rolled in Cuba for Coburg Banknote Inc.* Another Coburg connection with the night's events.

They stood there for almost another hour. There was much talk of loading levels and ships' manifests but Martin paid little attention. He was waiting for his own private moment of triumph.

It came when a line of men came along the deck, each carrying a wooden crate. Descending the steep accommodation ladder with some difficulty they piled the crates on the quayside. The FBI inspector came forward with a crowbar, inserted it under the nailed-down top of the nearest crate and levered. The nails groaned, the wooden cover rose and in the beam of a flashlight Martin looked down on the neat packs of green twenty-dollar bills.

'OK, boys,' the FBI inspector said. 'Let's head for home.'

· Twenty-five ·

The events of the spring of 1940 hit Pierre Coburg like blows from a pick-handle across his back. On 10 April, when the *New York Tribune* delivered the news that Germany had taken both Denmark and Norway, Pierre had laughed bitterly. 'Another opportunity for Emil,' he had said looking up at Rose and Martin from his place at the end of the breakfast table.

'What's that, Pierre? What opportunity for Emil?' Celine had asked as she entered the breakfast room.

Pierre showed her the headline. 'They'll need new currencies, ration books, identity cards. You don't imagine these orders will go to De la Rue in *England*, do you? They'll go to German companies, Givierke & Devrient or Imprimerie Coburg. And with the Janus machine the chances are that Emil will get a fat share of the pickings.'

Celine spooned some scrambled egg onto a plate and brought it to the table. She sat next to Pierre and reached out and touched his hand. 'What's the latest news on Janus?' she asked gently. 'When will Emil be sending you the specifications?'

Martin, watching from near the other end of the long table, marvelled at Celine's ability to calm Pierre. She had, it seemed to him, taken on a new role in the last month or two. His mother Rose seemed literally to have taken a back seat. She no longer sat next to Pierre at breakfast; she deferred to Celine in a way Martin had not noticed before.

'Have you heard from Germany?' Martin asked him.

'Emil won't be sending the Janus specifications,' Pierre said. 'Not until I've agreed terms.'

They were all looking at Pierre now. This was the first time they had heard of terms. The double head of Janus had always been the symbol of the separate but equal association between the two Coburg companies. Was the Janus press now about to seesaw that balance?

'What are Emil's terms?' Celine seemed most naturally the one to put the question.

Pierre looked at her, then down the table. 'All right,' he said. 'We'll talk about it.' He paused to organise his thoughts. 'A machine which will revolutionise banknote printing is in existence. It was developed and is owned by Emil. Admittedly I did not put money into it. I have no claim on it other than a brotherly agreement made at the beginning of this century, that we would share any technical developments.'

'So . . . ?' It was Celine again. 'Is Emil reneging on that agreement?'

'Emil is sitting pretty in Europe with German government contracts coming out of his ears,' Pierre said. 'Already Poland has a new, mostly Coburg currency. Now Norway, now Denmark. As the German army marches, my brother simply picks up more contracts. He should change his company symbol from Janus to Midas. Everything he touches turns to gold! Emil's terms will be given to me when I go cap in hand to receive them. I was summoned by cable this morning to meet him in Europe.'

'Will you go?' Martin asked.

'Will I hell!'

On 10 May 1940 the German army invaded Holland and Belgium. Day after day the *New York Tribune* carried unbelievable headlines. The French army reeled back. The British began to evacuate their troops from Dunkirk. By early June Italy had joined Germany and was moving into the south of France. The French government had evacuated Paris; Bordeaux was now the capital. Then, a month after the German offensive began, France surrendered.

As those blows rained one after another on the countries of western Europe, so Pierre Coburg reeled. Perhaps the changes in him had not all come in one month but it was in one short month that they were evident to those around him. All that ebullience and sometimes brutal energy seemed to have drained out of him. He walked alone in the gardens. Every servant knew that he had to be called the moment a radio news bulletin was announced or the *Tribune* arrived. He drank much more than usual. He declined offers to dinner parties and cancelled others. Nobody now, including even Celine, seemed able to get close to him. He was suffering a mounting rage of jealousy.

When Rose and Celine talked, as they did more and more that spring, they had no doubt that this cancerous jealousy of his twin brother was at the root of Pierre's difficulties.

'Let me tell you,' Rose said as the two women sat in her second-floor sitting room together, 'let me tell you that Pierre has *always* thought of Emil as his younger brother. Now he's not sure.'

'He's very sure,' Celine said. 'He's being overtaken by his twin brother.'

Rose looked at her coyly. 'Does he talk to you much?'

'Not like he used to.'

'Does he . . .' Rose left the sentence unformed. 'Do you . . . ?'

Celine shook her head impatiently. 'Up until a month, six weeks ago Pierre liked to touch me up in the library some nights. We were getting on fine. He was talking. Little company secrets. Stuff about him and Emil. He got drunk, he got frisky.'

Rose's eyes glistened. 'And . . .'

'And that's as far as it went. The news from Europe is a turn-off. He's just not interested.'

Rose pretended to think for a few moments. 'Perhaps,' she said. 'Perhaps you should try again.'

'What the hell for?'

'I've got a nasty feeling,' Rose said, 'that we could be talking about our future.'

'You think our future depends on me?'

'I think our future,' Rose said, 'depends on you persuading Pierre that he has to go to Germany to talk to Emil.'

'He'll never do that. He's got far too much pride.'

'You can put it to him that Emil is a member of a belligerent country, it's not safe for him to leave Europe. Suggest they meet in Paris. Yes, why not? It belongs to the Germans but it's not Germany. Yes, Paris.'

'Somewhere in France, maybe,' Celine said thoughtfully. 'That just might be possible.'

Rose nodded emphatically. 'Face to face I would still back Pierre against Emil.'

Celine sprang up and paced the room. Her mother watched her, watched her silk dress swishing round her knees, the movement of her hips . . . Men loved that movement. She no longer had anything much to offer Pierre herself, not at least what he wanted, that young, free swaying of the hips. But Celine had it. And was ready to use it. A little encouragement from her mother, a little advice about how . . .

'Another thing. Make sure you go with him to France. Not Martin. Play it right and this could be where you step up into place.'

Celine stopped in the middle of the room. Her face was set. 'I want you to take up that weekend invitation with the Lawsons,' she said.

'They didn't say when exactly.'

'Make them say this weekend. I've seen you do it before.' Celine smiled sardonically. 'And get them to invite Martin as well.'

'Martin won't go. You know he hates the Lawson girl.'

'I need the weekend,' Celine said. 'That's the deal.'

'It was good of Martin to go with her to the Lawsons',' Celine said pouring a brandy for Pierre.

He sat staring, mostly at the fire, in his favourite library chair. He wore a towelling robe and pale-grey cotton pyjamas. Until Celine had appeared he'd thought he would finish his cigar and go to bed. Today's news had been disastrous. France was to be divided in two by the victorious Germans. Both sides of the new line would need a completely new currency system. New printing contracts for Emil's Imprimerie Coburg now added up to considerable proportions of new currencies for Norway, Denmark, Holland, Belgium and in all probability two entirely separate parts of France. The French North African colonies were certainly going to change.

Celine sat on the arm of his chair. Her robe draped itself over his arm. He flicked it aside irritably and took the glass of brandy she offered.

Celine's finger scratched at the vee of hair in the neck of his pyjamas. 'Do you know you're a very hairy man?'

He sipped his brandy. 'You know what the world's going to look like by 1943, Celine?'

'No.' She left her hand where it was but kept her finger still.

'Do you realise that in a year or two Coburg Banknote Corporation could be finished?'

Celine rearranged her position on the arm of the chair. 'Just because of this war?' she said.

'Listen.' He gulped at his brandy. 'The Bureau of Engraving prints the currency of the United States. No way in there. De la Rue in London effectively prints for the countries of the British Empire. No way in there. Japan now controls an important part of China militarily and commercially. No way in there. The German victories have put every new European contract within the grasp of Emil. No way in there. So what are we left with?'

She scratched gently at the curling grey hairs on his chest. 'What *are* we left with?'

'Not much,' he said.

She slid her hand just inside his pyjama jacket.

He looked up at her. For the first time in weeks his brow cleared. He grunted, smiled.

She slid her hand further down so that the fingers passed over the hair on the dome of his stomach. 'I think you have to meet up with Emil,' she said softly. 'I'll go with you if you want.'

'I'm not kowtowing to my own twin brother,' he said.

'It wouldn't be kowtowing. After all . . .' she massaged down to the elasticated waistband '. . . all you say is true only if the situation remains as it is. But just imagine: FDR wins this election and takes the US into the war next year. What happens then to all Emil's contracts and plans if the US and Britain won? Which they would.'

He looked up at her smiling. 'It's a strong argument.'

'. . . To put to Emil when you meet him in Paris.'

Pierre nodded. 'He needs us because he needs insurance for the future. I could offer that in return for the Janus spec.' He grinned broadly. 'I'm feeling better.'

'So I see.'

It was the first time either of them had recognised in words what hands or thighs were doing.

'Celine, honey.' Pierre pretended shock. 'I'm your *grandfather*.'

'Are you going to let that make a difference?'

He laid his hands across her stomach and unbuttoned the large pearl buttons of her pyjamas. The silk fell open.

Neither of them had heard the door of the library open. The cry of horror was incoherent with shock and anger. As they swung their heads towards the door John Coburg was already half running down the long library towards them.

Their hands were still half hidden in cotton or silk pyjamas. They dragged them out as John Coburg reached them. 'Get up to bed, Celine!' he screamed. 'Now! Go up now. *Now!*'

She stumbled to her feet and looked down at Pierre, but he had not moved. 'Now!' her father screamed again, and she turned and fled from the room.

The two men faced each other, the son's face a bright unnatural red; Pierre's pale and suddenly dark-eyed. They were both thinking of the night John Coburg had been caught with Jack Aston.

'I don't care . . . I don't care about myself or what I've done,' John stammered. 'But I promise you this: if anything like this happens again, even if I think anything like this *might* happen again, I'll call in the police.'

Pierre got to his feet and walked past him. The long robe concealed the fact that he was trembling with anger.

'I'll do it, Pierre,' John Coburg shouted as his father reached the door. 'I'll finish you for good. I'll call in the police.'

Carefully closing the door behind him Pierre left the library.

· Twenty-six ·

Pierre's decision not to take her with him on his trip to see Emil was a heavy blow to Celine. She knew the reason of course. She knew her father had received a new lease of life as he relished the role he had adopted as watchdog over her. He seemed to see very little of Jack Aston these days. He was drinking less, watching more.

And Pierre was afraid, there was no doubt about that. To have the police called in by his own son would be a scandal he could not successfully surmount. In Rose's view her husband ought to have been hounded out of the house.

'Listen, Celine,' she said. And Celine turned wearily. All her life her mother's instructions, suggestions, interventions had been prefaced by 'Listen!'

'Listen to what, for God's sake?' she said. 'Martin's going with him to meet Emil. I'm not, because my father is threatening Pierre with the police.'

They were in Rose's sitting room a little before lunch on a fine day in the early summer of 1940. The *Tribune* had that day carried pictures of Hitler sightseeing in Paris.

'We could have done something about it. We could have drummed *him* out. Told him to go off and live with his darling Jack Aston or else.'

'It's too late,' Celine said. 'Pierre's changing. These last few months have hit him hard.'

'He doesn't look his old self,' Rose said. 'His doctors have told him he's a candidate for a heart attack if he doesn't let up a bit.'

'That won't stop him.' Celine poured herself a glass of lemon water and walked across the room to the window. The gardens of Island House were at their most magnificent. Across the tops of the trees the ocean sparkled blue-grey in the sunlight. Below her the grooms were taking out the horses for their daily exercise. Her own pair of red setters romped elegantly across the lawns. She turned her head. The chauffeur was driving her white

Bruzzelli sports car into the rear courtyard for its monthly service. She heard her mother's voice behind her but she had no desire to listen. After Pierre, all this, she was passionately convinced, belonged to her and to her alone. She thought for a moment of dispossession, inevitably by Martin, and moving to an apartment, however large, in Manhattan, and her stomach knotted. She loved banknotes, she loved contracts, the fight for new orders, meetings, urgency, success. The only way for a woman to get to the top of a corporation in America was to own it. That she was utterly determined to do.

In her orderly, logical fashion she sorted the opposition into three groupings. Pierre of course was free at any time to assign the company wherever he wished. But without interference, she believed that she could ensure that his will was in her favour. Martin was the most intractable problem of the three. He too was changing, getting older of course, getting more sure of himself. The problem of Martin could only be dealt with through Pierre. But the hub and pivot of her difficulties, she saw, was her father. While he held the sword of Damocles over Pierre, Celine knew that she could not hope to regain her influence over her grandfather. Therefore John Coburg had to be dealt with. She considered consulting her mother, then quickly rejected the idea. But she would get her mother's help.

She turned from the window.

'Really, Celine,' Rose said, 'you can be so cold. I was talking to you, darling. And you stand there as if you're deaf.'

'I was thinking,' Celine said slowly. 'I now know what we must do.'

Rose watched her in silence.

'You're going to help me.'

'Of course, darling,' Rose said uncertainly.

'Wait until you hear what I want you to do.'

'Anything.'

'I want you to invite Jack Aston for drinks.'

'No. Why, in God's name?' Rose flared, then stopped. 'Clever Celine. They haven't been seeing too much of each other lately, your father and Aston. Push them back together, then put the gun to his head. One breath of scandal and we'll have him jailed for five years for sodomy.'

'Go ahead and invite dear Jack,' Celine said. 'After all we're practically neighbours.'

At dawn the Pan American Clipper banked over Estoril and followed the line of the north shore of the Tagus as it began its descent on Lisbon Airport.

Pierre had slept much of the flight, and rising with the sun in the forward cabin windows and now shaved and dressed, he looked better than he had for months.

Martin had slept less well. It was not the narrow, rather hard, airliner bed that had kept him awake, nor the steady drumming of the engines. Much more it was the thought of seeing Alexina again.

It was now almost a year since he had seen her. He was now just nineteen years old; she less than a year younger. He looked back on last summer in confusion. The politics, the break with Alexina, the bizarre night with Elisabeth, the Führer at Lingfeld and finally the outbreak of war. The rush of events against which he had first fallen in love and then slept with a woman, a different woman, made his head swim. His decision now was to be a neutral in politics, to stand above, to be as many people in the United States yearned to be, isolated from what was happening in Europe. But also to be close to Alexina, if she would let him.

The airplane bumped and powered across the slender concrete runway, then swung left and taxied into the early morning sun towards a line of white airport buildings.

As Martin emerged from the cabin and came down the steps behind Pierre he was astonished by the number of aircraft on the apron bearing the German cross. He could see no Portuguese airplanes, no Spanish, one or two Italian light transports but mostly the silver-bodied, three-engined Junker 52, the workhorse of the Third Reich.

Entering the airport building he was astonished to see Elisabeth Oster coming towards them. Pierre smiled and stepped forward to clasp her in his arms. 'My dear girl,' he said, 'how good of you to meet us.'

When she was released by Pierre, Martin kissed her decorously on both cheeks. Pierre clearly knew she was coming to meet them. Equally clearly he had not considered it worthwhile telling Martin. It was just another of those examples of his grandfather's return to the breezy, confident Pierre of last year. Face to face with Emil he believed he could dominate him.

Elisabeth was laughing. 'Pierre didn't tell you,' she said to Martin as they were escorted by porters to a large German embassy Mercedes, 'my part in the war effort is a posting to our embassy in Lisbon. There are worse postings.'

'I'm sure,' Martin said. 'And how is Rolf? Was he with the army in France?'

Martin thought her face clouded slightly. 'No, Rolf is on special duties in Poland. Yes, important special duties.'

The car moved smoothly down the road toward the centre of Lisbon.

'Tonight,' Pierre said, 'I'm taking Elisabeth to dinner.' Martin waited while Pierre paused for effect. 'You, Martin,' he added, laughing, 'are going to entertain Oliver Sutchley.'

'Sutchley?'

Pierre nodded. 'You'll love him. And since he's English and works at the British embassy here in Lisbon, it's not possible, thank God, for him to dine with myself and Elisabeth. So the honour falls to you.'

They drove in to where the German embassy sat at the end of the grand boulevard. Martin was fascinated by the sheer impudent size of the swastika flying. In the early morning breeze it curled and uncurled, folded and unfolded in a lazy demonstration of the new confident power of Hitler's Germany.

He pulled his eyes away from the flag. 'Will it be difficult to get a French visa?' he asked from politeness rather than real concern.

Elisabeth's laugh trilled. 'Difficult? Difficult to get a visa to France? Why should it be difficult? After all, Martin, it is we, the German embassy, who now issues them.'

Pierre turned to her. 'We travel by train or boat?'

'We have arranged a Portuguese steamer to Bordeaux which is at this moment the seat of the French government of Marshal Pétain. From Bordeaux you take a train inland to Brive-la-Gaillarde and from there another train to Paris.'

'And what are the conditions like travelling in France?'

She squeezed his arm. 'All French resistance has ceased, of course. But we have conflicting reports.'

On the morning Pierre and Martin landed in Lisbon, Alexina Coburg was driving a Renault van through the back streets of a working-class suburb of Paris. It was a grey dawn matched by the long grey streets of garages and factories and blank walls with peeling posters urging Frenchmen to remember the Marne or Verdun.

Alexina was frightened. She had crammed her hair into a leather peaked workman's cap and smeared a thumbmark of motor oil on her cheeks. But she was never going to persuade anyone giving her more than a casual glance that she was a young Parisian mechanic.

There were no German soldiers to be seen, no road blocks, no gendarmerie. The ancient van bounced over the cobbles as Alex scanned the corners for the turn-off into the Rue Gassin. In the event it came sooner than she supposed. Braking hard she swung the Renault left and saw ahead of her a factory courtyard with a sign reading: Imprimerie Gerassimov.

Again there was no sign of life in the street. It was as if this part of Paris was deserted. Or perhaps waiting, watching from behind half-closed shutters. She shuddered at the thought and turned the van into the Gerassimov yard. Almost immediately a rusting metal-plate door was pulled back. She moved the van forward even before the screech of the door's metal rollers had ceased. Seconds later the van was in the glass-roofed plant and the metal door was being pushed closed.

She got out of the van. Her schoolfriend Andrée de Bretagne ran forward to kiss her, stopped and burst out laughing at Alex's feeble disguise. In the darkness behind them Monsieur and Madame de Bretagne rose anxiously from the wooden crates on which they were sitting. A long grey-green German army staff car stood behind them, the Occupation swastika on the hood.

There was no laughter now. 'So far so good,' Alexina said crisply.

Andrée, a pretty dark-featured girl, was opening the back of the Renault van.

'Enough food and bottled water to get you down to the Pyrenees, with one stop-over,' Alex said. 'Three blankets and three sleeping bags; one hundred litres of gasoline; one spare tyre; tools; a bottle of English whisky with the label removed of course; four litres of *vin ordinaire*; bread; and . . .' She knelt on the oil-stained cement and reached under the back of the van from which she pulled a shotgun.

'Let's pray we won't need it,' Monsieur de Bretagne said.

Andrée's mother hugged Alexina to her. 'You're a marvellous girl,' she said. 'A marvellous girl.'

Behind them there was a clatter on the iron staircase. Emil came down, his face unsmiling. 'You should go now, Georges,' he said to Andrée's father. 'Every hour that passes the organisation of our military government improves.' He indicated the upper window he had been watching from. 'It's clear outside,' he said. 'No patrols. Go south through Orléans, then head for Tours. My friend the general says the roads are clearer that way.' He shook hands with de Bretagne and embraced his wife.

'We know what this means to you, what you have done for us,' de Bretagne said.

Emil smiled. 'I can't think of it as treachery,' he said. 'Not betrayal of Germany. If there's any truth in all this madness I suppose I'm doing it *for* Germany, not against.'

Alexina and Andrée embraced. 'A *bientôt*,' they told each other and Alex stepped back to watch the de Bretagnes climb into the rocking Renault van.

Emil had the plate door open. As the Renault passed through he and Alexina ran quickly to the army staff car and climbed in. While Alexina cleaned up her face and threw the workman's cap out of the window, Emil drove rapidly through Argenteuil towards the centre of the city.

After minutes they both began to relax. The sun was rising, throwing colour onto the Seine on their right. 'Please don't get me into this sort of thing again,' Emil said, laughing now. He stretched out an arm and hugged her to him.

'No promises,' Alexina said.

He glanced at her and read the determination in her face. Releasing her he said: 'You know the dangers. You know no influence I have can help if it became a police matter, a Gestapo matter.'

'I know. But you believe it's right too, don't you?'

'At one time I didn't.' Without looking at her he said: 'Madame de Bretagne was right. You are a marvellous girl.'

Martin met Oliver Sutchley that evening by arrangement in the bar of the Hotel Bristol. Sutchley was a tall, stoop-shouldered, brown-haired Englishman, dressed in a well-cut dinner jacket. In the first ten minutes in the Bristol bar he had drunk three Martinis.

'Don't think of me as unpatriotic, old boy,' he said over the fourth. 'I'm a realist. And Winston bloody Churchill isn't.'

'You think he isn't?'

'Did you hear his last speech? The German army's at his throat – twenty miles away across the Channel there's the best army in the world and the biggest and most modern air force – and what does the lunatic say?'

Martin shrugged. 'What did he say?'

In a Churchillian growl Sutchley intoned: ' "We shall seek no terms, we may show mercy – we shall ask for none". Did you hear that? On the edge of defeat!'

Martin shifted uncomfortably. It sounded pretty crazy to him but it was surely what people wanted to hear. They didn't want to be told their government was desperately looking for peace terms. That's what had finished France when Marshal Pétain announced, off his own bat, that he was seeking peace terms. Even the best of soldiers don't fight on after that.

'You and I, old boy,' Sutchley was saying, 'we understand each other. We've got to stick together, OK? Pray for peace and we'll be all right.' He ordered another drink. 'It's not going to be long now, Churchill or no Churchill.'

Martin declined Oliver Sutchley's offer of dinner. An hour with him was enough. Perhaps he felt it was some sort of disloyalty to Alexina to be talking so warmly about the German dictator she despised. Or perhaps it was just that as a patriotic American Martin Coburg could not relate to this shifty, opportunist Englishman. Walking through the echoing colonnades of midnight Lisbon, Martin stopped to look at the floodlit swastika flying high over the German embassy.

France, in the high summer of 1940, was in a state of unbelievable chaos. As the German panzer divisions had sliced through Holland and Belgium and then rolled back the British and French armies in northern France, the great exodus had begun. Fuelled by incredible rumours of spies, of parachutists and of the insensate cruelty of all German soldiers, thousands then hundreds of thousands of Dutch, Belgian and French civilians began to leave their homes. It mattered not that the reality of the German advance was quite different: there were no parachutists dressed as nuns, no Germans in French peasant garb, no Hunnish fury unleashed upon the defenceless population. Yet nevertheless the exodus continued to grow. Great towns like Lille in the north of France saw the flight of over a half of their inhabitants and, as the countryside around emptied, the townships and villages south of Paris were engulfed by a tide of fleeing people. Hungry, thirsty and desperate, seventy thousand refugees surged into the small Corrèze town of Brive-la-Gaillarde; further south, Cahors, on the river Lot, population thirteen thousand, was swamped by a vast refugee army marching on the town. Over forty thousand people, exhausted, many old and sick, all at the limit of their endurance, camped in the market squares or besieged the railway stations for news of trains even further south.

Into this unbelievable chaos Pierre and Martin Coburg found themselves precipitated. By the end of June eight million people had travelled north to south, the length of France, until then the greatest single migration in the history of Europe. By the beginning of July and the signing of the Armistice a large proportion of those refugees were now fighting to return north to reoccupy farms and city apartments that they had abandoned only weeks before.

The French railway authorities tried to run a service, but with the French Ministry of Transport camping in a hotel without telephones in Bordeaux, it was an impossible task. As Pierre and Martin rattled west in a wooden-slat-seated local train from Bordeaux, they both knew that it might take them weeks to complete their journey to Paris.

On the sixth night out of Bordeaux they stopped in the small town of Souillac on the Dordogne river. The engine was uncoupled for use elsewhere and they joined a thousand travellers surging downhill to find food and accommodation in the centre of the town.

The small stone-flagged squares of the country town were crammed with people camping under the covered market or living from cars without gasoline or carts whose horses had been sold along the way. Thousands streamed through the narrow alleys off the Route Nationale 20, or fought for water at the single public pump in the Place du Puits.

As thousands tried to move north by road tens of thousands more were brought in by train from Toulouse or Bordeaux. Beyond the tiny market town of Souillac, for reasons nobody knew, there were no trains running north to Paris.

On the cathedral square the dust danced in a shimmer of midday heat. The medieval cathedral, almost Moorish with its array of domes, stood before them. Pierre was sweating until great dark patches spread from under the arms of his pale-grey suit. 'There,' he pointed as if he were personally responsible for positioning the man, 'a German sentry.'

They crossed toward the German corporal who stood, his rifle swung by its sling on his shoulder, his forage cap tipped forward against the sun.

Within five minutes they were drinking schnapps with a young officer in the signals room. Within less than half an hour, after much winding of handles and shouting into black bakelite mouthpieces, Pierre was speaking to Emil in the George V in Paris.

'Pierre, you old devil,' Emil could be heard bawling, 'where are you?'

'We're at a town called Souillac on the Dordogne river,' Pierre said. 'Very pretty but with no possible chance of a train north to Paris.'

The line crackled and hissed. Martin sitting on a stone bench in the high-vaulted room struggled to hear what Emil was saying. Did he hear Alex's name mentioned? Did Emil say he had brought Alexina with him?

Pierre was yelling into the handset. 'You'll what? You'll do what?'

Through more crackling and hissing Pierre listened, nodding, then gestured to the lieutenant to take the line. He turned away to Martin. 'We're in luck,' he said. 'Emil was just entertaining General von Henzinger to lunch in his suite. The general will put suitable accommodation in this area at our disposal.'

'But how do we get to Paris?' Martin said.

'We don't. There's a small flying club airfield less than twenty kilometres from here. Emil will fly down from Paris. The mountain's coming to Muhammad.'

Martin left, with difficulty, what he hoped was a suitable pause. 'Is Alexina coming with him?'

Pierre grinned hugely. 'She'll be a pretty young woman by now, eh?' He took Martin's shoulder in the painful grip of his huge fist which had tortured him as a child. 'Don't you worry, my boy. There'll be plenty to occupy you while Emil and myself are talking business.'

Beyond Souillac where the river Ouysse cuts its way through the limestone cliffs and follows a twisting path through bald rocky hillsides, the Château de Belfresnes stands guard at what was once a critical crossing point. Among the many chateaux of this much fought upon region Belfresnes passes almost unnoticed. It is small with perhaps no more than ten or a dozen bed chambers. But it is built high on an incomparable limestone cliff and its courtyard juts out onto a terrace with a view across the river and line after line of blue hills.

In 1940 the chateau was lived in by a Hungarian woman of an uncertain past who called herself the Countess Boritza. She was by now in her sixties and had lived at the chateau since the first war with an international selection of young lovers. When the young officer explained that he was to requisition the chateau for a few days during which important meetings were to take place there, the countess was delighted. She would be paid; she would be able to continue occupying her suite of rooms in the high turret; and she watched with pleasure the superbly built young German soldiers unpacking bedding and food and crates of wine for her important visitors' greater comfort.

Emil and Alex arrived the next day. From the terrace Martin had watched their car and its motor-cycle outriders twisting through the hills, disappearing behind limestone rocks and reappearing to climb the steep road toward the chateau.

Alex, in a wide-brimmed straw hat and a cream muslin dress, was seated next to Emil in the back of the open car. The driver was old Wilhelm from Lingfeld. Running across the main hall to meet them, Martin nearly knocked over the countess.

'Young man,' she said in her highly accented English, 'young man, why are you in such a hurry? Stop a moment.'

Martin stopped. 'My apologies, Countess,' he said hurriedly. 'I was going out to meet the new arrivals.'

He had already turned toward the door when she hooked his arm with the handle of her ivory walking stick. 'Martin,' she said. 'You must escort me out to the courtyard. Give me your arm. We shall greet the newcomers together.'

It was not by any means the picture he wanted to present to Alex after nearly a year apart but he had no choice. He offered the countess his arm and very slowly, her stick tapping on the ancient terracotta tiled floor, they passed under the main arch and out into the blazing sunshine. At that exact moment the outriders roared into the courtyard with the Mercedes directly behind.

He thought he saw Alex smiling. Certainly Emil was finding it difficult to hide his amusement.

Martin detached his arm and formally presented Emil and Alex to the countess. While Emil bent over the old lady's hand, Martin came forward to kiss Alex on both cheeks.

'What chaos!' Emil said. 'What indescribable confusion. Paris is beyond anyone's comprehension.' He was talking to the countess. 'You are very kind, Madame, to allow us to use your beautiful chateau for a few days. My brother, he's here already of course.' He turned to Martin. 'Where is the rascal?'

'He's upstairs in his rooms,' Martin said.

'Now tell him our guests are here,' the countess said gaily. 'And I will take Herr Coburg and his most beautiful daughter for an aperitif under the trees.'

Emil smiled and offered his arm. With Alexina they set off for the orchard where the countess took her daily glass or glasses of Suze in the shade.

It was almost twenty minutes later that Martin joined them and delivered the message that Pierre would take a bath and would join them for lunch. For a brief second Martin was sure he saw Emil's eyebrows rise. Then he leaned forward smiling. 'A glass of something for you, Martin?' He gestured to the soldier-waiter who was serving them and left Martin to make his own order. 'I was saying, Madame, whole *quartiers* of Paris are empty of people.'

'But of course,' the countess said. 'They're all down here in the south-west. But tell me, the theatres are still open, the restaurants, the night clubs?'

'Yes, in the midst of the administrative confusion with half a million German soldiers swarming all over the city and the *banlieue*, yet life continues.'

Martin turned his head and found that Alex was looking at him. He smiled and slowly she smiled back.

A half smile.

'You ask me what will happen, Madame,' Emil continued more seriously now, 'and all I can say is that I don't know. Will France become two countries? Yes, I suppose so. Perhaps. Perhaps not. Most important of all, what will the United States do? Will President Roosevelt be re-elected do you think, Martin?'

Of course Emil was talking about the twenty million counterfeit dollars.

'I think,' Martin said carefully, 'that the President's chances have increased since March. The opposition have not been as effectively organised as I'm sure they hoped.'

'I see.' Emil nodded. 'It is possible that the isolationists in America are short of funds.'

Martin smiled. 'I think it's possible, Emil.'

'Now, Madame.' Emil made a sudden turn to the countess, closing off his line of questioning to Martin. 'What are your own plans now that peace has returned? Will you stay in this most beautiful chateau? Will you leave for Paris or Berlin? Will you go back to Budapest, a city I so much enjoy? What will you do?'

'Monsieur Coburg,' she said, 'I am a penniless old lady. I had once thought, not so long ago, Monsieur, that the Château de Belfresnes was my dowry. Now I face facts. It is my pension, I shall sell it and take an apartment in Paris, where I will end my days in delicious depravity.'

Her rouged cheekbones stretched taut. Her red lips pouted. She ran her hand across the thin red-blonde hair. Alex was staring.

'My darling Alexina,' she said. 'To you growing old is inconceivable. To me it is a pain in the back when a gentleman, so rare these days, decides to lower his weight upon me. Ah,' she laughed as Alex blushed. 'Do you think then, my darlings, that age deifies a woman? When I am cut do I not bleed?' She stood suddenly. 'Come, Monsieur Coburg, let's go in to lunch. Let's drink *énormément* of the excellent champagne you have provided. Let's pretend for an hour or two that there's no war, or business meetings, or growing old.'

With Emil accompanying her they set off for the chateau.

Alex's eyebrows shot up. 'Are all Hungarian women like that?'

'God knows.'

'It's good to see you again, Martin.' She spoke quietly.

'It's a year almost,' he said.

'Since the day Elisabeth and Rolf were married.'

She was underlining that moment, the night before the wedding. Putting it between them before ordinary affections could smudge or obliterate it.

He was determined not to let her. The sunlight dappled her hair as they stood together in the orchard. 'Alex,' he said slowly, 'you never answered my letters.'

'No. Not letters like that. I saw no point.'

'Did you read them?'

'Some.'

'Don't you understand now that I thought you were going to marry Gregor?'

'You're saying that's why you slept with Elisabeth?'

'For God's sake, I didn't *know* it was going to happen. Emil dropped me in the woods.'

'And the fairy princess was waiting for you!'

His face tensed angrily. 'You knew it was going to happen. Why the hell didn't you warn me?'

She shook her head bitterly.

'Well, why?'

She looked down at the table, her fingers drumming on the cloth. 'Because I wanted you to have the choice, I suppose.' She moved round the table and looked out through the apple trees to the stone wall enclosing the orchard. 'When I realised what Emil and Pierre were planning, I thought I was going to go mad. I tore into Emil. I told him that all this Waldviertel myth was nothing but medieval shine that had to be washed off, abandoned. Women weren't filthy vessels to be cleansed by the holy penis of the lord or the priest or the first invited. It was a sick ancient custom, a custom designed for men. For their own salacious pleasure. In the Waldviertel, as you must know, it was as often as not a cover, an excuse for incest.' She broke off, tears in her eyes. 'And you fell for it. When I realised it had happened I could have killed Emil, you, and Elisabeth for submitting to it.' She looked up. 'Or maybe that wasn't too much of a sacrifice.'

'Alex . . .' He moved toward her.

She shook her head, keeping the table between them.

'We've got a few days,' he said. 'And you didn't, after everything that had happened, decide to marry Gregor.'

'That decision was taken out of my hands,' she said. 'He was killed in Poland.'

'I'm sorry, Alex.'

She nodded slowly. 'But I wasn't going to marry him.'

He was silent for a moment. 'We can't start at the beginning,' he said. 'I understand that. But we can make a new start, if you want to.'

They walked together through the orchard, the sunlight dappling her white dress. More than anything he wanted to reach out and take her hand. She seemed to know this as the back of their hands brushed against each other and she looked up at him and smiled briefly before looking away.

'Tell me about this last year,' he said. 'Did you ski? Did you skate at Hollenheim?'

'I spent the winter in the north,' she said more brightly. 'A nursing course in Hamburg.' She laughed and the shadows seemed to pass away. 'I learnt what very, very hard work is. Lectures from seven in the morning till midday. Practical work on the wards from two until six or sometimes eight. I got to know lots of girls from all sorts of different backgrounds. Girls who wanted to be more than just a *Hausfrau* or a breeding machine for the new Germany.'

They entered the ancient archway into the sudden cool of the wide hall. The thunderous voices of Pierre and Emil could be heard from the dining room with the countess's high screech of pleasure interwoven between. There was much laughter and the frequent clink of glasses.

'Thank goodness,' Alex said as they paused by the door, 'the two brothers are getting on well together.'

'They won't let business get between them,' Martin said.

She looked at him gravely. This time she did brush the back of his hand, slowly and deliberately. 'Let's have lunch,' she said, 'and listen to some disgraceful dreams of imperial Budapest.'

· Twenty-seven ·

The discussions between the two brothers began after lunch the first day and continued until late in the evening. A cold tray with cheese and beer was ordered up into the room which had been set aside for the meetings and Martin and Alex had dined with the countess. They had by now decided she looked like a giant bat with her rapid, swooping movements and the dresses which fell in great folds from her arms and floated and fluttered behind her. When she failed to elicit from them anything about the brothers' meeting she began to recount her stories of Budapest before the Great War. An unending succession of counts and archdukes had given her jewellery, always priceless, and had asked for her hand or tried to gain entrance to her boudoir. 'I am not a *putain*,' she assured Alex and Martin with a screech of laughter, 'but if men behave in such a silly fashion should we women not profit from it? My dears, I was from a family of great breeding, but little money. Some in those Hapsburg days boasted that they had never made love for love. But they were just *putains*. I, darlings, never made love for anything but love. If I accepted small presents from someone other than my lover it was only if Count Esterhazy's shade of ruby suited the colour of my hair, or if Count Balaton's diamonds, though large, were not too vulgarly set.'

'And did this life end with the Great War?' Martin asked.

'But not at all,' the countess said. 'I was still a young woman. Vivaciously attractive. Men wrote to me from the front telling me they would die for me. Some did. No, the life didn't end with the war but in the nineteen-twenties it moved. Opera and shooting parties gave way to skiing and tennis in the south of French. I think the truth is, darlings, that it became a little vulgar.'

When Martin and Alex stood outside her room later that night they were overtaken with gales of laughter. The champagne and Burgundy had done their work; the strain of listening gravely to the old countess was lifted. Any phrase of the countess's was enough to start them laughing again. 'I am not a *putain*,' Alex said.

'Certainly not if the diamonds are not too *vulgarly* set,' Martin responded.

A sound on the staircase brought them up. They both looked along the landing to where the countess was standing beside a huge mounted Chinese vase.

They faced her overwhelmed with embarrassment. Then she came forward smiling and kissed each of them on the cheek. 'Oh my darlings,' she said. 'Why shouldn't you laugh, even at me? You have so little time.'

Their embarrassment faded. The American boy and the German girl looked at her, baffled.

'Time?'

'So little,' the old lady murmured.

For a moment the three of them stood in the wide corridor. The countess smiled toward Alexina's door. 'Spend it together,' she said. 'Don't wait.' She flounced past them and disappeared at a turn of the corridor.

They stood awkwardly, facing each other. 'Well,' Martin said, 'I'd better say goodnight.'

Neither of them moved.

'But what if she's right?' Alexina said.

Martin touched her hand then ran his fingers up her arm to the rich curve of her shoulder. She moved closer to him. Reaching to put an arm round his neck she kissed him. The simple pressure of their lips brought their mouths open and their tongues danced slowly together.

The following morning the four Coburgs breakfasted together while the old countess took smoked salmon and scrambled eggs in her room. The atmosphere around the long refectory table laid for breakfast out on the terrace was, for Martin and Alex, unnerving. The two brothers were not their normal selves.

Looking out over the gorge with its sparkling river, Pierre was ebullient in a way Martin had never seen before. There was an element of theatre in the way Pierre behaved, pacing the terrace with his coffee cup waving in his hand. Emil, on the other hand, was unusually quiet. Not withdrawn or angry, but thoughtful, answering Alex or Martin with a slow smile. Perhaps, Martin thought as the two men retired with their briefcases and papers to the room upstairs, it was that Emil was quiet and confident; and Pierre was less certain of the way the discussions were moving.

In the great kitchen below the ground, the soldier-cooks the Wehrmacht had provided were packing a hamper. Sepp Jürgens the senior cook stood over them counting in the items, the Puligny Montrachet, the Château Margaux to drink with the cheese. He was a small fat man whose waistline very evidently suffered from his occupation. He was eating a great sandwich of French bread and cured ham as he waved his arm to encompass the stone-vaulted room. 'In the old days,' he said to Martin, 'they knew a thing or two about building kitchens, don't you think, young sir?'

'I'm not sure,' Martin said dubiously in deliberate provocation. 'It's not much like an American kitchen.'

'An American kitchen.' Pieces of bread flew from Sepp's mouth. 'An American kitchen. How could anyone cook a decent dinner in an American kitchen?'

'I guess it's been known,' Martin said smiling.

'Hah, you play jokes with me, young friend. But what I say is true,' Sepp insisted. 'Look at these ovens, look at that fire! Can you make fifty loaves at a time in an American kitchen? Could you roast an ox?'

'No.'

'Exactly my point. Now look at this.' He swung open a wooden door. 'My refrigerator!'

Martin and Alex peered into a huge dungeon-like room. With only a narrow aisle left to reach the stacked shelves at the back of the stone room, the flags were piled with blocks of ice. The intense cold seeped into the kitchen.

'Go in, go in,' the cook urged them.

Martin took Alex by the hand and together they stepped into the icy room.

'Why is it so cold?' Alex said.

Martin pointed toward a flight of rough-hacked stone steps in the back of the room. From them a draught of cold air came like a steady wind.

'Let's go see,' Martin said.

They could see that light came from below and as they approached the top of the stairs they could hear the roar of water.

'Some sort of underground river,' Alex said as they started down the rock steps.

Ten steps down they stopped in astonishment. A huge cavern opened up before them through which a river surged. Electric lights in the roof of the cavern threw weird shadows on stalagmites and stalactites, columns of limestone whose strange rondels made them seem as if they had been fashioned on a giant lathe.

They reached the bottom of the long, twisting staircase. The stone floor was damp as they crossed it following the course of the river until the electric light gave way to splintered beams of sunlight hitting the rock above their heads.

Forty or fifty yards further, away from the roar of the underground river, they reached the cave mouth. Thick foliage half obscured the sun and they pushed through the bushes to find themselves at the base of a narrow gorge. Bright purple flowers swamped their senses. They stood in one another's arms until they heard the German army cook calling to them, then they turned and slowly made their way past the roaring river, back up the stone steps to the kitchen.

'See, you young moderns,' Jürgens said. 'You think a cook should be content with an ice-box the size of a hat-box, or four snivelling gas flames on a cook-stove. Here, drink a glass of schnapps with me before you go off on your picnic.' He poured three large glasses of schnapps, looked round at the other three cooks, grunted and poured for them too.

Sepp lifted his glass. 'To the American kitchen,' he said. 'May it never come!'

They took an army *Kübelwagen* and drove down the twisting road among the yellow rocks to the bridge. Beside it one of the chateau's flat-bottom boats was beached and tethered to a post. Alex untied the rope and dragged the boat to the water's edge and Martin hauled the hamper from the back of the *Kübelwagen* and crunched across the pebble beach to place it on the boat.

The sun blazed down from a sky empty but for a few white rags of cloud and a tiny Storch spotter-plane reporting the movement of refugees on some distant road north. They launched the boat and pushed off with one of the blue and red banded oars. Alex insisted on rowing downstream and Martin sat in the stern of the boat, the tiller rope in his hand, the brim of his straw hat tipped over his eyes. Watching Alex, seeing the fall of her breasts as she bent forward to row, the glitter of sweat on her arms, the light puffing of the lips as she took the strain, he thought he had never felt so happy. From her face as she rested the oars he thought that her feelings were little different from his.

They rowed and floated downstream until they came to a deep cove in the river bank where the cliffs lifted clear from the water to a height of one hundred feet. Above them three separate streams gushed over the cliff and plunged down into the river. There was shade there from great chestnut trees which grew around the cove and the fall of water created an extraordinary coolness in the air.

They tied up the boat and unloaded the hamper. Taking the rug which was strapped inside the lid, Alex spread it on the ground beneath one of the giant chestnut trees. Martin had turned to watch the falling water bouncing and sparkling on the rock when he was suddenly aware she was no longer there. Calling her name, suddenly nervous, he brushed through a screen of bushes and stopped. She was poised for a fraction of a second, naked, on a jutting rock. Then her legs bent slightly and she propelled herself outwards, until she cut into the water below.

She had not seen him and he stepped back quickly behind the rock. It was not that he had not imagined her naked body before, but he had no conception of what the effect on him would be, seeing her like that. He went quickly back and was kneeling forward, unpacking the hamper, as she swam round the rock. He stood up and walked to the edge of the flat slab of the jutting limestone. Only her head was above the surface. Below her brown body rippled in the clear water. 'Are you coming in?' she said.

He nodded, beginning to unbutton his shirt. She slipped under the water, turned and swam along the line of the rocks. He undressed quickly and dived in.

For half an hour or so they chased and flirted in the water, pretending an indifference to their nakedness. When a fisherman rowed slowly past and seemed likely to choose the cove to stop in, they waved and called and splashed about until he decided to move on.

It was a flawless day. The trees waved above them in a soft breeze, the cigales chirped and trilled in waves of sound. When they had driven off the fisherman Alex swam towards the bank. Holding herself afloat by one hand on a jutting rock, she called to Martin. He turned and swam toward her. 'Look the other way,' she said. 'I'm getting out.'

He turned his back obediently and began to swim in a wide half circle. As he came back in the direction of the bank he could see that she was standing on the flat limestone slab, her towel wrapped round her tight across the breasts and tucked in underneath her left arm. Her legs were bare to above the knees. Her hair was already drying into thick golden strands.

He reached the rock and she threw him his towel and turned back to the hamper. He climbed out and wrapped the towel around his waist. The sun beat down hot on his shoulders; high above the river a pair of buzzards circled slowly in a dance of love.

They were both silent now as, highly conscious of the tenuous fastenings of their towels, they stretched out on the blanket opposite each other.

Minutes passed. Several minutes.

He reached forward slowly. She knew what he was about to do and she made no attempt to stop him. With the tips of his fingers he brushed her towel over her left breast at the point it was tucked in. The end loosened. Very slowly the towel fell from her.

She rolled forward slightly on her hip and stretched for the fastening of his towel. It fell away quickly. 'Equal,' she said, looking at his erect penis.

They were too afraid to make love. But for an hour they kissed and fondled and rolled on top of each other until one extra movement of her hand, one extra movement of exquisite friction against her belly and his spasm sent the sperm shooting.

She lay back gasping, one hand between her legs.

He looked down at her mouth shaped as if to scream. Then she jerked her knees up. Moaning.

He held out a hand to her and she pulled him close, so that she was half under him.

For moments they lay together until the sun began to sear his back and his sperm dried on the golden bloom of her skin.

They loaded the hamper into the boat and Martin took the oars. It was a different journey back. The current was strong and progress was slow. Huge grey-black clouds brought the rumble of thunder over the hills. The water slapped the side of the boat. The fisherman, content with cloud shadow, watched them curiously as he hung his line from the back of the boat.

They reached the stone bridge, tied up the boat and carried the hamper to the *Kübelwagen*. They had hardly spoken a dozen words since they left the cove.

The storm burst upon them with the ferocity that only weeks of blazing sunshine can produce. As they ran for the shelter of the stone bridge the rain was already slashing down, the thunderclaps following hard upon the flashes of lightning. From under the arch of the bridge they watched nature wreak its frenzy in the sky as rainwater gushed and coursed down the rocky bank. They sat on the ledge of cut stone a foot or two from each other and watched while, framed by the arch of the bridge, the storm moved away and the rain began to slacken.

'Do you think they'll come to an agreement, Emil and Pierre?' she said suddenly.

'They're brothers,' he said, 'they understand each other. They're from the Waldviertel. They're bound by a tradition they can't escape.'

She was, he saw, looking at him strangely.

'Perhaps they're no longer bound by the same tradition,' she said.

He put his arm round her waist and drew her close to him. 'What do you mean by that?'

'Emil's changed, you know. He bitterly regrets what he did last year, involving you as Elisabeth's first invited.'

'He must have known we'd hurt you.'

She shook her head. 'It's not only that. Not as narrow as that. He's seen for himself what Adolf Hitler really is. Where he's leading Germany.'

'From victory to victory,' Martin said.

She looked at him for a moment. 'He's leading Germany back into some Wagnerian make-believe,' she said. 'All mists and soldier-peasants and blood feuds. He's leading German civilisation to utter destruction.'

'Maybe you live too close to it. Seen from New York the new Germany doesn't look all bad.'

He could see she was angry.

'I think you believe,' she said, 'that it isn't important which Germany you support. Perhaps you don't really think there's any difference between the Germany of Goethe and the ordinary baker's wife or student and the Germany of these swaggering bullies who make people clean the ordure off the streets with their bare hands. Simply because they're Jews. I've seen that, Martin, in Vienna, with my own eyes.'

'Jesus,' he said, 'there are New York cops who ought to be in the penitentiary. They're exceptions. They happen in every country.'

'In my country, for the moment, they're not exceptions. They're state policy. They're part of a huge Nordic myth based on dimwit philosophers and pseudo-racial scientists. A lot of us at Munich University, professors and students, believe they're evil. You've got to take a stand, Martin. You, me, Emil, Pierre – we all have to.'

The rain had stopped but water dripped from the stones of the arch above their heads. The sun reappeared to dry the wet stone. A lizard emerged from a crack beside him and darted and stopped and darted again towards the light.

She stood up watching the sunlight glance through the raindrops dripping from the bridge. 'What you did with Elisabeth is unimportant. Except to me, of course. *That's* what Hitler's Nazi Party is about! His own family comes from the Waldviertel, for God's sake. Don't you understand that he's dragging Europe back into the fog of deceit and cruelty that we've spent centuries trying to struggle out of?'

She walked slowly from under the arch and climbed the slope towards the *Kübelwagen*. As he walked beside her, she said: 'I thought Americans rejected all this foul slush.'

He knew there was no use now in talking about neutrality, about Europe's politics not being America's concern, or his own. He watched her get into the *Kübelwagen*. Her face was set. She sat with her hands in her lap not looking at him.

He suffered a strong sense of defeat. But there was anger too. Perhaps Emil had changed, but Pierre still believed in bonds created by the wild tracks of the Waldviertel. Only his father, he realised for the first time, rejected the family myths. His father and now Alex herself. He climbed into the driving seat and started the *Kübelwagen*. But it all seemed to fit so well, the idea of a new Germany rising through the mists of its own ancient past. Something in Martin responded. Was that totally wrong?

They drove back the short distance up to the chateau without speaking. Inside at one of the great twelve-drawer desks an ancient Frenchman in a black frock coat was reading through a document, his lips moving, the French sentences emerging as a bee's drone. Emil was standing by his side. The countess was sitting on a Louis Quinze chair, cross-legged as if she were twenty-five rather than sixty-five, smoking a cigarette from an ivory holder. There was no sign of Pierre.

The old Frenchman finished his reading, removed his pince-nez and looked up at Emil. 'The document is complete, Monsieur. If the parties will sign.'

Martin and Alex watched as first Emil and then the countess signed the pages of stiff pale-blue paper.

'*Ça y est!*' said the Frenchman.

'You have made me so happy,' said the countess.

'I fell in love the moment I arrived,' said Emil.

Martin and Alex looked on in bafflement.

'Now the document of assignment,' said the Frenchman. 'If Ma'moiselle would sign here.' He looked toward Alex.

She came forward, half led by Emil.

'Just sign,' he said. 'Just sign.'

She bent and put her name to a single sheet of the blue paper. As she pondered over it she drew in her breath sharply.

'A little birthday present for you, my darling,' Emil said. 'From this moment you are the chatelaine of this most beautiful chateau.'

Martin turned and left the room. He knew that for Alex it should have been one of the happiest days of her life.

It was a hot night full of the sound of cigales and the wheeling, fluttering of huge moths.

They dined at a small table on the stone terrace overlooking the river. Soft light fell from the chateau windows above them. A pair of candles in brass candlesticks flickered on the table.

Emil and Pierre had hardly spoken. Alexina made one or two attempts to gain their interest then stole her hand to Martin's leg. 'Perhaps Martin and I should take our coffee into the drawing room,' she said to Emil.

He glanced across at Pierre who was pouring himself a brandy, pretending not to have heard, pretending he didn't care.

'No, stay,' Emil said. 'Someday the House of Janus will belong to you two. Stay and hear.'

This time Pierre's head came up. He swirled brandy in the balloon glass. Then nodded.

Alex's hand tightened on Martin's leg, communicating alarm.

Emil took the brandy decanter from beside Pierre and poured a glass for himself. 'I want to be as fair as possible in describing our differences. If Pierre wants to correct me, he's at liberty to do so.'

Pierre grunted into his brandy, turned his chair, crossed his legs and ostentatiously looked out into the dark hills on the other side of the river.

Martin, feeling the tension in Alex, realised suddenly that she *knew* something at least of what had passed between the two brothers.

'I believe,' Emil said softly in English, 'that the rule of Adolf Hitler will bring first Europe and finally Germany to its knees. I won't deny that Alex's arguments have been important in persuading me. Every German, everyone like you, Martin, who loves Germany, must face the truth. Wherever in the world this man sprang from, he must be destroyed. And he sprang from the Waldviertel.'

'So what difference does that make?' Pierre growled.

'Perhaps it means we have a special responsibility,' Alex said.

Pierre ignored her.

'We have a responsibility to do all we can, *not* to prevent Hitler's rush to disaster. We are beginning to hear stories of the fate of the Jews in Poland which chill the blood. I have received information that already plans are being drawn up to attack Russia. We are a state ruled by a lunatic. As one simple German industrialist, I know what I can do. I can't shoot him, I can't foment rebellion – but I am a manufacturer of a powerful economic tool. I make money. I print banknotes. One-thousand-mark bills for the Reichsbank. If I were to increase the supply . . .'

'It's a crazy idea,' Pierre said savagely.

'No. It will work,' Emil said deliberately. He turned to Martin. 'You know, Martin, that the strength of a nation's economy depends on many things. One of them is confidence in its currency. So . . .' He held both hands in the air. 'I will flood Germany and Europe with one-thousand-mark currency bills, genuine ones printed by me, distributed through banks in Europe. Within months Hitler's currency will be compromised?'

'Within three months,' Pierre said, still looking out at the hills, 'you will be in jail – and the name of Coburg, your name and mine, will be dirt in every central bank in the world. You do this, Emil, and you'll ruin me.'

'Pierre,' Alex said softly, 'when the US comes into the war, and we all know it will, the name of Coburg will be honoured as the first to resist Hitler.'

'The contents of graves are honoured,' Pierre said savagely. 'Corpses, dry bones. You're not going to do that to the Coburgs, Emil.'

Emil looked down at his drink. Martin took the decanter and poured brandy into the two remaining balloon glasses.

'Let Martin and Alex hear my proposal,' Emil said.

'Oh yes.' In the candlelight Pierre's face was flushed with anger. 'Having smashed his own company to smithereens, he now wants half my company. A fifty–fifty share in Coburg Banknote.'

Martin gaped.

'In return for the Janus,' Emil said.

'Which is rightly part mine anyway.'

'Which you refused financing for.'

In the silence round the table a nightjar shrieked across the river valley.

'I have made arrangements,' Emil said to Martin, 'for Dorotta, Alex and myself to escape as soon as, or even before, the Gestapo knows what's happening. I think it will take a few months. My plan is to come to New York and to join Pierre as a partner. Together we will make the House of Janus greater than it ever was. We will take on the aristocracy of banknote printing. And we will win.'

Pierre slammed the table. 'No. Because we'll be seen as the Coburgs, the people that committed the greatest sin possible in our world. Forgery.'

'There are greater sins by far.'

'Who will care? You will destroy the Coburg name.' He stood up, towering in his anger. 'I will not have it, Emil! Do you hear? I will not have it!'

They stood together on the terrace, disturbed, frightened by what they'd seen.

'They'll never come together on this,' Martin said.

'Of course not. Pierre's thinking of one thing only, the future of Coburg Banknote of New York.'

'What's so wrong with that?' Martin said defensively. 'What Emil's planning to do goes against the basic trust governments must have in their currency printers.'

'It's show, Martin. All front, you know that. You've seen them wheeling and dealing in China. You've seen them bribing for contracts. They're buccaneers, adventurers. Except now suddenly Emil sees there's something more important than the House of Janus.'

'It's crazy,' Martin muttered. 'He's risking himself, Dorotta and you for a temporary disruption of the German currency. It's childish!'

She hit him, a stinging blow across his cheek. 'It's not childish if you're a Jew on the run. Or a student at Munich University in Dachau Camp. It's not childish at all if your nine-year-old Hitler Youth son denounces you for anti-government talk!'

He was looking at her in shock. She became silent. Tears streamed down her cheeks.

'I promised to drink a *digestif* with the countess,' he said. 'Maybe I'd better go.'

She nodded, looking at him, willing him to make one step toward her. 'I'm sorry,' she said.

He turned away and walked quickly toward the staircase.

The blow fell less than an hour later.

'When you and Alexina are married,' the old countess had said, 'you must come to stay with me in my apartment in Paris.'

'We won't be married,' Martin had told her, the wine and whisky now having a marked effect on his speech. 'I told you. She thinks I'm a barbarian. She's given her life to opposing Hitler. Like a nun, damn it!'

The countess looked at him. 'She's not alone. Many hate what's happening in Germany. Many fear it. It is not something to be neutral about. Alex is right.'

'Listen,' Martin said, recklessly pouring himself another large whisky, 'I'm not a card-carrying Nazi Party member. I'm not even German, for God's sake.'

'Your beautiful Alexina is saying that doesn't make any difference. She's saying that evil must be seen to be evil.'

The internal telephone rang and the countess lifted the ivory and silver handset beside her chair. For a few moments she listened. 'Yes, he's here,' she said. 'Yes, I will give him your message.'

'Your grandfather wants you downstairs. Immediately, it seems. They have been searching for you all over the chateau.'

She watched Martin drain his glass. 'Your chateau as well,' she added, 'when you and Alexina are married. It was Emil's intention from the first time he saw it, you know.'

'What intention?'

'That the Château de Belfresnes should be for both of you. He has told me many times how happy that would make him.' She laughed. 'Ah, what strange people you Coburgs are! Look at Emil and Pierre, two great brutes hulking around the chateau talking, talking, laughing, laughing, fighting, fighting. Murder in their eyes one moment, the love of two brothers the next.' They walked to the door of the circular, turret room. 'There are some good things about having a tradition too.'

'Alex doesn't think so.'

'That's because we need to choose from the past with great care. I'm not sure,' she kissed him on the cheek, 'that you Coburg men are very good at that.'

He left the room and stood looking out of the arched window on the landing at the sweep of the river between the cliffs. He was drunk. He was angry, miserable, repentant, apologetic all at the same time. Most of all he was desperate to see Alex. He came down the winding staircase, his shoulder banging against the stone walls. He walked unsteadily along the lower landing until he reached the head of the main staircase. He could hear his grandfather's voice thundering through the lower floor. He focused with difficulty on the suitcases stacked in the hall and saw that some of them belonged to him.

Below him there was much banging of doors. Emil's raised voice said or rather shouted in German: 'Very well, if you want to behave like a spoilt child, behave like one.'

Pierre's voice, in English, roared as he entered the hall: 'So much for the spirit of the House of Janus.'

He appeared below, looked up and saw Martin. 'We're leaving,' he snarled. 'Now.'

Martin came down the staircase. 'I must say goodbye,' he said.

'We're leaving *now*.'

German soldiers had begun to take the suitcases outside.

Martin stood his ground. 'I won't go without saying goodbye,' he said.

Pierre looked at him as if he was about to hurl himself at his grandson. Then suddenly, strangely, his shoulders seemed to droop. 'I'll wait for you,' he said, 'outside in the car.'

Martin found Emil and Alex in the salon. They had been talking earnestly together and stopped when Martin entered. 'I've come to say goodbye,' he said.

Emil stood up and clasped Martin to him. 'Goodbye, Martin,' he said. 'I fear it will be a long time and perhaps in very different circumstances before we meet again. In the meantime, do not let Pierre do anything he would regret. He's an impetuous man.'

Again he pressed Martin to him, then released him and walked quickly out of the room. As the door closed behind him Martin turned toward Alex. She stood upright, her hands resting lightly on the back of a Directoire chair.

'There's nothing more to say, is there?' She smoothed her hands along the walnut rail of the chair.

'I don't know,' Martin said. 'I'm pretty drunk and I'm not sure how clearly I'm seeing things, but I've been talking to the countess.'

'She's a survivor.'

'She's also got a lot of common sense.'

'She told you to go back to New York and forget the whole dirty business here in Europe.'

'No.'

'What did she say?'

'I think she said we're all part of what's happening. British, French, Germans and certainly Americans too.'

'It's what I said.'

He shook his head. 'Not quite,' he said. 'The countess says we shouldn't throw away the past. We should choose from it what we want. Like a young woman, she said, going through the jewellery she has inherited from her grandmother.'

She came from behind the chair and stood in front of him and slid her arms round his neck. 'Perhaps,' she said. 'Perhaps.'

'I will always love you,' she said.

Out in the courtyard Pierre was hitting the horn. A long series of harsh blasts. 'Jesus Christ,' he said.

Then she kissed him.

· Twenty-eight ·

Reaching the foreshore Celine put the mare into a gallop. She found it difficult not to laugh out loud with the exhilaration of the moment. On the third finger of her left hand the diamond flashed in the sunlight and was answered by the sparkling of the waters of the Sound.

Island House stood on its long slope of hillside set out like the drawings for some English eighteenth-century home and garden. From the beach she turned and rode at a canter now, up the slope of the broad gravel alley which brought her to the front of the house. Merchant, one of the grooms, had seen her coming and was there to take the mare.

'Is my mother at home?' Celine asked him, already on her way toward the front door.

'No, Miss.' The groom grimaced at her back. 'She left for lunch with Mrs Tindale about an hour ago.'

Celine stopped and turned. She was bursting with impatience to tell someone. 'Is my father in?'

'I believe he's in his rooms, Miss. He went fishing early and I seen him come back about ten. Didn't go out since.'

She turned away and entered the house. Her father was coming down the stairs.

'A good ride?' he asked. 'Where did you go?'

'Along the foreshore. I like to get down to a good gallop.' She pressed the bell at the head of the servants' stairs. When she heard one of the maids coming up the uncarpeted stairs she called down to her: 'Bring a bottle of champagne and two glasses up to the library.'

'You've got a friend coming in for lunch?' her father asked, riffling through the mail on a silver tray.

'No. I thought you and I could share a bottle together.'

His eyes were raised to hers in surprise. He smiled. 'Very well.' He opened the door to the library. 'And to what do we owe this?' he said following her in.

'It's not unusual to drink a glass of champagne to celebrate, is it?'

'Ah.' He nodded. 'You've heard from Pierre and Martin. The discussions with Emil went well.'

'No.' She smiled slowly.

'But they've arrived in Paris?'

'No, they never made it to Paris. They met Emil in south-west France.'

'And you've heard nothing since?'

She opened a cigarette box and slowly took a cigarette. 'Not a word.'

'If it's not success in commercial battle, what are we about to drink to?'

'You've always told me commercial success isn't everything.'

'Perhaps because it always eluded me.'

He knew from the barely controlled smile of triumph that she was taunting him. It was a familiar smile he had seen a thousand times on his daughter's face when as a child she had gone behind his back to her mother to have an unpopular instruction countermanded. But they had drifted so far apart that she no longer had the power of irritation or pain. He sometimes asked himself if his newly assumed role of the watchful father was not more of an attempt to get even with Pierre than it was to protect his own daughter. Looking at her now as she lit her cigarette with those slow mannered movements she had copied from her mother, John Coburg registered how much he disliked her.

'As you know, Celine, commercial success isn't the only one that's eluded me.'

She waited while the butler entered the library with an ice-bucket and champagne glasses on a tray. He opened the bottle, poured two glasses and withdrew. They took a glass each.

'You must have felt it a success when you prevented Pierre taking me to Europe with him.' Again that smile.

'I did what I thought was necessary,' he said carefully.

'What I choose to do is my business,' she said in a flat, hard tone.

'You're nineteen,' he said. 'Unmarried. Whether I like it or not I'm responsible for you.'

She laughed. 'No longer,' she said.

'Is that what we're drinking to?'

She nodded, lifting her glass. 'That's what we're drinking to.' She raised her left hand, stretching her fingers to display the diamond. 'To my engagement,' she said. 'Jack Aston asked me to marry him this morning.'

They had emerged into the horror of the real world a few miles from the chateau. The great surge of peoples that had brought Dutch, Belgian and northern French down to the Dordogne and the Lot rivers was now fully reversed. Like water in an unsteady pot, millions of refugees were now flowing back north to their homes and farms. Against this tide of tired, angry, worried and distressed humanity it was impossible to proceed. The first night they slept in the car; the next morning they began to edge forward again, Martin at the wheel, Pierre grey-faced and burning with anger.

Hour after hour they moved forward and stopped. The sun beat down bringing the temperature inside the car to intolerable levels. Somewhere before Cahors the limousine came to a halt. A broken down cart blocked their way. An implacable stream of haggard faces flowing in the opposite direction offered no hope of persuading them to pull over.

'Pierre,' Martin said, the steering wheel burning in his hands, dust and sweat pouring down his face, 'let's go back. Let's go back to the chateau for a few days until this madness is over.'

Pierre sat slumped in the passenger seat. He had removed his jacket and rolled up his sleeves. His collar gaped loose. In eight hours they had covered less than twenty miles of the two-hundred-mile journey to the Pyrenees.

'If we turn back,' Martin urged him, 'we can go with the flow. By nightfall we'll be back at the chateau.'

'We'll find a hotel here,' Pierre growled.

Martin looked at him. A hotel? Was his grandfather crazy? With the population swollen by millions, what chance would there be of a hotel room?

'We've got money,' Pierre said, still looking straight ahead through the thick yellow dust of the windshield at a peasant struggling to right his collapsed cart. 'Money talks.'

Martin took a pull on the water bottle. He felt hung over, his temper on a short leash. 'Face it,' he said angrily, 'we're not going to find a hotel room tonight.'

'Listen to me, Martin,' Pierre said after a few moments, 'I can't go back. I can't go crawling cap in hand to my own brother. I've burnt my boats. I called him every name it's possible to call your brother. Get me back to New York City, Martin. I don't care how the hell you do it, just get me back there. I should never have made this trip. I should have stayed where I was. Negotiate from strength, Martin. Always negotiate from strength. Just get me back home.'

Martin looked at the huge figure next to him. His great head had slumped forward. He lifted his cigar to his lips and drew on it. 'What a goddamn mess,' he said, smoke breaking untidily from his mouth. 'What a goddamn mess.'

Martin sat with his hands on the wheel. To feel pity for this huge figure, so dominant in his life, was so unfamiliar that he felt sick to his stomach. He restarted the car and began to reverse it up the bank.

'We're not going back to the chateau?' Pierre said.

Martin shook his head. 'No. We're going back until we can turn west through the villages off the main road.'

'West?'

'To Bordeaux. It's still being used by United States shipping. We'll be able to pick up a berth there.'

In the library at Island House, Celine had watched her father's face crumple. He had not cried tears, but he had cried nevertheless. After a few moments he looked up at her. 'Why, Celine? Why did you do it?'

'That's not a question a father usually asks his daughter, when she announces her engagement to the most elegible bachelor in the Hamptons.'

'Stop fooling with me, please. Jack is twenty years older than you. We both know he's not your type.'

'What type is he, Dad?' she asked coldly.

He swallowed. 'I think you know what I mean. He's a quiet, gentle person. He's not interested in business. He lives very much his own life. He . . .'

'Jumped at the chance to be engaged to me,' she said.

'He's always wanted children. He's always felt he owes it to his family to have children.'

'You know what Jack Aston is,' she said sharply. 'He's bisexual. One side of his nature fights the other. He's not a happy kink.'

'I asked you why you're doing this.'

'You sound as if you don't approve. He's your best friend, isn't he?'

'He's my best friend, yes.'

'Of course you'll give me away,' she said briskly. 'Jack and I are thinking of the early fall for the wedding.'

He closed his eyes in pain.

She stood up. 'He likes girls, you know. He likes me. He's not a difficult man to deal with. Simple, in fact. Maybe even simple-minded.'

'What are you saying all this for? What is this all about?'

'You don't imagine I'm gasping with love for a seedy, middle-aged nancy, do you?'

'I don't think you love Jack, no.'

She nodded. 'Good. That's clear. Now you can have him back on one condition. You move out of this house and you stay out. I will brook no interference from you, do you understand?'

'My God,' he said, 'I knew you had no morals but I had not quite realised how totally devoid of humanity you were at the same time.'

'It's too late for lectures.'

'Yes.' He walked over and placed his untasted glass of champagne on the tray. 'When will you tell Jack you're breaking off the engagement?'

'As soon as you've packed your bags and gone.'

'As soon as you have Pierre to yourself.'

She nodded crisply.

'To do whatever foul things you want to with him.'

She looked at him for several moments. 'I'll choose how I run my life,' she said. 'Now you go and pack.'

They reached Lisbon a week later by a Panamanian-registered freighter from Bordeaux. One hundred and thirty-five passengers had bought sleeping room on the deck, mostly German Jews who had settled in France and who were now forced to be on the move again. Disembarking at Lisbon, bearded, indescribably filthy, Pierre and Martin shuffled forward in the long line waiting for their entry documentation to be completed.

A taxi from the port area cost them their last American money. Only by checking in at the Hotel Bristol where they were known from their last visit were they not turned away on sight.

Pierre had hit rock bottom. He was convinced that Emil was intending to destroy the Coburg Banknote Corporation. On the long journey to Lisbon long periods of total silence had alternated with a garrulous excitement in which he talked for hours, speculating, cursing Emil, vowing he would get even. Then he would drop into maudlin reminiscences of their boyhood in Waldviertel, of shooting rabbits together or illegally trapping deer when the winter was hard and food was desperately short.

'He has no pity, my brother Emil,' he had said as they were waiting on the only bridge across the Garonne river into Bordeaux. A mass of vehicles, carts, trucks, private cars with mattresses still tied to the roof, solidly blocked the ancient bridge. Between one vehicle and another there was so little room that people entering the city on foot were obliged to clamber across the top of vehicles to reach the other bank of the river.

Sitting in the by now battered limousine in the relentless heat, with the angry shouts of frustrated people and the neighing of crowded, frightened horses all round them, Pierre raged against his twin brother. 'You see, Martin, he's arrogant. He can't let the world take its course. He wants to intervene, shape it.'

'And you?'

'All I want is to own the greatest banknote printing business in the world.'

Suddenly the traffic moved again, jerkily at first, then flowing out of the bridge in a cacophony of blaring klaxons, shouting men and neighing horses into the heart of Bordeaux, the Armistice capital of France.

At Lisbon Airport Martin was informed that it would be at least two weeks before two seats would be available on the Pan American Clipper service to New York. He haggled, he pleaded a sick grandfather, he offered money. But in the end he could do no better than two tickets for mid-July.

For Martin the two weeks passed strangely. Part of each day was spent drinking with Oliver Sutchley in the Bristol bar. Part was spent ringing the German embassy to see if Elizabeth had yet returned from a period of leave. Mostly he was concerned with his grandfather. Pierre now passed all day in his hotel room, much of it in bed, his energy and vigour seemingly drained from him. Sometimes in the evening he would drink whisky and then his mind would seem to ramble through the past with Emil from the sunny village childhood to the betrayal of the last few days. 'Coburg Banknote,' he said, 'has always been more successful than Imprimerie Coburg.'

His lips trembled with anger. He gulped at his whisky, sucked hard on his cigar. It seemed nothing would control the trembling. 'But what will anything matter in a month or two? Emil will have pulled us both down. No central bank in the world will give a banknote contract to the Coburg *forgers*. The House of Judas!'

He scratched at his grey-stubbled chin. 'He must be stopped, Martin. For God's sake, we've got to stop him!'

Martin saw that he was close to sobbing.

The sight of Pierre, so much reduced, affected Martin strongly. He looked at his grandfather now as he sat up in bed with a bottle of whisky and noted the rheumy eyes and the twitch of the chin which once meant impatient decisiveness and now seemed all but uncontrollable.

He was not sure if he felt love for him. Not sure any longer that he felt respect. But he did feel deeply moved that life should so build him up and the avenging angel, in the form of his own twin brother, cut him down so hard. Was it pity then that was the cause of the turmoil inside him?

At night he walked the elegant eighteenth-century streets of Lisbon. Oliver Sutchley would be waiting for him in the Bristol to share a nightcap and explain why each day's news made Britain's defeat more certain. His contacts with the German Gestapo intelligence units, highly active in Portugal, were growing every day. Even Martin who didn't like the man felt bound to warn him that the British would shoot him as a spy if he didn't behave more circumspectly.

Below all this, occupying every available chink in his thoughts, were his feelings about Alex. He had reached the devastating conclusion that he could not love her. A girl who would destroy Pierre's life achievement for her own nineteen-year-old political ideas. Who would risk destroying everything Martin felt for her. Who was recklessly arrogant with the love he had wanted to give her. How could he love her?

He was too inexperienced to see that his seesaw reaction to Alexina was not the result of her political views or even some sense that she and Emil had deeply wounded Pierre. Instead it was the impossibility of facing life without her that he was reacting to, cultivating an anger against her, feeding on it until all elements of rationality were gone.

These were the nights he would feel a massive burst of rage against her as he roamed the ill-lit streets of the Portuguese capital watching the drifting street-walkers among the ill-lit colonnaded squares of the city.

Rambling, drunken sessions with Oliver Sutchley seemed his only release.

It was a few days before they were due to leave Lisbon. Martin had been lunching alone in the dining room of the Bristol. He sat at a table in the middle of the room which he had come to see as neutral territory. On the right, in a favoured section under the great windows, the Germans occupied a group of tables. On the left, in a dark corner of the dining room reflecting their current lack of success in the war, sat members of the British embassy, the captains of merchant ships, port shippers on their way home to join the army. In all public places where the Germans and British met at least one policeman was always present.

He was about to leave the table when he heard German voices in the hotel lobby. Looking up he saw Elisabeth Coburg detach herself from a group of Germans and hurry towards him. He stood up. Elisabeth stopped before him. In a voice that was strangely flat and formal, she said: 'Martin, I've just got back from Germany. A most appalling thing has happened at Lingfeld. Emil and Alex have been denounced to the Gestapo.'

· Twenty-nine ·

They had driven down the gravel drive to the house with old Wilhelm waving as they passed. The trees were bright summer-green and the sky between their gently moving tops was blue with a scud of faint white cloud.

Six members of the household, women in black dresses and white aprons, lined the terrace steps. The housekeeper who, now that most of the younger men were with the Wehrmacht, was the senior member of the staff, came out across the terrace. She came to a stop in front of them, her face unsmiling.

'Where is my wife?' Emil's voice boomed as he crossed the terrace. 'Has she gone into Munich for the day?'

Alex noticed the housekeeper's eyes were red. She had been crying. Or perhaps just not slept well.

Emil and the housekeeper exchanged formal greetings. 'Madame Coburg is not here,' she said.

Alex could see the tension in the woman's face.

'Munich, uh? The shops. Although when she sees what we've brought back from Paris for her . . .'

'There are two gentlemen here,' the housekeeper said quickly as two men in grey suits emerged from the french windows and walked across the terrace toward the steps on which they were all standing.

A strange cold breeze seemed to surround Alexina. Men like this, men in grey suits which were neither well nor badly cut, but tailored more with that neutral competence of a uniform, men like these she had seen emerging from the arch under the medieval town hall on Munich's Marienplatz. It was said that the Geheimes Staatspolizei, the police force everybody called the Gestapo, rented the cellar rooms of the old building from the municipality.

The two men came to a stop in front of Emil and Alexina. They were not young or clean cut as somehow Alex's terrified imagination was insisting they be. One was about fifty with the round face of a country shopkeeper.

The other was younger, pale-faced, his oiled dark hair combed back in straight slicks along the side of his head.

'Madame was taken away yesterday,' the housekeeper whispered quickly.

The man with the black hair came toward Emil. His lips seemed to Alex to move before the words emerged. He had long yellow teeth. 'Emil Coburg?' he said.

'Yes.'

'Inspector Krebs of the Munich Gestapo. You're to come with me.'

'Do I have the right to ask why?'

'No.'

'Am I under arrest?'

'If you like.' The Gestapo inspector shrugged his indifference at the letter of the law.

'Can I bring a bag?'

'No.'

'No clean clothes?'

The man's red lips parted. The yellow teeth smiled. 'We'll send them on,' he said.

His round-faced companion nodded.

'Our car's round the side of the house,' Krebs said. 'Get a move on.'

'Alex . . .' Emil turned toward his daughter. Krebs came forward and delivered a loud open-hand smack to Emil's cheek. 'Get going,' he said.

Emil turned in shock. His back was to Alex.

'And you,' Krebs said. 'Alexina Maria Coburg?'

'Yes.' She felt an overwhelming need to act with dignity. Krebs's assistant was already pushing Emil toward the car parked at the side of the house.

Alex drew herself up in anticipation of the inspector's next question. He smiled. 'Get your fat ass across there.' He jerked his head to the car. In that moment she realised that the battles of the future, beyond those for life or limb, would be for some shred of dignity to sustain her. 'Goodbye, Frau Kessling,' she said to the housekeeper, shaking hands with her before Krebs could stop her.

'Goodbye, Fräulein,' the housekeeper said, emboldened by her manner.

Taller than the man, Alex looked down at him, her lips compressed. Then she turned quickly away and walked ahead of the Gestapo inspector toward the waiting car.

*

At 2.30 p.m. on the day of the arrest Pierre returned from the Lisbon Gestapo office on Avenida Lisboa. Like many Americans fleeing through Portugal he had been astonished to discover that what was a foreign police organisation was housed in such a large and prominent building. But no government on the continent of Europe any longer had the power to refuse a Gestapo request.

Martin was waiting for his grandfather in the bar of the Hotel Bristol. He watched Pierre come towards him shaking his head.

'There is nothing to be done,' Pierre said heavily.

'You saw the head of the Gestapo himself?'

'Yes. A thick-built chap with a dirty collar. He wasn't forthcoming.'

'Did he tell you anything at all?'

'He told me that it was not Gestapo policy to discuss arrests. Or even to confirm them.'

'You offered him money?'

'It didn't work.'

'Good God,' Martin said, 'you were there over three hours. Did he say nothing?'

'Yes,' Pierre said. 'He finally agreed that Alexina had been arrested. Emil and Dorotta as well on the basis of the *Sippenhaft* law. Family guilt.'

'So where is Alex now?'

He was silent. 'Under arrest,' he said at length in a strangely even voice. 'In some Gestapo basement, I suppose. Being questioned.'

'She was denounced, Elisabeth said. That means by someone.'

'My Gestapo friend said, finally said, that Alex had been interfering with racial matters. You know what that means? It means she's been helping Jews. Did you know that?'

'I knew she had. Elisabeth knew as well.'

'Maybe others, too,' Pierre agreed. 'Too many others.'

'Will they go to prison?'

Pierre was silent.

'Did he say that, the Gestapo man?'

Pierre shook his head. 'They're finished, Martin. Finished.'

For the first time Martin's imagination lifted from reprimands by lecturing magistrates, to single nights in police cells, to month-long sentences even. 'Finished,' he said, dry-mouthed. 'What do you mean, finished?'

'It's a very tough regime,' Pierre said. 'It doesn't like opposition.'

'What does finished mean?' Martin's voice rose.

'Don't give me the melodrama,' Pierre said harshly. 'You know what finished means in Germany today.'

'That's what the Gestapo man told you?'

'The boss told me a lot of things, Martin,' Pierre said, draining his Americano and pushing his glass towards the barman for another. 'I took him to lunch.'

'You took him to lunch?'

'When I saw how the ground lay, I realised I was going to need his good offices.'

'To get them released?'

'No.' Pierre shook his head. 'That's beyond possibility now.'

'Then what?' Martin said. 'If we can't get them released why do you take a goon like that to lunch, for Christ's sake?'

Pierre looked at him. 'You're a good boy,' he said. 'But you're young. You don't understand. If there's nothing we can do for Emil and the others, certain steps have to be taken.'

'What steps?'

Pierre turned away from him, took his Americano and slowly half-turned back. 'It was my bounden duty,' he said. 'I made an offer to the Gestapo for Imprimerie Coburg, its engravings, plant and patents.'

'You dirty bastard!' Martin swung on his bar stool to face his grandfather. 'Are you a goddamn ghoul? Your twin brother is taken by the Gestapo and you go right off and make them an offer. Not an offer of every goddamn penny you own to get them released. You make them a slimy offer for the Janus patents you want to get your hands on!'

Pierre got off his bar stool and turned toward the door. But Martin was already standing next to him, his hand gripping his grandfather's arm. 'Denounced,' Martin said, 'denounced by who?'

'Take your hand off me, boy,' Pierre said icily. 'Or I'll knock you down.'

'You won't. You'll sit back on that goddamn stool and you'll tell me exactly what happened. And I'll tell you now that if it was you that denounced them, I'll kill you.'

They both faced each other, two men, several inches over six feet, in shock. In the last ten seconds the accusations they had made, the threats they had offered, would change their relationship for ever.

'I want you to tell me,' Martin said in a hard, quieter voice. 'Did you?'

Pierre faced him. 'Did I? No.' He paused. 'Did you?'

'For God's sake!'

Pierre threw two dollars onto the bar. 'For two weeks you've been mooning around the bars of Lisbon. Drinking too much. You've been talking to Sutchley, haven't you?'

'To Oliver Sutchley? So what?'

Pierre started for the door, Martin hurrying after him. 'Sometimes I wonder just how bright you are, boy. Oliver Sutchley speaks to the Germans, you know that.'

'I know he's pretty pro-German. What's that got to do with it?'

'You didn't get drunk with him?'

'I have, yes.'

Pierre stopped at the elevators and gave his floor to the attendant. 'Did you ever talk about Alex?'

'Probably.'

'Boasted a little about what a hell of a girl she was? About the Jewish family she'd helped in Paris?' The elevator arrived and Pierre stepped in and turned to face Martin. 'Did you, boy? Is it just possible?'

Aghast, Martin watched the elevator doors slide closed.

They hauled the body of John Doyle Coburg out of the sea off Montauk Point. He was unconscious but his oiled-cotton windcheater, acting as a rough life-jacket, had brought him to the surface. Of the two fishermen in the boat one was Dr Stephens of Montauk, a man who had seen more drownings and near drownings than he could remember. The principle he worked on was to assume life still existed, however much death was indicated. In this way he had saved many from drowning. In this way he condemned John Coburg to a life he had no wish to preserve.

Only Jack Aston was prepared to look after the brain-damaged husk of John Coburg. In the years to come Aston was to be seen lowering his invalid friend from the back of the pickup he had had specially converted, and wheeling his chair to the clapboard general store at Springs.

Late at night the airport lobby at La Guardia was seldom crowded. The cream-coloured carpet which ran the length of the room was soft underfoot. Gleaming leather cases were being carried by neatly uniformed young men. Passengers for Chicago and Minneapolis drifted from the restaurant toward the flight gate.

Celine stood at the Pan American desk and stared down at the young man in his powder-blue uniform.

'The Lisbon Clipper was early, Miss. Landing was half an hour before schedule.'

'Where are the passengers now?' she asked icily.

'Those waiting to be met are in the Clipper lounge, Miss. Some are still clearing customs.'

'Page Mr Coburg for me,' she said. 'Tell him I'll be in the President's bar.'

The clerk checked the list. 'There were two seats booked in the name of Coburg on the Lisbon flight, Miss.'

She nodded.

'But only one seat was taken.'

She frowned suddenly. 'Only one seat?'

'It appears Mr Martin Coburg didn't make the flight, Miss.'

PART THREE

· Daniel ·

· Thirty ·

I flew back to New York keyed to a fever pitch of excitement. I was Martin Coburg.

Somewhere I had a life story.

The Coburgs were rich, that much Zorubin had told me. They were the owners of the Coburg Banknote Corporation. That single fact in itself made understandable what I'd come to think of as my obsession with checking banknote serial numbers, guessing the length of time a bill had been in circulation from the fold-wear.

And then there was the question of Dorothy Curtis's Bank of England ex-husband, Oliver Sutchley, the man whose face I was sure I'd recognised that first night with Zorubin in the Pheasantry club in London. The odds were that I *did* know him.

And that, despite his denials, he knew me.

During the lengthy flight across the Atlantic I had had time to realise this wasn't going to be just the return of the long-lost son. The Coburg family, whoever it consisted of, had chosen not to know me. For whatever I had done, I had become a pariah.

I could have left it there. I had a new legal identity, cash in the bank. But as we came in to land at Idlewild, my heart was pumping wildly. I wanted to know. I wanted to know why I had been rejected. What I'd done or was thought to have done. For my sanity I needed to uncover four years of mystery. About the Coburgs. About why they had left me unclaimed in that hospital. About the nameless guilt I lived with.

I hauled my bag myself, half running through the brightly lit airport lounge out to the taxi rank.

I dragged open the door of a cab, threw in my valise and slid into the back seat. 'Take me to New York Public Library,' I said.

'You come back for the good weather?' the driver said for openers.

I barely heard him. I had already unzipped my bag, checking for a notebook, pencils.

The librarian, a tall earnest young man, reverently placed the thick envelope of clippings on the desk in front of me.

'This is your support material on banknote printing. Of course we have a whole collection on the subject in volume form.'

I told him the clippings would be fine and slid the wad of newspaper from the manila envelope.

Staring at me was a picture of a man. Big face, good-looking. Blond or white hair. He could have been me in thirty, forty years' time.

It was captioned: Death of Pierre Coburg in Washington, DC.

I read the story beneath the caption. President of Coburg Banknote, aged 69, died of a heart attack during a meeting at the Bureau of Printing and Engraving. His granddaughter, Miss Celine Coburg, 28, became President of the company at an emergency meeting of the board this morning in New York.

I turned the clippings. There was a mass of stories on Pierre Coburg. For over twenty years he had been one of New York's most eligible bachelors. Reports of liaisons were an inch thick; another wad of clippings showed him sailing and winter sporting. Always with a good-looking woman nearby.

Some serious items too: an invitation to the White House; dedication of a memorial to the victims of Waldviertel concentration camp; his appointment as president of the Security Printing Association of America. His death had been a minor news event. His death and his granddaughter's succession. The stories were all accompanied by a photograph of a tall, blonde girl, more like a model than a company president.

Another told the sad story of the death of her twin brother on the last day of the hostilities in Europe.

So this young woman was my sister. The good-looking old man was my grandfather.

Did I have a father and mother still alive?

I read back into the recent past. This was a bad time to have a death in the company. Coburg Banknote were pitching for a huge order from the Bureau of Printing and Engraving. The US Army in Europe and Japan was to have a currency of its own. Scrip it was to be called, an anti-blackmarket device dreamed up by the Treasury Department.

The order was clearly gigantic. More than that, I saw from the *Wall Street Journal* clippings, it carried prestige. A great deal of it. New standards of speed and colour were to be required. Paper-waste was to be less than four per cent.

Already, three months or more before Pierre Coburg died, Celine was chief negotiator for the company.

Interleaved with stories about banknote companies and printing contracts throughout the world there was a lot of material on Celine. A lot of photographs. Not surprising when you saw how sexy her competition was. But she was also, evidently, a very clever and tough lady. All the stories made it clear.

I leafed back. She was favourite for this winter's New York Woman of the Year Award. She spoke in a Sarah Lawrence debate on 'A woman's place . . .' She gave prizes at Vassar and endowed a chair of Business Studies at a women's college in Kansas City. Despite the big press stories on the day Pierre Coburg died, it was crystal clear that Celine had run the company since the war's end.

Her company?

Now here was something. A clipping from a technical journal, *Print and Printing News*. Turmoil in the normally calm backwaters of banknote printers. A brilliant young Italian engineer named Rino Giori was developing a new multi-colour machine, a possible world-beater. De la Rue in London were interested.

That was the news story. The back-fill was the story of the ten-year race to produce a hairline register multi-colour press. Rumours that the British were far advanced had proved groundless. No American company was seriously in contention. Except . . .

Except that Coburg Banknote Corporation of New York owned all rights and patents of the former Imprimerie Coburg of Linz. Imprimerie Coburg had belonged to Pierre's brother Emil Coburg: he and his family had disappeared into Waldviertel concentration camp. Thus the dedication of the monument to the victims and a donation to the Waldviertel Survivors' Association.

My pulse rate was up now.

I read on. It had been widely known before the war that Emil Coburg was working on an advanced banknote printing press. Even the name was known. Emil Coburg had called it the *Janus*.

But the Janus had disappeared. Sometime in the war the Janus had been moved from the Coburg factory at Augsburg. It was worth, ultimately, millions of dollars to its patent's owners, Coburg Banknote of New York.

Buried treasure.

The tall librarian came over to tell me politely that the section was closing. My excitement must have come over as a slightly threatening desperation. He told me I could keep the file until he had cleared the out-tags.

I didn't ask him what the out-tags were. I flipped back quickly to 1945 in the pile of clippings. There it was. The Coburg family, grandfather Pierre, John and Rose Coburg my parents, and, oh so sad, Celine, watching the coffin of Martin Coburg, killed in action, being lowered into a Long Island grave.

The empty coffin.

The librarian coughed genteelly. I was the last customer. But there was one more thing I had to do, one more item I had to find.

When *exactly* was I side-slipped to Roehampton Hospital, England? Sometime in November 1945. I remembered the fog, the river mists. OK, I flipped the old yellow clippings, square, rectangular, folded flat.

November 16, 1945. *Print and Printing News* again; *Washington Post*, a small story. *Wall Street Journal* a fourteen by ten: 'American Military Government Court, Munich, Germany. Today Pierre Coburg's claim was upheld to inherit the estate of his brother Emil Coburg, formerly of Lingfeld, West Germany.' The *Wall Street Journal* noted that the real estate value was negligible but the rights, royalties and patents of Imprimerie Coburg could prove of great value. Except, as *Print and Printing* pointed out, nobody knew where the patents were. Nobody had found patent, specification or the machine itself.

The Janus remained a buried treasure.

I stuffed the clippings back into the envelope and carried them over to the desk.

I was exhausted. I thanked the librarian and picked up my bag. Outside in the cool air I stumbled down the broad stone steps. It was still messy, it was still fog-bound, but a shape was emerging. A shape that began to scare the hell out of me, like those images of a top-hatted Jack the Ripper in a London fog.

I knew I was close to evil. I could feel its breath on my cheek. I hailed a taxi and told him to take me to a hotel. He asked, which?

I told him the Pierre.

It was only a moment or two later that I realised it was my subconscious writing black comedy again.

I didn't choose the day I arrived at Island House for the first time as Daniel Lingfield. I didn't choose the timing of my visit but I don't think I regretted it either.

I drove towards Montauk from the Hamptons knowing I must have done this a thousand times. But as I looked across the countryside and the ocean on my right, Long Island might well have been a tiny peninsula jutting from the underbelly of Australia. I recognised nothing.

Perhaps four or five miles from Island House I stopped to check with an old couple walking arm in arm along the straight hot road.

'Island House?' the man said. 'You go straight down this road and keep the ocean on your right, but keep your eyes on the left. Island House is the big one just after the crossroads. You can count on three miles, maybe four.'

As I thanked him I could see his wife was nudging him in the ribs. He turned to her, mildly irritated. 'What is it, Em?' he asked.

Her eyes never left me.

'Well, thank you,' I said again.

'You're Mr Martin, aren't you?' she blurted out.

There was silence in the singing heat. The engine of my Plymouth turned over fretfully. 'Yes,' I said slowly. 'I'm Martin.'

She backed away, just one step, then stood her ground. 'We all thought you were dead,' she whispered. Her husband had grasped her arm and was pulling her away from the car.

'You worked at the house,' I guessed.

'In the kitchen, Emma Hardy. You remember me?'

'Of course,' I said. 'I'm pleased to see you remember me. I was in hospital for a long time after the war. I'm not a ghost, Emma,' I said lightly.

She relaxed. 'Didn't think you were a ghost, Mr Martin. Just nobody told me you were still alive.'

I got back into the car. Emma Hardy had recognised me, but the family at Island House had written to the army that Captain Baxter's picture was not me. Baxter had left nothing to chance. He had sent out to each next of kin on the army's missing list something like an actor's composite of half a dozen pictures of me, close-ups, full length, in uniform and in civilian clothes. But he'd done more. He had meticulously recorded what we called my profile: that I spoke fluent German, that I was familiar with Kansas City and had certainly visited it many times, that I knew something of the chateau system of Bordeaux wines, even details of books he was able to establish that I had read. And yet with all this, nobody at Island House had recognised me. Like Elisabeth Oster, they had deliberately lied. There was no other possibility.

Emma's husband was tugging her away. 'We won't keep you, Mr Coburg. You won't want to be late.'

'For the funeral,' Emma Hardy said. 'Late for the funeral.'

Island House was bigger, older and genuinely more impressive than I had imagined. It was a mansion house which dated from around 1840 with fine late-Regency bowed windows and old brick, and wistaria climbing to elegant second-floor balconied windows. From where I parked my Plymouth I could see extensive gardens with shaded gravelled alleys running down towards the foreshore.

I was standing beside my car when a movement at the far end of the drive caught my attention. I turned to see a long black hearse leading a procession of three black Rolls-Royces. The convoy crackled slowly across the gravel drive and came to a halt at the front porch. I was perhaps thirty or forty yards distant. The driver of the hearse got out and mounted the wide arc of stone steps which led up to the house. His companion left the passenger seat and rounded the hearse to open the back. I stood in the bright sunlight as the birds flitted and twittered around me and a faint flavour of ozone was carried to me from the ocean.

I took a couple of steps forward but stopped as the glazed double doors of the house opened and four men carried out a coffin down the front steps and slid it reverently into the hearse.

Men and women dressed in black came out slowly and assembled on the top step watching as the hearse doors were closed on the coffin of Pierre Coburg. I could identify the principal actors from my reading of *Who's Who* and the *Society Register*. The man in the wheel-chair, thin-faced, haunted, was my father John Coburg. The older woman more or less next to him seemed to stare down indifferently at the scene before her. My mother Rose must have been in her late forties. She was tall and still beautiful in her maturity. Next to her was my sister Celine. Everything about her physical being reminded me of someone my memory could not reach out to.

This woman had a very special quality. A cutting edge that was apparent in the way she stood, in the way she gestured to the black-coated mortician's assistants to carry my father's wheel-chair down the steps, the way she indicated with a lifted finger who should travel in the second Rolls-Royce.

When members of the family had been allocated their cars, the convoy, led by the hearse, moved away down the drive. At the corner of the stable yard and at an upstairs window maids watched it go. A gardener stood and removed his cap. As a send-off it fell far short of what you might have expected at Storyville.

I got into my car and followed at a distance behind the convoy. As the limousines swung left at the gates to the drive I saw the face of Celine Coburg looking back at me from the rear window of her Rolls.

We drove at an appropriately funereal pace east toward Montauk Point. At the gates to the cemetery of the tiny clapboard church of St Peter-in-the-Fields two burly men stood in black jackets and striped trousers. The hearse passed through. The leading Rolls stopped for a moment as some words were exchanged between the gatemen and one of the occupants. The graveyard was on a light slope. It was small, not more than fifty yards by fifty, and the scar in the earth where Pierre Coburg's coffin was to be interred was close to the gate.

I accelerated slightly as the last Rolls passed into the cemetery and braked rapidly as one of the black-jacketed men swung the gate closed. My fender was a few inches from it.

'This is a family occasion, sir. The press have been asked to restrict themselves to this evening's press conference. All the financial papers have agreed,' he added.

'I'm a member of the family,' I said.

'I'm sorry, sir. Miss Celine's orders are perfectly clear.'

'I told you,' I said. 'I am a member of the family.'

The polite but strongly built man gave me a heavy push in the shoulder. 'Take off,' he said, 'I can smell a journalist a mile off. No goddamn respect.'

Next to me a light pleasant New England voice said: 'Beyond the pale, Martin. Like me, you're beyond the pale.'

I turned round to see a tall slim man, not young but with a young air. His thin brown hair stirred in the ocean breeze. 'You don't know me?' he said. It was a question.

'No, I'm afraid I don't.'

'You really did lose your memory.'

'Yes, sir.'

'If I told you I was Jack Aston, would that mean anything to you?'

The retainer at the gate was out of earshot. 'You recognise me as Martin Coburg?' I said.

'I'd be more or less prepared to swear in court that you were Martin, yes. Although the Coburgs would destroy me if I did.'

I absorbed that slowly. 'But outside of a courtroom you'd say I was Martin Coburg?'

He smiled. 'Or a very close imitation.'

We stood beside the chest-high stone wall that surrounded the cemetery. The ceremony was about to begin. The members of the family were arranging themselves round the large open green marble vault. I could just see from where I stood the inscriptions cut deep into the marble.

'Your grandfather much favoured the idea of family vaults,' Jack Aston said. 'He even had the ashes of his parents brought over from Austria.'

As the sunlight fell across the stone I read: Aloys Coburg 1841–1895, Paula Coburg 1856–1880. Below their names the stone read: Martin John Coburg 1921–1945 and Pierre Coburg 1880–1949.

'They say,' Jack Aston's voice was edged with hatred, 'that the stonecutters worked all night by flashlight to get the vault ready for Pierre.'

'You've got no great love for the Coburgs.' I turned to him. 'What did they do to you?'

He smiled bitterly. 'Would you like to hear what they did to *you*?'

It was almost dark when I drove over to Island House. So much of the past raced through my mind. It was like someone recalling his early childhood, uncertain whether he remembered an event from the past or knew it only from hearsay. Jack Aston had spared nobody, certainly not himself. I knew of his relationship with my father; of his brief engagement to Celine. I knew of Pierre's avaricious sexuality, of his affair with Rose and almost certainly with Celine. I knew of the Waldviertel Coburg past, of Emil and Dorotta and Elisabeth and Alexina. I knew of the growth of Emil's company; I knew of the Janus and that I was present on Pierre's last desperate trip to, as he saw it, save the Coburg Banknote Corporation. I knew much, but my weakness was that I didn't know how much. Or how little.

I stood in the hall at Island House examining the detail of floor tiles and plaster cornices in the hope that they might suddenly bring the past to life. When the butler returned it was to tell me that Miss Coburg had no intention of seeing anyone today. If I wished an appointment I should telephone her secretary at Coburg Banknote in New York City.

I told him no. I was going to see her *now*. He bristled but I could see he was scared.

I pushed him aside and opened the door he had used. I was in a book-lined room, long, elegantly lit with table lamps, and with a rich display of Persian carpets and leather armchairs. Next to the fire, Celine was standing with Rose. Each held a glass in her hand.

'You know who I am,' I said as I walked towards them.

'I know who you claim to be,' Celine said. Her mother, *my* mother, was nervous. Celine was perfectly relaxed.

'You can't keep this up,' I said.

She smiled an infinitely superior smile. 'Of course,' she said, 'it's possible you're right. It's possible you are Martin Coburg. How shall we ever know?'

I had imagined everything from sullen defiance to screaming denials. I never thought I would be confronted by an indifferent shrug of the shoulders.

She signalled to the hovering butler to leave us. 'I'll ring if I want you,' she said. 'I'll deal with this.'

I walked over to the drinks table and poured myself a scotch. For the first time her composure cracked. 'This is *my* house,' she said in a voice close to a snarl. 'You wait until you're offered a drink.'

I turned towards her, drink in hand. 'I don't know whose house it is at this very moment,' I said. 'We're going to find out.'

'There was a will,' she said coolly, 'a simple will. The business and property came to me.'

I sipped my scotch. 'You know that there's such a thing as unlawful influence.'

'Not relevant,' she snapped.

I looked at my mother. She was pale and lip-licking.

'Who took over,' I said softly, 'as Pierre's mistress when his son's wife could no longer offer enough *zest*?'

Rose was a caricature of a woman trapped. Her breath hissed in. Whisky spilled from her glass. She shot a wild look at Celine.

'Who was Pierre's mistress after *you*?'

'I don't know what you're talking about,' Rose said feebly.

'I'm talking about unlawful influence,' I said. 'I'm getting very close to talking about incest.'

Something gurgled in my mother's throat. Celine came forward. 'Your suggestions are distressing to my mother. What do you want?' she said contemptuously. 'Money?'

I had never seen such a steely quality in a woman.

'I want to know how it was that my grandfather, my mother and my sister failed to recognise my photograph when the US Army was trying to establish my identity in 1945.'

Celine smiled. 'But of course we recognised the photograph.' Her swift change of tactic had put her on top again. 'I'll tell you.'

'Let Rose tell me.'

Panic signals flashed from Rose to her daughter.

'*I'll* tell you, Mr Lingfield,' Celine said. 'Just listen. When the letter from the army arrived my grandfather, Pierre Coburg, called together the close family: Rose Coburg, myself and John Coburg. Our problem was to decide how we should answer the letter.'

'Why not just say, it's Martin Coburg?'

She ignored my intervention.

'The photographs *could* have been Martin Coburg. Same height and general build.'

'There are less than three per cent of American soldiers over six foot two,' I said.

'We're talking of individuals, not percentages,' Celine said coldly. 'Then there was a knowledge of German, which of course Martin had. And there was a familiarity with Kansas City . . . for what that was worth.'

'Put all the items together,' I said, 'and it was worth a lot.'

'We had to judge, Mr Lingfield. And we judged that Daniel Lingfield might well be Martin Coburg.' She shrugged. 'There was quite simply no way of knowing.'

Did she know she'd trapped me? Did she know that the evidence nestled under my arm? Did she know that to produce that evidence I would have to admit to a piece of the past which left me paralysed with guilt?

'So what was there for us to do? Pierre wrote a brief note saying the photographs were not immediately recognisable.'

'*She* wrote the letter.' I pointed at Rose. 'And it said the photographs did not resemble her son. I phoned the Department of the Army this morning.'

'What difference does it make who wrote the letter?' Celine said crisply. 'The letter was written. We all stand by it.'

'My father too?'

She pursed her lips. 'Ask him.'

'You bitch.'

'Why ask,' she said casually, 'if you know that he's incapable of recognising his breakfast? He has been for years.'

'I also know how it came about.'

She put down her drink. 'If you have any practical suggestions, I'm prepared to consider them. If you're short of money I'm quite prepared on the basis of this genuine doubt that exists to make you an *ex gratia* payment from my personal account. You've already received 75,000 dollars. I am prepared to provide you with a further 75,000 dollars, but don't make the mistake of believing that you have just completed a successful act of blackmail. Legally, *nothing* belongs to you, Mr Lingfield. Now, please leave.'

I had never hated anyone this much. I wanted to reach out and hit her. I saw that my mother's confidence was surging back. She looked at Celine proudly.

'I'm not leaving without an answer,' I said with much more assurance than I felt.

Celine nodded slowly. 'I see,' she said, 'that you're determined to rattle the skeletons in the Coburg family cupboard.'

'Why not?'

She raised her eyebrows. 'Have it your own way, Martin,' she said.

I was distinctly nervous. To be without a full memory of your own past is sometimes easy, comforting almost; but sometimes deeply disturbing. Especially when faced with this young woman's totally confident smile.

'You seem to be under the impression,' she lit a cigarette, as she spoke, 'that your family abandoned you in 1945. That we chose not to recognise your picture.'

'Am I wrong?'

'We certainly chose not to recognise your photographs. Of course we all knew it was you. But there was nothing new in our attitude.' She paused for effect. And she got it. 'None of us had spoken to you since the beginning of the war. None of us intended to speak to you ever again. So what possible reason could there have been for us to recognise the photograph? In Pierre Coburg's eyes you were no longer a Coburg.'

'No longer a Coburg,' I said. 'Why not?'

The only sound in the room was Celine blowing smoke across the glowing tip of her cigarette. 'Did your very partial memory tell you that you were a member of the SS?' she said scathingly.

I poured myself another drink.

'Of course it did. And I suspect your memory told you a great deal more.' Then with a sudden, unnerving transformation, her face flushed purple in anger. 'How dare you talk of unlawful influence on your grandfather's will? How dare you even come back here when you betrayed half our family to the Gestapo?'

I dropped my glass.

'Oh, yes,' she hissed at me. 'Before you left Portugal for the SS, every detail of the help Emil and Alex were giving to Jewish friends was on the desk of the Lisbon Gestapo. Passed on by you to a pro-Nazi Englishman named Oliver Sutchley. Does *that* name ring a bell?' she said with searing sarcasm.

'This is Sutchley's account of what happened?'

'It is.' She smiled, cold as ice.

'For God's sake, why should I do that? Why should I betray my own family?'

'You were young, ignorant and loyal. Loyal to Pierre. You told Oliver Sutchley that whatever happened Emil must be stopped. His plans to issue counterfeit German money would have destroyed the House of Janus, both sides of it.'

She knew she had me reeling. I tried to formulate the questions.

But there was no mercy in this woman.

'Get out!' she snapped. 'Before I set the dogs on you.'

I got into my car and drove quickly away from Island House along to the Point. I parked, looking out to sea, and thought that the only person I really wanted to talk to about all this was Vik Zorubin. But that, in the nature of things, was out of court.

I hated Martin Coburg. I hated the bastard.

I put the car in gear and drove at a dangerous speed towards the cemetery at Montauk. My headlights threw great shadows from the overhanging trees and I felt engulfed by a horrific nightmare or piece of surrealist theatre. The cemetery gates were open and I drove through, slewing to a stop on the gravel in front of the Coburg family vault.

The headlight burnt into the green marble: Martin John Coburg 1921–1945.

Sitting there in the car I blinked with fear. I was talking, thinking of Martin Coburg as someone else. But that arrogant young patrician in Lisbon was *me*. I could ask more questions, I could get more answers but the only way to deal with the dangerous schizophrenia which was threatening me was to leave Martin Coburg buried with the grandfather he had betrayed Alex and her parents for.

I reversed the car and drove slowly down the coast road. Deliberately I passed by Jack Aston's house. I could not bear to see him or my father now. I drove with a mind completely blank with pain; I drove with every intention of driving away from Long Island for ever.

I passed along the ocean road west until I could see the distant dome of light over New York City. I told myself what I had done I could never undo. However my young self made my flesh creep with revulsion, I was now Daniel Lingfield of Los Angeles, California. No part of me had ever been Martin Coburg of Island House, Long Island.

My mind eased a little. The guilt I felt was someone else's guilt. To believe that was the only way I could stay sane.

I drove through Queens and the image of the words on the green marble came up before my eyes. Almost as an hallucination in the headlights before me. I saw the deep incisions in the dark stone: Martin John Coburg 1921–1945.

Let it be.

· **Thirty-one** ·

Definitely.

I had made up my mind. I would go back to California on the first flight tomorrow morning.

Definitely.

Unless I phoned Zorubin in Berlin and asked him to come over and work for me.

No, I had made up my mind. Let it be.

Definitely.

I awoke next morning with a hangover composed fifty–fifty of alcohol poisoning and self-loathing.

Had I really done it? Had I really sent the German side of the family to their deaths? Had I really done it because I thought Emil Coburg was about to destroy his brother Pierre by printing counterfeit bills? Had I done it in the naive belief that the punishment for smuggling Jews into Spain was just a withdrawal of government contracts?

Martin Coburg was a self I didn't know then. He might have felt, believed any of these things. But one single idea returned again and again to my mind: if it wasn't me – who was it?

I lay in the big double-bed. Projected in my mind were pictures of Pierre from the newspaper clippings. Did he do it? Did *he* betray his brother to the Gestapo and yet still send contributions to the Survivors of the Waldviertel Association here in New York? Was he that evil? The press clearly didn't think so. His presence at the Waldviertel memorial ceremony was worthy of a news item each year.

My mind drifted. I called the desk to get me the times of the flights to Los Angeles this morning. While I waited I thought what I had to do to clear up and leave New York.

For ever.

I phoned Jack Aston. I thanked him for all he did for my father. I thanked him for what he'd told me about the Coburgs, about myself.

'What are you going to do?' he said.

'I'm going back to California.'

'And?'

'And nothing, Jack.'

There was a long, long silence on the line. 'What happened?' Jack's voice said flatly. 'What happened when you saw Celine?'

I saw no reason to be easy on myself. 'She took me by the scruff of the neck,' I said, 'she bounced me off a couple of walls and threw me out of the house.'

'What did she tell you, Martin?' the voice on the other end of the line said quietly.

'She told me I was responsible for the deaths of Emil Coburg and his wife – and Alexina.'

'Do you think you were?'

A long pause.

'Do you think you were, Martin?'

'Yes,' I said. 'I think I was.'

Somehow telling about my SS tattoo stuck in my throat. 'I've reason to believe it,' was all I could get out.

'You believe that *that* was why you never saw Pierre again after you returned from Europe? You believe he would have nothing to do with you?'

'It makes sense, Jack,' I said in anguish.

'It makes no sense at all,' he said quietly. 'It doesn't explain Pierre's will. I'm something of an expert on Coburg wills,' Jack said. 'I've had to be, in your father's interest. Pierre's will remained in your favour until the US Army reported you dead in 1945. After that he changed it. Apart from fairly minor bequests to Rose and your father, Celine became the main beneficiary.'

I had remained his heir until I was reported dead in 1945!

That didn't seem to be the act of a man who had cut off his grandson in 1940 in the belief he had betrayed the German family.

'Don't give up, Martin,' he said.

I knew what he was saying. I knew he wanted me to take up the sword against Celine. But I had no answer for him at that moment.

I said goodbye. It was a poignant moment. I didn't expect to talk to him again.

I jumped as the phone rang. I picked it up and a girl's voice told me I could get an American Airlines flight to Los Angeles from Idlewild at midday. I booked a seat and packed my bag, carried it down to the lobby and paid my bill. Let it be, I said to myself. Let it be.

As I left the hotel, I was fleeing back to the sunshine emptiness of my life in California. I had been worsted by Celine. I was on the run.

I took a cab and told the driver I wanted Idlewild. We were driving in silence down Fifth Avenue toward the Rockefeller Center. The line of automobiles bunched, moved on and came to a stop. The driver cursed. My head was turned to my left. I wasn't really looking at the imposing stone-faced building just twenty-five feet away. The bronze plate beside the entrance was too big to be discreet, too classy to shout the company name to the world. Silvered lettering read: Coburg Banknote Corporation.

I grabbed my bag and jumped out of the cab. The driver yelled even as my ten-dollar bill fluttered in through his window. Taxis were hooting behind us. A loud central-European voice was yelling at me.

I ran through the traffic and reached the sidewalk. Bag in hand I stared up at the building.

The doors were plate glass. The uniformed doorman opened one side and I walked in. Oak-panelled, marble-tiled. Another uniformed figure sat at a broad partner's desk. I crossed and swung my bag onto the desk in front of him. 'I want you to look after this,' I said in a manner so lordly Dorothy Curtis would have been proud of me. 'Which is the executive floor?'

'Fourteen, sir,' the man said. 'Can I have your name, please?'

'Coburg,' I said. 'Martin Coburg.'

He recoiled, half nodding. As far as he was concerned I was a distant member of the family.

By the time he had rounded his desk I had stepped into the elevator and pressed the button for the fourteenth floor.

The layout of the executive area made it easy. Two receptionists' desks formed the corridor. A door marked Arthur C. Jansen was on the left; another carrying the name Merril Soames was on the right. At eye-level on the most imposing of the three mahogany doors with thicker architrave and an eighteenth-century pediment, brass letters spelt out: The President of the Corporation.

I walked in. Behind me both receptionists had risen from their desks. In front of me, an attractive forty-year-old woman, becomingly severe in her dress, was standing, the telephone to her ear, a yellow pencil tapping her teeth.

I walked past her too, through the inner door and into a room with large windows in two walls, one looking over the Rockefeller Center, the other back toward Central Park. There were white panelled walls, a bad portrait of Pierre Coburg and photographs in silver frames on polished side tables.

Celine rose from behind the desk as I turned the key in the door behind me.

She said nothing. She wasn't frightened or alarmed. She didn't even give the impression she was put out. She picked up a telephone and said: 'Betty, don't have someone break the door down yet. I'm giving Mr Lingfield five minutes. After that, have someone standing by.'

She pointed to a chair. She smiled. 'Sit down,' she said. 'What can I do for you?'

Perhaps I was too baffled to speak. I told myself I was too angry. The truth is I just didn't have her experience in these one-on-one confrontations. Eyeball-to-eyeball, they'd started calling it in the business world.

Instead I said slowly: 'I think I've got a shock for you.'

She pursed her lips. I felt somehow I'd said the right thing. This was a woman who wanted to be in charge. Who mostly *had* been. Something coming out of the left field she found hardest to take. I was going to have to remember this in my dealings with her.

I waited.

'What sort of shock?'

I lit a cigarette. 'I've decided,' I said carefully, 'that I'm going to face the past. My past, Pierre's past. Your past. I'm going to go on and on – and if necessary on again, until I find out what really happened.'

'I've told you what happened,' she said coolly. 'After your gross betrayal of the German Coburgs to the Gestapo Pierre refused to see you again.'

'Is that so?'

She said nothing. But I could almost see her flinching.

'He wouldn't have anything to do with me?'

She nodded.

'And yet his will remained in my favour.'

Now she flinched.

'Pierre left it that way,' I tried to keep my tone level, 'until he thought I was dead. *He* didn't think I betrayed his brother's family.'

She took a deep breath. 'What counts is that he did alter the will.'

'What counts,' I said, 'is whether or not you and my doting mother ever showed him the photographs and data the army sent you.'

She smiled. 'And that you'll never know.'

Someone began knocking on the door.

'That I know already,' I said. 'And I'm as near as damnit sure it wasn't me who talked to the Gestapo in Lisbon.'

The phone rang and she picked it up. 'Mr Lingfield's leaving in a moment or two,' she said.

I took the key and unlocked the door. I could feel the presence of secretaries and security men on the other side.

'I won't give up,' I said. 'This is where my life ends or starts. So far I don't know which, but I won't give up.'

'Keep me informed,' she said, her tone less casual than the words.

I turned the door handle. 'I'll keep you informed. You'll know from the moment I tell you just how much your grip's loosening on all this.' I waved my hand at the panelling, the silver-framed photographs of prime ministers and presidents. 'I'll call you, write you, cable you.'

She nodded.

'Funny thing,' I said. 'When I left my hotel I was on my way to Idlewild to pick up a flight for California.'

'And now?'

'Now I'm still on my way to Idlewild, but my flight's going to be to Paris. I'm starting back in Europe, Celine. If anybody knows who turned the Coburgs over to the Gestapo, they're going to be in Europe.'

Her face was completely without expression. I opened the door. Two uniformed security men took a step forward. I turned back to Celine. 'I'll keep my promise,' I said. 'As soon as I've got anything, I'll cable you. Step by step you'll *know*.

· **Thirty-two** ·

Cross the river at the Pont d'Iéna. Run along the quayside. Look down from the rear window of the Paris taxi-cab to where Dorothy's yellow dress billowed in the grey-brown river.

Ten days ago.

I got out at the Boulevard St Michel and sent the cab on to check my bag into a small hotel on the Rue Rappe.

Paris held no magic for me. It was drizzling. Two o'clock in the afternoon. Cool rather than cold, but the booksellers along the embankment were wearing mittens.

I started making my way through the crowds of students and clerks and shop girls streaming back to work after lunch. Here and there a group of Foreign Legion paras in red berets sat at a café table. Tall, blue-black Africans sold leather belts from open suitcases on the sidewalk; Arabs offered couscous from brightly coloured street stalls; the smell of garlic and black French tobacco hung in the air.

At other times I would have loved this place, but the memory of Dorothy Curtis was too strong and that sense of isolation which can afflict Anglo-Saxons in Paris hung heavily upon me.

I turned at the Rue St Séverin and started counting the numbers opposite the church. The blue and white plate that said the right number seemed to apply to a small burgundy-painted second-hand bookstore. The windows were not that clean and the lights inside were dim. I pushed open the door and looked over my shoulder at the clang of the overhanging bell.

Nobody came out from the back room. I looked around at the walls lined with high bookshelves. The titles passing rapidly before my eyes were twentieth-century French and Anglo-American poets and novelists. In front of me a poster in English and German read: A meeting of the Waldviertel Survivors will take place above the Café de la République on Friday 2 May to commemorate the liberation of the camp. Members of the WSA and of any other survivors' associations will be welcome.

Waldviertel. A chill passed through my veins. The bottom part of the poster carried a simple black and white, pen and ink drawing of a barbed-wire fence and gnarled hands clutching at it.

I stood there for perhaps a full minute, my head bowed, desperately conscious of the tiny tattoo in my left armpit.

At some point I was aware that a man was watching me through the open door which led into the back room. He came forward, not tall but wiry. His face dark, lively, serious without being sombre. 'I'm Hans Emden,' he said. 'Can I help you?'

'You're connected with the Association?' I nodded toward the poster.

'I'm secretary of the Paris branch.'

'My name is Dan Lingfield,' I said. 'I would like to make enquiries about some people who were imprisoned in . . . Waldviertel.'

I had almost choked on the name. Nausea ebbed and flowed through me. He nodded. Not really encouragingly.

'The family name was Coburg,' I said.

I saw his face tighten.

'Emil and Dorotta Coburg and their daughter, Alexina.'

Immobile, he nevertheless seemed out of breath.

'And you, Mr Lingfield, who are you? A journalist perhaps.'

'No.'

'A private investigator?'

I knew he was playing for time. 'I'm a member of the family,' I said. 'My name was once Martin Coburg.'

'I see.'

I let the pause sink in. 'You were in the camp yourself?'

'I was in Waldviertel,' he said. 'Yes.'

In a shaft of sunlight dust sparkled. We stood for a moment in silence among the books and the smell of coffee drifting from the back room.

'Did you know the Coburg family?'

'Thousands passed through the camp,' he said. 'Mostly we didn't even know each other's names.'

'Do you have records of any sort?'

'We have a rough and ready *Todbuch*, a Death Book.' He turned and drew a heavy ledger from a shelf behind him.

He opened it with his back to me, leafed over pages that crackled drily and turned back toward me. 'Coburg. Here they are.' He placed the book on the desk. His hand remained on the page.

I ran my eyes down a list of names entered in a coppery ink in a continental hand.

So many names.

Then: Coburg, Emil (Executed 9.7.40); Coburg, Dorotta (Dead on arrival 9.7.40); Coburg, Alexina (Dead on arrival 9.7.40).

He closed the book with a snap. 'That's all we have on record,' he said.

I knew something was badly wrong. You didn't treat a relative in this cold disconcerting manner. No word of sympathy, nothing. Just 'Coburg. Here they are', and a Death Book dropped on the desk in front of me.

The catch spring hit the hanging bell over the door. An old woman came into the shop with a brown paper parcel under her arm. 'Do I disturb you, Hans?' she asked in German.

'No, no, come in, Magda,' he said. He took the parcel from her and unwrapped the books. Opening them one by one, studying the title pages, flipping them over to examine the bindings, he muttered to himself. 'These are very good, Magda. Very good editions. I can offer you three thousand francs and still do very well on the turn.'

'Give me a thousand and not a pfennig more,' the old lady said briskly. She turned to me. 'The man's a fool,' she said, 'at least to old ladies.'

They settled for fifteen hundred francs. To me her interruption had helped to defuse some of the tension I felt.

Emden walked into the back room and I heard a cash drawer opening. I leaned forward and took the Death Book. Opening it I found the Coburgs. Against Alexina's name, after *Dead on arrival*, was a note which had been obscured by Hans Emden's thumb. It read: See Anna Breitmann.

Hans Emden had emerged from the back room, a tin mug of coffee in one hand, three five-hundred-franc notes in the other.

Breitmann, Anna (Dead on arrival, 9.7.40). Papers given to Coburg, Alexina (9.7.40).

Hans took a long drink of his coffee, his dark eyes watching me over the rim of the tin mug.

I closed the book. 'Why?' I asked him.

He shrugged and handed the notes to the old lady. While she protested he had overpaid her, I said: 'What happened to Anna Breitmann?'

'Anna,' the old lady said. 'Anna was an angel. One day, I remember, she gave me two salted mackerel, *two*. Stolen from the SS cookhouse.'

Emden took her to the door. Closing it after her he looked back at me. 'Not all survivors want the details about them known,' he said.

'Alexina told you that?'

He didn't answer.

He shrugged. 'She survived.'

I found myself battered by strange emotions, by an extraordinary elation that this girl was alive. This girl I could never remember spending an hour with.

'When did you last see her?'

Emden put his head on one side. 'She came here once or twice,' he said. 'I don't know where she is now.'

'In Paris?'

'I said I didn't know, Mr Coburg.'

I turned toward the door and stopped. 'I mean her no harm,' I said.

'Good.'

Silence hung thicker than the motes of dust between us. I knew I was going to get no more from him. I glanced at the crude wooden donations box beside the desk. I reached for my pocketbook.

'Get out,' he said, his face as grey as death. 'Leave us alone.'

I did two things.

First, I went to the post office in the Rue Gaspar, called Vik Zorubin in Berlin and asked him to take the next flight to Munich.

Secondly, I kept my promise to Celine. My cable read: REAL GOOD NEWS STOP OUR COUSIN ALEXINA COBURG ALIVE AND WELL IN PARIS STOP MORE LATER STOP MARTIN.

Vik Zorubin arrived at Munich Airport wearing what looked like a dark-blue Navy surplus trenchcoat and carrying a scuffed leather Gladstone bag. His shoulders rolled, his great rubbery face split in a grin. 'So I'm on your payroll,' he said, extending his hand. 'Where do we start?'

'Before we start, Vik,' I said as we walked through the concourse, 'I've got the rest of the story to tell you.'

'OK.' He spied the bright red and white coffee shop in front of him. 'Tell me over a cup of coffee.'

I nodded. 'That way you don't leave the airport. When you've heard what I have to tell you might want to turn and catch the first flight back east.'

'Oh, no,' Zorubin protested with that unique brand of menacing amiability he could conjure up. 'I wouldn't go home without visiting the mountains, gazing at a few ski girls and roughing you up a little.'

We sat down in the service area and a girl in a red imitation stewardess uniform brought us coffee.

'Away you go,' Zorubin said, his thick-fingered hands flat on the white table between us.

I told him everything. When I reached 1940 I told him Pierre had come back from Lisbon alone. I had stayed in Europe in a crazy, young man's attempt to see Alex again. There was only one possible way of getting into the camps except as a prisoner.

He looked at me hard-eyed. 'So you joined the Allgemeine SS,' he said.

I nodded. 'I joined the SS.'

He said nothing for about thirty seconds. He stared at me with his dark expressionless eyes for what seemed to me a very long time indeed. Then he said: 'How long have you known this?'

'Since I met you in Berlin.'

A half smile. 'You had been to see Colonel Helm in Spandau Altstadt.'

'He told me my SS number,' I touched my left armpit, 'it meant that I was Martin Coburg, that I had volunteered in August 1940, and bought myself out a few months later.'

I lit a cigarette. He pulled an obscure Russian brand called *Stravka* from his pocket, slowly tore open the cheap paper packaging and took out a yellow corn-paper cigarette. 'Let's go back a step,' he said. 'You didn't join the Allgemeine SS to fight for the Führer.'

'I have a green sticker on my record. You know what that is?'

'I know.' He took a lighter and laboriously flicked at the wheel with his thumb. On the third or fourth try the spark became a flame. 'What made you call me in Berlin?' he said. 'Why not leave all this safely buried?'

'Yesterday I went to the Waldviertel Survivors' Association in Paris. Alexina survived the camp.'

For once his face registered something clearly recognisable as surprise. 'She's in Paris?'

'Almost certainly. But I can't get any further without your help.'

Zorubin got his cigarette alight, scowling at the taste. He sat back. He blew a smoke ring and it hovered like indecision between us. 'So my brief would be to find Alexina Coburg.'

'Will you take it?'

He puffed ruminatively. 'I already took it,' he said. 'From the French girl Andrée de Bretagne, you remember?'

'This way you get paid twice,' I said.

'OK.' He scowled again at his cigarette. 'You're not holding out on me?'

'Holding out?'

'You're not holding anything back?'

'You've got it all, Vik.'

'OK,' he said again. 'On one condition. If anything comes out that suggests you were an enthusiastic camp guard, I turn you straight over to War Crimes.'

I stretched out a hand. He took it and squeezed till the knuckles cracked. My knuckles.

· Thirty-three ·

We made plans. Zorubin would go straight to Paris and do all the conventional detective work on a trace for Alexina Coburg or Anna Breitmann. I would drive straight to Haus Lingfeld to confront Elisabeth.

Zorubin and I stood next to the Avis desk at Munich Airport. 'You're sure you don't want me to provide some muscle?' his heavy voice rumbled. 'You're not going to let her walk over you again?'

I smiled. 'Thanks, pal, for the vote of confidence.'

His flight was being called for the second time.

'See you in Paris tomorrow.'

He treated me to his savage smile and we parted.

I watched with some affection the powerful shoulders making space for himself through the crowded airport lounge. He was unanxious for me to see Elisabeth alone but I had some idea, perhaps hazily derived from my patrician background, that this was one woman I could deal with more effectively by myself.

I hired a car and drove across Munich and along the Perlacher Forest road. Here and there the foundations of new housing or a new factory was visible through the trees . . . I checked my speedometer. I should have reached the house by now.

I continued up the road for a further mile or two, then turned and drove slowly back. The gentle pitch of the red-roofed houses led my eye back from the road. I shook my head in irritation. Too many thoughts, memories, maybe even submerged memories were crowding my brain. I had overshot again. I turned the hired Ford into a side-street and reversed to regain the main road. As I did so I saw the name of the slip-road: Coburgstrasse.

I reversed again and drove slowly up the tiny road. It was lined with neat houses and two rows of fine old lime trees. I braked.

Give or take a few yards I was sitting on the very spot where a Teller mine had blown my memory to the four winds as the war ended. If I drove on, surmounting the rise in front of me, I should see Haus Lingfeld appear first as a gleaming slate roof, then a façade of golden stone and finally as a mansion set in an English parkland. But of course I wouldn't.

I put the car into gear, cruised up to the ridge and confirmed I was right. Small, newly built houses were arranged to follow the parkland slopes. I turned the car and came slowly down the drive. Something was bothering me about the houses. Was it the meticulous neatness of their layout? Was it their sheer uniform newness? Or was it something else? I looked again and this time it was obvious. They all looked so totally alike because they were empty. No curtains hung to break the architect's sweet dream of uniformity.

So if the houses were new, there was somewhere not so far away, a sales office, a show house. People who might well know where the Osters had moved on to.

Now that I knew what I was looking for it only took me a few minutes to find it. A large sign a few hundred yards down the road signalled that the construction company, at least for this block of perhaps sixty houses, was Maurice Eck GMBH.

Eck, the salesman in the office told me, was a builder of great reliability. He took a personal interest in standards of construction and a quality control guarantee was issued with each house purchase. Why was the road called Coburgstrasse? That, the young salesman, recently recruited from the north, did not know. Was there perhaps a poet of that name? Or composer?

'Do you know who owned this property before?' I asked him.

'No, sir. But it's one of the finest pieces of land hereabouts. The houses on the hill actually look over the original ornamental lake.'

Had he ever heard of the Osters, owners of the house at least up to a few years ago? He shook his head. He was an amiable young man, aware now that what he had hoped would be a sale was slipping away from him. 'They're the finest houses in the area,' he assured me dispiritedly as I turned for the door.

I stopped. Given pride of place among house plans and layouts was a photograph showing a group of people at some ceremony at the beginning of Coburgstrasse, the old lime-lined drive. A red ribbon stretched from one tree to another and a woman was advancing on the ribbon, large scissors in hand. She was Elisabeth Oster.

The salesman saw what he thought was renewed interest. 'Frau Eck,' he said, 'opening the development.'

The telephone book pointed me to the Ecks' house, a long riverside bungalow building of formidable modern luxury. As I came toward Elisabeth in the garden I wondered how she had adjusted to the demolition of Haus Lingfeld.

She stood, almost welcoming. She was nearly forty now, a tall striking woman in a pale-cream summer dress. As I reached the shaded garden table on the river bank she came forward and, to my astonishment, kissed me soberly on both cheeks.

For some moments neither of us spoke. Then she gestured for me to sit down. 'You know Lingfeld's gone, I suppose.'

I nodded, watching her.

'The best thing,' she said. 'By far.'

'Perhaps.'

A kingfisher swooped down the middle of the shaded river. 'Where's Oster?' I said.

'He gave me Haus Lingfeld as a divorce present.'

'Generous? Or not?'

'Not.' She smiled. 'It was the price of my silence.'

'About what?'

'About so many things.'

'About Alex being alive.'

She looked hard at me. 'That too,' she said.

'You know where she is?'

'No.' Elisabeth's shoulders dropped. 'She came back to the house just after the war. I sent her away.'

All the warm spring sounds of the river bank were silenced by the sudden splash of a jumping fish. I could imagine the loathing in my expression, but she was a hard woman, easily capable of rejecting dislike. Again she shrugged. It seemed the closest she was going to come to an apology.

'Why?' I said. 'Why, for Christ's sake, after all she'd been through!'

'Rolf told me to. He told me that unless I sent Alex away the American Coburgs would withdraw his denazification papers. You see, Martin, Rolf had a very . . . uncertain . . . war.'

'A lot of people had an uncertain war,' I said savagely.

She seemed to ignore my anger. 'I don't think of him as a murderer, not even now,' she continued. 'But he certainly did not deserve the papers which Pierre got him.'

'How did Alex fit into this?'

'The clearance papers were given to Rolf on condition that we frighten her away. In the atmosphere of 1945 it was not difficult.'

'But why?'

'Because of the court action, Pierre's claim to inherit his brother's estate.'

I shook my head. 'They wanted everything.'

'They always had.'

'Pierre too?'

'By the end of the war Pierre was a shell of what he had been. An old man long before his time. Celine,' she said with undisguised bitterness, 'decided everything.'

'So Alex was scared off.'

'She was officially dead, executed at Waldviertel.'

'What did you tell her?'

'I told her what I was told to tell her. That the American Coburgs were determined to acquire Emil's estate. That her life was in danger. She believed it because of what had happened.'

I took a deep breath. 'You were in Lisbon in 1940. Do you know who denounced Emil and his family?'

'I know,' she said quietly, 'who I told Alex did it. You.'

'It wasn't me,' I said.

She shook her head impatiently. 'We all know who did. We just don't know how. We just don't have *proof*.'

She leaned forward and, removing a beaded muslin from a jug of iced water, filled a glass and pushed it across the table towards me.

'Have you ever seen Alex since the end of the war?' I asked her. 'Do you know she's still alive?'

She hesitated for a moment or two, pursing her lips. 'Yes,' she said, 'she's still alive.'

'Where, where is she living?'

'When I last heard,' Elisabeth said carefully, 'she was a dancer. In a Paris cabaret.'

'A dancer?'

Elisabeth shrugged.

'Do you have an address?'

'Of course not. Would she risk a Coburg knowing her address?'

I lit a cigarette. We sat in silence for a moment, her eyes never leaving my face. Then she leaned forward and pushed the glass she had filled closer to me.

I took it and sipped. There was a little white wine in it, a refreshing iced drink. 'Why don't you inform the German courts that the original military government order was invalid, that at that time Alex was still alive?'

'It's all past,' she said. 'It's all a part of my life I want nothing to do with again. I'm like a lot of Germans of my age group. I didn't kill or encourage killing. If I was guilty of anything it was a sort of mindless patriotism. And then the war ended and all the lies began.'

'Why don't you inform the German courts that Rolf's clearance was false and that Alex is probably still alive?' I repeated harshly.

She was pale now, even regal in her straight-backed attitude as she sat opposite me. 'It's not the first time you've come to me as my conscience.'

'When I was at the hospital.'

'And later,' she said. 'When you came and saw that Rolf and I were prospering on the ruins.'

'Will you go to court?' I asked.

She paused for a long time. 'You know Rolf is to marry again?'

'Will you go to court?' I said gently.

She stood up. 'Yes,' she said, 'yes I will.'

'Not just because I asked you?'

She shook her head. 'No,' she said, 'because, after all the torture I went through to save him, he is hoping to marry Celine.'

As the afternoon sun fell on the cheap lined paper, I wrote at a stand-up desk in the Lingfeld post office. The cable to Celine read: ELISABETH DISAPPROVES MARRIAGE PLANS STOP WILL TESTIFY STOP MARTIN.

I knew I was on my way.

At six-thirty the next morning the door to my room in the Munich Hotel Opera opened without ceremony and four men entered. One was the hotel manager; the others were undoubtedly policemen.

I became fully conscious, stumbled into my robe and sat down on the edge of the bed while the inspector showed all the documentation. 'I have some important questions to ask you,' he said. 'I'd sooner do this at police headquarters.'

I got dressed and was taken to a service elevator at the back of the building which took us down to a small courtyard where two police cars were waiting. Ten minutes later I was sitting across the desk from the inspector and one of his assistants in the interview room of the Marienplatz headquarters.

The opening questions were brisk. The inspector clearly knew the answers in advance. But when I told him I was in Munich on personal business I knew I had said the wrong thing.

He made a note on the pad in front of him. 'You hired a car at the airport?'

'Yes.'

'What make?'

'A red Taunus.'

The inspector was suddenly silent.

'What's this all about, Inspector?' I asked with the same desperation and the same words I'd seen in a hundred movies.

A few seconds passed. The silence was some sort of signal to his assistant. While the inspector watched my face intently the assistant said: 'Last night Frau Eck was found in the woods by the river bank. She had been there some time.'

I looked at him, then at the inspector, incredulously. 'Dead? She's dead?'

'She received multiple fractures of the rib cage,' the assistant intoned, 'a fractured left ankle, and a greenstick fracture of the left femur.'

'But she's alive?'

'A savage attack, Mr Lingfield,' the inspector said. 'There were also severe injuries to the head.'

I could see he was playing with me with a degree of professional skill, the purpose of which I couldn't understand. 'Will you tell me if she's alive or dead, for God's sake?'

There was another of those silences while the inspector stared hard at me. After a three-second pause the assistant said: 'Dead.'

· Thirty-four ·

We were in an area of Paris I knew nothing at all about, an area of long cobbled streets lined with garages and decaying factory buildings. Tattered posters covered everything; ancient *Défense d'Afficher* signs were themselves half plastered over with announcements of Communist Party meetings or fights or vaudeville performances. Sometimes a school or a branch of the Crédit Lyonnais stood out from the greyness of the roof tiles and the kaleidoscope of peeling wall posters. In the back of the taxi Zorubin looked out and grunted as we passed the Metro Porte St Denis. It was a spring morning but the weather was trying hard to match our bleak surroundings.

I had been held for twenty-four hours in the Munich police station until one of Elisabeth's maids volunteered the information that she had seen a second car arrive, long after I had left in the red Taunus. This second car, a black Opel, had been parked off the road in one of the long walks which Herr Eck had landscaped to cut through the woodland.

This stolen black Opel, which had been found abandoned in a private car park the evening Elisabeth was killed, was undoubtedly the murder weapon. Its front fender was badly dented and splashed with blood, to which adhered tufts of Elisabeth's hair and strands of her clothing.

The Munich police were efficient and gracious about their error. By questioning the Sheraton hotel staff it was quickly established that I was there when Elisabeth was killed. A few minutes later, the recipient of ungrudging apologies, I was walking free across Marienplatz.

I flew back to Paris and found Zorubin at his hotel. He had had good co-operation from the French police but they had produced no lead on Alexina. Over a cup of coffee in the red leather and brass-studded hotel dining room I filled him in about Elisabeth. He nodded several times as I recounted the story but said nothing. I realised that as a cop in Boston he must have heard a thousand such stories.

'What did the guys in Munich think for motive?' Zorubin asked, hunched forward, his huge hands clasping his coffee cup.

'Robbery. The murderer lifted a necklace from round her neck.'

'But your guess is that was just a red herring? But it may not be. In most police work the obvious answer is the right answer. There's not a big Agatha Christie element in most killers. But just sometimes . . .'

I ordered croissants and some more coffee.

'The problem is, Captain,' Zorubin grimaced, 'if the killing was connected to the fact that she had promised to take the stand in court against the Coburgs, the killer or killers must have known of the result of your talking to her. But that's impossible. It's impossible for them even to have known that you were going to talk to her.'

'I guess so,' I said, as the girl brought more coffee and a wicker basket with half a dozen croissants.

'Unless,' said Zorubin, giving the waitress his most wolfish smile, 'they have people here in Munich and alarm bells began ringing back there when you left New York.'

I was feeling too guilty to tell him of my childish cables to Celine. Could she have got someone to Munich in a matter of hours? It seemed improbable – unless, as Zorubin said, she already had someone there, or thereabouts.

He savaged a croissant. 'She's got a lot riding on this, Captain,' he said.

We paid the blue Renault taxi having crossed and re-crossed half the railway lines of Paris since Porte St Denis. Even so the sign above the warehouse door in front of us read: Musée de la Danse Moderne, Porte St Denis.

We entered a dark-green clapboard building and followed a long corridor until we reached a half-glazed door. The room beyond was cavernous and dark but for a series of crude floor-mounted spotlights which illuminated line upon line of carefully framed posters for the *Folies Bergères*, the Moulin Rouge and the Lido.

A human version of the American bald eagle perched on a high stool turned, beak and eyes sharp, as we entered the room. She was a woman of incredible age, almost hairless, the flesh of her face so far attenuated that the eyes had become deep sunken and the nose a thin, hooked beak.

'Bonjour, Messieurs,' she said in a surprisingly strong voice. 'Come in. You're my first visitors today.'

I had the strong impression we were her first visitors that week or even that month. An intermittent draught carried pieces of paper trash the length of the room or swirled them round her stool. 'I am able,' she said, 'to guide you through the history of cabaret dancing in France without moving an inch.'

Zorubin grinned at her. 'They all say no one knew the game like Madame de Champellet.'

I shifted my feet about uncomfortably. 'Were you long in cabaret dancing yourself, Madame?'

She leaned from her stool and selected one from the bank of switches on her desk. Lights flicked on illuminating a set of photographs of perhaps the 1880s. Madame de Champellet was unrecognisable as the elfin figure posed in a photographer's glade or dressed as an improbable Roman legionary.

Zorubin turned and walked through a searchlight toward her. 'Now, Madame,' he said, his arms spread as he approached the old lady, 'let us move forward in time.'

'Ah, the twenties,' she said. 'Men love the twenties, the skirts so short, the morals so loose.'

'I mean after the war, Madame,' Zorubin said firmly.

'We're looking for someone.' I came towards her perch. 'We're looking for a particular dancer.'

The old woman stopped her restless shuffling.

'A girl named Alexina Coburg,' I said. 'Or perhaps she called herself Breitmann. A German girl.'

Madame de Champellet nodded slowly. Among her myriad creases it was difficult to say but I think she was frowning. 'There was a girl named Breitmann who danced with the Folies Bergères up to a few years ago. She called herself Alex. It's fashionable to have what they think of as an English show-name. Yes Alex . . .'

Both Zorubin and I stayed silent, afraid to disturb her train of thought. But a great bubble of hope was rising inside me that this bizarre old lady was about to direct us to Alex.

'The thing I remember so well about Alex,' Madame de Champellet said, 'was her magnificent legs. Quite the most magnificent long legs in Paris. A strong well-built girl, yes, the physique of a born show dancer. She never got beyond the chorus line of course, or a feature in a tableau.'

'Do you have a picture of her?' Zorubin asked.

The old lady shifted and humped her shoulders without replying. Her lips were moving in an effort to galvanise her formidable memory. 'I would propose,' she said at last, 'the spring line up at the Folies Bergères in 1947.' She flicked switches and light flashed around us. One single spot settled mid-way up the warehouse wall. A slight adjustment brought one girl after another into view. The first was inscribed simply Alex. She wore the plumed head-dress and five-inch heels of a show dancer. Her costume was minimal and revealed an extraordinarily beautiful body against the tawdry setting of gold lamé curtains. For a moment I stood feeling strangely breathless in my small moment of triumph. It was really Zorubin's expertise which had got us here and the old lady's phenomenal memory that had produced the picture of Alex. But I felt it my own triumph to have conjured this beautiful girl from the mists of my past.

Madame de Champellet had found Alex but did she know where she now worked?

The old lady was speaking: 'The following year she left Paris.' For a long time she thought, her lips again mumbling through the pages of her memory. 'She spoke English well, I remember. And of course the studies!'

I looked at her, no longer following her eccentric train of thought.

'She studied a great deal while she was in Paris, Monsieur. She enrolled at the Sorbonne, I recall. It was her ambition not to be a dancer for ever, you see.'

'What did she plan to be, Madame?' I asked her.

'She spoke very little about herself. She was a German aristocrat, I'm sure, but she said little. Whatever she planned to be I don't know but she was far too beautiful not to be some exceedingly lucky young man's wife by now.'

My heart sank. A married Alexina would be that much more difficult to trace. But I was feeling more than that. Some raw emotion.

How could I feel like this about a girl whose memory escaped me?

It took half a day at the chaotic Sorbonne to discover that Alexina Anna Breitmann had studied International Law and had received her licence in 1948. After that no one knew anything about her movements. We talked to girls from the *Folies* and the Bluebell Girls. Some knew Alex but none had any idea into what walk of life she had disappeared. Yet there was a theme running through the answers we were able to get. As a West Indian girl named Jo Metcalfe who seemed to be one of Alex's closest friends said: 'She left in such strange circumstances that it'd be hard to say anything with certainty.'

We were sitting at a café table below an enormous plane tree outside a former grainstore where the Bluebell Girls practised their routines.

'What were the strange circumstances, Miss Metcalfe?' Zorubin asked. 'You mean she just disappeared?'

The girl nodded her dark curly head.

'When you say she disappeared you do mean of her own choice?' Zorubin asked carefully.

The girl grinned. 'She wasn't white slaved as the phrase goes, if that's what you mean. Leastways I don't think she was.'

'So tell us how it happened,' I prompted her.

Jo nodded. 'She wanted out. We all knew that anyway. In the nicest possible way, Alex was a very superior lady. She wasn't going to dance in a chorus line until replacement day. She wanted to cut completely loose.'

'What about a guy?'

I watched Jo nod slowly. 'There was a man who used to take her out sometimes. A Frenchman. Much older than her. Polite, rich, lost one arm in the Great War – *that's* how old he was.'

'So if you had money to put on it,' I said, 'where is she now?'

For some moments Jo considered. The birds burst out of the plane trees and hurled themselves across the square. A demonstration of *infirmières* in white coats trailed through the square carrying bedsheets on poles bearing the inscription: Reinstate Docteur Marly. Nobody took a lot of notice.

Jo held her face in her long brown hands. 'She married him,' Jo said. 'That's my banker. After that I've just no ideas at all, gentlemen.'

We sat in Zorubin's hotel room. Me on the edge of the bed drinking coffee; Zorubin pacing, barefoot, shirt open to a hairy chest, a tumbler full of vodka in his hand.

Elisabeth's death had given me a terrible jolt. I had been in touch with the Munich police again but they had nothing. No leads. They were inclined to think it was exactly what it looked like, a sneak thief in a panic. I knew it wasn't.

I also knew I was being followed.

Between Zorubin's hotel and mine it was an easy five minute stroll along the river. Earlier that evening as I had walked along the Quai de Montebello I had become aware of a black Citroën slipping along the kerb behind me. When I stopped, the Citroën stopped. When I turned to stare at it, the headlights flicked onto full-beam. Then as I began to run back down the quai towards it, the Citroën swung away in a tight U-turn across the cobbled street and sped off along the river. It could have been an unmarked police car.

It could have been.

Zorubin's voice brought me back to the hotel room. 'We're nearly up with her.' His vocal chords seemed to throw the words at the flimsy bedroom walls. 'My guess is she took the old guy's offer and moved down south. It would account for the absence of farewells or forwarding addresses.'

'Maybe,' I conceded reluctantly.

He nodded vigorously. 'She was ashamed to tell the girls. She'd come on strong as someone who didn't sing for her supper. And now she's singing for a life-long meal ticket. It fits, Captain.'

Perhaps I just didn't want to hear it but my gut feeling was against Alex getting married, against the idea of her singing for her supper. 'You take the south of France, Vik,' I said. 'I'm going to hit the Sorbonne again. Some fellow student must know what happened to her.'

He came down to the lobby with me, shoes, no socks, wide-open shirt, glass of vodka. Madame behind the brass and mahogany counter sniffed disapproval.

Zorubin stopped one step above me and silenced the Madame with one of his savagely suggestive grins.

He put his arm round my shoulder. 'We're on the road, Captain,' he rumbled into my ear. 'Take my word for it.'

· Thirty-five ·

Leaving Zorubin's hotel I looked quickly right and left. There was no sign of the Citroën. I walked quickly down the quai. Across the Seine, Notre-Dame rose above the thin river mist. Lights sparkled behind stained glass. I fancied I heard organ music and voices singing.

The Citroën of course could have been nothing. A kerb-crawler looking for a streetwalker; a family admiring, as I was, the masterpiece in stone across the river.

But I still looked around me. Cars passed; couples strolled along the embankment; two gendarmes examined the women's silk underwear in Lutèce. Normal.

I turned onto the Boulevard St Michel, walked quickly through the drifting crowds, and turned into the side-streets between here and the Rue de Seine.

I had been walking fast. Now I slowed down, caught my breath and took out a cigarette. I was outside my hotel, a small hotel, with pre-war glass globes ranged either side of the entrance. A gust from the river took the flame off the top of my lighter. I watched, over the flame, the long black nose of a Citroën edging forward from behind a domed lottery kiosk.

I walked quickly up the steps of the hotel between the lighted globes. Pushing open the door, I stepped inside.

The Citroën was parked across the road, that much I could see from the window opposite the lobby bar. I peered hard at the figure at the wheel but the streetlights were too dim for me to make out more than a shape. Then the driver's door opened. One, two, three, four pug-nosed King Charles spaniels came tumbling out followed by an old lady, unsteady on her feet.

I went over to the bar, pulled up a stool and ordered a pastis. While the barman was pouring, the *patron* came across waving a pale-yellow envelope. 'A cable for you, Monsieur. *Télégramme Exprès.*'

I took the yellow envelope and tore it open. The cable read: ARRIVED PARIS RITZ STOP URGENT WE MEET STOP CELINE.

I could not restrain my delight. I laughed out loud, surprising the barman and the *patron*. Celine was in Paris, drawn here by my cables, by the fear of what I might discover next.

I came through the revolving door on the Vendôme side of the Ritz. Once settled at a table in the panelled Little Bar I ordered a scotch and asked for Miss Celine Coburg to be given a message that her brother was waiting for her.

She came down five minutes later wearing an ice-blue dress under a pale mink coat draping from her shoulders. Several customers turned on their bar stools to watch her as she sat on the deep sofa next to me and ordered Vichy water from the waiter who was almost immediately by her side.

For a moment we sat in silence.

'So what are you doing in Paris?' I said, unable to suppress my sense of triumph.

'I've a meeting with the regents of the Bank of France,' she said casually.

'When was that arranged?'

She smiled grimly. 'When I was on the plane,' she said. 'OK, I'm here to see you. Cards on the table.'

The waiter delivered the Vichy water and fussed about with canapés and ashtrays before withdrawing.

'Cards on the table,' I reminded her.

She nodded, playing with her hotel key marked President Wilson suite. After a long pause she said: 'So you believe that Alex is still alive.'

'I *know* it,' I said. '*You* know it.'

She picked up her glass and sipped at the Vichy water.

'You know it,' I said, 'because you bribed Elisabeth to warn her off when she came back to Lingfeld from imprisonment at the end of the war.'

'That's what Elisabeth says.'

'Said.'

Either she was a great actress or she really didn't understand. 'That's what Elisabeth said when you saw her in Germany?'

'That's what Elisabeth said just before she was killed.'

Her face was without expression. She needed long years of training for a performance like this – whether or not she already knew Elisabeth was dead.

'She was killed,' I said, 'the evening after she promised to testify against you, against the theft of Emil's estate.'

She smiled brilliantly. 'Overdose?' she said. 'Morphine was her solitary pleasure, I understand. What did the police have to say?'

I looked away from her.

'Do you know where Alex is?' she asked after a long silence.

'I will in a day or two,' I said.

'And what then? Why should she talk to you after what you've done to er?'

'Don't think I'm going to take your word for that.'

She looked at me sombrely, a look I was to remember afterwards, for her disconcertingly candid look. 'You were a young arrogant patrician,' she aid. 'Crossed in love and bitterly angry at what Emil planned to do to 'ierre's reputation. You denounced them, Martin. Not Pierre or me. 'ou.' She paused. 'I asked you what will happen when you find Alex.'

'Then you and the Coburg Corporation will be taken to court for theft of he estate of the Imprimerie Coburg.'

'Why should anyone want to steal a couple of old, deserted factories?)ne of them a burnt-out wreck.'

'Why should anybody want to steal the Janus?' I said.

Again she paused, nodding unhurriedly. 'I see you've done your nomework.'

'I have. I know how much you need that press. For the new US Government Scrip contract, for half a dozen new currencies up for tender n Europe. And I know about brilliant new presses being developed which vill leave Coburg Banknote a company without a contract to its name.'

I think she flinched. I like to think so. 'Does Alex know where the Janus s?'

'She must,' I said. 'Emil must have hidden it immediately before his arrest. It follows.'

She inclined her head. 'Whoever finds it, whatever their legal claim, could sell it on the black market. Any of the toffee-nosed banknote printers in the world would snap it up. Most of them without questions.'

'That would include you.'

'I guess,' she said slowly, 'the time has come for you and me to make a deal.'

'A deal?'

For a moment I thought my mind was playing tricks. I saw her lips pout, her legs swing out and back. All those tiny devices she must have used a hundred times throughout her career. 'You're crazy,' I said. 'I'm your brother.'

I watched the lift of the eyebrow, the sulky, disappointed line of the mouth. 'We always meant a great deal to each other, you and me.'

'I don't believe it.'

'We're Coburgs. We don't have to play by other people's rules.'

'*You* don't have to play by other people's rules. You and Pierre and even Rose.'

'And your father,' she said. 'Don't forget him.'

A passing hotel guest let his eyes linger for a moment on Celine. 'It's the only way to save Coburg Banknote.' She was brisk now. 'Fifty–fifty. We run the company together, you and me.'

I was shaking my head.

'You find Alex.' She leaned forward, the mouth a tense curved line. 'You find Alex and you buy the Janus patents from her.'

'You believe you can pull me in,' I said, 'as you did Pierre?'

'I believe what I'm offering you is what you want.'

'Jesus Christ.'

She put her hand on mine. 'It's the only way now,' she said softly. 'The only way to save the company.'

A great wave of anger rose in me. 'Don't you know that I don't give a damn for the company? Don't you know that even if it was mine I'd get rid of every goddamn dirty share of it as quick as I could?'

Her eyes were shining. The calm was shattered. Tears, rage, disbelief, everything passed in front of me. She was gripping my hand, kneading it, like a rejected lover. 'Martin,' she pleaded, 'Martin, don't say things like that. A business deal. A simple business deal. You and me against Alexina.'

I pulled my hand away and stood up. 'You're mad, Celine,' I said.

She stood up beside me, a tall striking young woman.

'You're not clinically insane, you're not certifiably mad, but when the courts strip you of all the trappings of power, when you're reduced to a prison number, not even a name, then I don't think your mind will be able to take it. No deals,' I said, and turned and walked through the bar toward the Vendôme exit.

I could feel the blood coursing, the pulse at the base of my neck throbbing. I was experiencing a form of elation I could not remember before. Celine was cracking. Her fear of my finding Alex was all I'd hoped it would be. Then my spirit dropped again as I remembered her thin-lipped insistence that it had been me who had denounced Emil's family. There are times, even listening to a compulsive liar, when you believe. I'm not sure how close I was to being convinced it was me, but however much I wrestled with the idea I found it impossible to throw it off. Of course Celine would deny he had done it, or Pierre had done it. Of course it was the one single hold she had over me.

And yet still something deep in my instinct said she was not lying. At this single moment she was telling the truth as she believed it.

I caught a cab outside the Ritz and rode across the river to my side of town. At Rue Jacob I paid off the driver and took a beer standing up against the bar at a small café.

It was late. After midnight I finished my beer and walked on down the Rue Jacob. It was a misty night with very little traffic about. Ahead I could see the two hotel globes glowing creamily.

In front of me where a building jutted I could see my shadow outlined against the wall. I saw, with a kid's delight, my shape double and treble until I was thirty feet tall.

Then I swung round in horror. The headlights of a black Citroën were needling towards me. Coming from directly behind up on the broad sidewalk, the Citroën gave me no chance of jumping clear.

There was no calculation in what I did. One step sideways and the rounded wing thwacked against my thigh.

I spun round and slumped, back against a doorway to a shuttered shop. The Citroën had turned; the headlights were again drilling into me.

As the car leapt forward, I ran. Behind me the tyres screeched, the engine roared. Shadows of my fleeing self were thrown across the façades of the old houses.

I flung myself sideways into an alley, slid to my knees, scrambled up and ran again, wildly, down the dark cobbled alley.

One moment I could see almost nothing, the shadow outline of dustbins, the shuttered windows, the deep doorways. Then a flare of white light engulfed me.

And the Citroën came screeching down the alley, overturning dustbins, so close I could almost *feel* it.

I had time to register that, ahead, the alley ran into a small square. I had time to register low old timber warehouses and the sharp detail of a rustling tin Michelin advertisement.

Then the car hit me. I went up, my raincoat billowing, was hit again by the top of the windshield and rolled over and down across the covered spare wheel.

I lay dazed in darkness.

And in silence. There was no sound of the Citroën's engine.

I tried to open my eyes but blood was running copiously across my eyebrows. The Citroën was standing in the square in front of one of the warehouses. The driver's door was opening.

I fought to blink the blood out of my eyes. There were footsteps approaching. Celine's tall shape came across the cobbles towards me. made the effort of a drowning man. I mobilised every single muscle in my body. I pressed down with my hands and feet and with a hoarse gasp I threw myself up and forward.

The impact bowled her over. I could hear screams of pain and shock as stumbled on.

I turned. She was already on her feet running for the car. My legs carried me a step or two, but my weight seemed to haul me backwards.

The Citroën's engines roared. The headlights flared in my face. This time I fell. As I hit the ground I saw, at eye level, the wheels hiss past me.

I lifted my head. The black car swerved, hit one side-wall of the alley and ripped off a door panel as it careered on, bouncing from one side to the other, trailing sparks and pieces of torn metal. When it crashed it seemed to climb a door frame, the front wheels six feet off the ground.

I dragged myself up. In the silence I could hear something dribbling. I walked forward. Gasoline was bubbling from the gas cap. Then a sheet of flame rose with a dull roar.

I ran forward. The driver's door had burst open. The fire and fumes obscured everything but a shape. I gripped a wrist and an ankle and hauled. The shape tumbled over me. Flames jetted from burning wheels. I leaned down and pulled with my last vestiges of strength. When she was safe from the fire I collapsed next to her.

Smoke-smudged and distressed by pain her face may have been, but I had no difficulty at all in recognising it from the photograph as Alexina Coburg.

· Thirty-six ·

What counted first of all with her was that I had thought it was Celine.

She told me I had shouted Celine's name as I hauled myself off the cobbles. And again at some point as she ran for the car.

We sat in my hotel room with cups of hot coffee, she leaning forward from the single armchair, me on the edge of the bed. The fog between us was thicker than anything that could have come off the river at the bottom of the street. It was a fog of fear, of suspicion and doubt.

She had washed the streaks of oil from her face and pulled back her hair into a chignon. In a dark blue sweater and blue skirt she looked wracked with indecision, deeply unhappy and totally desirable.

I poured brandy into her coffee. We had talked all night. Outside the rising sun showed as a lemon-yellow line against the slate roofs of Paris.

She was exhausted. 'I'm full of hate,' she said. 'Only a saint could survive a place like Waldviertel without hate and revenge as consolations. When Hans Emden told me you were in Paris, that you were looking for me, I was terrified. But I was glad too. Ever since I left the camp I have known I need revenge. For Emil and Dorotta and all those others who were betrayed during the nightmare.'

She shuddered. 'I was afraid, of course. But when you came looking for me at the bookstore, I knew I *had* to do something.'

'You've got to believe I meant you no harm, Alex.'

She paused, letting her head drop. 'You pulled me out of a burning car,' she said slowly. 'The truth is that one part of me believes you. But the other part needs my hate.'

'You've got to know,' I repeated, 'that when I came to the bookstore I meant you no harm.' I took a deep breath. I knew I had to put it into words, almost as much for myself as for her. 'I can't say that it *wasn't* me who denounced you. I just don't know. I can only say that now I mean you no harm.'

'You mean it might have been Martin Coburg. But it wasn't Daniel

· 285 ·

Lingfield.' She shook her head. 'That's too easy,' she said. 'That's far, far too easy.' She walked to the window, holding her coffee cup, watching the red rim of the rising sun.

I stood behind her. Very carefully I reached up and put my arm round her shoulder. For a minute or two we stood there. She was biting her lower lip. Tears were running down her face. 'Oh God, my God . . .' she whispered into the dawn light.

I left for London that same morning ten minutes after I had put her into a taxi. She was exhausted, suspended somewhere between relief and disbelief. We both needed time.

I also needed information. Someone in London must have talked, boasted, got drunk with Oliver Sutchley. Sometime, awash with pink gins, he must have said something about his relationship with the Coburgs.

By midday I was being served lunch on the Golden Arrow from Paris Gare St Lazare to Victoria Station, London. I had armed myself with copies of the *Herald Tribune*, the London *Financial Times* and *Time* magazine.

Business pages were all full of the new US Army Scrip contract which the Department of the Army was just about to award to Coburg Banknote. Another stop along the way of what seemed to be Celine's unimpeded progress. She was already a favourite subject with editors, the only corporation president you could photograph with all the glamour of a movie star.

More than that Coburg Banknote had greatly changed under her presidency. It was now a public company and had extended its Kansas City plant to make it capable of accepting the biggest security contracts. The company contracts with Washington, which had been recognised as exceptionally tight throughout the post-war Democratic period, seemed equally tight under Eisenhower. Indeed, Celine and her executive vice-president, Merril Soames, had, it seemed, sloughed off the slightly raffish impression of Coburg Banknote which had derived from Pierre's sticky-fingered delving in the China trade. This week, my twin sister, the President of Coburg Banknote Corporation, smiled confidently from the front cover of *Time* magazine, more confidently than she had in the Paris Ritz.

It was seven in the evening when I got to London. I checked in at the Regent Palace Hotel, dropped my bag in my room and took a taxi to Chelsea Barracks, the headquarters of Her Majesty's Brigade of Guards.

I had a little initial difficulty with the guard commander, a tall, awesomely military Irish Guardsman, but within half an hour I had talked myself into the office of the adjutant. He was an equally tall young man who looked and sounded as if he had just stepped out of the pages of P. G. Wodehouse but I saw that he wore an impressive row of medals on his chest and three discreet, red wound stripes on his Service Dress cuff. He was, himself, he explained, a Coldstreamer.

I must have raised my eyebrows.

'We're Irish Guards, Scots Guards, Welsh Guards, Grenadier Guards and Coldstream Guards here,' he explained. 'A headquarters unit for the whole Brigade of Guards.'

'So you would not yourself have known Sutchley,' I said. 'He was Grenadier Guards.'

'He was,' the adjutant said, pouring me a whisky and adding water. 'But he was known all right. Not liked, but known. Owed you money, you said?'

I nodded. 'Two thousand pounds. Dates from his days in Portugal.'

'The horses, I expect,' the adjutant said. 'Well, I can't make any promises, old chap,' he said carefully, 'but we do carry a small fund for this sort of eventuality. We'd need an IOU, of course.'

'A fund?' I said, puzzled.

'We don't like Guardsmen to have outstanding debts. Even a bounder like Oliver Sutchley.'

I explained quickly that I was not trying to get an old debt repaid by the fund. I wanted to know where Sutchley was now.

'Pushing up the daisies,' the young officer said nonchalantly.

'You mean he's dead?'

'Drunk in Soho last month. His usual haunt. Tottered out of a pub and collapsed.' He smiled. 'Not a pretty tale.'

'No,' I conceded.

'Appalling chap.'

I nodded. 'His wife lives in London?'

'Yes. Pleasant woman. Good family too. But all downhill once she met Sutchley. He introduced her to Soho.'

'She spends a lot of time there?'

'She's one of the Soho crowd. Boozing, betting, banging each other and pretending to be artists. I suppose one or two of them may be, God knows. But if you want to talk to her that's where you'll find her.'

I finished my whisky and thanked him for his help. We walked out across the wide parade square where long columns of young men in khaki were being drilled by a ferocious sergeant-major. 'You'll do your best, old boy,' the adjutant said, 'if there is any unfortunate publicity, to keep the name of the Brigade out of it?'

I promised him. At the gate the Irish Guards commander stamped to attention and saluted me as I passed.

It was a ten minute taxi ride to Soho. Perhaps I had been here before. But this visit offered no familiar feeling. The narrow courts and alleys were paraded by frowsy streetwalkers who seemed to believe it was enough to be a woman to be desirable. The pubs were better. I moved from one to another, drinking a half pint of bitter beer and asking the barmen if any of them had known someone named Oliver Sutchley. Or knew his wife. By my fourth or fifth pub I had established that though Vera Sutchley was known in most of the pubs in Soho, she was clearly no better known for paying her debts, whether they were gambling or boozing obligations, than her husband had been.

The Fitzroy tavern was a Victorian pub full of mature mahogany and decorative cut glass. It was also full of BBC radio producers and young sailors short of money at the end of their leave.

I eased my way up to the bar. 'Tyrone Power,' someone murmured in my ear. 'Have you ever had your portrait painted?' whispered another.

At the counter the barman was middle-aged, Irish and definitely heterosexual. 'Yes, sir,' he said as if he'd spent his youth in the Irish Guards.

I ordered a large Glenmorangie and stood sipping its unique, smoky taste until my whole tongue was alive with the flavour. Eyes flickered towards me and passed on. I stood around for a couple of minutes watching the drift of men through the bar. I doubt if there were three women in the whole pub.

The barman came down the bar. 'It's a quiet night tonight, sir,' he said. 'Most Saturdays it's more like something out of Dante's *Inferno*.'

I asked him if he wanted a drink.

The barman relaxed, one hand on the bar as he surveyed the clientele. 'Thank you, sir. I'll have a beer.'

'You ever get a woman named Vera Sutchley in here?' I asked.

The barman nodded. 'The redhead,' he said. 'Keep your hands on your wallet. She's over there in the corner.'

I paid for the barman's beer and turned towards the corner he had indicated. A tall red-haired woman of about forty stood with two men in tweed jackets. She was handsome in a drink-worn, slightly raddled way. Her clothes were, I guessed, originally expensive, but she managed to convey that faintly down-at-heel look of someone teetering on the brink of alcoholism.

For a few moments I watched her. She talked with some animation, a gin and tonic waving in her hand. Concentrating I could hear a few phrases in her beautiful bell-like voice. 'The four-thirty at Ascot . . . ran like a wet dream . . . last but one . . .'

'Did Oliver ever talk to you about the time he spent in Portugal?' I asked her when ten minutes later we were settled in a very different pub on the edge of Mayfair.

'You're a rather lovely young man,' Vera was saying, 'but I'd like to know where all this is leading.'

'There are some things in Oliver's life,' I said, 'that I need to know more about. Have you ever heard of the Coburgs?'

'I've heard of them, yes.'

I hesitated, wondering whether to give out now would be too early. 'I'm Martin Coburg,' I said. 'Does that mean anything to you?'

There was no coquetry now. 'Martin Coburg, the memory man.'

'That's what Oliver called me?'

She nodded. 'The Coburgs stopped Oliver's pension when he died,' she said.

'He was receiving a pension from Coburg Banknote?'

'Yes.'

I took a second or two to absorb that. A pension. For keeping quiet? 'This is for 250 dollars,' I said.

She inclined her head.

'I want to know the lot,' I said. 'Everything.'

'You know he was actually in touch with the Germans?'

'In Lisbon?'

She nodded. 'Early on in the war when he still thought they were going to wipe the floor with us.'

I was throbbing with excitement. 'Did he ever tell you about 1940 when the German Coburgs were arrested?'

She raised her eyebrows. It wasn't a question. She knew.

'He had something to do with it,' I insisted.

'A mailman, he said he was. OK. He delivered the bomb.'

There was a long, long pause. 'Who put the bomb in his hand?' I asked finally.

'The memory man,' she said flippantly. 'You did, of course.'

My heart jumped in my chest.

She laughed. 'Come back to my place and I'll tell you how it happened.'

*

We went straight back to her flat in Maida Vale, a big, rambling, shabby sort of place. The dishes were still in the sink, knickers and bras hung on a string across the bath.

'Gin and tonic?' she said.

'Why not? So what are you going to tell me?'

She smiled, lit the gas fire and went over to pour the drinks. 'You think I got you up here for my own low motives?'

I was silent. Too much misery flooded through me to care. I took the wad of 250 dollars from my inside pocket. The bills were secured by a band of broad blue paper tape. I wasn't sure her information had been worth it but I dropped the thin pack on the table.

'Wait a minute,' she said. She went into the bedroom. Through the door I saw her plucking at the bedsheets, straightening them.

I called through. 'Vera,' I said. 'I'm going.'

She came back and stood in the doorway. 'He really did believe in the German cause,' she said.

'You mean the Nazi cause?'

'Of course, but Oliver was not a clever man. Not a thinker, Dan.'

I stayed silent.

She began to wander round the room touching small objects, vases, picture frames, cigarette packets. 'He was devastated by the knowledge that he was mediocre. His family had been explorers and writers and sea captains for five hundred years. But poor Oliver was simply mediocre.'

'What was his job in Portugal?' I gave her a cigarette and lit it.

'Emil Coburg had tipped off the FBI that he had been ordered to work on counterfeit dollar bills intended to buy American politicians. Oliver was responsible for routing the bills through Lisbon. He did it. But it seems he also wanted to get on well with the people he thought were to be our new masters. He passed over the information about Emil Coburg's tip to the local Gestapo.'

I was taking deep breaths. 'You mean Sutchley did this off his own bat? You mean none of the American Coburgs denounced Emil and his family?'

She smiled. 'No. But they were prepared to pay Oliver a pension to make sure he would swear you did it.'

Even in my self-obsessed relief I could see the pain she had suffered. 'When did you find out?' I said. 'When did you discover what he'd done?'

She laughed, a tight, bitter movement of the garish lips. 'The day after he died,' she said. 'Widow's unhappy task, you know. Sorting through the papers. Looking for cash to buy a bottle of gin actually.' Her face hardened. 'When I found out, I sent the bastard off for a pauper's funeral.'

I sat down on the sofa. She gave me another drink. 'Have you proof, Vera? Evidence of all this?'

She went across to a bureau, an eighteenth-century piece of mahogany, and began opening and closing drawers.

'Got it.'

She was holding an envelope in her hand, a long grey official-looking piece of stationery.

'I think you should have this.' She handed me the grey envelope.

I pulled the letter from the envelope. It was from the City and Provincial Bank. It assigned a number to a safety deposit box Oliver Sutchley had left in their care.

'The relict,' she said, 'of Oliver Frederick Sutchley. You'd better have it. I checked for money and handed it back to the bank. Family photographs of better days. But there are a few papers. All the evidence you need.'

It was Saturday evening. Nothing could be prised from a British bank under any circumstances on a Sunday and I wanted to be back in Paris as soon as possible. 'Will you get the box for me on Monday?' I asked her.

'OK. And what?'

'Will you send it to the Hôtel Clemenceau, Paris?'

'OK.'

She stood looking at me, then took a pen from her purse and scribbled on a copy of the *Sporting Life* the address I had just given her. 'I've got an old friend who works for Air France,' she said. 'If you want I could get it to you before Monday evening.'

'I'm counting on it.' I leaned forward and kissed her on the cheek.

'That's all?' she said.

'That's all, Vera.'

'Change your mind?' She looked toward the bedroom.

'I guess not,' I said.

'A screw to remember?'

I shook my head.

She smiled. 'I always thought the moment Oliver was gone from my life I'd get lucky.'

I was standing at the door. 'You have.' I pointed to the 250 dollars.

'Who'd want to remember that?' She crossed to the door and opened it. 'Good night, gorgeous,' she said in her beautiful voice. 'Go now before I rip your fly.'

I took the night train back to Paris from Victoria. I suppose I had never felt like this before. Amid the shouting of railwaymen and clanking of steel wheels the train was run onto the ferry at Dover. I slept fitfully then lay in my bunk staring up at the lights flickering on the ceiling. All the dreams and images of guilt were only slowly leaking away. I had to force my mind to release me, force my mind to accept that I was not guilty.

I woke sweating in the confined compartment. We were stationary at a French station. A hanging clock face was set at three in the morning. The hour of the wolf, Vik Zorubin told me the peasants of Waldviertel say. The hour when most people die.

The train pulled forward, steel buffers clanked on steel buffers, steel wheels shrieked on steel rails. Men shouted. A pale-blue light illuminated a rail sign reading Rouen – St Jean. I turned in my narrow bunk. I dreamt of columns of men and women shuffling past me, their heads bowed, the dawn mists rising like sulphur fumes round their feet. So many, a voice was chanting, I had not known death had undone so many.

I awoke finally as the train pulled slowly through the Paris suburbs. The night had purged me, cleansed my mind for ever of the guilt that had beset me ever since that moment I woke in the army hospital outside Munich. As little as I knew about the way the mind works I felt that this one last night of perturbation was necessary. I was free; a new life was beginning.

Hans Emden had given me the address. Obviously Alex had told him to, though he had still seemed to do it with doubt and reluctance. I didn't blame him, after what he'd learnt from Alex about the Coburgs.

I paid off my cab and entered the glass and concrete building through the wide swing doors. For a moment I stood among the bustle of young German students and middle-aged businessmen. I found an official who checked my name with someone on the phone and directed me up a wide winding staircase and left into a waiting-room. I thanked him and went up to the gallery above. A notice read: Visas for the Federal Republic. I entered the empty waiting-room slightly mystified. It was large with ornate cornices and two long windows looking down on the square below. A double door, half open, led into another room from where I could hear a typewriter clacking busily. I took a seat on the modern Danish teak sofa. In front of me travel magazines were piled on a coffee table.

Through the partly open double doors I could see into the inner office. A middle-aged secretary walked past the opening. I heard her knock on an inner door and say: 'Mr Daniel Lingfield is in the waiting-room.' And Alex's voice said formally: 'Thank you, I'll see him now.'

The door opened. She looked totally different from the last time I had seen her. Instead of the pale washed face and torn sweater I was looking at a young woman in a dark well-cut coat and skirt, her tawny blonde hair was held back loosely, a pair of heavy black-rimmed spectacles in her hand.

She came forward. 'I'd prepared all the speeches,' she said. 'All the apologies. Now they've flown from my head . . .'

'You phoned Vera Sutchley?'

'As soon as Hans gave me your message.' She paused, looking at me across a distance of six feet. 'Can we ever recover from the past?' she said.

· Thirty-seven ·

We moved from place to place like desperate nomads, talking all day. I needed to absorb the detail of her life to know my own.

On a bench in the Jardin des Invalides we held hands while she talked shudderingly of Waldviertel.

It was a short journey in miles, she said, but it had taken over fifteen hours. With sixty-five people packed into each cattle car the day's heat was unbearable. No water had been provided, no food. The prisoners crowded into this fetid hell knew only that they were travelling east but the constant stops, the rattling progress for fifteen minutes before the long train again hissed to a halt, confused even those who were trying to guess their destination.

In cattle car number 72, Alex and her father had stood pressed tightly together. They had seen Dorotta driven into another truck. By nightfall on the next day Alex was convinced that the woman pressing against her back was dead. She had tried to speak to her, clearing her throat of dust and the acrid smell of their slatted prison, but the woman no longer even moaned. Alex knew too that a child and an old man had been trampled underfoot as they were all driven relentlessly onto the train. Somehow the feet of these crushed, terrified people had worked the two corpses into a corner. But that had been in the early hours of the journey, before the prisoners needed every ounce of strength to keep themselves alive.

By the following night most of the prisoners were locked in some private delirium. Some women were already dead. Nobody talked any longer. Some muttered in their standing sleep, some screamed.

With the first thin light of dawn Alex and Emil had turned their heads toward the barbed-wired gap above the low door. Gradually they were able to make out the shape of trees, then of small farm buildings. Then suddenly Alex heard a strange gurgle in her father's throat. She remembered clearly throwing her weight backwards against the dead woman behind her so that she could half turn to face Emil.

He was laughing!

'Oh, my darling Alexina,' he said. 'It's that meaningless irony of the gods. They're taking us back home.'

After a few more minutes the train had rattled and clanked off the main line onto a single-track spur through the forest. There was still no edge of sun in the eastern sky. A paleness streaked with grey gave enough light for Alex to see that they were pulling up at a long platform whose surface was roughly constructed of logs. Boarded walkways for the grey, menacing figures of the guards ran along the length of the high barbed wire which edged the far side of the platform. Between white Death's Head SS symbols was written in huge Gothic letters the name, Waldviertel.

An order had been shouted, a single incomprehensible word, and the grey figures seemed to hurl themselves at the cattle car, dragging back bolts, thundering on the sides with the base of their whips, shrieking at the prisoners, dragging them from the cattle cars.

Men and women who were barely strong enough to move stumbled down onto the rough surface of the platform, legs jerking like marionettes before they fell to their knees and were whipped, crawling forward, to join the line already stretching the length of the train.

It seemed to Alex to be a deliberate re-creation of the entry to Hell. Prisoners jostled and pushed as they flinched away from the guards' whips, screams of fear and anguish filled the woods. The dead and the dying were already being dragged from the train. Over two thousand people cowered in terror as a perfect dawn broke across the eastern hills.

Among the huge snaking line of people she tried desperately to cling to Emil. But a whip fell indiscriminately across her back and as she flinched away, fell, crawled and stumbled up she looked around to see his grey head turning, searching for her until he too was lost in the great dark mass.

It was shortly after they had been marched to the huge sandy Appel square that she saw Hans. He came out of one of the low wooden administrative buildings that surrounded the square wearing a prisoner's striped jacket but carrying a whip under his arm. He was walking slowly, reading from a sheet of paper.

Hans Emden was greatly changed since Alex had last seen him as he had turned to make his way to the Swiss border. His face was grey and his eyes were sunken. His head was shaved. His movements were sharp and nervous. He had that thin vicious quality of stamped tin.

'The prisoners with the whips are kapos,' somebody had whispered. 'Be careful, they can be worse than the guards. Pass it on.'

Alex had passed the information on, her eyes never leaving Hans

Emden's face as he walked towards the great dark mass of people on the Appel square.

The kapos screamed and kicked and whipped them into long lines. Hans Emden, she saw with dismay, was as harsh as any, acting under the negligent eyes of the dozen SS officers in charge.

She knew he had seen her. She knew that as he shouted and pushed the prisoners into line he was aware that he was moving toward her. She saw too that he did much more screaming and pointing than actual beating. She had, for a second, a small glimmer of hope.

He was standing before her, looking down the long line of prisoners. His hand fumbled for hers. 'Anna Breitmann,' he said as he pushed papers into her hand. He bawled for them to toe the white marks, and ran forward. Then still shouting orders he walked backwards down the line. 'Give me your transportation papers,' he said from the side of his mouth.

She fumbled in her coat, found the papers and pressed them into his hands. The line was forming up now, raggedly at first, men and women who had never been soldiers learning to dress ranks in seconds rather than days.

'You're on the execution list for tonight.' Hans had spoken like a stage ventriloquist, staring along the line. 'Your name is now Breitmann. You'll be all right.'

A group of SS officers had assembled at the far end of the front line. Hans ran toward them, stopped and bowed his head. Alex watched as the officers moved down the line. Even today, she said, she could remember the names of those prisoners called just in front of her: 'Altmann, Kurt . . . Siedman, Sophia . . .' the SS officer had droned. With each name Hans had stepped forward to present papers. 'Greim, Christina . . .'

'Dead on arrival.' Hans presented the woman's papers. She was the next in line now. Her face was blank with terror.

'739182,' the officer said.

Hans stepped forward. 'Coburg, Alexina. Dead on arrival, Herr Leutnant.' He handed over a fold of papers.

'Breitmann, Anna,' the officer yawned.

'Present, Herr Leutnant,' Alex had said.

The officer yawned again and passed on down the line. For a second only, Alexina's eyes had met the dark, blank eyes of Hans.

We got up and walked through a flock of pigeons pecking at the dusty gravel, then sat again at another bench as if movement was necessary to match or quell the turmoils of memory.

'After the war,' Alex said, 'I kept sane. God knows how. The only life I knew was as a camp inmate. Then I found I could make a living as a dancer, the only job I could get in Paris that didn't ask for a work permit. All the time I studied until finally, at the beginning of this year, I passed the examinations for the German Consular Service. Then one day, what seems a hundred years ago now, Hans Emden told me that you had been to his bookstore.' She was breathing heavily now. 'All those emotions I thought I had suppressed, all those emotions that centred on you, love, gratitude, hatred, fear, everything erupted to the surface. For twelve hours I was paralysed, literally unable to move. When I recovered I had refined all my feelings into one – hatred. Hatred for you. Disgust at the very idea that you had lived when so many died.'

We stood up again, propelled by strange gusts of feelings we could neither predict nor control. She reached up and hooked her fingers in the back of my collar, caressing me as we walked.

'You have no idea what it's like not to be alone.' She held tight to me.

'Celine is desperate,' I said. 'She won't be able to resist a claim from you to hand back Emil's estate.'

She frowned. 'For what it's worth. The Imprimerie Coburg is now nothing more than a couple of not very valuable building sites.'

'But the rights to the Janus,' I said. 'They're worth a fortune.'

'Not unless we *have* the Janus.'

'Emil didn't tell you where he'd hidden it?'

'He had no time to hide it,' she said. 'He was arrested the moment we got back from France.'

'We know Celine doesn't have it. Are you saying it just disappeared, got bombed, dismantled for scrap?'

She shook her head slowly. 'You don't remember?'

'Remember what?'

'That Emil relied on you to hide the Janus if anything happened to him. He asked you that in France.'

Then suddenly it hit me. 'Does that mean that's why I joined the SS, to go back after you were arrested to hide the Janus?'

She stopped and put her arms round me. 'It looks like it, darling,' she said. 'It's the only explanation that makes sense.'

We walked slowly along the Seine. We had talked the whole afternoon. Walked and talked.

As the sun set we had dinner in a small restaurant below her apartment on the Ile St Louis. We ate mostly in silence now, drained by the extraordinary day we had spent together.

I had never met someone like her. Someone with the same ability to speak so frankly, to risk rebuff. She had told me what she had felt for me when we were little more than children at Lingfeld. Then she told me, with that stunning frankness, what she felt now. 'We've lost too much time for it to be otherwise,' she said.

We left the restaurant and turned through great green-painted carriage doors into a courtyard within the ancient building. Ornate cast-iron staircases led up to galleries with apartments leading off them. We climbed the cast-iron staircase. Lights burned in the windows all around us. People moved inside their apartments, families, couples. 'But to destroy Celine,' Alex said, as if following a train of thought in her head, 'we must first find the Janus.'

We became lovers naturally, perhaps because we always had been. Standing with our arms round each other's waist in her apartment on the Ile St Louis, looking down on the Seine and the flickering reflection of the barge lights on the water, we had talked ourselves to a standstill.

It was somehow inconceivable to both of us that I should go back to the hotel. I turned toward her and kissed her mouth. Perhaps we both remembered that first time, that brief permitted moment of reconciliation at the Château de Belfresnes. Then we broke apart and walked together into the bedroom.

· Thirty-eight ·

Naked she was superb. We lay facing each other in the narrow bed, my fingertips travelling a patternless course over her body. Her mouth was drawn back in pleasure as I smoothed my hand across the minute golden hairs of her belly and down between her legs. 'I must get up,' she said, her arm tightening round my neck. I kissed her breast and, moving, let my tongue reach deep into her armpit.

I released her and she threw back the sheet which barely covered us to our knees and sat up on the side of the bed. Then, laughing, she propelled herself upwards and ran toward the shower.

I lay back in the bed and let the scents of lovers rise around me. I knew that what I had found was far more than my past. I knew that this tall, slender girl with dark-blue eyes, with long brown arms, with swelling breasts and blonde pubic hair was to be my future too.

I lay back in bed as she came out of the shower and I watched her cross and re-cross the room until she looked up, saw me watching her and smiled, her hands full of underwear. 'Lunch is out,' she said. 'We're entertaining a Franco-German group of industrial giants at the embassy. I'll be away by two.'

'I'll be here waiting for you.'

She stepped into her briefs and moved smoothly into a showgirl grind and bump across the room. 'At heart,' she said laughing, 'I'm a dreadful tart. I must admit,' she said, as she expertly slipped into her bra, 'that I rather enjoyed what I was doing to the men at the *Folies*.'

She came across to me and sat on the bed. 'Be warned,' she said, 'when we're married.'

It was the first time either of us had talked about a future that was not concerned with retribution or revenge. It was the first time in all the tumult of the last twenty hours that either of us had dared bring our future into the open.

I pulled myself up onto one elbow and caressed her thigh as she leaned over to kiss me. 'Will you be Mrs Alexina Lingfield?' I said.

'If you ask me to.'

'Will you marry me, Alex?'

'I will,' she said, tears rolling from her extraordinary Coburg eyes.

I took a shower, got dressed, made coffee and used Alex's phone to call my hotel. The *patron* told me there were no parcels from London but that a Mr Zorubin had called trying to contact me. He was at his hotel in Paris.

I called Zorubin straight away.

'Where the hell were you?' his voice rumbled down the line. 'I got back last night and I've been calling you ever since.'

'I was with Alex,' I said.

It took a moment for it to sink in.

'You've found her?'

'More truthfully, she found me. She works for the German consulate.'

'Jesus. And the printing press? The Janus?'

'She doesn't know where it is. But listen to this, Vik, she is damn near certain that Emil Coburg made it my responsibility.'

I could hear what I took to be vodka gurgling into a glass. 'OK, Dan,' he said, 'let me give you my report. I've got an idea we're going to be able to put two and two together.'

'I can come over right away,' I said.

'I'll give it to you on the phone. The south of France was a bust. Nothing, no trace. No problem now because you found her.' He paused to drink. 'OK. I took a ride up to Munich. An idea that had been eating at me for days: your SS records office in Berlin told you that after your officer training at Bad Tolz you disappear from the records, right?'

'His idea was that I was doing something unspeakable in Russia.'

'But in fact,' Zorubin said, as much triumph in his voice as I'd ever heard, 'in fact you were high-tailing for home. You deserted.'

'After I'd taken care of the Janus, if Alex is right.'

'She's right,' he said flatly. 'Let me tell you about Munich. I've got some pull with Archives, old Gestapo records of SS court martials. What do I find? One Untersturmbannführer Martin Coburg sentenced to death *in absentia*, for desertion.'

'Where does that take us?'

'To France, strangely enough. Listen, desertion was the main charge. Half a dozen minor charges covered illegal use of passes and movement orders . . .'

'And?'

'And appropriating a Mercedes truck and vehicle low loader, things the German army hauled armoured cars or even small tanks on.'

'I've got more nerve than I thought,' I said. 'You mean I had the Janus on the back of the low loader?'

'Nothing in the records says that, but it's a certainty. Not surprisingly they never found the low loader.'

I was intensely excited now. We only needed one more detail. Did Zorubin have it? 'Vik,' I said. 'Did the court martial record say anything about where the Mercedes truck was found?'

'Yes,' he said. 'In France.'

Then it hit me. 'Near the Dordogne river,' I said. 'It has to be.'

'It means something to you? A little place called Souillac?'

'It means a hell of a lot to me, Vik. It means I hauled the Janus to the chateau Emil had given Alex during the war.'

My mind was racing. Alex had sold the chateau. I knew nothing about law – had she sold the contents with the building? I arranged for Vik Zorubin to hire a car and drive down straight away.

Then I phoned Alex and caught her just before she was going in to lunch. When I told her she gave a whoop of delight that must have startled, or inflamed, the industrial giants.

When I reminded her about the sale there was a heavy pause at the other end. 'I'll call my *notaire*,' she said, 'and see if things have gone too far. Then I'll ditch the giants and drive down to meet Mr Zorubin there.'

I was exhausted with sheer exhilaration when I put down the phone.

Alex and I were on top.

Nothing could stop us now. Certainly not Celine. However many bundles of corporate lawyers she assembled.

I poured myself a scotch and phoned Celine. Perhaps it was a childish gesture. But it was something I needed.

That so cool voice. A change of mind?

'I'm sitting in Alex's apartment,' I said. 'I know where the Janus is.'

She didn't hesitate. 'Come over right away,' she said.

Putting down the phone, I drank my scotch and rang my hotel. Still no package from London.

I wanted that package. I wanted the complete documentary proof of my innocence. But I also wanted to get me a car and drive down to the chateau right away.

One more scotch. Phoned the hotel again without luck.

And decided to go round to see Celine.

Why?

I guess I wanted to taste my triumph before the lawyers held us at arm's length.

I wanted to see Celine hurting.

I came off the Place Vendôme and through the Little Bar. At the car hire desk I made arrangements for something fast to take me the 500 kilometres down to the Dordogne river.

Then I straightened my jacket and took the elevator up to the President Wilson suite.

I felt jubilant. The soft green carpet comfortably absorbed my footfall. I stopped at a window and looked down on the Place Vendôme. I had a moment's regret that Alex was not with me. But I knew there would be time.

Leaving the window, I followed the discreet gold on walnut sign pointing me to the President Wilson suite.

I turned at the second sign and faced the two white double doors.

One was open. Ajar.

I walked forward and stopped. Pushed the door until it swung open. Light streamed across a Chinese silk carpet in the parquet hall.

I called out. Then walked forward and pushed at the main door facing me. As it swung slowly on its hinges I saw, on the pale carpet, slowly revealed, the body of Celine. Her neck was broken, clear from the gigantic bruise at the neck, yellow and blue, and rag-doll angle of her head.

By some automatic reflex I swept my eyes across the room looking for the weapon. A Bouchon bronze perhaps, a candlestick. Nothing.

I knelt down beside her. There was no other sign of the struggle, no cuts on the hands or torn clothing. She had been struck one massive blow from a heavy object. Maybe even from behind.

I stood. Very, very slowly the shock began to ebb. Thought processes began to grope for an answer. I stepped back towards the door, turned and walked out into the corridor.

Alex! I knew her so little. I knew her not at all. She had killed Celine because she had to do it. Because somehow, this way, she had to assuage her thirst for revenge.

I remembered the words she'd used. 'I need my hate.'

Oh Christ. Alex! Had the Coburgs won after all? Had the face of the Waldviertel reared up in her mind in the moment of our triumph?

I rode the elevator down to the street. I had arranged for my hire car to be dropped at my hotel and the keys left with the *patron*. I walked out through the bar and was only aware I had signalled when a cab drew up in front of me.

I sat smoothing my hands across the cracked blue leather seats of the Renault. If the driver spoke I didn't hear him: my mind was blank.

I recognised the hire car outside the Hôtel Clemenceau, an English Jaguar. Fast as I'd asked.

Paying the cab I walked between the glass globes still lighted in daylight and into the lobby. The receptionist gave me the car keys and I turned back to the door.

The *patron* was emerging from a back room. He carried a tattered brown paper parcel tied with string, crudely sealed with red wax.

I took it from him wearily. A wave of fatigue flooded me, unbalanced me.

Perhaps I stumbled. Certainly the *patron* was holding me by the arm. 'Some coffee, Monsieur,' he said.

I sat on a bar stool while he got the coffee. The package from London was on the copper counter. I fiddled with it without interest. I knew the contents.

I tapped the corner of the parcel making it spin on the smooth copper surface of the bar. Nothing in it could be of importance now.

I plucked at the string and watched the red wax crack and tumble onto the shining copper.

I was within a millisecond of thrusting the package aside as the *patron* approached with the coffee. But my finger was hooked under a fold of brown wrapping.

I tore the paper toward me. Then tore again. From inside the crumple of cheap brown paper and string I drew a slender cigar box. The *patron* put down the coffee on the bar.

I flipped the cigar box lid. A note in an italic hand read: The earthly remains of Oliver Frederick Sutchley, a gentleman, wastrel and bum.

I had the feeling it was written in Sutchley's own hand.

My mouth was dry. I let the pink card flutter onto the long bar in front of me and looked down again at the cigar box. On top of a pile of papers was a wedding photograph of Oliver Sutchley and Dorothy. At the age of twenty-five his essential seediness had not yet shown through. Dorothy herself was slimmer than I remembered with a wide, sadly hopeful smile. I turned the photograph and dropped it onto the bar. Underneath it was a thick pack of documents secured by a rubber band. I slid a few out. They were large, ornate Russian share certificates all dated long before the 1917 revolution. Lenin and Stalin afterwards had made clear that capitalist investment in Tsarist times would never now be repaid.

Family photographs. Victorian upper-middle-class men and women certain that £2,000 a year from slum rents evoked the world's respect. Photographs of Sutchley at Eton, dark-eyed and evasive despite the Eton jacket and silk hat. Two franked tickets for the Orient Express. A carefully folded silk handkerchief . . .

More photographs. Mostly of garden parties against a background of Lisbon rooftops. Some single girls.

I was looking down at two typewritten pages of coarse orange foolscap paper spotted with the brown marks of woodpulp. The top page carried the black eagle wings on either side of the swastika set in the circle.

The paper was headed: Preliminary report to Gestapo headquarters organisation. The typed address was 1, Avenida Lisboa, Portugal. July 1 1940. It began:

> As senior Gestapo officer attached to the Reich Embassy in Lisbon I have the honour to report:
>
> On June 30 last the Embassy received an approach from Captain Oliver Sutchley of the British Embassy, a man known to Gestapo Hauptamt, Lisbon. The purpose of Sutchley's approach was given as the offer of information of the greatest importance to the interests of the Reich. Because the informant was British and because he was known to us as one sympathetic to our cause, I personally made an arrangement to meet him at a hotel we employed as a discreet house in the Lisbon outskirts.
>
> Mr Sutchley was extremely nervous. His information (the full details will follow this report) concerned an alleged attempt by Ausland Organisation in Berlin (since confirmed from that quarter) to introduce one million 20-dollar bills counterfeited in Germany by Imprimerie Coburg GMBH into the United States. The reported intention was to use the funds to support all possible alternatives to Roosevelt's candidature in the coming November US presidential election. Full report follows.

I looked at the Gestapo affidavit. On the grainy orange paper, stamped with the imprint of Gestapo Hauptamt, Lisbon, and signed by the interviewing Gestapo officer, this document had all the chilling authenticity of the murderous betrayal that it was. Oliver Sutchley was beyond vengeance but my stomach still twisted at the careless sweep of his signature in his fine italic hand. The sheer evil embodied in the ill-typed statement on its war economy orange paper left me breathless, my hands sweating. I folded the document. Staring up at me was a circular stamp of Gestapo Hauptamt.

Then the most terrifying shock I have ever experienced tore through my body and made me cry out loud in horror. *The Gestapo officer signing the document was Senior Commissioner Viktor Heinz Zorubin!*

· Thirty-nine ·

I drove out of Paris like the man possessed I was. Possessed by a dreadful fear that Zorubin would reach, *must* reach the chateau and Alex before I did.

I had tried to telephone from the hotel but there was no line. The local operator in Souillac had volunteered the information that the chateau had been empty since an old Hungarian countess had left there during the war.

The Jaguar was powerful and fast. The strain of its roadholding on corners was revealed only by the screech of tyres as I sped south across Paris. I saw red lights flash by me and saw other cars braking to a last-minute halt. Blaring motor horns followed me down the straight avenue named after Général Leclerc and across the cobbled Place d'Orléans.

I was now out onto the open road, the Nationale 20 to Orléans, Limoges, Brive and Souillac. Zorubin had started his journey immediately, I assume, after he had murdered Celine.

I allowed myself to think as the tyres pounded the road and the plane trees flashed past. Zorubin, whose strange physiognomy imparted an unusual charm to his manner, his way of walking, even the way he sat, the huge hands flat on the table before him. In that single moment reading his signature in the hotel lobby the charm had disappeared. I saw now his twisted, rubbery smile as infinitely threatening. It had been a long haul for him. I cast my mind back to the way we had met, or the way he had organised our meeting. I barely remembered now his cover story of service with the Boston Police Department and of course I had never for one moment thought to check. Or even to question his faint accent. Enough good Americans still retained some trace of a European past. Nor had I ever pursued the coincidence of our meeting at Eastlake Veterans Hospital, all that had been subsumed in my gratitude for delivering me from Cathy and the 'Reverend' John Hunter. And the further coincidence so much later that he should be working for a French Jewish family trying to locate Alexina. He had invested years in the search for the Janus, presumably as

Celine's man. But Zorubin was nobody's creature. The moment he had discovered the location of the Janus nobody was safe who had an interest in it – Celine, me . . . Alex.

My head was thumping, pacing my heart as I thought of the ferret tenacity with which he had pursued Alex.

As I raced through Orléans and onto the Châteauroux–Limoges road I blew a tyre. Like on a Coney Island Big Dipper operated by a madman I was swung once, twice, nearly blacking out, grazing trees and an oncoming truck until the skid lost its frenetic energy.

The car came to rest in the entrance to a field a few feet from the road. I climbed drunkenly out, my head spinning, my legs trembling. By the time I had changed wheels and got back onto the road I had lost nearly fifteen minutes. In my imagination I saw Zorubin's rubber smile of triumph.

I roared through Limoges with a Renault police van on my tail. But the Jaguar streaked away at the southern suburbs leaving the occupants of the trundling van to decide whether to phone ahead or to look for some other wrong-doer. It was 9.15. By my calculation I had something in the region of an hour to cover 130 kilometres, the last part a twisting hill road along the Dordogne gorge.

I didn't know that Zorubin was already turning into the courtyard of the chateau.

EPILOGUE

· Forty ·

Alexina's red MGB turned into the cobbled courtyard of the Château de Belfresnes and came to a stop beside the Simca with the Avis sticker on the rear window.

Getting out she walked slowly across the dark courtyard absorbing the scent of juniper and lime from the black hillsides around.

Absorbing the memories of the first time she was here.

The great front door was open and she passed through into the tiled hall. Only as her eyes became more accustomed to the dark could she make out the outline of the staircase and the gallery above. Then the moon emerged from behind a cloud and threw a long panel of light across the hall floor.

It was dank, eerie. But she told herself any house of this age, empty for seven or eight years, would be eerie.

She called out: 'Is anyone there?' Then . . . 'Mr Zorubin, Mr Zorubin . . .'

A crash and clatter greeted the words. Like a slate sliding from the roof. On the gallery a flashlight clicked on and a moving shadow came to the rail.

She could see he was a formidably square-shaped man. The head huge and round and his hair cropped quite short. 'You're Vik Zorubin?' she called up to him.

'I'm Zorubin,' he said. He came down the stairs towards her, the flashlight bobbing. She found, to her surprise, the man exuded a strange chill. Surprise because Dan had described him differently.

He stopped on the top stair. He had still not yet asked her hame although he clearly knew who she was. 'I've checked the generator,' he said. 'For this part of the house it's dead. For the kitchens and cellars it's working OK. Feeble but OK. So where do we start looking?'

She had to remind herself that this man was a friend of Dan's. She said: 'I'm Alex Coburg.' And held out her hand.

'Sure,' he said. 'But if there are going to be new owners around any time now, we'd better get moving.'

She let her hand drop.

'Now this machine must be twenty feet at least. Mounted on the low loader maybe even more.' She noted the heavy rumble of his voice. 'Tha suggests to me a barn maybe, a garage cut out of rock, this sort of thing.

'I've been thinking on the drive down,' she said, almost reluctant to tel him, preferring to wait until Dan arrived. 'I've been thinking there aren' too many places here to hide something that size.'

He smiled suddenly and she thought she got some idea of what Dan meant. It was a strange smile, wolfish and yet compelling. It told you this is a man you wanted on your side.

'When Dan and I were here before,' she said, 'we were shown a room through the back of the kitchen. As I remember, it led down into some system of limestone caves.'

'Caves?'

She smiled, trying to lighten the moment. 'This is the best-known region of Europe for caves. Almost every village here has its own *grotte*. Some of them run for miles underground.'

He nodded. 'OK, let's take a look.'

It was no good. She could not like the man. Or at least not warm to his brusque manner.

She led the way downstairs to the huge kitchen. There was electric light there, dim and sometimes flickering, but enough light to see the great iron stoves she remembered. And there, the door into the cold room.

She pushed it and stepped through. Zorubin followed her.

They walked between the long lines of now empty shelves then down the rough-stone, puddled stairs. From below the draught of cold air hit her in the face. A few steps lower she could hear the rush of water.

At the bottom of the stairs the huge cavern opened up before them. Dim flickering lights in the cavern roof threw shadows from the twisted columns of limestone. A narrow river plunged and rolled between jutting rocks.

Zorubin stood beside her. 'Is there any way in here from the road?'

'Yes, there's an entrance to the cave system just off the track up to the chateau.'

'OK,' he said and started forward.

The river turned away at this point but an arch of stone revealed electric light beyond. Zorubin ducked through the arch and emerged into a long, flat-bottomed cavern. At the far end moonlight showed through a thick screen of bushes.

In front of them, the shape of a huge machine stood under a tarpaulin on an old German army six-wheeled low loader.

She felt no jubilation. She was watching the face of Zorubin as he flicked his flashlight over the dimly outlined tarpaulin. She found she could not fathom his expression.

He walked up to the loader and kicked at the flat tyres, then he reached up to one of the tarpaulin ropes and with surprising agility pulled himself up onto the low platform.

She was cold now. Unhappy. Uncertain about this man.

She watched him take an Opinel wooden-handled knife from his pocket, heard the click of the blade into position then saw him slit the tarpaulin in great downward strokes.

She could not force herself to ask him why.

As the tarpaulin fell away she saw the Janus exposed, the dark-green paint cracked and flaking, the metalwork tarnished in the damp atmosphere of the cave. She wanted to turn and walk away. To run even.

Her eyes never left him.

She had, with a tremor of fear, the impression of something almost lustful as his hands roamed over the machine, pulling out drawers or sliding sections, muttering, grunting.

She took a step backwards. He had found something, maybe what he was looking for all the time, the steel name-plate screwed onto the flank of the machine.

She took another step away.

'Stay where you are,' he said, his eyes fixed on the name-plate.

She turned and ran.

Behind her she heard him leap from the platform as she raced for the bottom of the stairs.

Dan Lingfield's Jaguar took the winding road on screaming tyres, the headlights fingering the limestone rock shapes and the stunted hanging trees. A pale moon hung in the sky and light skeins of cloud drifted across it. Dan could see, across the gleaming river on his left, the outline of Château de Belfresnes's turrets and battlements high on the cliff.

Crossing the stone bridge he accelerated rapidly up the narrow road towards the chateau. Beneath the wheels, rock chips were thrown up clattering against the underside of the car. As he skidded round a bend the chateau loomed for a moment, silhouetted against the lighter sky. Then he was in the courtyard, two pairs of automobile rear lights winking a reflection as he braked.

The great medieval doors were wide open. As he ran from the car he could see some sort of light in the hall. In the mad panic to get to Alexina, the menace of Zorubin had become diffused, no longer human, a figure with powerful rolling shoulders and huge, blunt-nailed hands, but something that hung over the chateau, something that occupied any or all the rooms, the staircases, the mouldering, cobwebbed landings.

He was in the main hall now, running across it, heading for the stairs. Somewhere above he could hear something, movement, scuffling perhaps, and rapid footsteps.

The light in the hall came from a flashlight rolling across the tiled floor. He snatched it up as he reached the stairs, the light throwing huge shadows of balusters and newel posts on the crumbling plaster of the galleries above.

The scream was short, momentarily piercing, an animal cry that put ice in his spine. Then the most terrifying series of screams his imagination could conjure. And a dreadful baying sound, an animal in pursuit.

Then silence. A complete engulfing silence. Without realising it he had stopped on the first landing. His torch threw a long oval of light across the floorboards. He called in a voice that was no more than a harsh, barely human croak. He called Alex's name and heard no answer. He walked forward shocked by the realisation that his legs would hardly carry him. The ringing in his ears speeded and slowed, speeded and slowed. He called again and heard only that terrible grunting from above, a shuffling sound he could not identify.

And silence.

Running up to the next landing he saw that the moonlight flooded through open french doors from the terrace beyond. Perhaps the doors were still swinging, but he knew someone had passed through them only seconds ago. He threw himself forward and stopped dead. The sound was from *behind* him now, a ferocious high keening like an animal in a steel trap.

The flashlight beam jerked across the wall as he spun round then settled up the last flight of stairs. Zorubin sat there belching blood. His arms hung limply, the hands dripping onto the staircase. His head lay to one side, half severed by a great gash from which his blood pumped.

It seemed to Dan that he was shouting for Alex, for Alex, but he had no way of really knowing. Zorubin's button eyes were on him, indifferent it seemed to his draining life blood. Did he laugh? Or make some sort of ghastly attempt at laughing? Then he shuddered violently again and again as if he were suffering some prolonged orgasm. Slowly his weight took him forward and he pitched toward Dan down the last few stairs and rolled dead at his feet.

No passage of time had any significance. At some point he heard her sobbing. Against the moonlight from the terrace he saw her moving. The french door swung as she leaned against it, open-mouthed. In the torchlight he saw her face and bare arms were covered with blood. From her hand something clattered onto the flagstones. Automatically the beam of light sought it out. It was a kitchen cleaver, the wet blade chipped and bent.

· Forty-one ·

Sale of Daniel Lingfield's major shareholding in the Coburg Corporation and Alexina Coburg's one hundred per cent ownership of Imprimerie Coburg and its patents in the revolutionary Janus intaglio banknote printing system, was put in hand immediately. The proceeds, which would run to nearly 100 million dollars, were principally to be assigned to survivors of the Waldviertel concentration camp, Upper Austria, and distributed through Herr Hans Emden, President of the Waldviertel Association.

Several smaller donations were to be made to the garden staff and domestic servants of Island House, Montauk, Long Island. In Harlem a young man named Joe Williams, who, until suffering a serious accident, was considered an up-and-coming cruiser-weight fighter, had been informed that he was to receive the sum of 75,000 dollars. The news reached him, coincidentally, just one month before the lease became available on the late Henry O's Luncheon Club on Lennox Avenue.

To Rose Coburg events had moved at an astonishing speed. Within days of Celine's death she had been informed that the house and company were to be put on the market. She had been told not to expect a share of the proceeds.

She had packed four large suitcases that day and a jewel box and told a maid to get someone to help her take them down to her car. She allowed herself a final glance round the room and out across the gardens to the ocean beyond.

Leaving the bedroom where her small son had first found her in bed with Pierre she had descended the great Gothic staircase for the last time. At the door to Pierre's library she stopped, shuddering.

She desperately needed another drink.

The maid was still upstairs trying to find someone to help her down with the suitcases. It was bad form to be seen by the servants drinking in the afternoon.

She paused in the hall. Of course, there was brandy in the decanter on the library table. She pushed open the doors and went in. She was careful to close them after her. Quietly crossing to the drinks table, she took a decanter and poured herself a good measure.

Averting her eyes from the centre of the room she sat down in what had been Pierre's favourite chair.

It wasn't as though a daughter had died. She had never really loved Celine in that way.

She looked up now at the plain coffin on the long library table and heard the sounds of funeral cars on the gravel outside. Of course Celine had been wicked. She had been wicked to have kept Alexina from her inheritance; and to have sent the US Army photographs of Martin back without showing them to Pierre. She had been wicked to hire that monstrous ex-Gestapo man who had murdered Elisabeth and finally murdered her.

Rose poured another brandy. You would have thought Celine cleverer than that. Strange that she had never realised that all along Zorubin was working for himself.

She was drunk when the men in black suits came to take the coffin, waving her glass to give them permission.

She didn't clearly remember being driven to the graveyard. She saw, in a haze, Jack Aston manoeuvring her husband's wheel-chair; she thought she saw a black man with a broken nose; she saw people from the company she vaguely recognised. She saw her son and Alexina, his arm round her shoulder.

When the service was over Rose left Island House for ever.

They had all gone. Rose to God knows where; Jack Aston and John Coburg back to the cottage; Joe Williams to Harlem; ex-Colonel Buck to the new clinic he had just opened in Denver, Colorado.

Dan had shaken the last hand, thanked the last person for coming. Now he looked round and saw Alex, a tall figure in black, standing alone before the wall of green marble that fronted the vault. He walked slowly back down the gravel path and stood next to her. Their eyes moved down the incised and gold-lettered names:

Aloys and Paula Coburg.

Pierre Coburg.

Then, Martin Coburg 1921–1945.

He thought he felt the girl beside him shiver.

And finally, Celine Coburg 1921–1949.

He took Alex's hand and they looked up at the heavy gold lettering at the head of the green granite block: Vault of the Coburg Family of Waldviertel, Austria, and Long Island, New York.

Then they turned away.

Let it be.